Mills & Boon is proud to present
three super novels in one collection
by an author we know you love
and have made an
international bestseller

Enjoy these three books by rising star

Abby
GREEN

Keeping Her Close

Contains

In Christofides' Keeping
The Call of the Desert
The Legend of de Marco

May 2014

June 2014

July 2014

August 2014

Abby
GREEN
Keeping Her Close

MILLS & BOON

Published in Great Britain 2014
by Mills & Boon, an imprint of Harlequin (UK) Limited,
Eton House, 18-24 Paradise Road, Richmond, Surrey, TW9 1SR

KEEPING HER CLOSE © 2014 Harlequin Books S.A.

In Christofides' Keeping © 2010 Abby Green
The Call of the Desert © 2011 Abby Green
The Legend of de Marco © 2012 Abby Green

ISBN: 978 0 263 24675 9

024-0814

Harlequin (UK) Limited's policy is to use papers that are natural, renewable and recyclable products and made from wood grown in sustainable forests The logging and manufacturing processes conform to the legalenvironmental regulations of the country of origin.

Printed and bound in Spain
by Blackprint CPI, Barcelona

Abby Green deferred doing a social anthropology degree to work freelance as an assistant director in the film and television industry—which is a social study in itself! Since then it's been early starts, long hours, mucky fields, ugly car parks and wet-weather gear—especially working in Ireland. She has no bona fide qualifications, but could probably help negotiate a peace agreement between two warring countries after years of dealing with recalcitrant actors. Since discovering a guide to writing romance one day, she decided to capitalise on her long-time love for Mills & Boon® romances and attempt to follow in the footsteps of such authors as Kate Walker and Penny Jordan.

She's enjoying the excuse to be paid to sit inside, away from the elements. She lives in Dublin and hopes that you will enjoy her stories. You can e-mail her at abbygreen3@yahoo.co.uk.

In Christofides' Keeping

ABBY GREEN

This is for Lindi Loo and Lola,
my two favourite girls

CHAPTER ONE

RICO CHRISTOFIDES stifled his irritation and tried to rein in his wandering attention. *What* was wrong with him? He was in one of the most exclusive restaurants in London, dining with one of the most beautiful women in the world. But it was as if someone had turned the sound down and all he could hear was the steady thump-thump of his heart.

He saw Elena gesticulating and speaking with a little too much animation, her eyes glittering a little too brightly as she tossed her luxurious mane of red hair over one shoulder, leaving the other one bare. It was meant to entice but it didn't.

He knew all the moves. He'd seen countless women perform them for years, and he'd enjoyed them. But right now he felt no more desire for this woman than he would for an inanimate wooden object. He regretted the impulse he'd acted on to call her up once he'd known he'd be in London for a few days.

Curiously, he was being enticed by a tantalising memory. He'd glanced fleetingly at one of the waitresses as they'd walked in and in an instant something about the way she moved had registered on his brain, throwing him back in time—two years back in time, to be precise. He'd found himself thinking of the one woman who hadn't been like all the others. The one woman who had managed to smash through the high wall of defences he kept rigid around himself and his emotions.

For just one night.

His fist clenched on his thigh under the table. It had to be just because he was back in London for the first time since that night. He forced himself to smile tightly in answer to something Elena had said, which seemed to require that response, and to his relief he could see that she was off again, clearly loving the sound of her voice more than she cared if he was listening or not.

The night he'd met *her*—*Gypsy*...if that even was her name—they'd just come out of the club and he'd been about to tell her his name. She'd put a hand over his mouth, saying fervently, 'I don't want to know who you are...tonight isn't about that.'

Scepticism hadn't been far away. Either she knew damn well who he was, as he'd been splashed all over the tabloids for days before that night, or else... But Rico had found himself pausing as he'd looked down at her. She'd looked so lovely and young and fresh...and untainted. And for that moment, for the first time in his life, he'd pushed aside cynicism and suspicion—his constant companions—and said, 'OK, then, temptress... what about just first names?'

Before she could say anything and still believing deep down and with not a little arrogance that she *had* to know who he was, he'd held out his hand and said with a flourish, 'Rico...at your service.'

She'd placed her small soft hand in his and hesitated for a long moment before saying huskily, 'I'm Gypsy.'

A made-up name. It had to be. He'd chuckled, and he could remember even now how alien it had felt to allow that emotion to rise up. 'Fair enough. Play your silly game if you want… Right now I'm interested in a lot more than your name…'

Someone laughed raucously at a nearby table, jerking Rico out of the memory, but even so a hot spiral of desire ran through him and he had a sudden memory flash of hearts beating in unison, sweat-slicked skin, her sleek body around his in an embrace so velvet hot and tight that he'd fought just to keep control. And then her muscles had started to spasm around him, she'd given a fractured breathy moan, and he'd lost it in a way that he'd never lost it before or since.

'Rico, *darling*…' Elena was pouting at him, lips too blood-red. 'You're miles away. Please tell me you're not thinking of boring work.'

Rico stifled a cynical grimace. It was that very *boring work*, and all the many millions he'd made in the process, that had women like Elena hovering around him in droves, waiting for little more than a crooked finger to signal his interest. Even so, the acknowledgement couldn't stop him from shifting uncomfortably in his seat, very disturbed by the fact that he was being turned on not by the woman opposite him, but by a ghost from the past. Because that ghost was the one woman who hadn't fallen at his feet in sycophantic ecstasy when he'd singled her out.

On the contrary: she'd tried to walk away from him. And then the following morning she *had* walked away from him. But not before he'd left her on the bed, like a callow, unsophisticated youth. Regret burned him, and Rico didn't *do* regret.

He forced another tight smile and reached across for Elena's far too available hand. She practically purred when he took it. He opened his mouth to offer some platitude as a waitress walked past their table, and he frowned when his body inexplicably reacted—tightening almost as if it sensed something his brain hadn't yet registered. He looked up; it was the waitress he'd noticed on the way in. The waitress who had sparked a veritable torrent of memories.

Was he going completely insane? An evocative scent lingered on the air in her wake. He tried to sound casual, and not as if he was afraid he was going crazy. He looked back to his date. 'What scent are you wearing?'

Elena's lips curled seductively as she offered Rico her wrist to smell. 'Poison…do you like?'

He bent his head, but even before he smelt the distinctive perfume he knew it was all wrong. Nausea clenched his belly. He looked up again, as if drawn helplessly, to see the back of the waitress. She was taking an order at a nearby table. That evocative scent reminded him of—

Abruptly Elena pulled her hand from his with a barely disguised huffy sigh and stood from the table, smoothing a hand over one artfully cocked hip sheathed in silk.

'I'm going to go and powder my nose. Hopefully by the time I get back you won't be so distracted.'

Rico disregarded the reproach in her voice and didn't watch her walk away. He was transfixed now by the slim back of the petite waitress just a few feet away. She had a neatly shaped figure—firm buttocks, defined by the close-fitting black skirt which hid her legs to the knee, and slender but shapely calves and tiny ankles. Feet in low-heeled black shoes. So far so unremarkable.

His gaze travelled back up, past the plain white shirt, with just a hint of the bra underneath, taking in her hair, which looked a dark honey-brown but which he guessed might be lighter in daylight. It was densely curled, tied back into a tight bun, but he could already imagine the wild corkscrew curls that would burst free. Almost exactly like— He shook his head again, cursing softly. *Why* was that memory so hauntingly vivid tonight?

The woman turned slightly then, before stopping to respond to something the man at the table was saying, and it was enough to give Rico a proper glimpse of her profile. A small straight nose, determined chin, and a lush mouth with the slightest hint of an overbite—which he remembered thinking an adorable imperfection in a world obsessed with perfection. Certainty slammed into him on the heels of that thought—it had to be *her. He wasn't going crazy.*

His breath stopped. Everything went into slow motion as she finally turned and faced him directly. She was looking down at her notepad, scribbling something, juggling the big menus under her arm as she walked closer, and before he knew what he was doing, with something that felt horrifyingly exultant rushing through him, Rico stood and grasped the woman's arm, stopping her in her tracks.

Gypsy didn't know what was happening at first. All she knew was that someone had a tight grip on her arm. She looked up with a retort on her lips—and fell into steely grey eyes.

And stopped breathing, stopped functioning.

She blinked. Words died in her mouth. *It couldn't be him.* She was dreaming—or it was a nightmare. She was certainly tired enough to be sleep-walking. But she could feel the colour draining from her face, the peripheral noise fading into the background.

She was looking into exactly the same colour eyes as— There her mind shut down. *It was him.* The man who had haunted her dreams for nearly two years. Rico

Christofides. Half-Greek, half-Argentinian, billionaire entrepreneur, a legend of his own making.

'It *is* you.' He spoke her thoughts out loud in his deep voice, and sent Gypsy's brain into a tailspin. Very distantly she was aware of a voice screaming at her to run, get away. Escape.

She shook her head, but it felt as if she was under water. Was she still standing? All she was aware of was the dark depths of those deep-set stormy grey eyes, boring into her all the way to her soul, his hand tight on her arm. Midnight-black hair, slightly crooked nose, dark brows, defined jaw... It was all so familiar to her—except her dreams hadn't done him justice. He was so tall, towering over her, his shoulders so broad that she couldn't see anything but him.

Absurdly through the shock came the hurt—*again*—that he'd wasted little time in walking away from her the next morning. Leaving just an abrupt note which had read: *The room is paid for. R.*

A pointed cough sounded nearby. He didn't move, and Gypsy couldn't look away. Her carefully constructed world was crumbling into pieces around her.

'Rico? Is something wrong with our order?'

A voice. A female voice. Confirming what Gypsy didn't want to know by saying his name out loud. She registered dimly that it must be the stunning red-haired woman she'd walked past and noticed just minutes before. She couldn't believe now that she'd passed him so blithely, with no hint of warning.

But he ignored the woman and said again faintly, 'It's you.'

Gypsy managed to shake her head and at the same time somehow miraculously extricate her arm from his long-fingered grasp. She prayed that she could speak and say something that made sense. Something that would get her out of this situation and away from him. After all, it had been one night—mere hours—how could someone like him possibly remember her? After the way he'd left, why would he *want* to remember her? How could this awful fiery awareness be snaking through her veins?

'I'm sorry. You must be confusing me with someone else.'

Gypsy left him standing there and went straight to the staff bathroom, seriously afraid that she might be sick. Taking deep breaths over the sink, she felt clammy and sweaty. And all that was going through her mind was the imperative need to run, get away.

Ever since she'd found out that she was pregnant after their cataclysmic night together she'd known that some day she would have to tell Rico Christofides that he had a daughter. *A fifteen-month-old daughter, with exactly the same colour eyes as her father.* Gypsy felt nauseous again, but willed it down.

She could remember her terror at the prospect of becoming a mother, along with her instantly deep and abiding connection with the tiny baby growing within her. And with that had come the intense desire to protect her child. She'd seen how Rico Christofides dealt with women who dared to name him as the father of their child, and had had no desire to expose herself to that public humiliation. Even if she'd been certain that she could prove paternity.

Pregnant, and feeling extremely nervous and vulnerable at the daunting prospect of how Rico Christofides might react to the news, Gypsy had taken the difficult decision to have Lola on her own. She'd wanted to be in a strong and solvent position when she contacted him. Working as a waitress, albeit in an upmarket restaurant, was *not* the ideal situation for her to be in when dealing with someone as powerful as him.

Panic surged again. Gypsy didn't even see her own white face in the mirror. If she didn't get out of there *now*, Rico Christofides couldn't fail to recall the woman who had acted completely out of character and who, on a tide of desire so intense that she still woke sometimes at night *aching*, had succumbed to his masterful seduction and indulged in a one-night stand.

Making a fateful decision, uncomfortably aware that she was acting on blind instinct and panic but seeing no other solution, she splashed some water on her face and went to find her boss.

'Tom, please,' Gypsy begged, and mentally crossed everything. She hated lying, and especially using her daughter to do it. But she had no choice. Not with the father of her child just through the kitchen doors.

'I have to get home to Lola. Something has…come up.'

Her boss raked his hand through his short sandy hair. 'Jeez, Gypsy you really pick your moments—you know we're short staffed as it is. Can't it wait for another hour, until we have the main rush over with?'

Gypsy hated herself for this. She shook her head, already taking off her apron as she did so. 'I'm sorry, Tom. Really sorry—believe me.'

His face tightened and he crossed his arms. Gypsy felt the slither of fear trickle down her spine. 'So am I, Gypsy. I don't want to do this to you, but it's come to this: you've been late nearly every day for the past two weeks.'

Gypsy started to protest, saying something about the

inflexible hours of her daughter's minder conflicting with her shift hours, but her boss cut her off.

'You're a good worker, but there's a line of people behind you waiting to get a job here who won't let me down like this.'

He took a breath, and Gypsy's foreboding increased. 'If you leave like this now then I'm afraid you won't have a job to come back to. It's that simple.'

A vivid memory surged back of the moment she'd found out that the man who had turned her world upside down was none other than one of the world's most powerful men, and nausea returned.

The thought of going back out to the dining room and trying to function normally was inconceivable. She'd end up getting fired anyway for spilling someone's dinner into their lap, she was shaking so much. She looked at Tom and shook her head again sadly, already anticipating the drudge of having to look for another job, silently giving thanks that she had some savings to tide them over for a couple of weeks. 'I'm sorry, Tom, I have no choice.'

Her boss stood back after a long moment and gestured with his arm. 'Then I'm sorry too, Gypsy, because you're leaving *me* no choice.'

She couldn't say anything. Her throat was too tight. She gathered up her things and left through the back kitchen door, stepping out into the dark and dank alleyway behind the exclusive restaurant.

Later that night Rico stood at the floor-to-ceiling window of his central London penthouse apartment, hands dug deep into his pockets. His pulse was still racing, and it had nothing to do with the beautiful woman he'd said a curt and sterile goodnight to—much to her obvious disgust—and everything to do with a pretty waitress who had confounded him by doing a disappearing act.

She'd done a disappearing act the first time round, but he only had himself to blame for that. He grimaced; if he hadn't panicked… It still rankled with him that he'd let her get under his guard so easily. He could remember watching her sleeping, sprawled across the bed, feeling seriously stunned at the depth of his desire, *still*, and the depth of his response to her.

It was that and the overwhelming feeling of possessiveness which had driven him from the room as if hounds were snapping at this heels. He *never* felt possessive of women. But this evening, the minute he'd recognised her, it had surged upwards again, as fresh as if no time had passed. And she'd run. And he had no idea why.

He pulled out a small piece of paper from his pocket. He'd got her name from the manager of the restaurant, and his men had made short work of tracking her down. He now had Gypsy Butler's address—for apparently that *was* her name. He smiled grimly. He would soon find out what exactly he found so compelling about a woman he'd slept with for just one night, and why on earth she'd felt the need to run from him.

The following morning, as Gypsy walked home in drizzly rain from the local budget supermarket, pushing a sleeping Lola in her battered buggy, she was still reeling at what had happened the previous evening.

She'd seen Rico Christofides and she'd lost her job.

The two things she'd been most terrified of happening had happened in quick succession. She defended herself again: she'd had no choice but to leave last night— she'd have been in no fit state to work or deal with Rico

Christofides. Her legs felt momentarily weak when she recalled how he'd looked, and how instantaneous his effect on her had been.

He'd been tall and strong and devastatingly powerful. And still as bone-meltingly gorgeous as the first time she'd seen him across that crowded nightclub two years ago.

The night she'd met Rico had been a moment out of time—and most definitely a moment out of character. He'd caught her on the cusp of her new life, when she'd been letting go of a lot of pain. She'd been vulnerable and easy prey to the practised charm of someone like Rico Christofides. But she'd had no clue then just exactly who he was. A world-renowned tycoon and playboy.

Seeing him had made everything she'd ever known pale into insignificance. She knew if he'd been dressed like the other men in the club—in a natty shirt and blazer, pressed chinos—it would have been easy to dismiss him as being like all the rest. But he hadn't been dressed like that. He'd been dressed in a T-shirt and faded denims which had fit lean hips and powerful legs so lovingly that it had been almost indecent. An air of dangerous sexuality had clung to his devastatingly dark good-looks in a way that had left everyone around him looking anaemic—and awestruck.

But that in itself would have just made him a spectacularly handsome guy; it had been more than that. It had been in the intensity of his gaze across that heaving chaotic club—*on her*. Dark and mesmerising, stopping Gypsy right where she'd been dancing alone on the dance floor.

The impulse to get out of her tangled head and engage in something physical had called to her as she'd passed the club doors and heard the heavy bass beat just a short while before. It was a primal celebration of the fact that she was finally free of her late father and his corrupt and controlling legacy. When he'd died six months previously she'd felt more emptiness than grief for the man who had never shown her an ounce of genuine affection.

But when the gorgeous stranger had started to come towards her in the club, with singular intent, all tangled thoughts and memories had fled. He'd cleared an effortless path through the thronged crowd—and sanity had returned to Gypsy in a rush of panic. He was too handsome, too dark, too sexy…too much for someone like her. And the way he'd looked at her as he grew ever closer had scared the life out of her.

But, as if rooted to the spot by a magic spell, she hadn't been able to move, and had just watched, drymouthed, as he came to stop right in front of her. Tall and forbidding. No easy sexy smile to make it easier. It was almost as if something elemental had passed between them and this man was claiming her as *his*. Which had been a ridiculous thing to feel on a banal Friday night in a club in central London.

'Why have you stopped dancing?' he'd asked innocuously, his deep voice pitched to carry across the deafening beat, but even so she'd heard the unmistakably subtle accent.

He was foreign. As if his dark looks wouldn't have told her that anyway. A frisson of awareness had made her tremble all over when she'd noted his steely grey eyes, their colour stark against his olive skin. She'd shaken her head, as if to clear it of this madness, but just then someone had jostled her, heaving her forward and straight into the man's arms, into hands which held her protectively against his hard body.

Instantaneous heat had exploded throughout Gypsy's

body at the sheer physicality of him. She'd looked up, utterly perplexed, and had sensed real fear... Not fear for her safety, but an irrational fear for her *sanity*. On a rising wave of panic she'd used her hands to push against his chest and stepped back, answering tightly, 'I was just leaving, actually...'

His big hands had tightened on her arms—bare because she was wearing a sleeveless vest. Her light jacket was tied about her waist, her bag slung across her chest. 'You just got here.'

He'd been watching her from the moment she'd arrived. Gypsy had felt weakness pervade her limbs to think of how she'd been dancing: as if no one was watching.

And then he'd said, 'If you insist on leaving, then I'm coming with you.'

Gypsy had gasped at his cool and arrogant nerve. 'But you can't—you don't even know me.'

His jaw had been hard and implacable. Stern. 'Then dance with me and I'll let you go...' The fact that he hadn't been cajoling, hadn't been drunkenly flirting, had imbued his words with something too compelling to resist.

Gypsy's focus came back to grim and grey reality as she was forced to stop by the traffic lights. She didn't need to recall the pitifully pathetic attempt she'd put up to resist before agreeing—ostensibly to make him let her go.

But it had had completely the opposite effect. After dancing with her so closely that her body had been dewed with sweat and heat and lust, he'd bent low to whisper against her ear. 'Do you still want to leave alone?' To her ongoing shame and mortification, she'd shaken her head, slowly and fatefully, her eyes glued to his in some kind of sick fascination. She'd wanted him with a hunger the like of which she'd never experienced in her life.

She'd let him take her by the hand and lead her out of the club, seeing him as somehow symbolic of the cataclysmic events of the day that had just passed, during which she'd finally let go of everything that had bound her to her father.

She'd allowed herself to be seduced...and then summarily dumped like a piece of trash the following morning. She remembered seeing the curt note he'd left, and how cheap she'd felt—as if all that was missing was a bundle of cash on the dresser.

With an inarticulate sound of disgust at herself to be thinking of this *now*, the fact that she'd let a man like him—a powerful man *just like her father*—seduce her, Gypsy strode on across the road once the traffic had stopped. With any luck Rico Christofides would have become distracted by the vision of perfection he'd been dining with last night and forgotten all about her. *But he remembered you...* She realised that any other woman would be feeling an intensely feminine satisfaction that a man like him hadn't forgotten her, but *she* just felt panicky. *Why* on earth did a man like him remember someone like her?

A familiar sense of despair gripped Gypsy as she turned into her road, full of boarded-up houses and disaffected-looking youths loitering on steps. As much as she'd relished her freedom after her father's death, and as much as she wouldn't have minded living somewhere like this if she'd only had herself to worry about, it did bother her that her daughter's first home was in such a decrepit part of London. Even the nearby children's playground was vandalised beyond use, with just one pathetic swing left.

She sighed heavily, very aware of the irony that, but for her hot-headedness and determination to dissociate herself from her father, she might have been living in much more upmarket surroundings. But then she knew she could never have lived off her father's money—and she'd never have dreamed that she'd become pregnant after a one-night stand with a ruthlessly seductive—

Gypsy's heart stopped stone-cold dead in her chest—and it had nothing to do with the faintly menacing-looking youths crowded around the steps of a nearby house and everything to do with the stunning car they were eyeing up.

The gleaming black luxury vehicle with tinted windows should have belonged to one of the gangsters that had a stranglehold on the area, but Gypsy knew immediately it was a world apart from their cars. The gangsters around here could only *wish* to own a car like this.

And as she drew closer, and saw the back door swing open, her heart picked up speed, so that it was nearly leaping from her chest as she watched a tall, dark and powerfully built figure uncoil like a panther stretching lazily in the sun.

As if she didn't already know who it was, he turned to face her. Just feet away, and right outside her front door. No escape.

Rico Christofides.

CHAPTER TWO

GYPSY knew she couldn't run. The very thought was futile—as evidenced by Rico Christofides' clear determination to find her. *Why* was he so intent? All Gypsy had to do was picture the woman from last night and the contrast between them was laughable.

Today she was in her habitual uniform of too baggy jeans bought from a local charity shop, layers of threadbare jumpers to block out the January cold, sneakers, a secondhand parka and a woolly hat pulled down low over her ears and too wild hair. *He*, on the other hand, looked every inch the successful tycoon, in a long, black and expensive-looking coat, with the hint of a pristine suit underneath.

She saw his slaty grey eyes narrow on her as she approached. No doubt he was regretting his impetuous decision to find her. And then her skin prickled as she saw his gaze drop to the pram she pushed, with a sleeping Lola inside, obscured by the rainshield.

His daughter—oh, God—could he know?

Gypsy immediately reassured herself there was no way he could know. Why would he assume for a second that Lola was his? She just had to take advantage of the undoubted regret he'd already be feeling at seeking her out and get rid of him. As soon as possible—before he could see Lola and guess.

Even if he didn't guess she knew that once she told him about Lola he'd move heaven and earth to prove that she wasn't his—which was what she'd seen him do before. And then, when paternity was proved, he'd set out to control his daughter utterly. Exactly as her father had done to her once *he'd* had no choice but to accept her.

She knew this because Rico came from her father's world of powerful men who thrived on being ruthless. Men who dominated those around them.

As soon as she'd heard his name she hadn't been able to believe she hadn't recognised him. She even recalled overhearing her father speaking bitterly of Rico Christofides on more than one occasion: *'If you think I'm ruthless then don't ever cross Rico Christofides. The man is a cold machine. If I could beat him I would, but the bastard wouldn't rest until he'd resurrected himself from the dead and ruined me in the process. Some fights just aren't worth it, but I'd give anything to see his arrogance smashed…'*

Her father had been obsessive, and the memory of that almost grudging admiration had blasted away any chance that she might have contacted Rico Christofides before today.

The best that Gypsy could hope for was that that day wasn't going to be today, and that perhaps she could escape with Lola—go somewhere new, away from London—until such time as she could get her wits about her again and decide what was best for them both.

She was glad now of her plain and dowdy appearance. Rico Christofides must already be forming some escape route of his own. She'd help him along, agree with him that he must have the wrong person, and then he'd get back into his luxury car and be off, out of her life, until such time as she invited him back in, when she was ready to deal with him. With that assurance, she steeled herself and walked forward.

Rico watched the woman come towards him. For a second he faltered. Was this *her*? The woman approaching slowly looked impossibly plain from a distance, bare of any make-up or artifice. Pale. And her body was all but swamped in clothes that looked as if they'd just been dragged out of a skip.

And she had a child. Something which felt suspiciously like disappointment sent his brain reeling, and he clamped down on that emotion hard. A child was a complication. She came closer, and as he lifted his gaze back to her face he was already trying to come up with some excuse for having come all this way to find her, still doubting that it might be her. Perhaps he had been completely mistaken. Perhaps the name was a freak coincidence.

But then she drew closer, and all thoughts of children and complications fled as his body reacted with a helpless lurch of desire. It *was* her.

Despite her appearance, he could see the intensity of those huge green eyes now, framed with long black lashes, the delicate bone structure, her lush mouth. And her hair, with its irrepressible curls trailing out from under the tatty hat over her shoulders. It reminded him of the moment he'd first set eyes on her in that club. He'd been cursing himself for having gone at all, hating that he'd given in to weak restlessness, and then *she'd* walked in. Dressed in snug jeans and a vest top, completely at odds with the glitter of the too coiffed women who'd thronged the place. The expression on her face had been intense, as if she was being driven by inner demons, and it had resonated within Rico.

The firm swell of her breasts had been clearly outlined against the thin material of her top, and he'd watched, entranced, as she'd walked straight to the middle of the dance floor and started to dance with completely uninhibited grace. He'd seen plenty more beautiful women in his time, clothed and unclothed, but something about her lithe little figure, with its hint of sensual plumpness, had been more enticing than any gazelle-like beauty he'd ever known. With her tawny curly hair she'd looked wild, and free, and it had called to him on a base level too urgent to ignore…

She'd been exquisite. She *was* exquisite. Even though he could see at a glance now that she'd lost weight. Relief flooded him in a way that made him very nervous as she came to a standstill where he blocked the path. And along with the relief came irrational anger to find her living in such an obviously dangerous area. The anger surprised him; women didn't normally arouse feelings of protectiveness within him. He'd noted the local thugs with distaste after he'd knocked and got no answer from her door, and retreated to his car to wait. They'd tried to intimidate him, but after one quelling look they'd recognised the danger within him and maintained a respectful distance.

Right at that moment he'd completely forgotten that he'd just considered making his excuses and leaving. That was now the last thing on his mind.

Gypsy decided to pretend that she didn't know who he was, that she hadn't just seen him again last night. It was cowardly, she knew, but she was counting on him wanting to make his escape from someone who looked like a bag lady.

'Excuse me—you're blocking my way.'

He didn't move aside. Those penetrating grey eyes were fixed on her with unnerving intensity, and Gypsy could feel a flush of response rise up through her body as it reacted with dismaying helplessness to his proximity. As it was she was battling to keep back the images that threatened to burst free. Images of sweat-slicked bodies moving in desperate tandem, straining to reach the pinnacle...

'Why did you run last night?'

His deep voice cut through those disturbing images. Her lie fell out with an ease that would have had her horrorstruck in any normal circumstance. 'My daughter...I had to get home to my daughter.' And then she cursed herself. She hadn't denied that she'd *run*.

At that moment the rain started to fall more heavily, scattering the local teens around them. Rico Christofides gestured to her door, which was up a few steps. 'Let me help you with the pram.'

Panic rose. Gypsy protested, not wanting him anywhere near her place or Lola. 'No, really, I can manage...' But even as she spoke Rico Christofides took hold of the pram and lifted it bodily against him, as if it weighed no more than a bag of sugar. She had to let go or it would have become a tug of war. The irony that Lola could become an object of a tug of war was not lost on Gypsy at that moment.

The rain was teeming down now, flattening his black hair against his skull. Gypsy could feel drops of water falling down her back. When he gestured with his head, she had no choice but to precede him up the steps to the front door. In the manoeuvring that was done to open the door and get Lola inside, with Rico Christofides hanging onto the buggy relentlessly, he was in her tiny one-bedroomed apartment before she knew what was happening or could stop it.

He placed the buggy back down in the pitiful excuse for a sitting room with a gentleness that momentarily disarmed Gypsy. She was a little stunned. With a brusque economy of movement he shut the main front door and came back to shut her ground-floor apartment door. Now he was looking around, and asked, 'Have you got a towel?'

'A towel?' Gypsy repeated stupidly, knowing on some level that she was going into shock.

'Yes,' he said slowly. 'A towel… You're soaked through and so am I.'

'A towel,' she repeated again, and then, as if jolted by a stun gun, she came out of her shocked inertia. 'A towel—of course.' *Get the towel, let him dry off and he'll be gone.*

Gypsy walked on stiff legs to the tiny bedroom she shared with Lola and opened the cupboard to take out a towel. Coming back, she handed it to Rico Christofides, trying not to notice how huge he appeared to be in the small room.

Immediately he frowned and handed the towel back to her. 'You first—you're soaked. Surely you have more than one?'

Gypsy looked at it stupidly, and then gabbled, 'Of course.' She gestured jerkily. 'You take that one. I'll get another.' She tried not to let the mounting impatience she felt be heard in her voice. Why wouldn't he just *leave*?

Coming back to the sitting room, she saw him drying his hair roughly with big hands. He'd taken off his coat to drape it over a threadbare chair, and his impeccable suit was moulded to his strong frame, making her throat dry at recalling the body underneath.

He turned to face her, taking his hands down, leaving his short hair sexily dishevelled. He glowed with vitality and health, making Gypsy feel pale and wan.

He frowned down at her. 'You should take off your coat and hat…' He looked around. 'Do you have a heater in here?'

Reluctantly she pulled off her hat and started to undo her coat, knowing he was right; the last thing she needed was to get ill. She shook her head when those grey eyes settled on her again, expecting an answer, and flushed when they dropped imperceptibly to take in her shabby clothes as her coat slid off. She was very aware of her hair, which now curled in wild abandon around her shoulders, and could just imagine how frizzy it would be from the rain. She wanted to pull it back and tie it up. And she hated that he was making her aware of herself like that.

'Our heater broke this morning. The storage heating will come on in a couple of hours.'

Rico Christofides looked comically shocked. 'You've no *heat*? But you have a child—it's freezing outside.'

Gypsy flushed with a mother's guilt. 'This is the first day it's been broken. We'll manage until we can get a replacement…' She trailed off, suddenly thinking of the fact that now she was out of work her meagre savings wouldn't be stretching to cover a new heater. As if she could explain she'd lost her job because of him. How irresponsible was she?

She looked at Rico Christofides and recognised his wide-legged stance with dismay. He wasn't going anywhere any time soon. With extreme reluctance she finally said, 'Can I get you tea or coffee?'

His eyes narrowed on her once again. The barest hint of a smile tipped up one corner of his wickedly sensual mouth as he recognised her capitulation. 'I'd love a coffee, please. Black, no sugar.'

Stark, with no sweetener—just like him, Gypsy thought churlishly as she went into the kitchen to put on the kettle. All she could hope for now was that Lola wouldn't wake up and Rico Christofides would satisfy whatever bizarre lingering curiosity he had about her and leave. Soon.

Rico looked around the bare apartment as Gypsy moved about the kitchen and he suppressed a shudder of distaste. Without her presence right in front of him his brain seemed to clear slightly. Once again he questioned his sanity in pursuing her here, especially when his eyes fell on the battered-looking buggy which sat just feet away against the wall. His sane impulse was to come up with some plausible excuse—even just ask her why she seemed to be determined to pretend she didn't know him—but a greater overriding impulse was urging him to stay. Even if there was a child in the picture.

He could only make out the fact that her daughter was quite small, so therefore she must have had her since she'd been with him. And even though Rico knew he had no right to feel a surge of anger at that, *he did*.

Even just watching her pull off that damned unflattering hat and coat had scrambled his brain and made him almost forget the presence of the child. The quick movement of her small hands had reminded him of how they'd felt on him, stroking along the most sensitive part of his anatomy until he'd had to beg her to stop... He frowned. *Why* was she so intent on denying she knew him? And that night? Even if he had left the way he had, he knew it had been as cataclysmic for her too. The shocked look of awe on her face just after she'd exploded around him had told him that.

With no false pride he knew he was a good lover, but what he'd experienced that night with Gypsy had gone beyond anything he'd ever known before. *Or since*. It had shaken him out of his complacency. Was that why he needed to see her again? To recapture that moment? To see if it had been his imagination or something... *more*? He balked at that. He never wanted anything *more* with any woman. But that night with Gypsy had touched him on a level that had left him feeling an ache of dissatisfaction, and it had only grown since then, pervading everything around him and tainting the few liaisons he'd had with women in the interim.

He knew seeing her last night had thrown the fact that he'd been trying to recapture that fleeting transcendence he'd experienced with her into sharp relief. With that thought reverberating through his mind he heard Gypsy re-enter the room. He turned to face her and took the coffee she held out. She was avoiding his eyes.

Gypsy escaped Rico's gaze and occupied herself by going to peek in at Lola who, to her relief, was still sleeping peacefully, her cheeks pink and her rosebud mouth in a little moue. Long black lashes rested against plump baby cheeks. Gypsy's heart swelled, as it did every time she looked at her daughter, and at that moment she felt an overwhelming surge of guilt at knowing she was denying Lola's father knowledge of her when he stood only feet away.

She quashed it down, telling herself that she was doing it for good reasons, and straightened up, crossing her arms defensively over her chest. To her surprise she

saw that Rico Christofides had taken a saucepan from
the kitchen and was placing it in the corner of the room
where, to her dismay, she saw that he'd spotted a leak.

As he straightened up again she said, more caustically
than she'd intended, 'Look, what is it you want from
me?' The rogue thought that he could be there because
after seeing her again he'd been overcome with lust set
her mind spinning, before she realised how unlikely that
had to be.

Rico Christofides calmly sat down on the two-seater
sofa and indicated for Gypsy to sit down too. With a
barely disguised huff, which was really more fear than
impatience, she took the chair opposite the sofa. He took
a lazy sip of coffee before putting the cup down on the
chipped table.

'I'd like to know why you seem to be so determined
to pretend we've never met, when in fact we're intimately
acquainted.'

Gypsy blushed to the roots of her hair at the way he
said *intimately*. Tightly, she answered, knowing it was
futile to keep pretending otherwise. 'I am well aware
of the fact that we've met before, but I've no desire to
become reacquainted.'

He regarded her for an uncomfortably long moment
and then said, 'You may not believe this, but I regretted
leaving you the way I did that morning.'

A spasm of emotion made Gypsy clamp her lips together. She didn't doubt this was just a smooth move—he
most likely hadn't given her a second thought. Perhaps
he'd seen her last night and assumed she might be as easy
to seduce again. 'Well, I don't. And you're forgetting that
you left your kindly informative note.'

His face tightened. 'Contrary to what you might have
thought after that night, I'm not in the habit of picking

women up in clubs and booking into the nearest hotel for a night of anonymous sex.'

Gypsy burned inside, but shrugged nonchalantly. 'Look, what do I know or care? It's not something I gave much thought to.'

He sent a pointed look towards Lola's pram, and said ascerbically, 'Clearly I can see that perhaps one-night stands are a habit for you.'

Gypsy gasped in affront and sat up straight, hands clenched on her lap, 'How *dare* you? I'd never had a one-night stand in my life before I met you.'

He arched a brow. 'And yet,' he drawled easily, 'you were remarkably eager to throw yourself into the experience that night, *Gypsy Butler.*'

Gypsy's heart stopped. He knew her full name—of course he did; he'd found her. He'd be able to track her down no matter where she went now. They must have given it to him at the restaurant.

He asked now, 'So, that really *is* your name?'

Gypsy nodded, wanting him gone more than ever now, not liking the way he was making her feel so trapped, and said distractedly, 'My mother had an obsession with Gypsy Rose Lee, hence the name.' She left out the fact that for a good portion of her life she hadn't been called by her birth name at all. As far as she was concerned that part of her life had ended when her father had died.

Forcing her mind away from those memories she said, harshly but quietly, mindful of Lola, 'Look, what is it you want? I'm busy.'

He cast her a scathing glance. 'Busy trying to get away from me, for some reason.' His eyes narrowed on her, and she felt like a tiny piece of prey in front of a predator, with no escape in sight. 'And at high cost—

especially when I happen to know that your disappearing act last night lost you your job...'

Gypsy held in a gasp but said shakily, 'How do you know that?'

His shoulder moved minutely, 'The waiters were remarkably indiscreet and loud.' Taking her by surprise, Rico Christofides asked then, as if it had just occurred to him, 'Where is your child's father?'

Sitting in front of me, she thought hysterically, and schooled her features, hitching up her chin in an unconscious gesture of defiance. 'We're alone.'

'You have no other family?'

Gypsy shook her head, and tried to ignore the feeling of vulnerability his words provoked. Rico Christofides was grim. 'Which proves my point, don't you think? You slept with me and at least one other man soon after—for I can't imagine that you had left a small baby in the care of a stranger while you were with me that night.'

Gypsy shook her head, aghast at the thought of leaving Lola like that while she went off to spend the night with someone. 'Of course I didn't. I would never have done something like that.'

Rico Christofides looked almost smug. She'd proved his point for him, albeit erroneously, because of course she hadn't slept with anyone else since him. With panic galvanising her movements, making them jerky, Gypsy stood up with clenched fists at her sides. 'Look, Mr Christofides, you're really not welcome here. I'd like you to leave.'

It was only at his sharply drawn together brows and the way his head snapped up that Gypsy ran over what she'd just said and realised with sick horror its import.

He rose slowly and looked down at her, frowning, and Gypsy felt the horror spread through her when he said,

'You know who I am. So you *did* know who I was that night?'

She shook her head, feeling sick, the possible future implications of her knowledge too much to consider right now. 'No...no, I didn't. It was only the next morning... when I saw you on the news...'

It had been just after she'd read his note and realised he'd gone. She'd seen the TV in the corner of the room, on a news channel and on mute. He'd obviously been watching it before he'd left that morning. To her utter surprise she'd seen *him*, clean-shaven and pristine in a suit, looking almost like a different person, walking down the steps of an official building surrounded by photographers and an important-looking entourage. Gypsy had raised the sound and watched with mounting horror as she'd discovered exactly who Rico was.

'And yet you never contacted me once you knew... you still left...' He said this almost musingly, as if trying to work her out. Gypsy knew that in his world women who wouldn't take advantage of a one-night stand with a man like him would be few and far between.

She nodded her head vigorously. 'Yes, I left.' And then, far more defensively than she liked, 'I got the hint that morning when I woke and you were long gone, leaving a note which made me feel like a call girl, and to be perfectly honest I have no interest in discussing this any further. I'd like you to leave *now*. Please.'

At that moment, to Gypsy's utter horror and a spiking of panic, a cry came from the pram—which turned into a familiar wail as Lola woke from her nap and demanded attention.

CHAPTER THREE

So she *was* upset with how he'd left her. Rico forced his mind from that intriguing nugget of information. He could see that she was torn between wanting to go to her child and wanting him gone, and then she blurted out, over the ever increasing wails, 'Look, now is really not a good time. Please leave us alone.'

Please leave us alone.

Something about those words, the way she said *us*, the hunted look about her face, made Rico dig his heels in. There was some bigger reason she wanted him gone. She felt threatened. That much was crystal-clear.

And, to his utter surprise, the child's piercing wails were not making him want to run in the opposite direction, fast. Gypsy's words, her whole demeanour was intriguing him, and he hadn't found much intriguing at all lately. He wanted answers to her behaviour, wanted to know *why* she wanted him gone so badly, and her crying baby wasn't about to deter him.

That realisation shocked him slightly, as his only experience with kids to date was his four-year-old niece and her baby brother. While they amused him—especially his precocious niece—his younger half-brother's besottedness had left him perplexed. He just didn't really *get* the whole kids thing. And certainly had no intention of having any himself any time soon—not after the child-hood he and his brother had endured... But that path led to dark memories he wasn't prepared to contemplate now.

With a brusqueness brought on by those thoughts Rico bit out, 'Shouldn't you see to your child?'

With obvious dismay at his intractability, Gypsy went over to the pram and pulled back the cover. Immediately the child stopped crying, just a few snuffles now as Gypsy cooed at her and leant in to pick her up.

In that moment Gypsy's plea to *please leave us alone* resonated in his head. Rico's skin tightened over his bones imperceptibly. He was aware that he'd tensed and stopped breathing. As if he had some prescience of something about to occur, something momentous. Which was crazy...

Gypsy lifted out the solidly warm weight of her still sleepy daughter, unable, despite everything, to keep an instinctive smile off her face. Lola was a happy little girl—rarely grouchy, invariably even-tempered and smiley—which was impossible not to respond to. Gypsy might have castigated herself for her behaviour that night, but she'd never for one second regretted Lola, or contemplated not having her.

Gypsy automatically started to take off Lola's outdoor jacket, as she would be warm after her nap, and tried valiantly to ignore the fact that Rico Christofides would now be looking upon his own flesh and blood for the first time. Pushing that scary thought away, she thought surely now he'd balk at the reality of a toddler and leave them alone?

A child demanding attention was hardly conducive to discussing a one-night stand? Surely he'd see that she wasn't in the market for that again? But even at that thought her lower belly clenched with desire, as if in denial.

Lola's coat was off, and she sat up in Gypsy's arms, more awake now. Having spied Rico Christofides she looked at him shyly, leaning into her mother more, sticking her thumb in her mouth—a habit she'd developed as Gypsy had tried to abstain from using pacifiers.

With the utmost reluctance Gypsy followed her daughter's gaze, knowing what Rico Christofides would be looking at: a delicately built toddler, with wide slate-grey eyes ringed with long dark lashes, slightly darker than pale skin, and a shoulder-length mop of golden corkscrew curls which habitually refused to be tamed. She was adorable. People stopped Gypsy on the street all the time to exclaim over Lola.

At that moment Lola took her thumb out of her mouth and looked at Gypsy, while pointing at Rico Christofides, and said something unintelligible with all the confidence of having uttered a coherent word.

She gave a determined wriggle that Gypsy knew better than to resist, and she had no choice but to put Lola down on her feet and watch as she toddled, still a little unsteady after her nap, over to Rico Christofides, to look up, clearly certain she'd get a warm response. When he just stared down at her, with a slightly shell-shocked expression, Gypsy felt foreboding surround her like a thick ominous fog.

Lola looked from Rico back to Gypsy and then, uncertain because of his lack of response, she came back and held her arms out to Gypsy, who picked her up again and held her close.

'What did you say her name was?' asked Rico after an interminable moment of tense silence, and Gypsy nearly closed her eyes in despair. *He knew.* He'd have to be blind not to know. They had exactly the same uniquely grey eyes, and now that Gypsy had seen him again she could see they shared the same determined chin...and forehead. She was his feminine miniature—a stunning biological example of nature stamping the father's mark on his child so that there could be no doubt she was his.

'Lola,' Gypsy replied faintly.

As if forcing himself to ask the question, not having taken his eyes off Lola yet, he asked hoarsely, 'How old is she?'

Gypsy did close her eyes now—just for a second. The weight of fate and inevitability weighed her down. She was to be given no reprieve, and even if she did try to bluff her way out of this now, and run, she'd have to change her identity to evade Rico Christofides. An impossibility, considering her already precarious circumstances.

'Fifteen months...'

'I didn't hear you,' he said quickly, curtly.

Gypsy winced at the harsh tone of his voice, and said again, with fatality sinking into her bones along with a numbness which had to be shock, 'Fifteen months.'

For the first time his gaze met hers, and she could see what was burning in those increasingly stormy grey depths. Stark suspicion, realisation, shock, horror...all tangled up.

'But,' he said carefully, *too* carefully, 'that's impossible. Because if she's fifteen months old then, unless you slept with someone else directly after me, that would make her...*mine.* And as you haven't contacted me then I can only assume that she *isn't* mine.'

Gypsy's breath became more shallow. She tightened

her hold on Lola, who was beginning to pick up on the tension. That sense of guilt surged back; she couldn't deny him this, no matter who he was. She looked directly at Rico Christofides and swallowed. 'I didn't sleep with anyone else. I haven't been with anyone else...since you.' It killed her, but she had to say it. 'And I wasn't with anyone just before...you.' She didn't think it worth mentioning now that she'd only had one previous lover, in college.

Again too carefully, Rico Christofides said slowly, 'So what you're saying is that your daughter is mine? This little girl is my daughter?'

Gypsy nodded jerkily, going hot and cold in an instant. A clammy sweat broke out over her skin, making it prickle. And at that moment, with impeccable timing, clearly bored with the lack of attention, Lola started to squirm and whinge.

Gypsy seized on the distraction. 'She's hungry. I need to feed her.' And she fled like a coward into the kitchen, where she put Lola into her highchair and started chattering to her saying nonsensical things. She knew she was in shock, close to hysteria—and acutely aware of the man just feet away, who now had the power to rip their lives apart.

Rico wasn't sure if he was still standing. He'd never been so thoroughly shocked, taken by surprise, blindsided in his entire life. All of the control he took for granted had just crumbled around him like a flimsy façade, and he saw how precarious it had really been since he'd taken control of his life at the tender age of sixteen.

He knew anger was there, but couldn't feel it quite yet. He was numbed. And all he could think about was how it had been just those four words which had made him stop: *please leave us alone*. All he could think about was what it had been like to look into that little girl's eyes for the first time and feel as though he'd missed a step, even though he hadn't even been moving.

When she'd toddled over to look up at him with such innocent guile his heart had jolted once, hard, and he'd felt as if he was falling from a great height into an abyss. An abyss of grey eyes exactly the same unique shade as his own, which he'd inherited from his own father. Right now, the most curious sensation flooded him—as if an elusive piece of himself was slotting into place, something he hadn't even been aware was missing from his life.

It was too much. Acting on blind instinct, he crashed out of Gypsy's apartment, through the main door and to his car, where his driver jumped out. Gasping, Rico yanked open the car door and reached inside for what he was looking for. He realised belatedly that it was still raining as he pulled out a bottle of whisky and unscrewed the top, holding it by the neck before taking a deep gulp of the amber liquid.

His driver quickly ducked back into the car, clearly sensing his boss's volatility and his need to be unobserved. With his hand clenched around the bottle, clarity slowly returned to Rico and he welcomed it. This woman had betrayed him in the most heinous way. The worst way possible.

He'd believed that his own biological father had turned his back on him, but in fact he hadn't. His mother and his stepfather had seen to it that he had believed it, though.

And here was Gypsy Butler, repeating history, blithely bringing up his own daughter—his flesh and blood—

clearly with no intention of ever letting him know. She'd tried to get him to leave!

He'd vowed at the age of sixteen that he would never be vulnerable or powerless again. That vow had become his life's code when he'd finally found his father and learnt just how terribly they'd both been lied to—for years. Since then, for him trust had become just a word with useless meaning.

The flimsy chance which had led him to choose that restaurant last night made him shudder in horror; at how close he'd come to never knowing of his own daughter's existence. He looked back towards the still open front door and took in the shabby excuse for a house. Resolve solidified in his chest, and he threw the bottle of whisky back into the car.

He knew that his life was about to change for ever, and damned if he wasn't going to change their lives too. There was a deep primal beat within him now not to let Gypsy or his daughter out of his sight again. The fierce and immediate possessiveness he felt, and the need to punish Gypsy for her actions, were raging like a fire within him.

Gypsy was shaking all over, and had to consciously try to calm herself as she finished feeding Lola and listened out for Rico's car taking off. The speed with which he'd left the apartment had in equal measure sent a wave of relief and a wave of anger through her. While it was her worst nightmare to be in this situation, *how* could he reject his daughter so summarily?

She felt a surge of protectiveness for Lola, and cursed Rico Christofides while acknowledging that she'd expected this to be one of his possible reactions. Straight denial and rejection—just as her father had done with her initially.

She told herself that this was a good thing; she'd salved her conscience by telling Rico Christofides, and Gypsy knew that in the long run they'd both be better off. At least she could tell her daughter as she grew up who her father was, and that it just hadn't worked out between them. Guilt hit her again when she thought of how her daughter might perceive the disparity in their circumstances, but Gypsy reassured herself that—as she knew well—the fact that Rico Christofides was a multibillionaire did not a father make.

Her own life had been changed for ever when her ill and penniless mother had begged her father to take Gypsy in. He'd been the owner of the company where Mary Butler had been a menial cleaner. An impossibly rich man who had taken advantage of his position and taken her to bed, with all sorts of promises, only to drop her and fire her as soon as she'd told him she was pregnant. Unable to get another job or make rent payments, she'd soon become homeless.

Gypsy had spent her first few months in a women's refuge, where her mother had gone after she'd given birth at Christmas time. Slowly her mother had built up her life again, finding more menial work and eventually getting them both a council flat in a rough part of London.

Gypsy had known from a very young age that her mother wasn't coping, and she'd learnt to watch out for the signs so that she could take care of her. Of them both. Until she'd got home from school one day and found her mother passed out on the couch, with an empty bottle of pills on the floor.

The emergency services had managed to save

her—*just*. And the only thing that had stopped them from putting six-year-old Gypsy straight into foster care had been her mother's assurance that she would send her to live with her father. And so Gypsy had eventually gone to live with the father who had never wanted her, and she'd never seen her mother again. She'd only found out later that her father had comprehensively shut her mother out of Gypsy's life.

Forcing her mind away from sad memories, she strained to listen out for the car and still couldn't hear anything. *What was he doing?* She made sure that Lola had a firm grip of the plastic cup she was drinking from and stood up, heart thumping. The door to the apartment was still open, and she crept over to close it.

With one hand on the door, she heard heavy steps. *He was coming back.* Panic made her clumsy as she tried to shut the door completely, but it was too late. A hand and foot prevented her from closing it, and as she jumped backwards in shock at how quickly he'd moved she heard a laconic drawl, edged with steel.

'You didn't think it would be so easy to get rid of me, did you?'

CHAPTER FOUR

She watched, dry-mouthed as Rico Christofides stepped back into the room, closing the door with incongruous softness behind him, angry grey eyes narrowed intently on her, face impossibly grim. Rain clung in iridescent water droplets to his hair and jacket. She had an awful feeling of *déjà-vu*—the same feeling she'd had that day when she'd found her mother unconscious. Everything was about to change and she was powerless to stop it.

The anger she'd felt moments ago at thinking of him rejecting Lola dissipated under a much more potent threat. Just as her father had belatedly and reluctantly swept in and taken over when she'd been six, now Rico Christofides was about to do the same. This was the other reaction she'd expected and feared.

She fought through her fear and bit out through numb lips, 'I don't want you here, Mr Christofides. I never intended you to find out—'

He uttered a curt laugh. '*Clearly* you never intended me to find out. How serendipitous, then, that I just happened to choose *that* restaurant last night, out of the many thousands in London.'

His sensual mouth firmed, and he looked angry enough to throttle Gypsy, but she felt no sense of danger.

'Believe me, it makes my blood run cold to think how close I came to never knowing about this.'

Gypsy heard herself say, as though from a long way away, 'You didn't let me finish. I didn't intend you to find out *like this*. I was going to tell you...at some stage.'

He arched an imperious brow, derision all over his handsome face, 'When? When she turned ten? Or perhaps sixteen? When she was a fully grown person who'd built up a lifetime of resentment for the father who'd abandoned her?' His voice became blistering, his accent thickened. 'Undoubtedly that's what you'd planned, no? Feed her lies and tell her that her father hadn't wanted to know her? Couldn't be bothered to stick around?'

Gypsy shook her head. She was feeling nauseous at the condemnation in his tone. 'No, I...I hadn't planned that at all. I *was* going to tell her—and you—I promise.'

It sounded so flimsy to her ears now. The fact was she'd just proved him right; she'd planned on keeping this from him indefinitely and it made Rico's eyes narrow even more. Gypsy could see the effort it was taking for him not to reach out and shake her. Or perhaps even worse. For the first time she did feel fear, and stepped back.

He noted the move with disgust. 'Don't worry, you and your promises are so far beneath my contempt right now I wouldn't touch you with a bargepole. If you were a man, however...' He didn't need to finish that sentence.

Gypsy bit back the impulse to explain that she'd wanted to use her degree, set up as a practising child psychologist and be solvent before she went looking for him to deliver the news. She'd known how defenceless she would be to someone like him unless she could stand on her own two feet and demonstrate that she was successfully independent. And this situation was proving exactly how right she'd been to be scared.

Yet even now she was impossibly aware of him physically. The way his suit clung to his powerful frame, the way his hands on his hips drew the eye to their leanness. Hips which she could remember running her hands over as he'd thrust into her so deeply that sometimes she still woke from dreams that were disturbingly real...

Half dizzy with shock, and a surge of very unwelcome lust, Gypsy sank down helplessly into the chair behind her. Rico Christofides just looked at her, without an atom of sympathy or concern, even though she could feel her blood draining southwards and knew she must have gone white. She was scared to stand in case she fainted. But she drew on the inner strength which had got her through years of dealing with her domineering father and stood again, albeit shakily.

At that moment a plaintive cry came from the kitchen, and they both turned to see Lola looking from one to the other with huge grey eyes and an ominously quivering lip. Gypsy could see that she was picking up on *her* distress, and moved to take her up and hold her.

With Lola securely on her hip, she looked back to Rico Christofides, slightly shocked to see a stricken look on his face. She steeled herself and said, 'Look, please leave us be. You know now—you know where we are. I don't want anything from you. *We* don't need anything from you.'

He dragged his eyes from Lola to her, and Gypsy felt the cold sting of his condemnation like a whip against her skin. 'Well, I'm afraid that's just not good enough— because I want something from you. *My daughter.* And, until such time as she can speak for herself, *I'll* determine what she needs.'

His effortlessly autocratic tone made chills run up and down Gypsy's spine. It reminded her so much of her father. She instinctively pulled Lola closer. 'I'm her mother. Anything to do with her welfare is *my* decision. I chose to have her on my own. I'm a single mother.'

His eyes speared her then, and she saw a suspicious light. 'You must have deliberately led people to believe that I'd refused to come forward to acknowledge my own daughter. Am I even mentioned on the birth certificate?'

Gypsy blanched and recalled how she'd lied about knowing his identity when asked in the hospital. She'd reassured herself that if she hadn't seen the news that morning she wouldn't necessarily have realised who he was. All of this behaviour; the lying was so unlike her.

She shook her head quickly and visibly flinched when he made a move towards her. For a second she thought he'd rip Lola out of her arms and take her away. Lola started to make sounds of distress.

Rico stopped dead still and said, his face pale with anger, '*Damn* you to hell, Gypsy Butler. How dare you refuse to name me as her father. You *knew* who I was.'

Gypsy was trying not to shake, and to pacify Lola at the same time, keeping her voice carefully calm. 'I was protecting her, protecting us.'

As if aware of his daughter's distress too, he surprised Gypsy by lowering his voice. But that didn't make it any less angry. 'From *what*? You had no right to take that decision.'

Gypsy couldn't speak. How could she explain to this man that once she'd found out she was pregnant she'd known for sure that he could not be told until she was ready to deal with him?

He was waiting for her response, for her justification. She blurted out, 'I saw you on the news that morning.'

He frowned.

Gypsy went on, 'I saw you come out of court after you'd reduced that woman to a wreck—and all because she tried to prove that her baby was yours.'

Rico slashed a hand through the air and said curtly, 'You know *nothing* of that case. I was making an example of her so that no other woman would be inclined to think they could take advantage of me in such a way.'

Gypsy hitched up her chin. 'So how can you blame me for not running to tell you of *my* pregnancy? You made it clear when you left that morning that you didn't want to see me again, and then I saw how you dealt with a woman who claimed to be the mother of your child.'

Rico bit back the urge to tell Gypsy that he'd regretted his hasty departure; he'd phoned the hotel straight after the court case was concluded, hoping against hope that she mightn't have left. But she had. And he was not about to reveal that weakness now…especially not now.

Gypsy watched as Rico's face became even more implacable and hard. She conveniently left out her myriad other reasons for not telling him. The memory of that woman's humiliation in the face of Rico's cold and very public displeasure was still etched on her brain.

His voice was utterly icy when he spoke. 'The difference in this case is that I *know* we slept together. I'd only ever met that woman socially before, and because I rejected her advances and she had some paltry circumstantial evidence to suggest we might have been intimate she tried to prove that her baby was mine. I insisted on a paternity test and a public court to prove my case.'

Gypsy shivered inwardly. He was as ruthless as her

father had said. 'But you ruined that woman's reputation, dragging her through the courts.'

His face was stony. 'She brought it all on herself. She was convinced I wouldn't want to risk the publicity to prove I wasn't the father. I gave her an opportunity to avoid it and she refused, believing I'd be an easy target and pay her off to keep her quiet. Within weeks of the court case she'd admitted who the real father was and was forced to make do with his meagre million euro fortune. Believe me, she does *not* merit your sympathy.'

Gypsy wondered now at the woman's sense of delusion. Anyone could see that Rico Christofides was not a man who would bow to pressure. She tried not to let his explanation sway her, but deep down she had to admit she was surprised. Even so, she asked, 'And yet you believe that Lola might be yours?'

Rico's eyes went to Gypsy's, and something that flared in their depths made her go hot in the face. 'Apart from the fact that you've told me she is, I can be fairly certain that she's mine because the protection I used that night split. When you assured me you'd be safe, I believed you.'

His words fell into the vacuum they'd caused. To Gypsy's horror, all she could remember was that moment when he'd held back from sliding into her to put on protection. Even that had caused her to entreat him desperately, 'Please, Rico…don't stop now. *Please*.' If anything, she was probably to blame for the protection failing because she'd rushed him. And then she had promised him she'd be safe, fully believing that she had no cause to worry. But she hadn't taken into account how erratic her cycle had grown in the months after her father's death…

He continued, cutting through her shameful memory,

'You dare to ask me this after you ran from me last night, knowing I was the father of your child? You ask me this when looking at her is like looking into a mirror for me?' His mouth twisted. 'But don't worry. I'm not so naïve that I won't get a paternity test done just to make sure. Your insistence that you want nothing from me only leads me to believe that you *do*.' He laughed harshly. 'You can hardly expect me to believe that I managed to impregnate the one woman in the world who wants not a cent of my fortune?'

He didn't allow her to interject.

'Perhaps you intended coming after me when she was old enough and skinny enough from malnutrition that your story would pluck at the heartstrings of the public with maximum effect? Or perhaps you just relish the twisted power of knowing you're denying your own daughter her paternal heritage? You'll do what you can to bleed me dry even while keeping me away from her?'

Gypsy clutched Lola even closer, and in an unconscious move shielded her daughter as much as she could from Rico. She felt fierce as she gave a scathing look around the pathetic flat. 'Do you really think that I would choose to bring up my daughter in *this* just so that I could hatch some cunning extortion plan? Or that I revel in the fact that we're dependent on dodgy storage heating? I am a good mother, and despite our challenging circumstances Lola has wanted for nothing. She is well fed, looked after and loved. She is an extremely happy and secure child.'

Rico looked at Gypsy. Her huge green eyes were luminous, and he realised that the sky had darkened outside. The rain was a torrential downpour now, and he could hear the insistent drip-drip of the leak in the corner and feel the damp in the air.

He could not understand this woman. This whole situation. He was certain he was Lola's father—he *felt* it in his bones in a way he couldn't explain and didn't want to articulate to this woman. So why hadn't she fleeced him from the moment she'd found out she was pregnant? Especially as she'd known who he was. None of this made sense to him.

He asked again, 'Why didn't you tell me?'

Gypsy looked away. He saw her bite her lip. Finally she looked back, and he saw trepidation in her eyes, and something that looked suspiciously like fear. 'Because I wanted to protect my daughter and do what was best for her.'

Rico shook his head, uncomprehending. His brain was quick, faster than most, but right now it felt as if treacle had been poured into it.

'What on earth are you afraid of?'

And Gypsy just said simply, 'This.'

'You're not making sense, woman. How can your present situation be better than what I could have offered?'

At that moment Rico had a vivid insight into how it might have been. The shock of finding out that Gypsy was pregnant, but then coming to terms with it. He would never have had to wonder about her. He would have had her in his bed all this time, to sate himself until he was done with her. A curious sense of loss assailed him.

They could have worked out some mutual arrangement with Lola... But even as he thought that, he knew he wouldn't be happy with a *mutual arrangement*. Things had escalated way beyond that now. Gypsy owed him. He'd missed out on fifteen months of his daughter's life. His daughter looked at him as if he was a stranger because he *was*.

He fought not to be distracted by remembering the

illicit thrill which had run through him to hear Gypsy's admission that she hadn't slept with anyone else since him—that he'd been her only one-night stand. She'd been slightly gauche and innocent that night, and she'd been so tight around him—almost like a virgin. At that memory a wave of desire engulfed him.

Gypsy's chin came up and Rico drew on all his control, fought the impulse he had to stride forward and plunder her soft mouth, caress the delicate bones of her jaw.

'There are plenty of people surviving on a lot less than I. Money isn't everything, and I didn't relish the prospect of being hauled through the courts and the tabloids to prove your paternity. It was my decision to have Lola, therefore she's my responsibility.'

Rico fought back the barrage of questions. He sensed that there was a lot more to it than that. But right now he needed to get them out of this godforsaken place. He would have plenty of time to question Gypsy later. She was proving to be an enigma of monumental proportions, but he had no doubt that despite what she said she had an agenda. Every woman did.

CHAPTER FIVE

GYPSY hoped Rico would just take her explanation and leave it at that. She didn't like the look on his face now, though, it was far too determined. And Lola was being far too quiet.

Gypsy turned her head to see that she was just looking at Rico, with big, watchful eyes, thumb in her mouth. Mrs Murphy, Lola's minder, had commented plenty of times that Lola was an 'old soul'.

And then Rico said, 'Get your things together. You're coming with me.'

Gypsy's head whipped around so fast she nearly got whiplash. 'What?'

'You heard me.' Steel ran through his voice. 'I want you to get whatever you need and pack it up. We're leaving this place *now*.'

Gypsy shook her head, panic trickling through her even as the prospect of being whisked away from this flat held undeniable appeal. With anyone but him.

'I'm not going anywhere with you. *We're* not going anywhere.'

Rico folded his arms. 'Why? Because you've got work to go to later?' He clicked his fingers then, as if remembering something. 'Oh, but that's not right, is it?

You walked away from your job last night. Not a very responsible thing to do if you're a single parent, is it?'

Gypsy blanched. She'd forgotten for a moment.

And then, as if thinking of something, Rico asked abruptly, 'Who was minding Lola last night?'

Immediately Gypsy was defensive. Her hackles rose—he was already sounding far too proprietorial. 'Mrs Murphy from down the road. She's a retired qualified childminder who looks after Lola in the evenings for some extra cash.'

He bristled. 'You leave *my* daughter with a stranger in this armpit of a street?'

Gypsy bristled right back. 'She's not a stranger, she's a lovely woman, and Lola has always been perfectly safe with her.' Gypsy's conscience struck her then. She knew that if she'd had a choice she wouldn't have been leaving Lola with anyone. 'And,' she added hurriedly, 'Mrs Murphy comes here to mind her, as Lola is usually already down for the night when I go to work.'

'When you *used to* go to work,' Rico amended. He slashed a hand in the air, 'Here or there, it doesn't matter. This street is a minefield of drug abuse and gangs. I won't have you here for one more night.'

Shaking inside, because her worst fears were manifesting themselves, Gypsy said, 'You can't just come in here and turn us upside down like this.'

'Oh?' Rico sneered. 'Because you have such a lovely set-up here and such a perfect routine?' His voice rang with determination. 'This place is not fit for a dog, much less a small child. You are coming with me and you will stay with me tonight.'

Right then Lola reached up to touch Gypsy's face, and she could feel how cold her small hands were. Guilt rushed through her. The storage heating still hadn't come on, and Gypsy knew that even when it did its heat output was not great. Without the supplementary heater things would be bleak, and far colder than usual. It was freezing, it was damp, and she was horribly aware of the leak in the corner—and the fact that Lola had just got over a bad cold.

Rico Christofides couldn't have picked a worse moment to confront her. *Or a better one,* she realised bitterly.

'What's wrong with her?' Rico asked sharply, his eyes on Lola, who Gypsy could feel getting heavier in her arms.

Weariness struck Gypsy. 'She's tired. She didn't sleep well last night, and she only got a small sleep in the buggy just now.'

Something even more determined crossed Rico's face then. 'I will carry you both out of here bodily if that's what it takes, Gypsy, don't think I won't. We have to talk. You owe me this. And I refuse to stay here a moment longer.'

To her utter shame, Gypsy could feel the fight leaving her. She couldn't in all conscience deny him the chance to talk things over. 'Where are you proposing to take us?'

'To my apartment in town. It's infinitely more comfortable there. I have a housekeeper who can keep an eye on Lola while we talk.'

Feeling as though she was being carried aloft on white water rapids, with the utmost reluctance, Gypsy finally said, 'OK—fine. We'll come with you.'

And then things moved with scary swiftness. Gypsy put a drowsy Lola into her buggy while she got together a bag of essentials. She balked at Rico's assertion that they wouldn't spend another night here, and resolved to make him see he couldn't just waltz in and change their lives, but she packed a small suitcase just in case, knowing well that with a small child she couldn't afford not to be practical.

Finally she was ready, and saw Rico had his coat on again and stood in a wide-legged stance, waiting. He'd asked her about a car seat for Lola, and she'd explained that the buggy seat doubled as one. She'd heard him on his mobile phone, barking out what sounded like orders in Greek. Now he just watched her with cold eyes. So unlike the seductive man who had danced with her in that club that night—not that his effect on her was any less now.

She pushed aside the memory ruthlessly. Her hands were full with bags, and she looked to Lola's pram.

Before she'd articulated anything he moved and said, 'I'll take her. You lock up.'

And before Gypsy could protest or say a word she watched as Rico detached the seat from the buggy frame, as if he'd been doing it all his life, and then lifted the seat up with an ease Gypsy envied. Seeing him cradling the seat with Lola in it made something primal and treacherous rush through her. She wanted to snatch her daughter back from him, and yet her eyes pricked ominously. Gypsy forced the tears aside, knowing that to show any emotion to Rico Christofides would show him weakness—and she couldn't afford to be weak.

Once the flat door and main door had been closed and locked, Rico let Gypsy go to the car first in the teeming rain, accompanied by the solicitous driver, who held an umbrella over her head. He put her bags in the boot, before helping her into the car. When she was settled, Rico strode forward, Lola protected by his coat. Once at the car, he handed her in to Gypsy, who was all fingers and thumbs securing the seat belt around the chair. Lola was bone-dry and contentedly sucking her thumb—which made Gypsy feel peculiar inside.

As the car slowly pulled away from the kerb she remembered something. 'The buggy!'

Rico all but ignored her, officiously making sure that her own seat belt was fastened. Gypsy wanted to slap his hands away when she felt them brush against her thigh, hating the shiver of heat that went through her lower body. He was far too close, as she'd had to move to the middle of the back seat to accommodate Lola's chair. His musky and uniquely masculine scent wound around her, threatening to make all sorts of memories flood back. It was humiliating in the extreme when he clearly didn't feel the same way, at all.

And who could blame him? Gypsy thought wearily, knowing that she looked not far removed from a homeless person. The only smart clothes she owned were her work clothes, and they were useless now...

He finished and straightened up, and said grimly, 'That pram is the least of your worries. By the time we get to my apartment there will be a new one waiting.'

Gypsy tried not to let the quiet warm luxury of the car seduce her. 'You can't just do this, you know...just because you're her father.'

He turned a blistering grey gaze on Gypsy, and she tried not to quail beneath it. The space in the back of the car was claustrophobic. 'The moment you decided to leave me out of the equation was the moment you started stacking the odds against yourself. I have just as much right to my daughter as you, and now that I know of her existence I will move heaven and earth to ensure that she grows up knowing me.'

He turned away to look out of the window, his profile austere, jaw clenched.

Gypsy closed her mouth firmly. She knew that there was no point in remonstrating further right now. Men like Rico Christofides and her father switched off when they weren't hearing what they wanted or expected to hear.

Gypsy turned her head too, her stomach in knots, aghast at how easy it was to just stare at him. She looked out of her own window as London slid past in bleak greyness. She just hoped and prayed that when he saw the reality of living with a toddler even for a few hours he'd be all but paying them to go home.

Before long they were in the much more salubrious area of Mayfair. Clean streets, expensive cars, and even more expensive-looking people. It had stopped raining, almost as if they'd left the black cloud behind over Gypsy's dismal street. Distaste curdled her insides; her father had had an apartment here, where he'd housed his various mistresses.

Rico's car drew to a smooth halt outside a sleek building with an awning over the pavement. A doorman rushed to the car to open the door for them. Gypsy got out and extricated Lola, who had fallen asleep during the journey. She stood on the pavement with Lola in her arms, blinking, feeling a little as though she'd been transported to another planet, and half hoping that she might wake up in a minute and see that this had all been a bad dream.

With not a word, and barely a glance, Rico took Gypsy's bags and led the way into the building and into a lift, where he pressed a button that said *P*. She grimaced to herself. *The penthouse*—of course.

When they emerged from the lift into a plush corridor an apartment door stood open, and Gypsy could see an ample-figured middle-aged woman taking delivery of a myriad assortment of boxes, directing the men to somewhere inside the apartment and saying, 'We need it all set up as soon as possible, please.' Then she saw Rico and broke off with a smile. 'Mr Christofides—you're back already! As you can see it's all just arrived. The men won't be two ticks getting it put together, and then I'll make sure it's set up to your satisfaction.'

Rico brought Gypsy from behind him, his hand on her back, making her feel as if she wanted to arch into it. She stood stiffly, Lola heavy in her arms.

'Gypsy, this is Mrs Wakefield—my housekeeper.'

The warmth in his voice made Gypsy suck in a breath. It reminded her too much of how he'd seduced her so easily. She avoided looking at him and smiled tightly at the openly curious woman, who now looked to Lola.

'Ah, what an absolute cherub. Now, you must be tired and famished. I thought she might be sleeping after the car journey, so I've got a little makeshift bed set up in the sitting room if you want to take her through and lie her down.'

More than a little stunned, Gypsy meekly followed the motherly woman through a gleamingly modern reception area to a huge open-plan room decorated in dark greys and muted tones. A bachelor pad if ever there was one.

Mrs Wakefield showed Gypsy where to lie Lola down, and she even had a cashmere blanket to put over her. She confirmed Gypsy's suspicions when she said chattily, 'I have five girls myself, but they're all grown up now. They grow so fast—mark my words, you won't even see the time fly by before she's turning your heart in your chest with boyfriends and wanting to go out all night.'

Gypsy made some trite comment, but she was very aware of Rico, who had followed them in and was standing silently by. She could feel his censorious gaze. No doubt his housekeeper's words were reminding him of how much he'd missed already.

With a promise to return soon, with some tea and sandwiches, she left them alone in the huge room. Gypsy fussed over Lola for a moment, wanting to avoid looking anywhere near Rico.

He asked then, 'Is it normal for her to sleep like this?'

Gypsy finally stood up and crossed her arms. His question unsettled her, making her defensive. 'She's just catching up. And she normally has a nap in the afternoon anyway.'

Rico's jaw was tight. 'How would I know this?'

Gypsy just looked at him, quashing the dart of guilt, and watched as he took off his coat with jerky movements, before flinging it down over the back of a chair. He started to pace, and Gypsy felt that weariness snake over her again. She hadn't realised how tired she was. But she was exhausted.

In an effort to put some space between them, she moved away and looked around. Floor-to-ceiling windows looked out over London, where clouds made it seem darker, the skyline soaring against them. Despite the grim weather it was enchanting. And completely impractical.

She turned around again, determined, despite the pathetic state of her own flat, not to allow Rico to railroad them. 'We can't stay here for long. This place is a recipe for disaster with a toddler.' She gestured with a hand towards a low glass table. 'There are sharp edges and corners everywhere. Lola's far too inquisitive at the moment—she'll get hurt.'

Rico stood with hands in his pockets, grey eyes narrowed on Gypsy, who could feel a flush rising over her chest and her face. All of a sudden she felt hot, and wanted to take off some layers.

'I will make sure Lola is protected. Within twenty-four hours this apartment will be child-proofed. You'll have to come up with more than such a flimsy pretext to deter me, Gypsy.'

Suspicion and a trickling of cold horror gripped her then, and she asked, 'Those men...what were they delivering?'

Rico ticked off on his fingers. 'A pram, a cot, a changing table... I told my assistant to make sure all the basics were bought and delivered. You can let me know what's missing.'

Gypsy's hands dropped to her sides. 'But...I just came to talk...for one evening...one night. We are going home tomorrow. I have work to find, and Lola's in a routine.' Hysteria was rising. 'You have no right to presume anything. We don't need all that for one night, so you're just going to have to get it taken away again.'

Rico advanced on Gypsy, and she fought not to snatch up Lola, turn and run. He came and stood before her with a look of almost *savage* intent on his face, in his eyes, and Gypsy knew that this was the moment she'd realised just how formidable he was going to be.

'That child is my daughter. I have missed fifteen months of her existence—fifteen months of her development and watching her grow. As far as she's aware she has no father. It doesn't matter that she might be too young to realise the import of that now, *I* do. Know this, Gypsy Butler: as of this day, and from now on, I am in her life and your life. And you, with no job and living in a hovel, are in no position to argue with my wishes.'

Conversely, even as his words horrified Gypsy, she felt on more even ground. She knew what she was dealing with now. She asked, 'Are you threatening me, Rico? Are you saying that if I were to leave with Lola right now, walk out of here, you would bring down the full force of your power on us?'

A muscle jumped in his jaw. His eyes were so dark they looked almost black and not grey. Eventually he said with chilling calm, 'That's exactly what I'm saying. If you were to walk out of here right now, the only way I would allow it to happen was if you were to leave *alone*.' He smiled, and it was feral, 'But, based on the evidence of how determined you've been to keep her from me and all to yourself, I don't think you'll be doing that.'

The implication that he would quite happily let *her* walk away sent something dark to Gypsy's gut. 'You're right. I wouldn't dream of leaving my daughter behind. As for our situation—yes, we're vulnerable, and certainly in no position to fight you should you decide that it's necessary. So of course I'm not stupid enough to encourage your wrath. I know how men like you operate, Rico Christofides. You have no compunction about squashing the opposition just so long as you get whatever it is that takes your fancy at the time. We'll bow to your wishes for now, as we have little choice, but I don't doubt that as soon as you've seen the reality of setting up home with a small child you'll be throwing us back to where we came from, so you can get on with your self-absorbed existence and your bid for world domination. And as far as I'm concerned that moment can't come soon enough.'

Gypsy stopped talking. She was breathing hard. Rico was just looking at her, far too assessingly, and she

cursed herself for having said too much. But, as she knew
well from experience, it *would* be utterly futile to fight
with someone like him. Better to indulge him, let him
play out his father role, and wait for him to get bored.
She had no doubt he would—especially with red-haired
beauties like the one last night waiting in the wings. At
the thought of him sleeping with her something even
darker clenched in Gypsy's gut.

Just then Mrs Wakefield bustled back into the room,
with tea and sandwiches, and Lola woke up, struggling
out of her makeshift bed. Gypsy rushed to help her off
the couch, and automatically lifted her away from the
hazardous glass coffee table. Lola slipped out of her
hands again, like a wriggling eel, and toddled over to
the huge window, fascinated by the staggering view.

She pointed when a bird flew past and exclaimed,
'Birdy!'

Mrs Wakefield finished putting out the tea and went
over to make friends with a clearly delighted Lola. After
a few minutes of largely nonsensical but earnest chatter
from the toddler, she turned to Gypsy, 'She's a sunny
one, isn't she?'

Gypsy smiled wryly, glad of the momentary distraction. 'Most of the time, yes. But woe betide anyone who
gets close when she's tired or hungry...'

Mrs Wakefield held out a hand, and Lola took it trustingly. 'Why don't we go off for a little exploring and let
Mum and Mr Christofides have their tea?'

Before Gypsy could protest Lola was happily toddling
out of the room with Mrs Wakefield, not a care in the
world at leaving her mother behind. And while Gypsy
felt proud, because it was a sign of a happy and secure
child, she also felt absurdly hurt.

When she turned around Rico was holding out a chair

at the larger table for her to sit down, and he said mockingly, 'Don't worry. She's not going to kidnap her or spirit her away.'

Gypsy said nothing, just sat down, still a little shocked at what had spilled out of her mouth only moments before. Clearly she was feeling far too volatile at the moment to be sure of remaining calm and rational. With grim reluctance she finally slipped off her coat, knowing they wouldn't be returning to her flat any time soon.

Rico poured tea and pushed some sandwiches towards Gypsy. She was avoiding his eyes again, and he was still reeling slightly at her outburst. The fact that she was projecting something deeply embedded within her onto him was obvious. He suspected it was the same thing that had stopped her from automatically telling him about her pregnancy. But what?

His interest piqued, he vowed, among everything else he'd already set in motion, to look into Gypsy Butler's life for clues. The fact that he knew nothing about the mother of his child did not sit well with him. If he had ever contemplated having a child with anyone, he knew he was the kind of person to have chosen someone based on cool logic and intellect. The mother of his child would not be left to fate and circumstance, the child would not be conceived in a moment of blind passion— His stomach clenched. But that was exactly what had happened…

But, he reassured himself, he had the means to control that. To control *her.* He watched her eat the sandwiches with relish, and wondered how long it had been since she'd eaten properly. Her baggy shapeless clothes hung off her petite frame, and that slightly plump litheness he remembered so well was gone. Even so, he conceded reluctantly, it did nothing to diminish her appeal or douse his desire.

Abruptly he stood, cup in hand, and went to look out of the window. He didn't like the way she could rouse him so effortlessly, or the way he cared even for a moment that she'd grown thin. And especially he didn't like the way he felt inclined to do everything in his power to restore that vivacious health.

He turned to face her and she was looking at him with big wary eyes. Very like the way Lola had been looking at him in the flat. Her hand was clenched around her cup, a tiny crumb at the corner of her mouth. Her wildly curling hair lay around her shoulders, reminding him of that free spirit image she'd projected when he'd first seen her, which had pulled him to her like a magnet. It made him think for an uncomfortable moment that perhaps she *was* someone who wouldn't be influenced by his wealth.

He steeled himself and reminded himself of exactly what she'd done to him. *The worst thing possible.* Distaste and disgust for the type of woman she was, for the type of mother she was, rose up within him and he welcomed it. On the evidence of her reluctance to inform him about Lola she might not be a gold-digger, but she was something worse. She was the kind of woman who wouldn't hesitate to marry another man and have him bring her daughter up as if she were his own, uncaring of the cataclysmic fall-out that would ensue.

He reacted to the way she was still looking at him, with trepidation mixed with a kind of defiance. 'You *do* know that I'll never forgive you for this, don't you?'

CHAPTER SIX

'YOU *do know I'll never forgive you for this, don't you?'*

The words resounded in Gypsy's head as she lay wide awake in the softest bed imaginable much later that night. It had taken ages to put Lola down after she'd been fed, bathed and changed. The penthouse was far too exciting for her—plus the attention of not only Rico but a clearly besotted Mrs Wakefield, who had been the soul of discretion even though Gypsy had seen her looking assessingly from Lola to Rico.

To see Lola running around the cavernous rooms had made Gypsy's chest ache, very aware of how cramped their own space was…

Mrs Wakefield had shown Gypsy around the entire apartment, and brought her to an enormous suite where a cot had been set up by the king-sized bed. An impromptu nursery had been made in the dressing room. A huge bathroom completed the suite, and Gypsy had seen from a brief look into Rico's own rooms, stamped with his masculine touch, that he had an even larger suite.

The housekeeper had told her how to get around the kitchen, and shown her where everything was. Gypsy had been bemused more than shocked to see the fridge and cupboards were already stocked high with an assortment of baby food, and the formula she'd requested. There had even been baby monitors, so that Gypsy could keep one with her as she moved about the apartment in case she didn't hear Lola wake.

Lola slept nearby now, and Gypsy could hear her baby breaths, light and even. Usually the sound comforted her, but her stomach hadn't unclenched all evening—or, in truth, since she'd seen Rico just last night. *Just last night.* It was hard to believe that within the space of twenty-four hours she was ensconced in his apartment. But then, she surmised grimly, she'd feared exactly this kind of autocratic takeover all along.

And yet her conscience niggled her. While he was being just as controlling as her father had been, she couldn't deny the fact that, unlike her father, Rico was showing nothing but signs of accepting Lola.

He'd come into the kitchen where she'd been making herself some cocoa after putting Lola down for the night and said coolly, 'I've arranged for my doctor to come in the morning. He'll take swabs from Lola and I, and we'll have paternity proved within the week.'

Without giving her a chance to say a thing, he'd continued relentlessly, 'I don't see any point in your going anywhere until we have the results of the paternity test, so you will remain here for the week. Once it's established that I'm Lola's father, the first thing we will see to is amending the birth certificate so that my name is added.'

Utterly remote and cold, he'd inclined his head then, and said, 'If you'll excuse me? I have some work to attend to in my study. I trust you know your way around now?'

Gypsy had nodded, intimidated by this ice-cold man. 'Mrs Wakefield was more than helpful.'

'Good.' And without another word he'd strode out of the kitchen.

Gypsy had heard a sound then, on the baby monitor. Straining her ears, she'd just been able to make out that Rico must have gone in to look down on Lola. Her heart had lurched treacherously at realising that. There was silence for a long moment. She'd heard his breath, and then something indistinct that sounded like Spanish.

With a shiver, Gypsy realised that even if his initial acceptance of his own flesh and blood wasn't mirroring her father's cold rejection of *her* the outcome would be the same. Rico was staking his claim, vowing not to let his daughter be taken away from him. Vowing to make Gypsy pay...just as her father had done to her mother—albeit for different reasons.

In Gypsy's case, once Social Services had been involved, and her father had had no choice but to acknowledge her, he'd made sure that Gypsy had never seen her mother again. It had only been in later years that she'd discovered that her mother had died alone in a mental hospital just a few years after that awful day.

Gypsy had always suspected that nothing much had been wrong with her mother other than a tendency to depression, which could have been exacerbated by her birth and their tough circumstances. She'd been a mournful woman, prone to pessimism, and not very strong. But nothing that a little support mightn't have helped.

Her father had cut Mary out of Gypsy's life ruthlessly, and even though he'd had information as to her whereabouts he'd refused to help her at all. He'd let her be sucked into the labyrinthine mental health-care system, eventually to die. After her father's death Gypsy had found heartbreaking letters from her mother, begging for his help, begging for a chance to see Gypsy again. It had been almost too much to bear...

Gypsy sighed deeply and tried her best not to think of that now. Tried not to think of how it had killed her inside to realise the night she'd met Rico that she had found it so easy to gravitate towards a man of her father's ilk. Was there something within her that resonated with powerful and ruthless men, despite what her father had done to her and her mother?

She sighed again, and turned over to face where Lola slept so peacefully. Her father was gone. And, while she might be in this untenable situation with Rico now, she was *not* like her mother. She would not be so easily separated from her daughter. She was infinitely stronger and more resourceful. They would get through this, and she would *not* let him consume them utterly just because he craved control.

The following morning, early, Rico sat at the breakfast bar in the state-of-the-art kitchen. The *Financial Times* couldn't hold his interest. He looked around and grimaced, seeing for the first time exactly what Gypsy had seen yesterday evening. The place *was* a potential minefield for an innocent toddler. Watching how Lola had gleefully run around last night, having to be plucked from danger every two seconds, had made him sweat. He'd never had to account for a small child before.

His heart clenched at recalling her vibrant energy, and how right it had felt to have her here—how quickly he'd felt that if anyone so much as looked at her the wrong way he'd want to flatten them.

She was beautiful—more beautiful than anything he could have imagined. She was bright, sharp, inquisitive. And, he had to concede grudgingly, all the evidence pointed to the fact that Gypsy was indeed a good mother.

Finding Gypsy in the kitchen making hot chocolate last night had made him feel unaccountably off-centre. Because she'd looked *right* in that domestic milieu. It had been almost as if he couldn't remember a time when this penthouse had just been his London *pied-à-terre*, a place where he invited his mistresses for transitory pleasures. The sense of triumph had disturbed him, making him sound more caustic than he'd intended when he'd outlined his plans for the week.

When he'd gone to look in on Lola as she'd slept, a wave of emotion he'd never felt before had nearly felled him. His hand had shaken as he'd reached out to stroke soft skin—soft as a rose petal. And he had known in that moment, as he'd looked down at her flushed and downy cheeks, at the riot of golden curls around her head and that tiny, fragile and yet so sturdy body, that he was possibly falling in love for the first time.

As for her mother... Rico welcomed the hardness that settled in his chest at just thinking of her. All he felt for Gypsy was a singular irritating desire, which he hated to acknowledge, and the need to seek vengeance. To make her bend to his will. To punish her for keeping their daughter secret from him.

Just then he heard Lola's cry come from the baby monitor, which Gypsy had obviously left in the kitchen last night. She cried out again, and the cries became more forceful as she woke up. Rico tensed all over. Silently he cursed Gypsy. Why wasn't she attending to their daughter? Perhaps something was wrong?

Feeling a very unwelcome sense of panic, Rico was about to stride from the room when he heard Gypsy's soft, sleep-filled and husky voice. 'Good morning, sweetheart...'

He heard the rustle of movement but still couldn't relax; hearing Gypsy's voice was sending a new kind of tension through his body.

'Did you sleep well, my love?'

Lola cooed in response, and Rico heard the sound of kisses. Heat flooded his body.

'I bet you did...you're my best girl, aren't you?'

With an abrupt move, Rico shut off the monitor. The problem was she was *his* girl now too, and the sooner Gypsy came to terms with that the better.

He finished his coffee with one gulp and went to his study to make some calls.

Gypsy was just finishing feeding Lola her breakfast when Rico walked into the kitchen. Immediately her heart thumped hard, and she felt self-conscious in the same baggy jeans and an ancient college T-shirt, with her hair dragged up and held in place with a big clip.

Lola grinned happily at Rico, sending specks of food flying as she waved her spoon around and chattered in baby-speak. Immediately aware of how pristine Rico was in comparison to her, in his dark trousers and white shirt, Gypsy leapt up to get a cloth and wipe the floor.

His voice came curtly. 'Leave it. Mrs Wakefield will see to it.'

She flushed, but sat back down again. 'I don't want to give her any more work to do.'

Rico smiled tightly. 'While your concern is commendable, Mrs Wakefield has a veritable army of cleaners under her, so don't worry about it.'

He leaned back against the fridge and looked with such indulgence at Lola that Gypsy found it hard to breathe. Then his expression changed visibly to something much cooler as he looked at her. 'I trust you slept well?'

She nodded, watching as Lola grabbed her cup. She was getting to that age when she was determined to do everything herself. 'Yes. Very well. I'm lucky that Lola has always been a pretty good sleeper, and she was tired last night.'

'*You* look tired,' he said abruptly, and when Gypsy glanced up she could see his face flush, as if he was angry with himself for noticing.

She shrugged, feeling even more self-conscious and haggard. 'I've been working hard...' She amended it, '*Was* working hard.'

He obviously noticed her T-shirt and asked now, 'You went to London University?'

Gypsy busied herself cleaning Lola, who squirmed to get away. She hated having to tell him anything, but nodded and said, 'I studied psychology, and specialised in child psychology.'

'When did you graduate?'

'Two years ago.' Just weeks before she'd met Rico in that club. Not that she was going to mention *that* now.

Rico finally walked over to the coffee machine, and with his intense regard off her for a moment Gypsy could breathe again. She cast his broad back a quick glance. 'I'll need to go out today to get some things for Lola. I need nappies and some other supplies.'

Rico turned around and leaned back easily against the counter, coffee cup in hand. 'I've taken the day off work. My doctor will be here in about an hour to take the swabs and then we can go out together. We can get what you need, and there's a park near here where Lola can play for a bit. We'll have to stay out of the apartment anyway, as people are coming in to child-proof it.'

Surprise washed through Gypsy at the speed with which Rico was adapting his world to accommodate Lola—and also, she had to admit, the fact that he wasn't already gone to work, having left behind an impersonal note, or indeed no note. On the contrary, he was taking a day off. She couldn't remember one instance when her own father, or her vacuous stepmother, had taken a day off for her. Not even on school sports days. Not even on the day when she'd come to her father's home to move in. His cold housekeeper had brought her to a room and told her to stay there until dinnertime.

Feeling unaccountably threatened, and vulnerable from the memory, Gypsy said churlishly, 'Afraid that if you turn your back we'll be gone?'

Rico's eyes flashed, but he took a lazy sip of coffee and drawled, 'Let's just say that trust is certainly an issue.'

She couldn't say anything in response. She didn't want to let him know how much he was surprising her. 'We'll be ready after I've washed and changed Lola.'

Rico put down his coffee cup then, and for a second Gypsy could have sworn that something intensely vulnerable flashed across his face. But it was gone before she could be sure.

'Good,' he said curtly, and watched as Gypsy's jaw tightened in response.

She lifted Lola up to take her out of her seat. Rico had to school his features. For a second an impulse had risen up out of nowhere to offer to help with Lola. It had come out of a desire to get to know her better, to know her routine, watch what Gypsy did with her. Rico forced himself to remember that if he hadn't seen Gypsy in the restaurant he'd still be unaware of the fact that he was a father.

Gypsy walked into the bedroom later that day, exhausted, and succumbed for a moment to sit on the bed. She felt upside down and inside out. After the genial and twinkly-eyed doctor had been and gone that morning, having taken swabs from Lola and Rico, Rico had changed into jeans and a thick jumper and they'd gone out, wrapped up against the cold. Clearly he didn't trust them to be further than ten feet away from him.

They'd gone to the local shops, where Gypsy had bought what she needed, insisting on paying, much to Rico's obvious chagrin. He'd looked ridiculously out of place in the local pharmacy. And then they'd gone to a local park, where Rico had largely ignored her and focused on Lola, who had basked happily in this new friend's attention. Now, after holding herself so tightly for hours, and being so excruciatingly aware of Rico's physicality, Gypsy's defences were extremely shaky.

Rico's unquestioning certainty that Lola was his still stunned Gypsy. And the fact that Lola was out in the living room right now, playing happily with Rico, made Gypsy feel very funny.

Gathering her energy again, she went to the nursery to get a bib for Lola's dinnertime. When she opened the door she gasped out loud, belatedly remembering Rico's scathing looks at her flimsy nondescript clothes that morning. She'd heard him making sporadic calls on his phone during the day but hadn't thought much of it till now...

In shock, she took in what had to be thousands of pounds worth of clothes for her and Lola, hanging up or put away in drawers. The temporary nursery had been moved to a little ante-room off the bathroom, and was kitted out with even more accessories.

A potent memory of her father made her vision blur with anger. At the age of thirteen she'd been mesmerised when she'd seen the profusion of beautiful clothes he'd bought for her—until she'd realised to her shame and horror that they were all either too big or too small. And that he'd bought them specifically for her to wear socially, at his side, not out of any genuine paternal affection. He'd forced her to wear them, reading her acute embarrassment as ungrateful thanks. He'd had no comprehension of a daughter on the threshold of puberty, with a rapidly developing body.

And now Rico had taken a decision to do more or less the same thing. At no point during the day had he even asked her opinion. Or suggested that they go shopping together. Not that she would have complied, she knew grimly, but it would have been nice to be consulted. He was *buying* them—throwing money at the problem.

Gypsy gathered up some of the baby clothes, with their ostentatious designer labels, and stalked into the living room, where Rico was standing at the window with Lola held high, pointing things out. He looked around, those grey eyes glowing, only to rapidly cool as he took in Gypsy's stiff stance.

'What's the meaning of this?' She held the clothes out stiffly, some falling to the ground.

Rico's eyes flashed as he turned to face her. 'You're both in dire need of new wardrobes. I can provide that.'

'I've already told you,' Gypsy spat, 'we don't need you, or your money. To spend money on clothes this expensive is pure extravagance. There's enough in there to clothe an entire village of babies, not just one. As it is, Lola's growing so fast that she'll have outgrown most of them before she can even wear them.'

Rico's face tightened, a muscle moving in his jaw, and Gypsy felt like a complete bitch. Because she had the strangest sensation that she'd just hurt him.

'I will provide for my daughter. That is non-negotiable. And while you are with me, under my roof, you will *not* go outside the door looking like a bag lady.'

'God forbid,' Gypsy muttered caustically, somehow relieved that Rico was retaliating, 'that we should embarrass the great Rico Christofides.' She put down the rest of the clothes and held her hands out for Lola, who squirmed to get to Gypsy. 'It's time for her dinner now.'

After an interminable moment full of crackling tension Rico finally handed her over, and bit out, 'I'll be in my study for the rest of the evening. If you're so concerned about the excess of clothes, take out what you think she won't need and I'll have them sent back.'

And then he walked out, and Gypsy inexplicably felt like a complete heel.

A couple of hours later she sat by Lola's cot, watching her fight against sleep, her eyes getting heavier and heavier. And Gypsy was still fighting that feeling of guilt. Because Rico was all at once confirming every one of her worst suspicions and yet confounding them at the same time. The image of Lola in his arms earlier was still clear, and she knew she'd been a coward in not acknowledging how it had made her feel—knew too that her knee-jerk reaction to the clothes had come from somewhere that had much more to do with painful memory than the present situation.

* * *

In his study at the same moment, Rico looked impossibly grim as he picked up his phone. When someone answered, he bit out tersely, 'Gypsy Butler. I want you to find out everything you can about her. Money is no object.'

When he put the phone down Rico took another gulp of whisky from the bulbous glass and passed a weary hand over his face. Women caused not a ripple in his life: they were there, they were willing, and he always chose the most beautiful and experienced. *Until that night*, when everything he'd thought he knew had blown up in his face...

No woman, *ever*, had made him want to simultaneously throttle her and kiss her. His mouth curled up in a feral smile. Kissing Gypsy certainly would help assuage the near-constant ache in his groin, but he could well imagine the resistance she would undoubtedly put up. She tensed whenever he came near her, but he could see the signs of attraction. It hummed between them like a current of electricity.

Domination of this woman was rapidly becoming his life's obsession, and sensual domination over her rebellious nature was going to be sweet indeed. For the first time since he could remember work was taking a back seat in his life. Going shopping was something he hadn't indulged in in a long time. It had reminded him uncomfortably of the night when he'd met Gypsy in the club, and he had ducked into an all-night pharmacy to get protection, like an out-of-control teenager.

He'd felt uncomfortably exposed when she'd pointed out his impulsive gesture to spoil his daughter. How could he explain to Gypsy that he wanted the chance to lavish everything on Lola that he'd been denied up till now? He'd felt exposed and weak; no one had made him feel like that in a long time and he didn't welcome it.

Perhaps when he'd had Gypsy again he would be able to see clearly how best to slot her into his life. She had to want *something*, despite her apparent moralistic outrage at his wealth; she'd made a big song and dance earlier, insisting on paying for everything—Rico couldn't remember the last time a woman had insisted on paying for anything—but once he knew what it was Gypsy wanted, what her weakness was, he would manipulate her to his ends. The most important thing for now was to ensure that he bound both Gypsy and Lola to him as tightly as he could. They weren't going anywhere for the foreseeable future.

The following evening Gypsy fumed and seethed. She paced along the huge window in the living room and glared at the view. The apartment was quiet. Mrs Wakefield had gone home and Lola was asleep.

When they'd woken that morning Gypsy had found a note from Rico.

I'll be at the office all day. Call me if you need anything.

He'd listed a number. Gypsy had breathed a sigh of relief, but had momentarily felt an uncomfortable spiking of something suspiciously like disappointment.

It had been later, when she'd been in the hallway, putting the last of the bags full of new clothes she'd decided she and Lola didn't need—which was most of them—that she'd noticed the tabloid newspapers.

Mrs Wakefield had confided to her that they were her weakness, and that Rico got them delivered each day for her. Something had caught her eye, and she'd opened the top one out to see a grainy picture of Rico, herself and Lola in the park the day before.

Rico had Lola in his arms, and Gypsy stood to one side smiling. She couldn't even remember that she had been smiling, and it felt like a treachery to see it now. The headline screamed out: *Tycoon Rico's secret family!*

In horror, Gypsy had thrown the paper down. With anger boiling upwards she'd tried to call him, but hadn't been able to get past the clipped secretary who'd said officiously, 'I'm terribly sorry but Mr Christofides can*not* be disturbed at the moment if it's not urgent. I'll pass on a message?'

Gypsy had bitten out, 'Tell Mr Christofides that his *secret family* would like to talk to him.'

He'd planned it—she knew he must have planned it. To make sure that it was out there in the public domain that he had a child. So that they wouldn't be able to make a move without being followed.

Sure enough, when Gypsy had rung down to the doorman he'd sounded bewildered and confirmed that, yes, there suddenly seemed to be hundreds of photographers outside the door. To think that she had been *surprised* by Rico's apparent willingness to spend time with them.

The apartment door opened at that moment and Gypsy turned round, hands clenched into fists at her sides. With her heart thumping she waited, and watched as Rico's powerful frame appeared in the doorway. He was tugging at his tie and looked tired. She quashed the concern.

'Thank you for calling me back today.' Sarcasm dripped from her voice.

His eyes burned a dark grey, no expression on his face. 'I got the message.'

Gypsy was starting to shake at his non-response. 'Do you know that if I hadn't seen the tabloids and had gone out with Lola we would have been ambushed by the hundreds of photographers outside? As it was we couldn't leave all day, and to keep a toddler cooped up in an apartment—even one as large as this—is not a pleasurable experience.'

He walked further into the room and pulled off his tie, flicking it down onto a sofa while his large hand went to open the top button of his shirt. Gypsy wanted to back away, but couldn't as the window was already at her back.

'I heard about the tabloids getting pictures. There were bodyguards waiting outside. You would have been protected.'

Gypsy threw up her hands. 'Oh, I'm sorry—is that something I'm just meant to know by osmosis? And what good would bodyguards have been with a hundred paparazzi snapping pictures of me and my child?'

He came closer, and Gypsy could see the glorious olive tone of his skin, that stunning bone structure, and the slightly crooked nose which hinted at a past which contained violence. Despite his urbane exterior, a sense of barely leashed danger oozed out of him.

His mouth was grim. 'I didn't call you back because I was involved in intricate negotiations and could *not* break away.'

Gypsy smiled bitterly. 'Oh, I'm sure you were. Nothing is as important as *negotiations*, or making your next million.'

His eyes flashed at that, but he just said, 'I knew you and Lola were safe. If I'd thought for a second you were calling about something serious—'

Gypsy gasped. 'That *was* serious! Our safety was

compromised, and we were forced to stay inside like fugitives. Not to mention the fact that our faces are all over the tabloids and everyone is wondering who this *secret family* is.'

Horror trickled through Gypsy at the thought of people digging and finding out about her history. She had a very real fear that if Rico found out who her father had been, and what she had done when he'd died, he would hold it against her—use the information to make her seem like a weak mother. And if he ever found out about her mother's mental instability…

Fear galvanised her as she squared up to Rico. 'I'm leaving in the morning. Taking Lola with me, back to our flat. Your plans are not going to work. I have rights as Lola's mother. I've given you a chance to see her, but I will not let our lives be turned upside down like this.'

Gypsy went to stalk past Rico, but he caught her arm in a bruising grip.

She looked up and tried not to be aware of how tall he was. 'Let me *go.*'

His mouth was a grim line. 'You're not going anywhere, Gypsy. We don't have the test results back yet, and that mob outside will follow you and hound you until they know every last detail of your life.'

He articulated her fears exactly. Bitterness blinded her. 'Which is exactly what you planned, isn't it? You expect me to believe that you didn't *know* about the pictures? Tell me—is one of those filthy editors your friend? Can you feed him stories when you want? Manipulate things to suit you? Manipulate *us*?'

It had been one of her father's favoured *modus operandi*—the manipulation of the media.

'*No.*' Rico sounded incensed, insulted. A muscle clenched in his jaw. 'Of course not. The paparazzi are always on my trail. I'll admit I was aware of them lurking yesterday—and, yes, I'll admit that the thought of some pictures turning up didn't bother me too much. But I didn't anticipate this level of interest.'

His hand was still on her arm, making Gypsy feel all sorts of sensations, making her forget why she was so angry. He was so close—too close. She tried to pull away but his hold increased. She felt desperation rise.

'Let me go, Rico. You had no right to expose us like that, and you didn't mind the thought of pictures turning up because you had to realise that it would constrain our movements. No wonder you went back to work today. I'm taking Lola tomorrow, and we'll leave London if we have to.'

Rico whirled her so fast that Gypsy lost her balance and only stayed standing because he gripped both her arms. He stared down at her and she was mesmerised by his eyes. He shook his head, and his harsh hold on her arms inexplicably gentled, even though he was silently telling her of his refusal to let her go. His eyes roved her face, and Gypsy's mouth tingled betrayingly where his eyes rested on it for a long moment.

To her utter chagrin and horror she couldn't remember exactly why she and Lola had to get away so badly. She was back in time, staring up at Rico for the first time and thinking that he had to be looking at someone else—he couldn't be looking at *her* like that.

His hands drew her closer, and Gypsy felt her feet moving against some dim and distant will she was trying to impose.

Rico was finding it hard to remember what they'd been talking about. He was forgetting the tinge of guilt he'd felt at Gypsy's accusation. While he certainly hadn't intended for them to be hounded by the press, he *had* seen the advantage in allowing it to become public knowledge that he had a daughter. But now, as he looked down into Gypsy's deep green eyes, all that faded.

His voice was rough and deep. The words felt as if they were being pulled out of him. 'Dammit, I still want you. I couldn't forget about you, no matter how hard I tried. That's why I came after you.'

Gypsy fought the clamour of her pulse, threatening to suck her under. Everything she'd been angry about was disappearing under a wave of need so strong it was making her shake. She fought not to give in to Rico's pull, and said scathingly, 'You were thinking of me even as you slept with that woman the other night?'

He smiled, and it was pure danger, 'Jealous, Gypsy? Because if you are then surely that means you haven't been able to forget about me either.'

'Damn you to hell, Rico,' Gypsy said shakily. Too many nights when she'd woken aching for this man's touch were mocking her now.

'Well, if I'm going to hell then you're coming with me.'

He pulled her right into him, and her T-shirt and jeans were no barrier against his long, lean, *hardening* body. A tremor of pure arousal shot through her as his head descended. For a split second Gypsy tried to articulate something negative, but their breaths were mingling, and then his mouth was slanting over hers with expert precision and she was lost…

She was back in time, on the street outside that club, after putting her hand over Rico's mouth because she didn't want to know his name, because she didn't want any kind of reality to intrude on the moment. And he'd pulled her into him and kissed her for the first time.

The kiss then, as now, had been the culmination of

an intense build-up. His mouth was hard and firm, and yet soft enough to make her melt and yearn and lean into him even more. Tacitly telling him of her approval, of her desire. Rico groaned deep in his throat and deepened the kiss, plundering Gypsy's mouth, finding her tongue and stroking along it with erotic mastery. His hands had moved down to clasp her hips, fingers digging into her waist. Her hands clung to broad shoulders. She could feel her hair loosen from its topknot and fall down over her shoulders.

Between her legs she was burning up, the ache she'd been feeling for two years growing more acute with each passing second, with the tantalising promise of fulfilment. As if reading her mind, Rico pulled her even closer, his big hands spreading around her buttocks to lift her against him slightly, so that she could feel his arousal more fully.

And all the while their mouths clung, and a desperation was building in the kiss, as if they'd both suddenly realised the depth of the passion they'd been missing for two years. Gypsy strained higher, her hands going to Rico's head, where her fingers tangled in silky strands, keeping his head against hers. Not allowing him to escape...

With another guttural moan, Rico impatiently found and pushed up Gypsy's T-shirt, smoothed his hand up over her waist and belly to cup her breast. With a gasp she couldn't hold back she tore her mouth away from Rico's and looked up—dazed, dizzy.

At that moment a little squeak came from the baby monitor. They both tensed and froze. The red mist of arousal cleared from Gypsy's brain and the present moment came back. She was plastered to Rico's front, all over him like a clinging vine. And his hand cupped her lace-covered breast intimately.

No other sound came from the monitor, but Gypsy used the impetus to push roughly away from Rico, who stood there looking dishevelled and utterly gorgeous, cheeks flushed, eyes so dark they looked black in the dim lighting. More buttons on his shirt had been opened. Horror gripped her. Had she done that?

She backed away and hit the window, was glad of the support. She felt as though she might just slide down it and land in a heap of sprawled limbs. 'I don't know...' she began shakily '...that was...'

'That,' Rico said grimly, sounding utterly composed, 'was something we will return to—without interruption.'

Gypsy shook her head, and quivered as Rico strode forward and caged her in, putting his hands either side of her head on the thick glass.

'We've just proved that this desire has not died. If I were to seduce you right here and now I could have your legs around my waist and take you right against this window.'

The carnality of his words made Gypsy blush brick-red, even as the image in her mind strangled any denial she might make. She just shook her head again—pathetically.

Rico brought a finger to her cheek and trailed it slowly and sensuously down over her jaw, and lower, to the V of her T-shirt which rested just above her cleavage. His eyes met hers. 'You won't be going anywhere, Gypsy. Not until I say so.' A chill entered his voice. 'And if you do, I'll find you. So you see, no matter where you go, I'll simply bring you back. You and Lola are mine now, and I always claim what's mine.'

At that moment the monitor sprang to life again, and Gypsy jumped. A plaintive wail sounded. *'Mama...'*

'I hate you, Rico.'

He smiled, and it didn't reach his eyes. 'I hate you too, Gypsy. But conveniently enough our desire seems to exist in spite of our mutual antipathy.'

Gypsy finally managed to bring her hands up to knock Rico's down, and on extremely wobbly legs, feeling perilously close to tears, she left the room to tend to Lola.

CHAPTER SEVEN

RICO sat heavily on the couch once Gypsy had left. In truth his legs felt profoundly unsteady. His heart was racing and, despite the coolness he'd just projected, the taste of Gypsy, the feel of her, the scent of her, had all acted like the most powerful aphrodisiac. If they'd not been interrupted by Lola just now, he wouldn't have been far from freeing himself from his confining clothes, pulling off her jeans and surging up and into her moist heat against the window he'd just taunted her with. He burned with a need he'd only felt once before—the night he'd met her.

He reeled at realising how quickly passion had blazed—literally within minutes of arriving in the door from work. But something about the way she'd told him that she intended to leave had unleashed a wave of possessiveness and desire inside him so strong that it still astounded him.

Through the baby monitor he heard Lola's cries abate, and Gypsy saying in a voice that sounded suspiciously husky, 'What is it, sweetie? You woke up?'

Even at that Rico tensed all over again, and cursed volubly. And then the monitor went suddenly silent, as if Gypsy had realised he might hear them and had turned it off, and he had to restrain himself from going down to the room and demanding irrationally that she put it back on.

That Friday morning Gypsy got the call which meant the inevitable end of life and freedom as she and Lola had known it. In a curt voice Rico wasted no time in informing her that he had the paternity test results and they were positive.

You could have saved your precious money, Gypsy wanted to hurl at him but didn't. She merely listened to him tell her that he'd be home soon to talk to her, and put down the phone.

While Mrs Wakefield gave Lola some lunch, Gypsy paced the floor of the living room. Every nerve in her body was coiled tight, and had been ever since that kiss three nights ago. Since then she'd done everything possible to avoid being alone with Rico—much to his evident and mocking amusement. His steel-grey eyes followed her with heavy-lidded intent whenever they were together—which hadn't been that often, as he'd been working till late most days, confirming for her that he would fall into a predictable pattern of work. Even that hadn't induced feelings of recrimination, only something suspiciously like disappointment.

Her motivation had changed from an intense desire to get away from Rico and his autocracy to the treacherous desire for her own self-protection. She was already so vulnerable to him, and now she was even more vulnerable. Because clearly her mind had absolutely no control over her body. And her body wanted Rico so badly that she dreamt of it when she slept and craved it when she was awake.

She hated that she could be so weak, that even

knowing Rico was intent on controlling them she could still desire him so badly.

Just then she heard the unmistakable sound of his return, and went to see him standing at the door of the kitchen, taking in the sight of Lola happily chirruping away with Mrs Wakefield, causing a circle of destruction around her highchair. He had a look on his face that made Gypsy's heart twist, and then he said, sounding suspiciously gruff, 'Mrs Wakefield, I'd like to introduce you to my daughter—Lola.'

Mrs Wakefield smiled affectionately. 'Well, I could have told you that the minute I saw her. She's the image of you.'

As if just becoming aware of Gypsy's presence Rico turned his head, and all that warmth was gone in a flash. She shivered. He hated her. He really hated her now that he had incontrovertible proof that he was Lola's father.

He turned back to Mrs Wakefield and asked, 'Would you mind taking Lola for a walk when you've finished here? I have some things to discuss with Gypsy.'

The older woman said yes easily, and Rico looked back to Gypsy and said curtly, 'My study—now.'

Feeling like rebelliously stamping her foot and saying no, Gypsy took a deep quivery breath and followed his tall, broad figure down the hall and into the study. It was dark and book-lined, with all sorts of modern technology humming silently.

Rico turned and watched Gypsy enter the room, shutting the door behind her. Feeling acutely aware of her effect on him, and not liking it one bit, he sat on the edge of his desk and crossed his arms.

She looked at him with that familiar wary defiance, and a part of him felt the need to soothe, to protect and comfort. She looked incredibly young and innocent—her face clear of make-up, her hair pulled up high into a ponytail of crazy corkscrew curls that he wanted to loosen over her shoulders. But he quickly quashed the impulse.

This was what desire did to you. It clouded the ability to think straight. To see what was real. And what was real was this: Gypsy was *not* innocent. She might not be mercenary in a monetary sense, although the jury was still out on that, but she was mercenary in a far worse way as far as Rico was concerned. She would have quite happily kept Lola from him—perhaps for ever. And it was clear that she was not going to give him any straight answers. She trusted him about as much as he trusted her—that much he suspected they would agree on.

Bitter, futile anger rose *again* in acknowledgement of what he'd missed out on, but Rico pushed it down. He had to be cool, controlled. Stake his claim and leave Gypsy in no doubt as to who held the power between them.

He saw her hitch her chin up imperceptibly. 'You wanted to talk?'

He inclined his head slightly. 'As I told you earlier, I now have proof that I'm Lola's father.'

Gypsy crossed her arms across her chest, inadvertently pushing her breasts forward. Rico kept his gaze lifted with an effort, and shifted irritably on the desk.

'And…?' Gypsy asked, with all the hauteur of a queen.

Rico bit back a reluctant smile. He had to hand it to her for bravado. No one stood up to him the way she did. And he admired that, even if he didn't like admitting it.

'And that means that I am now going to exercise my

rights as her father to care for her, provide for her and protect her—as befitting my heir.'

Gypsy's generous mouth tightened. 'You can do that all you want. Just let us get on with our lives and we can work out some custody arrangement.'

Rico sneered. 'You think I am going to allow you to return to that hovel of a flat with *my* daughter?' He dismissed the very notion with a slashing hand, making Gypsy flinch slightly. Perversely that made him contrite, and angry for feeling it. 'I am not interested in custody arrangements. And I am certainly not interested in being forced to stay in the UK so that I can drive into that ghetto twice a month to see my daughter for a few measly hours.'

Gypsy's arms fell, her hands clenched into fists by her sides. 'We'll take you to court. You can't do this.'

He arched a mocking brow. 'You'll take me to court with *what*? Your leftover tips from the restaurant? Believe me, Gypsy, any court you drag me to will be packed to the rafters with my own people. The best that money can buy. Do you honestly think that any judge will look favourably on a mother who wilfully cut the father of her child out of their lives for no apparent good reason? What judge will deny me my right to have access to Lola when they hear how you took it upon yourself to make her solely yours?'

He saw how she paled in the dim light, how she swayed for a moment, and with a silent curse he nearly got up to steady her. He saw her visibly compose herself. He could almost hear her brain whirring.

He decided to go for the jugular. 'You have no job. You have no prospects, despite the degree you say you have. To work you're going to need childcare, better childcare than a pensioner down the road, and to afford childcare you need to work. It's a catch-22.'

White-lipped, her green eyes huge in her face, Gypsy bit out, 'So tell me what it is you want.'

Rico relished the moment before speaking. He had Gypsy exactly where he wanted her. 'What I want is the fifteen months you owe me. You and Lola living with me for fifteen months, so that I don't miss out on another day of her development.'

This time Gypsy did sway, and Rico got to her just in time to lead her over to a chair and sit her down. In seconds he was back, with brandy in a glass. She waved it away, saying distractedly, 'Don't drink...'

He put the glass down, but stood over her and restrained himself from hauling her up and shaking her. She was acting—she had to be. This apparent vulnerability couldn't be real. And what on earth was wrong with the prospect of fifteen months living in the lap of luxury?

She looked up then, a hopeful light in her eyes. 'Fifteen months...and then you'll let us go?'

Rage bubbled inside Rico's gut. How delusional *was* she? And why did her eagerness to get away from him cause a spike in his gut? 'Not as such... But I *am* willing, after fifteen months are up, to help set you up in employment, help you find somewhere to live...help you get back on your feet. Providing, of course, that I have full and unimpeded access to Lola and a say in her future.'

Her mouth tightened again, and he could see her hands in fists on her lap.

'And in the meantime you plan on dragging us around the world with you? What kind of a life is that for a small child? She needs a routine, Rico, not a billionaire playboy father. Or are you planning to leave us in a sterile apartment like this one and visit whenever the mood strikes?'

Gypsy looked up at Rico and felt as if her neck might snap. She was so tense. His words were whirling sickeningly in her head, and along with them his obviously smug sense of satisfaction at having got her exactly where he wanted her. She needed space. She had to digest this—even though she knew with fatal certainty that what he said was true: she wouldn't have a leg to stand on in court, and had no means to get there. And, she had to acknowledge heavily, she only had herself to blame. If she hadn't taken the decision to keep Lola a secret who knew how things might have developed?

He answered her now, coldly. 'On the contrary. My main base is in Greece. I live between Athens and the island of Zakynthos. Most of my business is conducted there. This is actually my first visit back to London in… two years.'

The way he said the words, as if he was remembering that night, made the air crackle between them. Feeling claustrophobic, Gypsy blurted out before she could censor her words, 'You're not going to…to demand that we get married…?'

Rico looked down at her. He was far too close. He arched one brow. 'Is that what you'd like, Gypsy? Is that what you're holding out for? Nothing less than matrimony?'

Before she could say that it was the last thing in the world she wanted he continued. 'Curiously, I have no desire to marry someone who believes that she has the divine right to play God with a child's life. Any wife

I choose will understand the concept of honesty and trust.'

Standing up, because the feeling of claustrophobia was getting worse, and not liking they way he'd said he had no desire to marry her had impacted her somewhere very secret she bit out, 'Men like you don't even know the meaning of *trust* or *honesty*. And if I had to go back in time I'd make the same decision all over again.'

Gypsy expected Rico to move back to give her space. But he didn't. He brought his hands up to her arms and held her. Gypsy tried to pull away but his hold tightened.

Her words had hit a nerve. His eyes flashed, his jaw tightened. 'I'm not finished. I haven't told you the other thing I want.'

Gypsy's whole body was tensed against the inevitable effect of Rico's proximity. They were practically touching. All she'd have to do was take a deep breath and her breasts would push against his chest. Anger at realising that, and wanting it, made her lash out. '*What?* Haven't you asked for enough? What more can I give you?'

He looked at her for a long moment, his steel-grey gaze intent, focused. And then he said, with devastating simplicity, '*You.*'

His words sank in, slowly, and with it came an awful trickling of heat through her veins and into her belly. She started to struggle in his arms. 'No...*no*... I won't have it. I don't want you.'

But Rico just kept on holding her and said, 'Stop lying to yourself, Gypsy.'

He brought his hands up to her face, fingers around the back of her head, holding it. His thumbs were warm on her jaw. To her utter horror she could hear her breaths coming, hard and shallow. She put her hands over his, as if she could pull them down, and entreated with everything she had, all her secret vulnerabilities where this man was concerned, 'Rico...*please* don't do this.'

He shook his head. 'I can't *not* do this.'

And with his big hands cupping her face and head, crowding her utterly, he lowered his head to hers and took her lips in a kiss of soul-destroying and surprising sweetness. As if all the tension and animosity between them was an illusion. If he'd been hard and forceful it would have been easier to remember to fight, but this... this was something else entirely.

Gypsy emitted a sound that was somewhere between a moan of capitulation and frustration. Rico urged her even closer, and she could feel him taking out her hairband and letting her hair fall, combing through it and twining long strands around his fingers. Her treacherous hands dropped.

And meanwhile his mouth was on hers, getting hotter and harder, opening her to him. He stroked his tongue along hers, enticing her to explore. And Gypsy felt her legs weaken.

In mere seconds the world shifted, and Gypsy found herself straddling Rico's lap on the chair, facing him, her legs either side of his powerful thighs. His hands were still on her head, allowing no quarter as he brought her face back to his and set about undoing every one of her defences. With a moan Gypsy had to place her hands on his chest, to stop herself falling forward completely, but that action transmitted the heavy beat of Rico's heart right through to her bones.

His hands came down to her waist, searching for and finding the bare skin between her jeans and top, stroking sensuously. Gypsy was aware that she was arching her back, but couldn't stop it. She was in another world where time and reality didn't exist. And, weakly, she resisted reality.

When Rico started to pull her T-shirt up, after only a moment of hesitation Gypsy lifted her arms and let him pull it off. Rico sat up straighter, and a new urgency infused the desire-laden air around them as he pulled her into him and pressed kisses against her neck and throat, down to the valley between her breasts.

Gypsy clutched his head, trembling all over, aching to get closer, and as if Rico heard her silent plea he shifted them subtly, so that the apex of her thighs came into direct contact with his burgeoning arousal.

She gasped and pulled back, and in that moment she realised that Rico had somehow undone her bra and was pulling it down her arms, baring her rosy-tipped breasts to his gaze.

'So beautiful…' he breathed. 'I've never forgotten this… I've dreamt of this…'

Something about his words melted Gypsy inside, and with her hands spread on his shoulders all she could do was suck in a breath of pure pleasure as he cupped one breast and then brought her forward to his mouth, so that he could lick teasingly around the aureole before flicking his tongue against the hard nub.

The bare skin of her shoulders was incredibly sensitised by her hair, and before Gypsy knew what she was doing she was blindly tearing off Rico's tie and opening the buttons of his shirt with feverish hands, all while his mouth was wickedly bringing her closer and closer to the edge of delicious sensation.

Finally, with his shirt open, Gypsy spread her hands across his broad chest with its smattering of hair, revelling in his innate strength. Rico broke away from her breast and, heavy-lidded, Gypsy looked down, her eyes roving over the stark planes of his gorgeous face, marvelling that he desired her like this. A burgeoning feeling of something awfully like tenderness rushed through her, disorientating her for a moment. It unsettled her, because she'd felt it the night they'd slept together, and finding him gone in the morning, leaving nothing but that note, had been like a slap in the face.

But he didn't give her time to dwell on that, to allow it to filter through and break the moment. Bringing her close again, he caught her mouth and kissed her until she was dizzy. One of his hands moved down over her soft belly to flick open her jeans, and she gasped open-mouthed into his kiss. His other hand came around and slid down between her jeans and her bottom, caressing the flesh, moving her in even closer, so she could feel how hard he was. In that moment he thrust upwards, and even though their clothes acted as a barrier the sheer memory of his potent size and strength made stars explode behind Gypsy's eyes.

Instinctively her hips moved, seeking more friction. He was relentless, kissing her, his hot mouth moving down, finding a breast and suckling. One hand kneaded her bottom, pulling her closer, and his other hand delved under the opening of her jeans to the apex of her legs, underneath her pants, where one finger found the moist centre of her desire and rubbed, back and forth, as he rhythmically thrust against her.

Almost sobbing, because on some level Gypsy knew that he was only displaying his control over her, showing her how weak she was, she couldn't save herself from the ultimate surrender. With a cry, she felt her body tense and peak, before falling down into spasms of pleasure so intense that her hands dug into Rico's shoulders as if he was her anchor in the storm.

To her absolute horror, as sanity came back in slow doses, she could feel her body still clenching spasmodically. She was half naked, *in his study*, and had just been brought to orgasm for the first time in two years with little more than heavy petting.

On roiling waves of shock and horror Gypsy pulled Rico's hands away and scrambled up. Her jeans were undone, half off. Her breasts throbbed, her body ached— and Rico sat there, sprawled in sexy abandon, with his shirt open and his hair dishevelled.

She saw her T-shirt and whipped it up, pulling it on with shaking hands, not caring if it was back to front or inside out. Or where her bra was. With a strangled cry of something she couldn't even articulate she fled from the study.

All she heard behind her was a dark, knowing chuckle.

Fleeing straight to her bedroom, Gypsy locked herself in the bathroom, turned the shower onto steaming, stripped and got in. Only once she was under the powerful spray did she give in to tears of humiliation and anger. Rico had proved his point. He held all the power—over her situation, over Lola, and—possibly worst of all—*over her*. Because if she couldn't remain immune to Rico how could she protect herself or Lola, when inevitably he would lose interest in being a father and reject them both?

When she felt composed and had changed into a poloneck top and fresh jeans, Gypsy wound her damp hair up and stuck a clip in it. Taking a deep breath, she went back out to the living room—where, to her dismay, she saw Rico standing looking out of the window. No sign of Mrs Wakefield or Lola yet.

Rico turned to face her, hands in his pockets, and Gypsy cursed the fact that he hadn't gone back to work—knowing that it was hypocritical of her, because if he had she'd have found fault with that too. Looking as cool as a cucumber, and not as if he'd just made love to her within an inch of her life on a chair in his study, Rico held out a piece of paper to Gypsy.

She had to go closer to get it, and all but snatched it out of his hand. She glanced at him before reading it. 'What's this?'

'It's a press release.'

Gypsy read the print.

After a break in relations, Rico Christofides and Gypsy Butler would like to announce their joyful reunion, together with their daughter Lola.

She looked up from the paper and felt shaky all over. 'Is this really necessary?'

He nodded curtly. 'Absolutely. They will dig and dig until they know who you are, who Lola is, and what her relationship to me is. We give them that, and a staged photo, and they'll leave us alone...'

Gypsy could feel her blood drain southwards, and was barely aware of Rico's narrowed look. 'They won't dig if we give them this?'

His look was far too assessing, and Gypsy tried to hide her fear of people finding out about her past, terrified that Rico would use the knowledge in some way to strengthen his position. He shook his head. 'No, they'll still hound us to a certain extent, but it won't have the same intensity...'

Gypsy handed him back the paper. 'OK, then, go ahead with it.'

Rico said smoothly, 'I already have.'

Gypsy's eyes clashed with his. 'Of course. How could I forget? You act and then ask later.'

Rico shrugged nonchalantly. 'I know what I want and I go after it. Now,' he said crisply, and looked at his watch, 'my driver is downstairs, waiting to take you to your flat, where you will pack up the rest of your things. Bring back only what you can carry. I'll have my assistant box everything else up and ship it to my home in Athens.'

'But what about the flat?'

Rico's lip curled. 'My assistant will look after informing the landlord. No doubt it'll soon be snapped up by the next unfortunate individual who has to live there.'

Gypsy bit back words of protest, knowing they were futile. 'Then what?'

'Then...' Rico came close to Gypsy, but she backed away, not liking the way butterflies took off in her belly. 'Tomorrow we travel to Buenos Aires for my nephew's christening, which is in a few days. I'm to be his godfather. I also have some business to attend to while we're there.'

Intrigued despite herself, Gypsy asked, 'You have a nephew?'

'He's my younger half-brother's son.' Almost accusingly he said, 'Lola has cousins: four-year-old Beatriz and six-month-old Luis. My brother Rafael and his wife Isobel are looking forward to meeting you and Lola.'

Gypsy felt a little overwhelmed to suddenly discover that he had family—that he was going to be a godfather and that Lola had cousins. It made her feel a curious wrenching inside. *Family.* Lola might never have known. It was something Gypsy had always longed for—a brother or sister, even cousins. But both her parents had been only children, and she'd been her father's only child.

In something of a daze, she let Rico guide her out to the hall. She put on her coat and went down to the car. All the way to her flat, and as she packed up her paltry belongings, Gypsy was still in a bit of a daze. Finally she looked around and heaved a sigh. The flat looked even worse now that she'd been living in Rico's penthouse for a week. Even she couldn't stomach the thought of bringing Lola back here...

She looked down and made sure she had her most important possession: an old box full of mementos of her mother—photos, and those letters she'd found in her father's study after he'd died. She didn't care about anything else.

She sat down heavily on a chair for a moment, feeling emotion welling within her, but she stayed dry-eyed and just felt inexplicably sad and fearful that despite everything she was destined to watch as Lola received the same treatment she'd got from her own father.

And yet Gypsy had to acknowledge the utter shock Rico must have felt to find out about Lola. But from that first moment he'd taken it on board and assumed Lola was his. At no point had he rejected her, or ignored her until he'd got the results of the paternity test back. She had to admit grudgingly, for the second time in the space of a few days, that in spite of his autocratic take-over of their lives he hadn't been acting exactly as she'd feared.

Gypsy had borne little physical resemblance to her father, and he too had insisted on a DNA test once he'd been forced to take her in—even though he'd known of her existence. With the proof that she was his, he'd just looked at her, shaken his head, and said, 'It'd be easier

to look at you if you at least took after the Bastions…
but there's nothing. You're all your poor, stupid, mad
Irish mother—and with that hair you look just like the
gypsies she named you after…'

Gypsy blinked back the memory, her focus returning to the room. In a way, she thought, at least Lola *did*
resemble Rico. That must be why it was easier for him
to bond with her.

With a last desultory look around, she stood up, picking up the bags. Making sure she had the box, she left the
flat for the last time. On her way back to the penthouse,
the prospect of facing Rico and the future he'd outlined
for them made the emotions clamouring in her chest feel
much more ambiguous than she liked to admit.

The following day, after they'd arrived at a private airfield and been shown onto a plush private plane, Gypsy
thought back to that morning. In a hive of activity, while
getting ready for the trip to Argentina, Rico had reminded
her of completing the necessary paperwork to have him
added to Lola's birth certificate.

Then he'd curtly informed her, 'The paparazzi are
outside waiting. They know they're going to get a shot of
us leaving, so I'd appreciate it if you could bring yourself
to wear some of the clothes I bought for you. Also, in
Buenos Aires there are a couple of functions I have to
attend—not to mention the christening…'

In other words, Gypsy had surmised as she'd packed
angrily, leaving behind her own shabby clothes, she'd
better dress the part from now on. And he was also
informing her that he expected her to be at his side in
public…

She turned to him now on the plane, as she held Lola
on her lap as they took off, but he was engrossed in some

paperwork, giving her his slightly crooked profile, which only made him look more dangerous.

Stifling a sigh, Gypsy looked out of the window as England dropped away below them and felt as though a net was tightening around her, slowly but surely.

A couple of hours into the flight, after Lola had exhausted the length and breadth of the plane, and had been fed and changed, she was asleep on one of the reclined seats near Gypsy, the seat belt tied securely over her blanket, thumb stuck firmly in her mouth.

Gypsy looked from Lola to Rico, and flushed when she caught him staring at her. She blurted out what had been on her mind earlier. 'Are you suggesting that we appear in public together...like some sort of...couple?'

His eyes narrowed. 'I've released a press statement to the effect that we are...*together*, so, yes, I am going to make full use of you by my side. I need a companion in public, and of late have not had anyone to fulfil that role.'

Gypsy's heart beat fast, and to counteract it she said waspishly, 'The redhead wasn't fit for public duty?'

Rico smiled, and it made him look years younger, more carefree... *Lord*, thought Gypsy, remembering when he'd smiled at her like that the night they met.

'You're inordinately interested in this redhead.'

Gypsy snorted inelegantly, but couldn't look away. *Had* he slept with her? She hated that she wanted to know, and that she cared. She balled her hands into fists, nails scoring her palms.

'I'm not interested in the slightest,' she lied. 'I would just like to know what the public perception of my role is likely to be if I'm to be seen by your side.'

'I'd say it's likely to be that you are the mother of my child, who is also sharing my bed. And if it's any consolation I didn't sleep with the redhead that night; seeing you again rendered me all but impotent.'

Gypsy flushed and struggled to control her wayward response to hearing that admission. She asserted hotly, 'I will *not* be sharing your bed.'

He shrugged, and released her from his gaze to look back to his work, then said, 'We both know if I started kissing you I could have you on the bed in the back of this cabin within minutes... But with respect to our daughter I'll desist from making my point here and now.'

Gypsy choked back something rude...but couldn't for the life of her stop her mind from imagining Rico coming over to her seat, trapping her with his arms and bending down to kiss her, before lifting her up and carrying her to the back of the plane...to that bed...where all she could imagine was a tangle of limbs, olive skin contrasting with pale skin...

What was wrong with her? Gypsy opened her belt and got up to go to the bathroom. Only once she was locked inside, and after splashing cold water on her face, did her pulse finally return to something close to normal. She looked at her face in the mirror, eyes huge. She was terrified that sleeping with Rico would crumble her precious defences...he already had so much control—too much control. If he had *her*, then he would have it all.

She'd been too young to fight against her father's control, and he'd tried to wipe away every last trace of who she really was. She couldn't forget that. She had to fight Rico for her own preservation and Lola's. She *had* to.

Gypsy woke to a gentle prodding, and opened her eyes to see Lola's big grey ones staring up at her, alongside Rico's. He was squatting by her side, holding her. She was awake in an instant, her back protesting as she'd fallen asleep sitting up.

Lola smiled at her, small teeth flashing, 'Mama... fly!'

Gypsy smiled tightly, hiding her momentary sense of disorientation at knowing that Rico had obviously taken care of Lola when she'd woken, and had been watching her sleeping. Lola was picking up more and more words every day now, generally repeating back any words said to her. Gypsy automatically went to reach for her, but Rico took her over to sit on his lap. Gypsy saw that his paperwork was put away.

He glanced at her and said, 'We're landing shortly. Buckle up.'

And just like that he was settling a completely contented Lola in his arms, and securing the seat belt around them. It made her think again of how at ease he'd been with Lola from day one. And he was growing in confidence around her, having no apparent qualms about picking her up or playing with her. He'd shielded her from the glare of the paprazzi cameras as they'd left the penthouse that morning, cocooning her within his arms. This side of Rico was one she hadn't anticipated, and while she still didn't doubt it was temporary, while the novelty lasted it unsettled her more than she liked to admit.

She couldn't help asking curiously, 'Have you always wanted children?'

Rico sent her a quick look, his hands huge around Lola, making something ache in Gypsy's chest. She qualified. 'That is...you seem very comfortable with Lola...'

Rico felt his daughter's plump and solid little body curved into him so trustingly, and knew without a moment's hesitation that he would lay his life down for her. Gypsy was looking at him with those huge eyes, her hair tumbled around her shoulders in glorious abandon. Her question unsettled him. He'd never thought about having children—had never wanted to have children. How could he explain that the concept of fatherhood had always mystified him, having had no good experience to call on?

But the day he'd seen Lola for the first time he'd suddenly *known* instinctively what it was. And as he'd come to terms with it, he had been able to feel so much more of his father's pain and loss. And also to hate his stepfather even more for his cruel treatment. And…a hardness settled in his chest…he could also hate Gypsy a little bit more for denying him this basic right.

But he couldn't articulate this to the woman who sat across from him, the woman he'd found himself staring at while she slept, looking so innocent. It had taken all his restraint and control not to pick her up out of her seat and carry her down to the bedroom to slake his lust. He hated wanting her so badly. He wanted to be able to control his desire. He wanted to be immune to her charms, unmoved by her wild beauty which called to him as strongly now as when he'd first seen her.

He schooled his features, afraid she might see something of the turmoil within him. 'Whether I wanted children or not is no longer a relevant question. I have Lola, and the reason I'm comfortable with her is because she is *mine*, my flesh and blood, and I will do everything in my power to protect her.'

CHAPTER EIGHT

THE fervour of Rico's words still rang in Gypsy's head as they sped along the wide Buenos Aires boulevards to Rico's brother's home, where they were going to be guests. A trickle of sweat dropped between her breasts even though the car was air-conditioned. It had been like walking into a baking oven, stepping off the plane into the bright Argentinian sunshine just a short while before.

Rico had warned Gypsy how hot it was likely to be, but even in light linen trousers and a shirt she was still hot. Luckily there had been some summer dresses and light clothes amongst Lola's new wardrobe, and now she was all decked out in a gorgeous polka dot dress, complete with sandals and matching pants.

Sitting in a baby seat, she looked out at the view with big eyes, turning to smile winningly at Gypsy every now and then, or to point and exclaim intermittently, 'Car!' or, 'Woof! Woof!' when she saw a dog.

Rico was sitting in the front, alongside the driver, conversing in Spanish. He looked back at Lola indulgently when she pointed out the umpteenth car. 'Very good, *mi nenita…*'

Gypsy had to swallow an inexplicable lump, and looked out of her own window. She wondered if there would come a time when Rico might look at *her* without that censorious, unforgiving light in his eyes, and despaired that she even wanted that.

She could see that they were in a more residential area now, with huge houses just visible behind tall trees and flowering bushes. The car slowed, and a set of ornate black gates opened to reveal a long drive which led to a huge open courtyard and a stunning house.

On the steps Gypsy could see a beautiful slim woman with short dark hair holding a chubby black-haired baby, and beside her a tall dark man who bore a striking resemblance to Rico. It had to be Rafael—his half-brother. And between their legs danced a small dark-haired girl in worn shorts and a T-shirt, bare feet. The sight comforted Gypsy, who hadn't really known what to expect.

They got out. Gypsy was all fingers and thumbs on Lola's straps, but finally managed to extricate her. She went shy at the sight of so many new faces and leant into Gypsy, her thumb in her mouth.

Rico was by her side then, a hand on her back, and Gypsy felt slightly comforted. They walked forward, and any trepidation fled at the huge smile on Rafael's wife's face as she walked forward to meet them, embracing Gypsy warmly, and then Rico.

'It's *so* lovely to meet you, Gypsy. And Lola—isn't she a sweetie?' Gypsy was surprised to hear that Isobel sounded quite English, and also *looked* more English than Argentinian.

Gypsy was aware of the two brothers greeting each other warmly, but with a certain reserve she couldn't put her finger on. She smiled at Rafael in greeting, and could see that up close there were distinct similarities. But where Rico's eyes were that cold steel-grey, Rafael's were dark brown. And he didn't have the air of suppressed danger that seemed to surround Rico like a cloak of darkness.

The introductions were quick and chaotic. Beatriz their four-year-old daughter, was adorable, with big chocolate-brown eyes, and clearly excited to meet her new cousin.

Rico surprised Gypsy by picking Beatriz up and making her squeal with delight, before saying, 'Once Lola is settled in you can get to know her...'

Beatriz smiled and said, 'OK, Uncle Rico.'

In a flurry of being ushered inside, where a homely housekeeper appeared, wiping her hands on an apron, and more introductions, Gypsy deduced that Rafael and Isobel were blissfully happy. It oozed from every cell of their beings and throughout the house as Isobel led Gypsy on a whirlwind tour.

Standing at a bedroom door some minutes later, Isobel apologised, saying with a grimace, 'I'm sorry—you must be absolutely exhausted. I know how arduous the flight can be from England; I went to school there, near my father's family. But here I am chattering on when all you probably want to do is wash and rest.'

Isobel was cradling her smiley baby easily, and Gypsy felt in that moment that they could be good friends. She'd never had a close female friend before. She smiled shyly, feeling a sudden weariness wash over her. 'To be honest, it's all been a bit of a whirlwind...but I'm very happy to meet you too—and your children are gorgeous.'

Isobel grimaced again, but smiled. '*Most* of the time, as I'm sure you well know.'

Gypsy shared a complicit smile and appreciated Isobel's lack of questions when she and Rafael had to have dozens. Just then Rico appeared, and Isobel gestured to the huge luxuriously furnished room through the open door. 'I hope this will be suitable for you both, and Lola. I've set up a cot for Lola in the room off the dressing room, so she's close by. I've also left baby monitors in there if you want them at night. If you need anything else just shout. Someone will bring your bags up shortly, but get some rest in the meantime. We'll eat at about eight, after the children are in bed.'

Rico's voice rumbled through Gypsy. 'Thank you, Isobel, we'll see you later.'

With a little wave Isobel walked quickly down the corridor. Gypsy and Rico still stood at the bedroom door. With a hand on her back he propelled her inside. Gypsy clutched Lola to her like a lifeline as she realised something very scary on investigating the rooms. One bedroom, one bathroom, one dressing room and one smaller room, where a cot and changing table had been set up.

She whirled to face Rico. 'This room is surely for me and Lola. Where's your room?'

He crossed his arms. 'Right here.'

Gypsy backed away and shook her head. Rico had changed on the plane, into a pair of faded denims and a dark polo shirt, and he was all too devastating to her equilibrium like this. 'No way. We are not sharing a bed. Obviously Isobel has assumed we're a…a couple. I'll have to let her know.'

Gypsy walked purposefully forward, but Rico stopped her with his arm. Lola, the little traitor, squirmed out of Gypsy's arms towards Rico, and she had to let her go when he reached for her. Looking far too smug, he said, 'You will do no such thing. She's gone to a lot of trouble to set this room up, and would be mortified to think that you're not happy with the arrangement.'

He shrugged insouciantly. 'All we have to do is share

a king-sized bed. You can put pillows down the centre, if you like. Or is it that you're just afraid that you won't be able to help yourself from ripping my clothes off?'

Gypsy balled her hands into fists and felt another trickle of sweat go down the small of her back. 'You're just playing with me. You can't seriously expect me to believe that there aren't a dozen more bedrooms here that you could use.'

'It's not up for debate, Gypsy. Now, you can go and bother Isobel with this tiny problem, when she's got her hands full with her kids and organising the christening in two days, or you can just let it go and be an adult about it.'

Once again Gypsy felt like stamping her foot. What was it about this man that made her regress to a mental age of fifteen? But steel resolve straightened her spine. 'Fine. If that's the way you want it, I will have no problem keeping my hands off you. But know this, Rico Christofides, if you so much as breathe near me I will scream this place down.'

Rico smiled a shark's smile. 'You might scream, but it won't be to keep me away from you.'

Gypsy flushed, remembering how abandoned she'd been the night they'd slept together. And the other day in the study. No self-control whatsoever. Mortified, and burning up inside with humiliation but determined not to let him see it, she held out her hands for Lola, who just looked at her, quite content in Rico's arms. 'I should feed her now. She'll be hungry.'

Rico said easily, 'Why don't I feed her and let you wash and rest? I'll bring her back up when she's ready to go down for the evening. Beatriz is probably driving her parents crazy wanting to see her again anyway.'

And just like that he took responsibility for her

daughter. Feeling thoroughly disgruntled and at odds with everything, her emotions see-sawing wildly, Gypsy could only watch as Rico walked out with Lola high in his arms, chattering away happily.

Still muttering to herself, Gypsy had a brief shower, and when she emerged in a voluminous fluffy robe, feeling half-human again, there was a smiling girl putting away their clothes. *Their clothes: hers and Rico's.* That curious ache settled in her chest again, and Gypsy stuttered her thanks as the girl melted away discreetly.

The bed looked both terrifying and more inviting than anything she'd ever seen and, feeling as if surely she could snatch ten minutes of a nap, Gypsy lay down.

She woke much later, when dusk had fallen outside, to the familiar sound of Lola's cry. Instantly she was awake, and saw Rico come into the room with an obviously cranky Lola in his arms. When she saw Gypsy she started to wail even louder. For the first time since she'd met him again Rico didn't look his assured self. He actually looked *worried*.

Gypsy pulled her robe tight around her, wishing she had taken the time to dress, and took Lola, whose wails decreased almost immediately.

Rico said tightly, 'I'm not sure what's wrong with her. She ate some lunch and played with Beatriz, and then suddenly she started crying…'

Gypsy knew it would be all too easy to make Rico feel bad, but that knowledge didn't sit well. She couldn't do it. She looked at him, trying not to notice how gorgeous he seemed in the dim light of the room, in the intimacy of this situation like any domestic couple with their child.

Smiling wryly, she said, 'Welcome to cranky and tired Lola. She can go from upbeat and happy to heartbroken in an instant. It's been a lot for her to take in today, that's all. She just needs to wind down and get to bed... I'll get her a bottle and put her down.'

Rico surprised her by saying he'd get the bottle, and while he was gone Gypsy bathed Lola and changed her for the night. She couldn't help sensing his relief at knowing that he hadn't been at fault for upsetting Lola and that she was OK.

When he came back Gypsy was rocking Lola back and forth. She took the bottle from Rico and, after testing it, gave it to Lola, who was already falling asleep after a few greedy gulps. Rico stood with a shoulder against the doorjamb, watching them, and Gypsy felt huge relief at escaping from his intense scrutiny when she put Lola down and those long-lashed eyes closed in exhaustion.

She came out of the small room and pulled the door partway closed behind her, making sure to leave the baby monitor on in the room.

Rico said, 'I'll have a shower and see you downstairs, if you like. Dinner will be ready soon.'

Gypsy nodded, and as soon as she heard the shower going raced out of the robe and into a plain black dress and slingback heels, tying her hair back at her nape to tame it as much as she could. Escaping downstairs before Rico might emerge with just a towel around his waist seemed like the most important thing in the world.

She'd taken the second baby monitor with her, and as she approached the reception area a maid appeared as if from thin air and showed Gypsy into the main drawing room. Gypsy blushed to the roots of her hair when she saw Isobel sitting on Rafael's lap, their heads close together, his arms about her waist, her arms around his neck.

Isobel jumped up the minute she saw her, an impish

grin on her face. 'I'm sorry, Gypsy, we didn't see you... Would you like an aperitif?'

Rafael stood too, and greeted Gypsy so urbanely that he defused her embarrassment. By the time Rico appeared, in a snowy-white shirt and black trousers, Gypsy was explaining to Rafael and Isobel about her name. As soon as Rico came and stood near her, though, her voice dried up in her throat at imagining sharing a bed with him that night.

The housekeeper appeared and called them through for dinner, which was served in a wood-panelled dining room.

Gypsy sat back after the dessert and patted her belly, trying to ignore Rico's steely gaze across the table. She looked at Isobel. 'That was too delicious for words...'

Isobel smiled. She was sitting directly opposite Gypsy, to Rafael's right, with Rico beside her at the head of the table. 'It's nice that it's just us this evening. I understand that you're going to a function tomorrow night and that's lucky for you as you'll get to avoid the arrival of our other guests and the ensuing mayhem of preparations for the christening.'

Instinctively Gypsy leant forward. 'Is there anything I can do to help?'

Isobel waved a hand. 'Not at all. It's all in hand. Believe me, it's just lovely that you're here.' She sent a mischievous look to Rico. 'According to Rico, we should never have believed that he might one day appear with a ready-made family.' She continued. 'What was it you said on our wedding day? Something about not offering a return invitation any time soon?'

Rico looked steadily at Gypsy and she was caught by his gaze, unable to read it or escape it. A muscle ticked in his jaw, and then he drawled, 'Well...since I can't remember issuing a proposal, I'd say what I said then still holds firm…'

Gypsy was only vaguely aware of Rafael's sharp intake of breath, and the discreet look between him and Isobel. Gypsy burned inside with humiliation, which was made worse because she knew his statement *shouldn't* bother her—especially not after he'd succinctly outlined his requirements for a wife. But before she could come back with some witty rejoinder, to show how he hadn't affected her even when he *had*, the door opened and Rafael and Isobel's nanny came in.

She said something to Isobel, who stood up, apologising. 'It's Luis. He won't settle. Please excuse me?'

Wanting desperately to escape, Gypsy half stood and said, 'I should check on Lola.' But to her dismay Isobel waved her back down. 'Don't be silly. Have your coffee and I'll check on her for you.'

Feeling sick inside, Gypsy sat back down and couldn't meet Rico's eye. Thankfully Rafael seemed happy to cover the gap in conversation, and Gypsy let the talk flow over her. She hated that she felt so hurt by Rico's comment. He'd all but stated that he wouldn't be marrying Gypsy if she was the last woman on earth, even if she was the mother of his child. And she didn't even *want* to marry him! He was welcome to the tall, sleek, blonde heiress-type he'd undoubtedly go for. Or the sultry red-head—even if he said he hadn't slept with her.

After what she deemed an appropriate amount of time she excused herself, saying to Rafael, 'The jet lag is catching up with me. If you don't mind, I think I'll go to bed.'

Praying that Rico wouldn't follow her, she breathed a sigh of relief when she heard Rafael continue the conversation. She all but ran up the stairs, and practically bumped into Isobel, who was coming back down.

Isobel touched Gypsy's arm and asked gently, 'Are you OK?'

Gypsy nodded. She felt like bursting into tears, but held it back.

Isobel bit her lip and said, 'I didn't mean to say anything to cause tension between you and Rico. I'm so sorry... I saw the way he was with you, and I guess I just assumed...'

She looked so mournful that Gypsy blocked out her pathetic need to know what Isobel meant by *I saw the way he was with you* and shook her head. 'No, it's not you at all. Believe me. It's just...things aren't exactly how they seem with me and Rico...we're not...*together.*'

Isobel groaned. 'And I put you two in the same room. I am *so* sorry. Look, I'll move Rico—'

'No!' Gypsy said forcibly, anticipating Rico's retribution, and forced herself to say calmly, 'Don't—really. It's fine, honestly. Our relationship is not to be a cause of concern to you.'

Isobel took Gypsy's arm and walked her back down the corridor towards the bedrooms. 'If it's any consolation, I think I might know a little of what you're going through...' she confided.

Gypsy frowned. 'But you and Rafael seem so...' She trailed off, remembering intruding on their intimate moment.

Isobel smiled ruefully. 'Oh, we are *now*. But, believe me, it wasn't always like that.' She shook her head, 'Considering their background, and the damage their father—' She stopped and clarified. 'That is the damage Rafael's father, Rico's stepfather, did to them both, it's easy to see where they get their drive and arrogance.

And Rico had it so much worse than Rafael, because he was someone else's son. Rafael doesn't even know what happened between Rico and his biological father when he left at sixteen to go and find him in Greece.'

Reeling inwardly at this information, Gypsy repeated, 'He left at sixteen?'

Isobel nodded. 'After a beating that nearly put him in a hospital. If he hadn't turned on his stepfather that day and fought back, who knows what might have happened? As it was, he saved Rafael from years of further abuse…' Isobel turned to Gypsy at the door of the bedroom. 'Look, if there's any way I can make this more comfortable for you, let me know.'

Gypsy forced a smile. 'I will. And thank you.'

Isobel hugged Gypsy impulsively before walking away.

When Gypsy had let herself into the bedroom she stood with her back to the door for a long moment while silent tears slid down her cheeks. The other woman's easy affection had pushed her over the edge of her control.

She wiped at the tears that wouldn't seem to stop and told herself angrily that she *wasn't* crying at the thought of a proud sixteen-year-old being beaten so badly that he'd left home. She'd already begun to suspect that Rico was a much more complex person than her father. Hearing that intriguing snippet about his and Rafael's childhood made her want to know more, and that was dangerous. Along with the ever-increasing proof that when it came to *his* daughter he was proving to be nothing like her own father.

He was making Gypsy pay, yes, just as her father had done to her mother—but not because she'd asked him to acknowledge Lola, but because she *hadn't*.

And while his words tonight should have comforted

her, telling her of his intention that they would never formalise their relationship just for the sake of their daughter or because he might gain more control over them, they had done anything but. The words had scored through her like a serrated knife.

Suddenly anticipating Rico striding into the room, Gypsy hurriedly dressed in her nightclothes and got into bed, hugging one side. She put a pillow in the centre as a warning to Rico, but she had no doubt after that comment downstairs that he'd be as likely to try and seduce her as he would be to give Lola up.

Rico came into the room and saw the slight shape under the covers in the bed. A small bedside light threw out a dim glow, and Rico walked over to look down on Gypsy where she lay sleeping. He cursed softly when he saw the unmistakable sign of tear-tracks on her cheeks, feeling his chest tighten. He did not welcome the unbidden emotion where this woman was concerned.

Dammit. He'd just had to endure the worst look of reproach from Isobel, and Rafael's clear disapproval. He hadn't told them, however, that he had regretted the words as soon as they'd come out of his mouth. He'd wanted to snatch them back as soon as he'd seen the colour leach from Gypsy's face and her eyes grow bruised. It had been a cheap shot designed to hurt, and it had.

Rico was disconcerted by this need to hurt Gypsy, because it hinted at a desire to force her to push him away. When really he knew he didn't have to make much of an effort there. He was surprised she hadn't hit him the other day, after he'd seduced her in his study and all but exploded like an inexperienced teenager in his pants. What had started out as an exercise in domination over her had turned rapidly into something completely out of his control.

Gypsy hated him, but perversely that thought didn't give him the same satisfaction it might have a few days ago. His mouth thinned. He had done something or he represented something that she despised. It was becoming more and more clear that something lay behind her reasoning for not getting in touch with him when she'd found out about her pregnancy.

She kept making comments about *men like you*, or *I know how you operate*, and it was beginning to seriously get on his nerves. And yet she'd had an opportunity earlier to make the most of his discomfiture when he hadn't known how to deal with Lola's bad behaviour, but she hadn't. She'd been generous and had put him at ease, assuring him it wasn't his fault.

And he'd repaid her by making a snide comment.

He was used to people looking for a weakness and exploiting it, and she hadn't done that. She was full of shadows and secrets which he was only now beginning to unravel. She didn't trust him, she didn't want his money, and she fought her attraction to him as if her life depended on it. And he wanted to know why. Right at that moment, despite the most urgent desire he'd ever felt for a woman burning him up inside, he felt the need to proceed cautiously, suddenly wary of what further vulnerabilities intimacy might bring.

'I owe you an apology.'

Gypsy's hand tightened around her coffee cup. It was just her and Rico in the bright and airy breakfast room. When she'd woken this morning she'd been inordinately relieved to find Rico's side of the bed empty. He'd already taken Lola downstairs to eat with Beatriz, Isobel and Luis, and Isobel had insisted on taking Lola off to play with Beatriz.

So now it was just the two of them, and she had to have misheard. She looked at him warily. 'Apology?'

He nodded once, curtly, the lines of his cleanshaven face stark. 'What I said last night was unforgivably rude. You are the mother of my child and deserve more respect.'

If Gypsy hadn't already been sitting down she would have fallen. She got the distinct impression that those words had cost him dearly. She might be the mother of his child but he still despised her for what she had done. But then her heart thumped—was he saying that he *would* marry her? She went hot all over, and clammy at the same time.

As if Rico could see the direction of her thoughts he said mockingly, 'While I don't envisage such a union between us, I had no right to say it so baldly. Suffice to say, I still don't relish the thought of marrying a woman who thinks nothing of keeping the father out of his child's life.'

Gypsy's chin hitched up. So he was apologising not for what he'd said, but how he'd said it. Fresh hurt lanced her, mocking her attempt to deny it. 'I didn't think *nothing* of it. I had my reasons and they were good ones.'

Rico leant forward, suddenly threatening. 'Yes, about those reasons... You've not been entirely forthcoming in that area. You're determined to believe the worst of me— that's been clear since the moment we met again—and you've obviously thought the worst since you knew who I was. That's why you never contacted me, isn't it? While I find it hard to believe, I'm willing to bet that you slept with me that night because you truly *did* think I was just some anonymous person, and not one of the wealthiest men in the world.' He said this with no arrogance, just stated the fact.

Gypsy's skin tightened across her bones and she confirmed his suspicion, saying faintly, 'I didn't know anything about you till I saw you on the news that morning…'

Her brain whirred sickeningly. He was issuing a direct challenge and skirting far too close to the truth. He couldn't know about her father; he couldn't know the dramatic step she'd taken after he had died. If he shared the antipathy her father had felt for him, he'd use that for sure. And he couldn't know about her mother's mental instability. He wouldn't understand—few people would—and he would use all that information to make her appear an unfit mother.

She was aware on some level that this fear was coming from a visceral place, not necessarily rational, but she couldn't control it. She didn't see herself ever being able to trust Rico. She couldn't remember the last time she'd trusted anyone.

How could she, when her formative experiences had been learnt so painfully at the hands of someone who hadn't even been as powerful?

She reiterated. 'As I told you before, I had no desire to be dragged through the courts, and your departure that morning had left me in no doubt as to how reluctant you were to see me again.'

He seemed to consider saying something for a long time, and eventually he said roughly, 'I told you the day I came to your flat that I regretted leaving you the way I did.'

Gypsy swallowed. She'd dismissed his words as an easy platitude at the time, but now they skated over her skin and made little tremors race up and down.

His mouth tightened into a thin line. 'I rang the hotel…most likely just after you would have seen me on the news…but you'd already left…'

Gypsy stopped breathing. She had the vaguest recollection of a phone ringing as she'd walked away from the room, but she had assumed it was coming from somewhere else. That had been *him*? To say what? That he wanted to see her again? But even as she thought that, and her heart clenched treacherously, she realised that she'd known who he was by then…so she would still have run, disgusted at having let herself be seduced so easily by someone like him. She'd still been raw after her father's death—especially as she'd just found out the extent of his cruelty to her mother.

Gypsy tore her eyes from his and looked down, feeling very wobbly inside. 'You say that you rang. Whether you did or not is a moot point now.'

'Clearly.'

Rico's voice was harsh enough to have Gypsy's eyes meet his, and something in those grey depths made her breath hitch.

And then, moving abruptly, Rico put down his napkin and stood up. 'I have to go into my office here today. The event we're going to tonight is black tie—it's for a charity I'm patron of. Be ready to go out at seven p.m.'

Gypsy watched as Rico strode powerfully from the room, and when he'd gone the absence of his intense energy made her sag like a lead balloon. She'd been to dozens of society charity events, as her father had been patron of many—but only to enhance his ego, avail himself of tax benefits, and occasionally to dip into the funds for himself.

He'd never got caught. He'd been too good at creating smoke and mirrors so people didn't ask questions or looked the other way. But Gypsy had known, though she'd always been too terrified of the potential punishment if she did something as audacious as call the police. But nevertheless her father had managed to punish her for her knowledge.

Once again she was being hurtled back in time. With effort she forced her mind away. She'd never wanted to be party to something like this again, and here she was, right in the middle of it. She let familiar cynicism wash over her as she thought of the prospect of the evening to come, but knew it was a weak attempt to avoid the thought of going out on Rico's arm in public.

She couldn't even drum up the disgust she'd expected to feel at the thought of seeing Rico posture and preen purely to raise his profile. She had an uncomfortable presentiment that he would confound her expectations again.

That evening Gypsy sat beside Rico at the head table, in a thronged and glittering ballroom in one of Buenos Aires' best hotels. She was incensed that her distaste for this milieu was being constantly diminished because she was so distracted by how gorgeous Rico looked in a classic black-tie tuxedo.

Isobel was minding Lola, and had kindly helped Gypsy to get ready earlier. She'd endeared herself to Gypsy even more when she'd confided with feeling that she and Rafael had a pact that they'd only go to charity events if and when it was absolutely necessary, and only if Rafael could promise that he would try to extort as much money as possible out of the assembled Buenos Aires elite. After they'd given over their own generous donation, of course.

Gypsy had been happy with her appearance once

Isobel had left. Her hair was straightened and twisted into a classic chignon, and her plain dark green silk dress, sleeveless and with a cowl neckline, fell to the floor. She looked the part—the part she'd been trained well to play by her own father when it had suited him to act out the role of devoted parent, which had only ever lasted as long as they'd been on public display.

When Rico had come into the bedroom earlier and asked, with a horrified glance at her head, 'What have you done to your hair?' Gypsy had felt like a gauche teenager again—acutely self-conscious and aware that she just didn't have the right *look* for this world.

Defensively she'd touched her hair and said, 'Isobel straightened it for me. It's tidier like this... I thought for the dinner—'

But he'd just said curtly, 'Come on, we'll be late,' and strode out of the room, making Gypsy want to slam and lock the door behind him.

Now she looked resolutely away from Rico, and tried not to let the fact that his powerful thigh was brushing against hers intermittently bother her. But she couldn't pretend to herself that she wasn't affected, and squirmed inwardly at the thought of Rico knowing.

Suddenly a hush descended on the room as a compère got up and signalled to the crowd. She heard Rico sigh deeply beside her and snuck a look. His face was expressionless, but his jaw was tight, and she knew in that instant that he too hated this. Reeling at that information, she watched dumbly as he got up with fluid athletic grace after being introduced, and walked to the podium with thunderous adoring applause resounding around the room.

Up until that point Gypsy hadn't taken much notice of what the charity in question was, but now she recognised it as one of her father's own pet projects. One that he'd taken funds from. Her face burned with mortification at the realisation, and also at the weak fear that had led her to keep quiet about it when she'd been younger.

Rico was talking now, and Gypsy became quickly mesmerised by the simple articulacy of his words and his obvious genuine passion for the cause. A few people shifted uncomfortably around her; clearly they'd just expected him to get up and smile and say nothing of any consequence. But Rico was not going anywhere yet.

He knew his subject well. He was listing facts and figures that made her feel dizzy, and he was not afraid of mentioning the unpalatable stuff that people at an event like this preferred not to hear. To her knowledge he hadn't even brought a piece of paper, but with simple eloquence he put it to the crowd to put their money where their mouths were and started an impromptu bidding session—the prize being a new car of the winner's choice, from him. She could see exactly what he'd done; he'd embarrassed them into action, and now they couldn't bid fast enough.

The woman to Gypsy's left, who had been introduced as the co-ordinator of the charity, shook her head and smiled conspiratorially. 'I don't know where we'd be without him. He consistently shakes people out of their complacency and inertia. If only everyone could be as dedicated. There are far too many poseurs and charlatans standing in as concerned philanthropists.'

Gypsy swallowed painfully.

Finally he was finished—once an obscene amount of money had been bid. Everyone started to stand up and move about. Rico was coming back down to the table and, to Gypsy's surprise, with singular intent he grabbed her arm and said succinctly, 'OK I've had enough. Let's get out of here.'

Gypsy trailed after him, seeing the way people approached him but then stood back as if intimidated by his grimness. She almost felt sorry for them. 'Don't you want to stay? Talk to people?'

He glanced back at her. 'Not unless they want to pay for my time and donate more money. Do *you* want to stay?'

Gypsy all but shuddered and shook her head eagerly. 'No.'

A questioning gleam lit his eyes for a second, but then it was gone, and he led the way until they were back in the car and driving away. Rico was already opening his bow-tie with a grimace, and the top button of his shirt. Gypsy was transfixed by his hand, those long fingers...

Suddenly his hand stopped moving, and with a panicky feeling in her gut Gypsy met speculative grey ones. He quirked a small smile. 'If you keep looking at me like that I'm going to do something about it. I meant what I said in London. I want you, and I intend to have you, Gypsy. On my bed, underneath me...'

Her face flaming now, Gypsy hissed, 'Stop that right now.'

He shrugged. 'It's going to happen, Gypsy. We might not trust each other, or even like each other very much, but that's beside the point. I won't force you, though. You'll admit you want me too before we sleep together. I'm prepared to wait...for now. But I'll warn you I'm not a patient man.'

Gypsy tried to look away but couldn't. She felt hot inside at his obvious intent, and extremely susceptible having witnessed Rico at that charity event—having seen his clear distaste for the whole scene and his obvious determination to beat the cynics at their own game.

Right now she felt very confused, because the man she'd just seen working a jaded crowd to his advantage was someone she very possibly wanted to like her. Feeling very shaky inside, she mustered up a futile and rebellious, 'Don't hold your breath...'

CHAPTER NINE

THREE days later they were sitting on Rico's plane again, winging their way back to Europe—to Greece. Rico was immersed in work at the back of the plane, and Gypsy had Lola curled sleepily on her lap, exhausted after exciting days getting to know her new cousins. She was already worshipping the ground that Beatriz walked on, and doting on Luis as if he were her own brother.

Gypsy had met Rico's mother—a small dark woman with the saddest eyes she'd ever seen. It had been clear that no familial love existed between the brothers and her, despite Isobel's valiant efforts to include her in everything. She hadn't even looked all that surprised or overjoyed at being presented with a brand-new granddaughter.

But, more than that, Gypsy couldn't get over how, in the space of the last three days, her impression of Rico had changed so much.

After witnessing his distaste at another society charity function the night after the first outing, she'd ascertained that, while he wanted to contribute something, he had as much cynicism for the monied elite as she did. Even more disconcerting had been his reaction to seeing her hair straightened again. He'd growled at her in the car.

'I don't want to see your hair like that again. In future leave it alone.'

His words had had a seismic effect on her after years of having it drummed into her by her father that she looked like an unkempt mess, not fit for polite society. Feeling more and more uncomfortable at clinging on to her prejudices, the following day Gypsy had asked Isobel if she could use the computer in the house study, and she had done what she should have done as soon as she'd found out she was pregnant. She'd run a Google search for Rico.

She'd read as much as she could, with a sinking heart and a sick feeling her belly. Far from her father's assessment of Rico—which she realised now must have come out of petty jealousy—Rico Christofides was universally lauded as one of the cleanest entrepreneurs in the world. He played harshly and ruthlessly, yes, but always fairly.

Her father's name was even mentioned in a couple of articles, citing instances when he'd tried—stupidly, by all accounts—to take over some of Rico's interests. Rico had merely swatted him back like an inconsequential fly. No wonder her father had hated him so much; he hadn't been able to beat him. And he'd been humiliated in the process.

Gypsy had even seen that while they'd been in London Rico had been involved in extremely delicate negotiations to save an electronics plant on the verge of collapse in northern England. If it had gone under it would have pushed an already economically challenged area over the edge. But Rico had managed to pull it back from the brink, and not only that but also to create more jobs in the process...

She'd felt even sicker, because those were the

negotiations she'd taunted him about that day in the penthouse, when they'd been stuck inside thanks to the paparazzi.

She heard movement beside her, and looked over to see Rico take a seat on the other side of the cabin. Treacherous flames of desire and illicit excitement feathered through Gypsy's veins. He put his head back now and closed his eyes. Gypsy felt a lurch in her chest at seeing faint dark circles under his eyes. And when she recalled how gently he'd held Luis the day before at the christening she felt something even scarier.

Suddenly his head snapped back down. Those eyes opened and looked straight at her. Heat flooded her face when she recalled how she'd woken only that morning to find Rico on one arm, staring at her with a wicked gleam in his eye, his broad and powerful chest bare.

She'd watched, instantly awake and breathless, as he'd taken the pillow from the centre of the bed and thrown it to the other side of the room. Suddenly filled with nebulous emotions, acutely aware of how much she'd misjudged him, she'd entreated huskily, '*No*, Rico,' terrified he'd see her vulnerability.

But he'd just come closer and closed the gap between them. His skin had been hot and silky as he'd trapped her under one arm, bicep bulging. '*Yes*, Rico. I find that my patience is running very thin.'

Every nerve-point in Gypsy's body had come alive, treacherously telling of her inability to deny this desire. His head had lowered and his mouth had slanted over hers, stifling anything else she might say. After a futile moment of trying not to react to his kiss, to his proximity, Gypsy's mouth had opened and Rico had plundered ruthlessly, tongue stabbing deep, making Gypsy's back arch.

Her hands had instinctively clung to his arms, fingers digging into hard muscle. Before she'd known how he did it, the buttons of her pyjama top were undone and he was spreading the sides apart to bare her breasts to his gaze. The hardening rosy tips had tingled as he'd brushed a hand over one, and then the other.

Gypsy's breath had come fast and shallow, and when he'd lowered his head and mouth to suck one tip deep she'd all but bucked off the bed, so sensitised it had hurt.

Just as his hand had been travelling down to the waistband of her pants, a mewl had come from Lola in the other room.

They'd both stopped, waiting, and it had come again—stronger. Louder. She'd woken up. With a veritable turmoil of tangled emotions and frustrated desires in her belly Gypsy had pushed Rico away and got up, hastily buttoning her top again. Reluctantly she'd looked back to the bed, to see Rico lying there, arms behind his head, the sheet just managing to hide the extent of his arousal, chest broad and awe inspiring, gleaming dark olive with a smattering of masculine hair.

He'd smiled wickedly and drawled, 'Next time we won't have a convenient interruption. I can promise you that…'

Gypsy had fled.

Now, as Rico's far too assessing eyes looked at her, she burned all over. She wasn't sure if it was her imagination, but she thought she'd caught him looking at her periodically over the last couple of days with a speculative gleam. He just arched a brow now, and asked laconically, 'So, did you find anything interesting on the internet?'

All the heat that had just warmed Gypsy's cheeks leached out. 'What do you mean?'

'You know exactly what I mean,' he said easily. 'Isobel told me you'd been on the internet, and it's an easy thing to check the history. I think you possibly found out everything but my shoe size.'

No wonder he'd been looking at her; he *knew* she'd been snooping. The heat flooded back—and she hadn't even found out anything about his personal life, his real father in Greece, or what had happened to him between the ages of sixteen and twenty, when he'd burst on the scene having become a dotcom millionaire overnight.

Gypsy's arms tightened across the sleeping Lola, causing her to shift slightly. Stiffly she said, 'I felt that perhaps I owed you the benefit of the doubt. I realised that I really didn't have much basis for my...' She faltered tellingly.

'*Prejudice* I think is the word you're looking for.' And then he shocked her by saying, 'Perhaps we're both guilty of the same thing. After all...you've given me very little to go on...'

Gypsy quivered inwardly at the thought of one of his many minions checking her out. 'There's nothing much to tell.'

Rico turned to face her more. 'And yet I find that's really not the case at all. You're quite the enigma. You patently didn't come after me for the easiest gold-digging opportunity in history, but the ease with which you can navigate a high-end charity event tells me you know that world. And yet you were living in a hovel when I found you.'

For the first time Gypsy felt that perhaps she could tell Rico something of her life, but then that visceral fear surged up: despite what she knew about him now, she still couldn't trust him. It held her back. There was too much at stake. He might play fair in business, but would he play fair in personal matters—especially those concerning his own daughter? He'd said he wouldn't ever forgive Gypsy for what she'd done. It was only now that she knew a little of his personal history that she could see how it might have shaped his need not to be seen rejecting his own child.

She reiterated stiffly, 'There's really nothing to tell.'

After locking eyes with her for a long moment, until Gypsy felt breathless, Rico said, 'Why don't you take Lola and get some sleep in the bedroom? I still have work to do.'

And, as much to escape as anything else, Gypsy took his suggestion and left.

A few hours after doing some brain-numbing work which had more to do with blocking out the erotic memory of kissing Gypsy that morning, and how hard it had been to let her walk away, than any actual need to work Rico stretched and stood up.

He prowled silently to the back of the plane to look in on Gypsy and Lola, and stopped just inside the doorway with an ominous tightening in his chest. Gypsy lay on her side, her hair in a stream of curls around her head, knees up and her hand protectively on Lola's chest, co-cooning her. Lola lay in complete abandon, legs and arms splayed. Gypsy had put pillows on Lola's other side to prevent her rolling off the bed.

A fierce sense of possessiveness rose up within him, and it encompassed the two people on the bed—not just the little one. The constriction in his chest not easing one bit, he walked in and pulled a blanket first of all over

Gypsy, and then a smaller one over Lola. Neither one moved. He stood watching Gypsy and tried to battle the maelstrom of emotions she so effortlessly aroused.

He'd told her she was an enigma, and she was. Information on her background was starting to trickle through, and what he'd learnt so far had him reeling. He'd just given her a chance to tell him herself, but she hadn't. And he wanted to know why she was so reluctant to tell him of her past.

It was becoming harder and harder for him to cling on to his sense of injustice that she'd kept Lola secret from him. It was also becoming harder for him to remember why he didn't want to shackle her to him in marriage. The prospect, once so repugnant, now had a distinct appeal. He couldn't lie to himself that he wasn't a little envious of what Rafael and Isobel had together, and, while he didn't imagine he'd ever experience that for himself, he certainly wasn't averse to trying to create a home based around family…and mutual desire.

All Gypsy's behaviour in the past few days had pointed to her sharing a very similar moral compass to Isobel's, and he knew Isobel was not a woman who would choose to have a child and decide not to tell the father without good reason.

Gypsy's presence by his side at the social functions had been a revelation. In the past he'd had to deal with sulks and moues of disappointment from mistresses or dates when he'd wanted to do his bit and then leave as soon as possible. But he'd got the distinct impression that Gypsy had as little time for those events as he did. She'd had no desire to ogle the A-list celebrities, or talk inanities with the sycophants who all wanted a slice of him—or more accurately his fortune. In the space of two nights he'd found himself instinctively seeking her

hand and relishing finding that she was right behind him
without a murmur of dissent—if anything she'd shared
his look of mild distaste.

And what was even more disconcerting was the
ease with which he'd slipped into something that felt
extremely domestic. Coming home to Lola each night,
checking on her. Listening to Gypsy get up to soothe
her if she woke during the night. Feeling the bed dip as
she got back in and *aching* to just pull her close to him
and make love to her until he could satisfy himself that
what had happened between them had been a figment
of his imagination.

He had a sinking feeling, as he watched her now and
felt the familiar throb of desire, that it would prove to
be anything but. He'd told her arrogantly that he'd wait
for her to come to him, confident that she'd be mindless
with desire for him, but he'd been the one to lose control that morning. Vulnerability clawed upwards again.
He'd control this desire, wait until he knew more about
the mother of his child. Make her *want* him as badly as
he wanted her. Space. That was what he would have to
impose—even if it killed him.

Lola squealed happily as Rico threw her in the air again,
only to catch her in safe hands just before she touched
the glittering azure water of the pool, which was half-
indoors, half-outdoors. Rico had explained that this was
the winter pool and was heated. Gypsy had seen another
idyllic outdoor pool from the terrace where they'd had
breakfast that morning.

'Again!' Lola screeched ecstatically, her favourite new
word, which she'd picked up from Beatriz. Gypsy stifled
a wry smile to see that Rico was fast discovering the

perils of an indefatigable toddler who'd just discovered an exciting game and the power of language.

Her heart clenched to see Lola so happy in this environment—especially when she thought of their less than salubrious home in London and felt the familiar guilt. There, Lola had been lucky to get a go on the one non-mangled swing in the bleak park. Here... Gypsy sighed as she looked around from the seat she sat on. Here was paradise.

They'd landed in Athens late last night and transferred straight onto a smaller plane, which had borne them across southern Greece to the island of Zakynthos. In the surprisingly cool night air Rico had ushered them into a Jeep and had driven them himself to his villa, which was near the private airfield.

Gypsy had been too exhausted to take much notice of their surroundings last night, and had been barely aware of the friendly housekeeper Rico had introduced as Agneta. But she *had* been disturbingly aware of a new coolness from Rico. Gone were the hot and intent looks, but she was determined not to let it bother her. Rico was undoubtedly trying to unsettle her again.

This morning, when she'd carried Lola down to breakfast, she'd been in awe at the beauty of the simple yet expansive villa unfolding around her. Everything was bright and airy, with huge glass windows showcasing the fabulous views of the Mediterranean.

Agneta had met them with a wide smile and led them to where Rico was reading a paper and eating breakfast on a shaded terrace. Gypsy had been surprised, once again, that he was there and hadn't already left to go to work. She'd also been more than bemused to see a state-of-the-art highchair waiting for Lola, and she'd noticed the discreet child-proofing that had been done throughout the villa.

Rico had stood when they'd arrived, and enquired, 'I trust you slept well?'

Gypsy had just nodded and garbled, 'Yes, thank you. Our rooms are most comfortable.' Which was a huge understatement. She didn't want to admit that she'd actually missed Rico's presence in the room last night—*in the bed*. Even though she'd told herself staunchly that she'd been relieved to be shown to a suite of rooms of her own.

There was a dressing room, bathroom and sitting room. Not to mention the huge bedroom, with a four-poster bed complete with diaphanous muslin curtains drawn back. And Agneta had shown her into an equally generous ante-room which had been set up as a nursery for Lola. Gypsy had had to swallow an emotional lump, and had put it down to tiredness.

But that same lump was threatening again now, as she watched Rico and Lola frolic in the water, both sets of identical grey eyes smiling. So she knew it had nothing to do with tiredness. With each day that passed Lola was getting more and more attached to Rico. She went into his arms with no hesitation, and was already using him as someone to go to when she didn't want to do something Gypsy wanted her to do.

With that revelation making her feel uncomfortable and crabby, not to mention the far too provocative sight of a half-naked Rico, she approached the side of the pool with a towel, indicating that Lola should get out.

'She'll be impossible to put down for a nap after lunch if she gets too excited now.'

Those two sets of grey eyes turned to her, and Gypsy felt inordinately petty. But even though Rico's eyes flashed he waded to the edge of the pool and handed Lola over. Predictably, she began to protest at having her game cut short.

He drew himself out in one fluid motion which made Gypsy's breath hitch. She avoided looking at where the water sluiced off his body. She could only be thankful that he wore board shorts and not something more insubstantial.

'I should go into Athens for a few hours to tend to business. Go ahead and have dinner without me. I'll probably be late.'

Gypsy barely looked up, too afraid of what she might see. She had an awful prickling feeling that she'd *hurt* him.

As Rico sat in his car in the bumper-to-bumper traffic in central Athens his suit chafed, and he longed to rip off his tie and open his shirt. He cursed himself. He'd always loved coming back to Athens, and the anticipation of work, of seeing his mistress or the prospect of taking a new one. But that didn't appeal any more. All he could think about was the reproach in Gypsy's eyes as she'd taken Lola from him at the pool and the feeling that he'd done something wrong. And also how much he'd prefer to be there, and not here.

He cursed himself again for his weakness. The child was making him soft, and frustrated desire was clouding his brain—that was all. He cursed his vow to exercise restraint and let a new sense of anticipation fire through him as he thought of grilling his employees to see what else they'd found out about Gypsy.

By the end of their first week living at the villa Gypsy knew her nerves were wrought tight. Rico was there every morning, to greet them and have breakfast. He'd play with Lola for a while, and then disappear in a helicopter to go to Athens and work. Most evenings he'd make it back for dinner and they'd have stilted conversation—stilted because every time Rico tried to navigate into more personal waters Gypsy clammed up.

She'd heard the helicopter some time ago, and now waited with her heart thumping unevenly for Rico to appear for dinner.

When he did, striding into the room as silently as a panther, he took her breath away—as always. He'd obviously just showered and changed. His hair was still damp, slicked back from his high forehead. The dark shirt and faded jeans made her think of that night she'd seen him in the club for the first time.

She gulped and looked away, thankful for Agneta's presence as she came in with the first course. Rico asked after Lola, and Gypsy told him that they'd taken a drive to a nearby beach and had a picnic. On their first day he'd given her the keys to a Jeep, telling her it was hers to use.

He finished his starter before her and sat back, appraising her with those unreadable silver eyes.

Gypsy felt more and more hot, wishing she'd put on something lighter than a cotton jumper and a pair of jeans. 'What is it?' she finally asked. 'Have I got something on my face?'

Rico shook his head, and then smiled, causing Gypsy to feel momentarily winded. He reached out a long arm and his fingers took a strand of her hair, letting it slip between them. His eyes met hers. 'Who made you believe you should straighten your hair?'

His touch was affecting her far too much. Gypsy

pulled her head away and Rico finally let go. She pushed her unfinished starter away, her appetite gone.

Rico leant forward. 'Gypsy, either you tell me something about yourself or fifteen months of living together is going to get very tired, very quickly. And if that's your plan then give it up—because it won't work. You owe me.'

She bit her lip and played with her napkin, feeling as though she was about to walk into a chasm with no bottom in sight. 'My father... He never liked my hair left curly.' She was trembling now. She'd never spoken of her father to anyone.

'He was a fool,' Rico growled softly.

Gypsy flicked him a glance and looked away again, somehow heartened by the glint in his eye. It reminded her of an expression he had sometimes when looking at Lola. 'He used to tell me I looked like the gypsies that lived at the side of the road...so if we ever went out in public he'd insist I had it straightened.'

'Even as a child?'

Gypsy nodded.

'What about your mother? What did she think?'

Gypsy tensed perceptibly, but even Agneta coming in to take away the starters and deliver their main course didn't divert Rico's attention. He merely repeated the question when they were alone again.

Gypsy looked at him. 'My mother got ill when I was six, and I went to live with my father.' She didn't think it worth mentioning that the least of her mother's worries at that time had been the state of Gypsy's hair.

Rico put down his fork. 'They weren't married?'

Gypsy shook her head.

'Tell me about her.'

Gypsy thought back and let a small smile play around

her mouth, unaware of how Rico's gaze dropped there for a moment. 'She was Irish...and poor. Very naïve—too naïve. My father was her boss; he seduced her, and promised her all sorts of things, but when she fell pregnant he didn't want to know.'

Rico asked sharply, 'How do you know that?'

Gypsy looked at him, not really understanding the vehemence behind his question but suspecting something had hit close to his own experience. 'I guess I don't, for certain. But I know my mother kept him informed of our whereabouts and he never showed up or helped us financially. It became more obvious when she got ill and wanted him to take me in. He refused at first.' Gypsy couldn't hide the bitterness in her voice. 'He took me once he'd had a paternity test done, of course.'

She focused back on Rico and asked, 'Did something similar happen to you?'

Rico held a delicate wine glass in one hand, twirling it in long fingers. She could sense his tension.

He didn't look at her, but said, 'Something like that. My mother had an affair with a rich Greek tycoon, and when she fell pregnant he ran home. She was forced into a marriage of convenience to save her family's reputation before it became common knowledge that she was pregnant.'

He looked at her. 'Except that's not exactly how it happened.' He went on, 'I left to find my father when I was sixteen, determined to confront him for leaving us. When I eventually found him, here on Zakynthos, he had lost nearly everything and had less than a year to live. He'd always believed that my mother had had a miscarriage. He told me that he'd begged her to marry him, but that after the supposed miscarriage she'd told him to leave and never come back.'

His mouth was a grim line. 'So all those years were wasted; he thought I'd never been born, and I believed he'd not wanted to know me. And my stepfather had made my life hell because I reminded him every day of another man in my mother's bed.'

Gypsy felt emotion rising up. 'Rico…I'm so sorry. I can't imagine how bittersweet it must have been to meet your father only to lose him again.'

Rico laughed harshly. 'Don't get too romantic about it. He was a bitter old man by the time I got to him, and the best thing he did for me was leave me his ailing taverna—which I did up and sold on at a profit a few years later.' He inclined his head. 'And I changed my name, so at least I gave him that in death.'

Gypsy couldn't meet his eye; in many respects they'd trod a very similar path. She felt as if a huge lump was constricting her throat, but managed to get out, 'I can see why you were so angry to find out about Lola… I truly wouldn't have kept her from you if I'd thought I could trust you.'

'And why couldn't you trust me, Gypsy?' he asked silkily.

She looked at him. 'I still don't know that I can. From the moment you came back into my life…*our* lives… you've dominated and controlled. I grew up with someone who lived his life like that, and I know a little of what it's like to be resented for being there. I didn't want to risk putting Lola through that.'

His eyes glittered dark grey in the gathering dusk. 'It would seem as if we're at something of an impasse. You admit you can't trust me, and I'm not sure that I can forgive you for keeping me from Lola.'

Gypsy tried a wry smile, but it came out skewed. 'We only have to endure this for fifteen months and then you can get on with your life.' That damned lump was back in her throat. 'You can find someone who can match your exacting standards of moral behaviour.'

Rico reacted viscerally to the fact he'd just revealed so much about his past and to that provocative statement— even though he hated himself for reacting. He reached out to take her chin, drawing her face around to his. She wouldn't avoid him. He felt her clench her jaw against his hand, and even that had a hot spiral of desire rushing through him. 'You won't be going anywhere until we've dealt with this desire between us, Gypsy. Unfinished business, you could call it.'

Gypsy tried to pull her chin away, but couldn't. She gritted out, 'Well, let's go to bed now and get it over with, shall we?'

His eyes flared in response, and Gypsy could see something hot in their depths. Even though it caused an answering quiver in her belly, she immediately regretted her rash words. He finally let her go and sat back, draining his wine glass before saying nonchalantly, 'This will happen the way I want it, Gypsy, and it won't be to prove a point. Provoke me all you want, but you'd better be ready for the fall-out.'

Gypsy threw down her napkin and left the room.

Rico curbed the urge to drag her back and plunder her mutinous mouth. Desire was a heavy ache within him, and far too many ambiguous emotions were roiling in his chest. As for what he'd said about forgiving her—he was very much aware that forgiveness was something that had stolen over him while he wasn't even looking. He still felt regret for having missed out on Lola's early months, but no more anger towards Gypsy—and that realisation was cataclysmic.

* * *

That night Gypsy slept fitfully. She'd checked on Lola after dinner, but had been too restless to go to sleep straight away. It had seemed crazy to stay confined to her bedroom just to avoid Rico. Remembering the pool and how enticing it had looked, and the fact that it was heated, had encouraged her to think she might exercise herself to exhaustion.

It was only when she had been on the brink of walking into the pool area that she'd heard a sound and seen powerful arms scissoring in and out of the water. Mesmerised, half hidden behind a big plant, Gypsy had watched with bated breath as Rico had stopped and floated lazily on his back.

He had been completely naked. His long sleek body illuminated only by the moonlight and a few dim spot-lights. Nearly tripping in her haste to get away before he saw her, Gypsy had fled back up to her room, knowing that nothing would be able to eradicate that potent image from her brain.

Now she'd woken again, and flipped onto her back, sighing heavily. She thought she'd heard a mewl come from Lola, but wasn't sure if it had been a dream or not. She got up to investigate, just in case.

At the doorway to Lola's room Gypsy felt her breath stop when her eyes registered the sight before her. Rico was asleep on a chair in the corner, his long jean-clad legs spread out before him, wearing a worn T-shirt which he must have pulled on after his swim. Powerful arms cradled the sleeping form of Lola to his chest.

Lola's legs were curled up and her thumb was in her mouth, her other hand curled trustingly on Rico's chest. For a second Gypsy feared she might cry out, so intense was the emotion ripping through her.

Controlling herself with an effort, she could see that

though Rico might be asleep he must be uncomfortable. On bare feet she padded over and, bending down, barely breathing, carefully started to put her hands underneath Lola to lift her up.

Immediately Rico's hands tensed in an instinctively protective gesture, and his eyes snapped open. Silently Gypsy communicated with him, and willed down the response of her body to his proximity, suddenly very aware of her short nightdress.

Relaxing his hold, Rico let Gypsy lift Lola away. Her legs went weak as her hands felt the hard contours of Rico's chest. Carefully she stepped back and placed Lola down into the cot, pulling a blanket over her, and prayed that Rico would be gone when she turned around.

But he wasn't. He was sitting forward, elbows on his knees, looking at her with slumberous eyes. One lock of midnight-black hair had fallen over his forehead. Hot all over, Gypsy backed away to her bedroom and watched with widening eyes as Rico stood up and prowled towards her.

Taking her by the hand, he put a finger to her mouth before she could say anything and looked at Lola. Gypsy nodded and let him lead her out. Her heart palpitated at the thought that he'd come through her bedroom to get to Lola, having obviously heard the same cry she'd heard earlier.

Expecting him to let her go now they were out of Lola's room, with the door pulled behind them, Gypsy tried to pull her hand away—but Rico wouldn't let go. She looked up, and all she could see were two burning pools of stormy grey.

She knew that look. She *ached* for that look. She'd seen that look in dreams for two years. But even so she shook her head. The need to protect herself against this final capitulation was strong. She opened her mouth to speak, but Rico put his finger there again and came close, backing her against the wall and pressing close, so close that Gypsy couldn't think. All she could see was that image of him naked in the pool. Heat exploded low in her belly.

His voice was low and sultry. 'This is inevitable—as inevitable as it was that night two years ago. We've both been waiting for this…wanting this…'

Gypsy shook her head again, futilely, and Rico speared his hands through her hair either side of her face, his thumbs on her jaw.

'You're mine, Gypsy, and there will be no more waiting. Your body tells me what you refuse to.'

And he bent his head and kissed her passionately, tipping her head back so that he could stab deep with his tongue. Desire was instant and overwhelming. Gypsy didn't have a hope. She was a bundle of vulnerabilities, and at every turn this man was only making her feel more vulnerable, giving her little to cling onto in the way of protection.

Feeling impotent, and angry at her weakness, Gypsy fought fire with fire. Stroking Rico's tongue with hers, she exulted in his hitched breath as he recognised her capitulation.

Gypsy's hands came to his T-shirt and snaked underneath. She needed to feel his chest. Moving her hands over him, she felt how his belly contracted when she scraped her nails over the smooth skin and moved higher, through the covering of hair, finding the blunt nipples.

Impatient to see him, she pulled at the T-shirt. He ripped it off completely. He bent down for a second, and Gypsy felt herself being lifted into his arms and carried to the bed before Rico put her down again, sliding her down his body so that her nightdress rode up over her thighs.

She tried to move back, but with his hands on her waist he wouldn't let her budge. His eyes were burning down into hers. She couldn't look away, and felt heat flood her cheeks when he rocked his hips against her and she could feel the thrust of his erection against his jeans and her belly.

Liquid heat seeped between her legs and Gypsy squirmed. Breathless, she reached up and wound her arms around his neck, searching for and finding his mouth, savouring the firm fullness of his lower lip. His big hands moved to her bottom, underneath her pants, which he pushed down as he caressed her, coming back up over the indent of her waist and pulling her nightdress upwards.

For a split second Gypsy hesitated, her pants around her thighs and her nightdress bunched up just under her breasts. And then, with a deep shaky breath, she lifted her arms and let Rico pull it up and off all the way. Dimly, she knew he would not deviate from his mission. And the clamour in her own pulse told her that, no matter what she might protest, she was as hungry for this as he was.

She felt her hair fall down over her shoulders, and watched as Rico reached out to twine the strands around his hand. She brought up her hands to cover her breasts and he smiled down at her wolfishly. 'It's a bit late for modesty, don't you think?'

Gypsy bit her lip. Rico bent down and pressed a kiss to her shoulder. Shuddering, she let her head fall back, and she felt his hands come to her pants, pushing them down her legs completely.

She was barely aware of him taking something out

of his jeans pocket before she heard the button snap and the zip come down. They were gone, and he stood before her naked and proud.

Unable to stop herself, she let her gaze drop almost greedily. A part of her balked at his size, despite having been with him before, but another part *thrilled*.

Hoarsely Rico said, 'Touch me, Gypsy…please…'

She reached out and closed one hand around his length, feeling a shudder go through his big frame. She'd touched him like this on that first night too. He moved closer, put his hand to the back of her head, and while she kept her hand on him, moving up and down, he tipped her face up to his and kissed her.

He trailed his other hand down her body, caressing the side of one breast, its full outline, causing her own hand to stop momentarily. Then he continued down over her waist and her belly.

Mouths fused, Gypsy groaned deeply when she felt his hand seek between her legs, pushing them apart, stroking through her curls to where she burned wetly for him. Her hand stopped moving on him again for a moment when she felt the slide of his fingers along her wetness, slipping inside.

Her body clenched in an automatic reaction.

He tore his mouth away and said harshly, '*Dio*. How could I have forgotten how responsive you are…?'

Gypsy made a soft mewl. She ached all over. Her breasts throbbed, their peaks so tight and hard they almost hurt.

As if sensing her building agitation, Rico took her hand from him and pushed her back onto the bed. 'Gypsy, I don't know if I can go slowly…'

She lifted her head, feeling all at once slumberous

and wide awake. Half incoherent with lust, she replied, 'I don't want slow.'

She vaguely heard the ripping of a packet before he was back between her legs, hair-roughened chest crushing her breasts. Blindly she drew up her legs and reached for his buttocks, her hands feathering along his hips.

He put one arm under her back, arching her up to him, and as he thrust into her he bent and sucked one nipple deep. Gypsy had to bite her hand to stop crying out loud.

With his steady thrusts, past and present mingled into one moment for Gypsy. She'd always thought she'd imbued their night together with something *more* than it was. That it couldn't possibly have been as earth-shattering as she remembered.

But what was happening now *was* even more than she remembered. Little fires danced all over her skin. Sweat dewed her body. She burned and ached at the same time for the elusive pinnacle. Her hips moved in tandem with Rico's. He was a master of torture, bringing them close, only to pull back again. Constantly hovering near the edge.

Close to emotional tears that she didn't have the strength to hide, Gypsy husked, 'Rico, please...'

And finally, unleashing his full awe-inspiring power, Rico gave in to the devil inside him and drove Gypsy over the shattering edge before letting himself fall behind her.

After a brief respite, it was Gypsy who turned to Rico and started to press tiny kisses all down his chest and hard belly. He tensed as she found that rapidly recovering part of him and took him into her mouth.

Sucking in a breath of pure arousal, struggling to

retain control, he reached down to pull her away before she made him explode completely. Drawing her up so that she straddled him, he shifted her with big hands on her hips so that her hot, wet core slid down on him, encircling him in that tight heat.

With his legs bent, Rico clenched his jaw not to come just at the sight of Gypsy finding her rhythm, sliding up and down his shaft, which felt fuller and harder than he could ever remember. His hands cupped her breasts, thumbs flicking her nipples, before he came up to take one and then the other into his mouth.

In some dim recess of his mind, as her movements became more frantic, as she pushed him back and bent down over his chest to press a kiss to his mouth, her hard nipples scraping against his chest, Rico knew that any hope he'd had that their night together hadn't been as stupendous as in his memory was blown to smithereens. Because it had just been eclipsed.

CHAPTER TEN

'I KNOW when you're awake, Gypsy. You go very still and your breathing changes. I was aware of it every moment you lay pretending to sleep in Buenos Aires.'

Gypsy opened her eyes and met Rico's grey ones. Her heart thudded painfully and her cheeks flooded with colour. She couldn't bear to think of how wanton she'd been last night. Or how easily she'd capitulated.

He was propped up on one elbow. The curtains were open and she saw that he was cleanshaven and wearing a white shirt and jeans. Panic gripped her, and she would have thrown back the cover but remembered that she was naked.

'What time is it? Where's Lola?'

'She's dressed and downstairs, with Agneta and her grandson. He's the same age.'

Gypsy looked at him suspiciously. 'You changed her nappy?'

Rico grimaced. 'Yes, after a few attempts.'

Something in Gypsy's insides melted but she fought it. 'I should get up.'

Rico leaned back and put his hands behind his head. 'Go ahead. I'm not stopping you.'

Gypsy bit out, 'I'm naked.'

He said with a mock-lascivious leer, 'I know.' And

then more seriously, when she didn't move, 'Are you telling me that after last night you feel modest?'

Gypsy all but groaned, and went even redder. Her hands clenched on the sheet and she looked around desperately for something to cover up. Taking pity on her, Rico got off the bed and went to the bathroom, coming back with a robe. He wouldn't turn around, though, and watched mockingly as Gypsy contorted herself to get into the robe without revealing anything of her body.

Her body upon which she could already see the marks of having been made love to. Eventually she stood up, but gasped when Rico grabbed the lapels of the robe and pulled her into him.

She looked up, her belly spasming treacherously. 'Rico, we can't—not here, now...'

'As much as I'm looking forward to making love to you again, Gypsy, I won't right now. What I am going to say is this: I don't want to hear one word of regret or recrimination. You'll be moved into my rooms as of today, and Lola will be set up in the suite adjoining mine.'

Gypsy went to speak, but Rico cut off whatever she was about to say when his mouth slanted over hers and he took advantage of her open mouth. Within seconds the flames of passion rose around them, and before Gypsy knew it Rico had stopped kissing her and she was clinging helplessly to his T-shirt. She saw the burning intent in his eyes and it made her tremble in response. How could she deny that she wanted this too, after last night? She'd be the worst kind of liar.

Amidst the desire heating her blood trickled something cold, though—Rico was just controlling her, dominating her exactly as he'd been doing all along. It made her say now, as she stepped back and willed her legs to hold her up, 'I won't say anything about regret or re-crimination, but I want to keep my own room. We have a baby monitor. If I go to you we can still hear if Lola wakes up.'

Rico trailed one finger down over her flushed cheek and spoke musingly. 'Still so sure that you have something to be afraid of?'

Gypsy bit back the words trembling on her lips. She *did* have something to be *very* afraid of—and it had to do with the fact that the thought of inviting such intimacy with Rico was terrifying to her equilibrium. What was left of it.

Rico said now, 'Fine—have it your way. As long as you're in my bed every night…or I'm in yours…the geographics aren't important.'

And over the next two weeks Rico proved that Gypsy's independent stance was really just a mockery. If he went to her bed he didn't leave till the morning, and then usually only to stroll provocatively naked across the hall to his own room. And if she woke in his bed he wouldn't let her leave easily. So invariably all they were doing was using their own rooms to change and wash.

Even more disturbing, when she saw Rico return from work in the evenings on the days he went to Athens, she was aware of a spreading warmth she couldn't dampen down, no matter how much she tried.

It emanated right from her heart outwards, and it encompassed Rico now, as he strolled out to the terrace where she played with Lola as the sun set over the sea in the background.

'*Kalispera, mi pequeña,*' he said, before plucking Lola up and planting a kiss to both cheeks, which had her giggling delightedly.

'You'll confuse her with two different languages,' Gypsy mock-scolded, slightly breathless at the way her body responded to the hot look Rico gave her. In that moment a part of her yearned for him to come and kiss her too, and she hated that she did. Wanting that kind of intimate display of affection was dangerous, because it meant she wanted more.

'Nonsense,' Rico dismissed arrogantly. 'She's my daughter therefore she is of above average intelligence and will be bilingual by the time she's three.'

Gypsy's heart thumped so hard for a moment that she put her hand up to her chest, afraid Rico might hear it. This easy banter made her feel weak with longing. Forcing herself to push down the treacherous and confusing desires of her heart, she got up abruptly, brushing grit off her jeans.

With Lola still in his arms, happily trying to pull his tie apart with chubby hands, Rico said, 'There's a function in Athens tomorrow night. I'd like you to accompany me.'

Gypsy stifled a grimace. 'A charity event?'

Rico smiled. 'No, it's a party to celebrate the opening of a friend's new hotel.'

'Oh…' Gypsy faltered. What could she say? She couldn't hide here on the island for ever, but the thought of going out in public with Rico when her feelings for him were see-sawing all over the place was very dangerous. But of course she couldn't explain that—and he'd wonder what was wrong if she gave an excuse. She shrugged, 'OK…'

'Good. I'll have Demi come pick you up around four and bring you over in the helicopter. I'll meet you at the hotel.'

Still breathless, Gypsy followed Rico as he strode back into the villa with Lola. 'Wait—what about Lola?'

He halted and turned back. 'Agneta will be here. She can watch her overnight.'

Gypsy gasped. 'We'll be gone all night? But I've never left her alone for a night.'

That familiar implacability came back into the lines of Rico's face. 'Which is why it seems to me that it's a good idea to start now. I get invited to things all the time, and it's more practical to stay in Athens. We could bring her with us if we had a nanny, but as we don't…'

Gypsy felt the wrench of being parted from Lola already. 'We don't need a nanny. I can take care of her—'

'Not all the time.' Rico's tone brooked no argument, and he turned to stride inside again, throwing back over his shoulder, 'Now that you've brought it up, I'll arrange to have some nannies sent to the villa for interview in the next few days.'

'You're doing it again.' Gypsy almost had to run after Rico, watching as he handed Lola over to Agneta, who indicated that she would feed her. When Agneta had left with Lola, Rico turned to her with a dangerous look on his face.

'I am a busy man. Part of this fifteen-month deal is that you are by my side as my companion. We can't do that with a baby. She will be fine. Rafael and Isobel have a nanny for exactly that purpose.'

'That's Rafael and Isobel,' Gypsy said, afraid he'd hear the bitterness in her voice. 'They're different.'

He came close then, and Gypsy backed away, suddenly intimidated by the dangerous light in his eyes. 'Why? Because they're a real couple?'

'Something like that,' Gypsy flung at him, hoping he'd stop coming towards her. But he didn't.

'There's no reason we can't be that, Gypsy...we have desire...'

Gypsy spluttered, shocked to feel a rush of something that felt disturbingly like *hope*. 'That agreement you mentioned is *your* agreement. If you can recall, I didn't have much say in it. And Rafael and Isobel have a lot more than desire. You don't even *like* me!'

Rico stopped, a muscle in his jaw pulsing. 'I think it's safe to say that what I feel for you is undergoing something of a metamorphosis. And, to be perfectly honest, fifteen months is looking less and less palatable. I envisage a much longer union. It's practical on every level...especially when I don't see any sign of our desire waning...'

Feeling sheer panic at his cold words, and wanting to know what he'd meant by saying his feelings were changing, let alone the prospect that he'd want to lock her into some sort of loveless but passionate union, she blurted out, 'Well, I can't guarantee that my desire will last much longer. And I'm sure your ego won't relish taking to bed a woman who doesn't desire you any more. So perhaps you should think of that before you make any rash pronouncements.'

The words were stupid—inspired by panic and completely untrue, much to her own dismay. If anyone was going to lose their desire she had no doubt it would be Rico. She saw his expression change and knew she had to run—fast. She did turn, as if to flee, but Rico caught her easily with his arms around her waist. Gypsy struggled against the inevitable way her body was already responding and half kicked out fruitlessly as Rico carried her into his nearby study, shutting the door behind him.

Her back was against the door and Rico was crowding her, saying dangerously, 'You were saying?'

Gypsy couldn't open her mouth. As Rico spoke his fingers made quick work of opening the buttons of her shirt. His hips ground into hers, and with his hands he pushed apart the shirt, baring her lace-covered breasts to his gaze.

Her breasts heaved with the effort it took just to stay standing, and even though on some level Gypsy was aghast at her instant response she couldn't help it. She could feel her nipples harden and push against the lace of her bra, and Rico saw it too, a feral smile curling his lips as he cupped her breasts and brushed his thumbpads over the straining peaks. Gypsy bit back a moan.

'I don't see any evidence of your desire waning. *This* does not happen to everyone…' Rico's voice was guttural. 'It's been instantaneous between us since we met. Do you think it'll burn out when a two-year absence couldn't dampen it?'

Gypsy fought through the waves of desire threatening to suck her under and said defiantly, 'Nothing lasts for ever.'

With anger and desire crackling between them, Rico took Gypsy's mouth in a bruising kiss. Her treacherous hands acted independently of her will and went to his tie to pull it off. Frantically she opened the buttons on his shirt, hearing some pop and fall to the ground. While her hands were on his belt he pushed down the lace cups of her bra, freeing her breasts to his mouth, where he sucked and nipped gently at the sensitised peaks.

Gypsy pushed down his trousers and freed his heavy erection. Rico flicked open her jeans and pushed them down, along with her panties.

'Kick them off and put your legs around my waist.'

Gypsy nearly wept with frustration when her jeans got stuck, bending down to pull them off before reaching up again to cling onto Rico's neck and shoulders as he took her legs and wrapped them around him. They hadn't even moved from the door.

With one smooth and powerful thrust he embedded himself within her. Gypsy gasped out loud, clutching him tightly as he slowly withdrew and then thrust in again. He loosened her hold and set her back against the door, putting some space between them so that he could bend his head and take one rosy-tipped breast into his mouth as he thrust rhythmically.

When he took his mouth away from her breast Gypsy opened her eyes and looked at him. His cheeks were slashed with colour, his face stark with need and passion, his eyes nearly black. With a welling of emotion she acted completely instinctively and clasped his face in her hands, bringing his mouth to hers.

As they approached their shattering crescendo their mouths clung, and Rico swallowed her loud moan as she clenched around him more powerfully than he'd felt before. Then he let himself go, and spilled his life seed into her with such an intensity of feeling that when it was over he could only bury his head in her neck and try to remember which way was up.

They stayed like that for a long moment, the air cooling their hot skin, still intimately joined, and Gypsy stroked Rico's hair, not even aware of the tenderness of her gesture.

In that moment when Rico felt Gypsy's hand in his hair, something fundamental within him changed for ever. He might have just impregnated her. And, if truth be told, he hoped he had. Reeling with that knowledge, he couldn't deny it any more. He had to face up to the fact that his feelings for Gypsy had changed utterly.

Resolve gave him the strength to move, and he carefully let her down, holding her when her legs weren't steady. He could feel the tremors still running through her body. He handed her her clothes, before picking up his own and putting them on. Never in his life had such intense urgency dictated his actions. He winced inwardly. 'Are you all right?'

Gypsy looked up from where she'd just pulled her jeans up. She looked dazed. 'I...think so.'

Rico frowned, fear tightening his insides. 'Did I hurt you?'

Gypsy blushed and shook her head, her hair falling forward to hide her expression from him. 'No...you didn't hurt me.'

With that sense of resolve running through him and gathering force, Rico tipped up her chin. Her cheeks were flushed, lips swollen from his kisses, eyes huge. He had to curb the resurgence of desire. 'If you think our desire is on the wane, or that this is something that happens more than once in a lifetime, then you're a more cynical person than I thought you were.'

Gypsy looked at Rico, her heart pounding all over again. He was looking back at her with an indecipherable expression on his face.

'But...you're not a once-in-a-lifetime person.'

His mouth tightened. 'You don't know what I am, Gypsy, because since the morning after we met and you found out who I was you've had me sized up and boxed away.'

Gypsy felt little flutters enter her belly, along with a panicky feeling. 'I don't know what you're saying, Rico.'

'What I'm saying is that you have to open up to me, Gypsy. You need to trust me. I'm not letting you go, but I'm not going to put up with your blinkered view for ever. I am in your life and in Lola's life for the foreseeable future. For that to work we need to agree on things like a nanny, and you need to be by my side when I need you.'

Inwardly shaking at his assertion that she needed to trust him and feeling extremely exposed to think that he'd made love to her just to make a point, Gypsy blurted out, 'Just like I need to be available for a quickie when the mood takes you?'

Rico's thumb moved back and forth over Gypsy's skin. All he said was, 'We both wanted what just happened. Don't pretend you didn't. And, just as I've never before picked up a woman in a club for a night of anonymous sex, I've also never felt that same urgency we felt just now. You have a unique effect on me, Gypsy Butler.'

Just then they heard Lola's chatter. Agneta had obviously finished feeding her and was looking for them. Feeling very flushed and disheveled, Gypsy pushed past Rico to open the study door, and tried to pretend that everything was normal when the world felt anything but.

At the door she turned and said to Rico, while avoiding his eye, 'I'm quite tired tonight. I'm going to go to bed early. *Alone.*'

Rico said with a mocking drawl, 'Don't worry, Gypsy. I won't come to your bed this evening. I'll be gone early in the morning, but be ready to come to me in Athens at four o'clock tomorrow.'

That night, sleepless in bed, *aching* for Rico despite her words, Gypsy lay and stared at the ceiling in the dark. She needed to think but her mind was disturbingly fuzzy. She'd got the distinct impression from Rico's comments earlier that he saw some sort of future for them. But what, exactly? And was she brave enough to ask him?

She turned over on her side and looked out of the window to where the sea was just a black mass, with the small lights of boats flickering on and off. Rico was right. She'd prejudged him and misjudged him every step of the way.

He was nothing like her father in the business sense. And she now knew from his own personal history why he'd been so adamant that he wanted Lola. But still, that didn't account for the way he'd so instinctively taken to fatherhood. He was nothing like her father in that regard either.

Shamefully, she had to acknowledge that part of her reaction could have come from jealousy at seeing how unreservedly Rico had accepted Lola. She'd never received that from her own father. She could also see that a lot of his initial arrogance had most likely been due to shock, and perhaps a fear that she might try to run away again. He'd done everything he could to make sure they didn't leave his side.

But more than all of that was the way she felt about him. She couldn't help but remember the way he'd been that night they'd met for the first time. The magic that had infused the air as the dark and handsomely seductive stranger had put her at ease, made her laugh, and then made love to her with an intensity that had left her in pieces. Knowing Rico as she did now, she suspected that he'd indulged in a much lighter, less cynical version of himself that night. Perhaps because he had been unburdened by his anonymity, just as she had been.

If she was truly honest with herself, amidst all the turmoil of her pregnancy and finding out who Rico was, the one thing that had superceded everything else had been the hurt that he'd left her so coldly. And yet he'd admitted that he'd regretted it, that he'd tried to get in touch with her.

Gypsy's heart squeezed. She didn't think she could ever hope that Rico would look at her with the tenderness she'd seen between Rafael and Isobel, but right now her silly heart couldn't help longing for it. She couldn't fool herself into thinking that whatever rapprochement was between them would absolve her of her actions in his eyes.

The crows of doubt mocked her for even *thinking* that she might be falling for him. It had only been a few weeks since she'd met Rico again—how could she trust her feelings when her daughter's future happiness was at risk? Who was to say that Rico wasn't just seducing her to keep her and Lola in his complete control, only for him to lose interest and move on, having torn their lives apart?

The old fear was still strong, making her feel as if she should be suspicious of the way he was bonding with Lola. She hated it, but it squeezed like a vice around her heart; it was ingrained within her after years of living with a man who had bullied and controlled her because he'd resented her, the reminder of his weakness. A man who had thought nothing of letting her mother die because she was socially undesirable, and because she'd forced his hand so that he'd had to acknowledge his daughter.

Thoughts and memories roiled sickeningly in Gypsy's head until she finally fell into a dreamless sleep.

* * *

Gypsy looked at herself in the mirror of the wardrobe in a luxurious suite at the brand-new hotel that was opening that evening. A car had met her from the helicopter at the airport and whisked her here to the hotel, where she'd been met by a veritable entourage.

Up in the suite there had been a wardrobe of different outfits, and once she'd picked one out the team had set to work. The hairdresser had even smiled and said to her, 'I'm under the strictest instructions not to straighten your hair.' Gypsy had just smiled back weakly, feeling a plummeting sensation in her belly—as if she were falling over an edge into a dark chasm of the unknown.

Now she was on her own again, and twisting and turning to see herself, feeling all at once ridiculous and disturbingly *sexy*. The dress was a dark gold colour, fitted and to the knee, with just one wide strap over one shoulder, leaving the other bare.

High-heeled gold sandals looked like the most delicate things she'd ever seen and her hair was down, with Grecian-style gold bands holding it back from her face. She wore simple gold hoop earrings.

It was only then that she noticed the tall, dark and looming shape lounging against the door behind her. She whirled around, feeling very exposed. Rico was stunning in a black suit, white shirt, black tie. He straightened up and strolled towards her, and she could see that he was holding a champagne bottle and two glasses. Immediately her stomach roiled at the sight, but she clamped down on it; surely now she could take the opportunity to get over that awful teenage trauma?

Rico stared at her as if he'd never seen her before, raking his eyes up and down her body, and then he said simply, 'You look beautiful.'

Gypsy grimaced and wanted to squirm.

Rico smiled. 'Say, *Thank you, Rico.*'

She looked at him and felt an alien lightness bubble up. She smiled too. 'Thank you, Rico. You look lovely too.'

He poured champagne into two flutes and handed her one. Gypsy instinctively held her breath as she took a sip. It slid down her throat like an effervescent sunburst and she almost shouted with relief. She'd gone clammy for a moment, expecting to feel the old urge to be sick. But it hadn't come. She took another sip, relishing it.

Rico touched his glass to hers and said, 'You look like you've never tasted champagne before.'

Gypsy caught his eyes. 'Not for a long time.'

He arched a brow and asked, 'Secrets of a hell-raising youth?'

Gypsy hid the dart of pain and said, 'Hardly.'

A delicious coil of tension settled in her belly as she took Rico in; he was so tall and broad. His face all planes and shadows and hollows.

On an impulse, she blurted out, 'What happened to your nose?'

Rico stiffened. She could see his hand tighten on his glass, but then he said, 'My stepfather, the day I left Buenos Aires… He left me with a token of his affection, and a constant reminder that your own flesh and blood is your only real family.'

Gypsy remembered Isobel telling her how Rico had nearly had to be hospitalised.

'Was he responsible for the scars on your back too?' She'd noticed the faint silvery lines criss-crossing his back one morning when Rico had got up to go back to his own room, and she'd felt them while making love, but she hadn't had the nerve to ask about them. Until now.

Rico's mouth was a thin line. 'Yes, more of my

stepfather's legacy for not being his biological son. It's hard to get out of the way of a belt when you're small...'

Sheer horror tightened her gut, and she had a sudden stark understanding of how important it was for him to be there for Lola.

Gypsy went close and reached up her hand to touch his jaw. Her voice was husky. 'If I'd been there I would have stepped in the way, so he'd hit me instead.'

She looked up at him. A part of her couldn't believe what she'd just said, and another part felt fiercely that she'd meant every word. Even now anger bubbled low to think of anyone beating Rico, or hurting him.

Realisation hit her like a thunderbolt. *God*, she'd fallen for him. There was no luxury of *falling* about it. She was already deeply and profoundly in love with this man.

To her relief, before Rico might see something of her realisation and her reaction, he took the champagne and put it down before taking her hand.

His voice sounded rough, and impacted upon her somewhere very raw. 'We should go downstairs. The grand opening will be any minute now, and I have a speech to make.'

Feeling as though the earth had shifted on its axis, Gypsy followed Rico out, her hand tightly clasped in his. All the way down in the lift she looked resolutely at the floor, terrified that if she looked into his eyes he'd know immediately.

Rico stared at the elevator door on the way down, Gypsy's hand in his. He was still reeling from her simple assertion that if she'd been there she would have taken the blows for him. He knew she'd been sincere because she'd looked shocked once the words were out—as if she couldn't believe she'd said them.

The only other person who knew the extent of what Rico had been through at the hands of his stepfather was Rafael, because he'd suffered too—albeit not to the same extent—and many times Rico had felt that Rafael wanted to say something similar. That if he could have borne the brunt of that man's anger he would have. But he'd never articulated it the way Gypsy just had, with such sweet simplicity.

Taking a deep breath just before the doors opened, Rico gripped Gypsy's hand more tightly momentarily, and she squeezed him back in silent communication. His chest expanded, the door opened, and they stepped out and into the melee.

Rico had made his speech and was now back at Gypsy's side, holding her hand again. A guilty part of her revelled in this newly proprietorial touch and she grimaced inwardly. She could never have imagined *this*—wanting to be claimed so publicly by him.

They barely needed to circulate, as a constant stream of people came to *him*. The only time he crossed the room it was to another couple, and Rico slapped the man on his back playfully. He introduced the handsome man and his very pregnant wife to Gypsy. 'I'd like you to meet some newlywed friends of mine—Leo Parnassus and his wife Angel.'

The wife smiled shyly, one hand on her large bump. Gypsy asked how far along she was, and they started to chat about pregnancy and birth. She could feel Rico tense by her side, and when the couple had moved on he turned to her and said, 'I don't know anything about your pregnancy, or the birth…'

Guilt rose up, so much more poignant now, and immediately fearing some kind of reprisal Gypsy took her hand from his. 'I'm sorry... I didn't think...' she started.

But Rico took her hand again and shook his head. 'No, it's not about that. I'm not angry about that...not any more. But I'd like you to tell me some time, OK?'

Gypsy nodded, feeling herself fall even further into the chasm. But just at that moment, with absolutely no sense of foreboding whatsoever, she heard someone near them declare shrilly, 'Oh, my *God*! Alexandra Bastion, is that *you*?'

CHAPTER ELEVEN

GYPSY's blood went cold. Unbeknownst to her, her hand had tightened painfully on Rico's. The woman came over and grabbed Gypsy's arm. Gypsy recognised her through the fog of shock. They'd gone to school together—a remote and very exclusive boarding school in the Outer Hebrides in Scotland. The furthest place her father had been able to find to send her.

'Alexandra—I don't believe it! It's been—what?— seven years since we left that place? How *are* you? What have you been up to?'

The woman's eyes went appreciatively to Rico. Clearly she was looking for an introduction. But Gypsy was incapable of speaking, and suddenly, on top of this shock, she knew the taste of the champagne was making itself felt and that she was going to be sick.

As if realising her turmoil, and no doubt thinking the woman was mad, Rico put his arm around Gypsy's waist and said urbanely, 'I'm sorry—you must have the wrong person.' With a smooth move he glided them away.

Gypsy got out through numb lips, 'I need a bathroom.'

She could hear the woman behind them saying to someone, 'How strange. I could have sworn that was Alexandra Bastion…and *who* was that guy?'

Her voice faded away, but Gypsy felt clammy all over and knew that if Rico hadn't been holding onto her she might have fallen.

In seconds they were in the lift and going upwards, a wall of tense silence between them. Gypsy took deep breaths and concentrated on not being sick, but all she could think of was the champagne sloshing around her belly, and she knew it had been that woman who had sent her back in time.

As soon as they were in the suite she ran for the bathroom and closed the door, hunching over the toilet bowl as the contents of her belly came up. She was aware of the door opening and Rico coming in. She put out a hand and said weakly, 'No, please…go away.'

But, predictably, he ignored her. She heard water running, and then she felt a damp cloth against her face and it was wonderful. Eventually, when her stomach was empty, Rico helped her up and handed her a toothbrush with toothpaste already on it. She brushed her teeth and splashed water on her face. And then Rico lifted her into his arms, despite her weak protest, and took her over to one of the ornately covered chairs and sat her down.

He went and sat on the corner of the bed, near the chair, and just watched her, hands linked loosely between his legs. Gypsy knew without him saying a word that she had to talk. *Now.* With a tight knot in her belly, she took a deep breath.

'When I was fifteen years old my father found me tasting champagne from a leftover bottle after one of his parties.' Her belly tightened at the memory. 'He dragged me into his study, opened a new bottle of champagne and forced me to drink the lot. He wouldn't let me leave the room until I had. When I was sick all over the floor he made me clean it up, and told me that perhaps I'd remember that lesson if I ever wanted to taste champagne again.'

She looked at Rico. His eyes bored into hers and he said, 'Your father was John Bastion.'

Gypsy couldn't even feel surprised that he knew. She just nodded wearily. 'When did you find out?'

'Before we came back to Athens.'

So he'd known for the past few weeks, but said nothing.

He saw the question in her eyes and said, 'I wanted you to tell me yourself. Why didn't you want to tell me about him?'

Her heart clenched. She bit her lip. Where to start? Hands closed tight in her lap, she finally said, 'Because I hated him, and from the day he died I wanted to forget that he'd existed.'

Rico frowned. 'Where did *Alexandra* come from?'

'He didn't want me. The only reason he took me in eventually was because he was a so-called pillar of society and Social Services couldn't understand why he wouldn't. He had to; he wanted to avoid negative press attention at all costs. But the minute I was under his roof he insisted on changing my name to Alexandra, and he spread the word discreetly that he'd adopted me out of the goodness of his heart. He didn't want anyone to know I was his biological daughter. He was ashamed to be reminded that he'd had an affair with a cleaner. He was ashamed of everything about me—especially as I wasn't some sleek blonde, like his own mother or his new wife.'

Rico stood up and started to pace. He turned around. 'And what about your mother? Where was she?'

Gypsy's hands tightened. She looked down. 'We weren't well off at all... Where I was living with Lola was a palace compared to where we were. She couldn't cope. She tried to kill herself...that's why she wanted me to go to my father. He insisted they send her to a mental hospital for psychiatric assessment...and without any resources or anyone to speak for her she got lost in the system, forgotten about. She died there when I was about thirteen, but I didn't find out until after my father died and I found a letter from the hospital.' She didn't mention the heartbreaking letters from her mother.

'Your father and stepmother died in a plane crash?'

Gypsy looked up again and nodded. 'Over the English Channel, coming back from France.'

Surprising her, he asked, 'Why were you in the club that night, Gypsy?'

Feeling the quiver of trepidation in her belly, but knowing that if he investigated further he'd find out everything anyway, she told him. She smiled wryly, but it felt a bit skewed. 'As I was officially my father's next of kin, despite public perception, I received everything in his will. He'd never got around to making sure I wouldn't, which is undoubtedly what he'd planned, but as he believed he was infallible he hadn't counted on sudden death...

'That night...the night of the club...it was six months after his death and I'd just received and signed over every single Bastion asset and property to all the charities he had been patron of and had stolen from for years. I felt so guilty that I'd never been brave enough to report him to the police it was the least I could do. I donated the rest of his money to psychiatric care and research. I insisted it was done anonymously. I didn't want any media attention. And I'd also just reverted back to my own birth name, which was easy as it was on my birth certificate. I was finally free—from him and his legacy. I didn't want a penny of his money. Not after what he did to my mother and how he treated me.'

She shrugged. 'I heard the beat of the music and I wanted to dance, to celebrate being free...'

Rico came and sat back down heavily on the bed.

Gypsy continued with a rush, wanting to make Rico understand. 'He knew that I knew about his transgressions with charity funds, so when I was seventeen he took me to a charity event and auctioned me off to work for a summer with that charity's operation in Africa.' Her mouth twisted. 'It was to get me out of his hair, but also a punishment and a way to demonstrate his control. I had the last laugh, though, because it was the best experience I ever had and it inspired me to want to study psychology.'

She bit her lip. 'He spoke of you. He was envious of your fortune and said you were ruthless. That was another reason I believed the worst about you. I assumed your methods were the same as his...'

Rico's lip curled. 'I never had anything to do with the man. I had no respect for the way he did business.'

Feeling unaccountably sad, Gypsy said, 'I know that now.' She stood up abruptly. Emotions were bubbling too close to the surface. She'd never revealed this much to another living soul and she suddenly felt too exposed. 'Look, do you mind if we don't talk about it anymore? It's in the past now. Alexandra Bastion never really existed. I'd like to go home to Lola tonight, if it's possible.'

Rico stood too, tall and powerful, his face and eyes unreadable. Gypsy nearly sagged with relief when he said, 'Of course it's possible. I'll call Demi now. Why don't you get changed and we'll go?'

The whole way back to the island, and then to the

villa, Rico was silent, and Gypsy was grateful. Once they got inside, though, and they'd both looked in on Lola, who slept peacefully, Rico trailed a finger down Gypsy's cheek and said, 'We'll talk in the morning...we need to talk about this.'

His steely tone brooked no argument. Of course he wasn't going to let her revelations end here. Reluctantly Gypsy nodded briefly, and Rico stepped away and strode from her room, leaving her alone.

And that night, for the first time in a long time, she slept like a baby.

The following morning Gypsy revelled in waking up to Lola's chatter as she waited contentedly for someone to come to her. She had a prickling sensation over her skin, as if something momentous was going to happen. And she couldn't forget the revelation that Rico had already known of her past. Perhaps not everything, but enough, and yet he'd wanted to wait for her to tell him. He hadn't used it against her.

It made her feel slightly panicky inside, with the sensation of no walls of defence left standing. What would happen now?

Gypsy dragged herself up and went to greet Lola, who said ecstatically, 'Mama!', and stood to greet her. Gypsy took her out and held her close, breathing in her delicious scent and feeling her solid weight. But already Lola was squirming to get down and be off exploring.

It was only when she was escaping out through the bedroom door that Gypsy realised she was looking for Rico, who appeared at that moment, cleanshaven and gorgeous in jeans and a T-shirt, and swung Lola up in his arms, much to her delight.

He looked at Gypsy, no discernible expression on his face. 'I'll take her down if you want to get dressed.'

So we can talk.

He didn't say it, but he didn't have to. He now had all the knowledge, all the power. Gypsy hated the way she automatically imagined the worst, but she'd had years of dealing with exactly that.

A short while later, dressed equally casually in jeans and a long-sleeved top, Gypsy joined the mayhem that was Lola's breakfast-time. Agneta was there too, cooing at Lola, who was happily holding court. Gypsy came in and had some coffee and a croissant, but she couldn't swallow past the huge lump in her throat.

When Agneta took Lola off, insisting that she would get her changed and dressed, Rico finally put down his napkin and stood.

'Will you come into my study?'

Gypsy looked up, and something dark made her say, 'Oh, so you're *asking* now?'

It was a mistake, because Rico glowered and all Gypsy could think of was the frantic coupling that had happened between them in there. With warmth suffusing her cheeks, she followed Rico.

Once in the study, Rico turned around to face Gypsy. Instinctively wanting to protect herself, she crossed her arms. Rico hitched one hip on the edge of his desk, and Gypsy fought not to let her gaze drop wantonly to where his jeans stretched over hard thighs.

'I had no idea you went through so much at the hands of that man.'

Gypsy looked at Rico before glancing away. His gaze was so intense. She shrugged. 'How could you have known? No one knew except for me.'

'That's why you didn't want to tell me about Lola, isn't it?'

Gypsy swallowed painfully. Her gaze swung back. 'It was a large part of it, yes. But, no matter what you believe, I *did* intend telling you. I just wanted to be in a better position…so you wouldn't see me as weak…and the thought of being dragged through the courts to prove paternity *was* daunting. I didn't want people finding out that I had been Alexandra Bastion and wondering where the family fortune had gone. I had never imagined that I might become pregnant. I truly did believe I'd be safe.'

Rico winced. 'I told you about that court case. It was just unbelievably bad timing for you to have seen it that very morning.'

Rico stood from the desk and started to pace, making Gypsy's pulse race. She crossed her arms tighter across her chest.

He stopped to face her and in an uncharacteristically impatient gesture ran a hand through his hair. 'Look,' he began, 'it's clear now that we both had our reasons for reacting the way we did—you in your decision to keep Lola to yourself, and me for wanting her with me from the moment I knew about her.' He shook his head. 'I thought you were just like my mother—wilfully keeping me from Lola just because it served your purposes. And the thought of Lola possibly being brought up by some other man some day…enduring what I had…was too much to contemplate.'

Gypsy balked at the thought of *another man*. There would be no other man. Not ever. Not any more.

She bit her lip and said quietly, as that assertion rocked through her, 'I was just so terrified that you would be like my father…*worse*…because you were even more powerful than him. All I ever was was an inconvenient pawn to him.' She looked at Rico. 'I thought you would sweep in and take us over, remove me permanently from Lola's life the way my father did my mother.'

Rico shook his head. 'I was angry, yes, but I never thought of taking you away from Lola. I will admit that I saw a future where Lola was in my life and you were sidelined...but I don't see that future any more.'

'You don't?'

He shook his head. 'No.' His voice was a little gruff. 'I see a future with all of us together. I don't want this to end in fifteen months. I don't want to let you and Lola go. I want more than that, Gypsy. I want us to be a family...'

Gypsy started to tremble from her feet up. What Rico was saying was so huge. Massive. He wanted them to stay together. For ever? It was all at once the most exhilarating thing and the most terrifying. And in the midst of it all was her bone-deep ingrained fear and panic.

That snide voice was reminding her that men like Rico were masters of getting what they wanted. That he *had* swept in and taken them over. Look at them now—living on an island, effectively cut off from everything and everyone. And she had no idea how Rico really felt about her. He might be able to forgive her now, but what if that resentment was still there, buried and festering away? What if his desire waned and he wanted another woman?

Gypsy shook her head and started to back away, noticing the flash of Rico's eyes. He stood up straight at the desk, and his quick anger at her less than compliant response seemed to add fuel to her reasoning.

'You want me to agree to your plans just like that?' She snapped her fingers. 'You've been in our lives for a month, Rico, and suddenly you think that we can be a *family*?'

His frame bristled with energy. His jaw was tight. 'You're just saying that because it's hard for you to trust me.'

'Don't patronise me, Rico. From the word go you've stormed in and had it all your own way. This is exactly what I was afraid of.'

'Gypsy—' he sounded frustrated now '—you're not being rational.'

Something deep within Gypsy was surging up— something that had been buried for a long time. 'I am *not* my mother, Rico. I am not mentally weak. I have skills. I can take care of myself and my daughter.'

'I'm not saying you can't. What I'm saying is that I want to be there too. I want us to be together.'

'Because you want to control us.' Gypsy knew now that she was being irrational, but she couldn't stop.

'*No!* Dammit, Gypsy, no. Not because I want to control you but because I love Lola. I don't want to be separated from her and I—' He stopped abruptly, concern etched on his face. 'What? What is it?'

He even came towards her, but she waved him back— if he touched her now... For a heart-stopping moment she'd thought he was about to say he loved *her*, and when he hadn't...she'd felt like collapsing. Of course he loved Lola. And he wanted to do what was best for her. A million miles from her own father. Suddenly Gypsy felt ashamed.

Rico's voice was tight. 'Look, what is it going to take for me to prove that you can trust me and that I'm not like your father?'

Gypsy lifted stinging eyes to Rico and, with a guilt that nearly crippled her, said the one thing she wanted least. But she couldn't stop it—as if on some level she thought if he could prove *this* then she would gladly give him everything, even if he didn't love her.

'I want to know that you will let us go if we want to—that you won't cut yourself off from Lola just to punish me.'

With his features pale and stark, Rico said nothing for a long moment, and then he walked out of the study. Before Gypsy could wonder what he was doing he came back and held out a key. She saw that it was the key to the Jeep.

'Go on—take it. I've instructed Agneta to pack up some things.'

Numbly Gypsy took the key and looked up into Rico's eyes. They were a cool slaty grey. 'You're just going to let us go? Right now? Like this?'

His mouth was a thin line. 'That's what you want, isn't it? That's what it's going to take?'

Suspecting he was just proving a point, but feeling utterly confused and bewildered, and thinking that perhaps even Rico had had enough by now, Gypsy nodded dumbly. She'd meant that she wanted him to assure her that he would let them go *if she wanted*, but now she realised that she might not have trusted that either. And through all of that was the heart-searing realisation that he *could* let her walk away—because she meant nothing to him.

Things happened quickly, and through it all a numbness settled over Gypsy as bags were put in the boot of the Jeep and as she strapped a bemused Lola into her chair. Poor Agneta was looking on, wringing her hands as if she had done something wrong.

Rico stood back. The only thing he said was, 'This

doesn't mean you're out of my life. Lola will always know I'm here.'

Gypsy got into the Jeep and held herself together as she started it up with a shaking hand. She had no earthly idea what to do or where to go. She was proving her point, and it was a disaster. But she drove out of the villa anyway, and set off along the coast road.

Almost immediately a plaintive wail came from the back of the Jeep. 'Papa!'

In her shock, Gypsy nearly swerved. Hearing Lola call Rico *Papa* for the first time, as if she'd just made the connection now that they were leaving, undid her completely. She had to pull over to a layby because her eyes were so blurred with tears.

And then Lola was wailing in earnest at Gypsy's distress.

The two of them were sitting there sobbing when suddenly Gypsy's door was wrenched open and Rico stood there, demanding, 'What is it? Did you crash? What's wrong?'

But Gypsy couldn't get a word out. She was crying too hard, even though Lola's wails had stopped and she was saying tearfully from the back, 'Papa… Papa…'

Rico took his attention to Lola and said wonderingly, 'She just called me Papa…' And then, soothingly, 'Everything is OK, *mi pequeña*—do you want to go home?'

Clearly Lola did something to indicate the affirmative, because then Rico was lifting Gypsy expertly into the passenger seat and suddenly they were turning around and driving back to the villa.

Through a blur of tears Gypsy saw Rico take Lola out and kiss her, before handing her to a relieved-looking Agneta, saying something in Greek which had Agneta nodding and smiling. And then he was at her door and lifting her out before she could protest. In all honesty Gypsy felt as weak as a rag doll.

Rico took her straight up to his bedroom and sat down on a chair in the corner with her on his lap. Gypsy was still sniffing and taking big convulsive breaths. Wordlessly Rico handed her a hanky, and she blew her nose loudly.

When she was more composed, and becoming very aware of sitting on Rico's steel-hard thighs, she tensed.

'Now...' he said. 'Do you believe that I'll let you go if you want to?'

Gypsy's heart beat fast. She looked at him suspiciously. 'You weren't far behind us.'

'Answer the question, Gypsy Butler. Do you believe that if you really want it, I'll let you go?'

Slowly she nodded her head, because she *did* believe it. In all honesty she'd believed it even before he'd orchestrated his little enactment.

He said now, 'I was following just to see that you were OK. You looked shell-shocked—I was worried. And,' he added, 'it's good that you believe me, because I'm never going to let you go again.'

Gypsy couldn't even gasp or act affronted. She just felt sadness well upwards. Tears formed again. She felt him tense, as if expecting a fight, and rushed to explain. 'It's not that I want to leave, I don't. But I don't see how loving Lola is going to make you happy in the long run—won't you want to meet someone else and settle down?'

Gypsy waved a shaking hand, not letting Rico speak. The tears were back, constricting her voice. 'I mean, Lola adores you, and you adore Lola, and it's the best thing I've ever seen, and I know now that you would never hurt her like my father did me...' She gulped in a breath. 'But it's going to get awfully embarrassing because...' Her heart thumped hard once, and then it spilled out. 'Because you see I adore you too, and I don't ever want you to send me away, and I *do* trust you, but it's scary because I've never trusted anyone, so I didn't believe it, and you won't thank me for these feelings when you want to move on...'

Rico shifted so that Gypsy fell into the cradle of his lap. He brought his hands to her face and wiped away the tears, and said gently, 'Can you stop talking and crying for one minute?'

There was such warmth in his voice that it shocked Gypsy's tears into stopping. She hiccupped once. And blushed when she could feel the press of his arousal against her bottom. How could either of them be thinking of *that* at a time like this?

'Gypsy Butler...' Rico began, making sure she wasn't looking anywhere but into his eyes, which *glowed*, making her heart beat fast. 'Can you not tell how deeply and irrevocably in love with you I am?'

Wordlessly, shock hitting her, she just shook her head.

'Well, I am. I was about to tell you earlier, but then you looked as if you were going to faint. I started falling for you when I saw you in the club that night. I was ready to walk out, bored beyond tears, cursing myself for having gone in at all—and then you walked in, and I couldn't look away. You looked so wild and free and totally different to anyone else.'

His thumbs stroked her cheeks, and Gypsy could feel herself leaning against him, melting all over.

'And then...that night...it was magical. I felt like I'd

met the one person who connected with the real *me*. Not the tycoon. And I was such a fool to leave you like that in the morning, but I was freaked out by how much you'd made me feel: possessive, and yearning for something I'd never even noticed I wanted before...'

'It was like that for me too,' Gypsy said, feeling shy, still not really believing she was hearing this.

'And then you were gone, and all I knew was that I'd spent the night with a temptress called Gypsy and I didn't even think that was your real name. For the past two years you've haunted my dreams and my life. I tried to recreate what I experienced with you but it never happened. I was growing increasingly cynical and delusional and then I saw you again. I thought I was dreaming you up.'

'But...just now...you let me walk away...'

An intense light lit his eyes. 'To be honest I didn't think you'd go through with it. But then I realised I had to let you go, or else you never would have trusted that I *could* let you go. You and Lola mean everything to me, but if you're not happy here then I would never keep you against your will. I have to warn you, though, I'll follow you wherever you go...'

He drew her head down to his and started to kiss her, as delicately and tenderly as if she were made of fine bone china. Impatient with his restraint, Gypsy deepened the kiss, her tongue stroking erotically along Rico's until she heard him groan and finally he gave in to his passion.

She was being lifted from the chair, and suddenly they were tumbling onto Rico's bed and his hands were everywhere, desire rising to fever-pitch as they both struggled to be free of conflicting clothes, needing to forge a deeper union.

Finally, blissfully naked, Gypsy arched her whole body against Rico's hard physique and revelled in his indrawn breath. He pressed her down and moved over her, both hands framing her face, her hair spilling out around her head.

He looked down at her, and nothing but love shone from his eyes.

'There's just one other thing.'

For a second something familiarly panicky skated over Gypsy's skin, and she asked warily, 'What?'

He waited for a moment, a wicked glint in his eyes. And then said finally, 'If it's not too scary a prospect, and if I promise not to ever control you but to give you all the freedom you want, will you trust me enough to marry me, Gypsy Butler?'

Love and passion infused every cell, and she felt the final release of all her old fears. She smiled up at Rico tremulously and reached up to caress his jaw. 'I trust you with all my heart, and our daughter's life. And I'd love to marry you.'

Rico saw the tears forming in her eyes and started to kiss her again, moving over her body so that she could feel his hardness. He growled mock-seriously, 'No more tears. I won't allow it. Only smiles and laughter from now on…and love.'

He joined their bodies, and Gypsy gasped at the exquisite sensation, too distracted to think about crying any more even if they were happy tears.

EPILOGUE

LOLA handed Rico's phone back to him and lisped through her two missing front teeth, 'There you go, Daddy, now you have the *newest* newest ringtone.'

Rico repressed a grimace when he thought of the effect the last ringtone had had on a recent high-powered meeting, and said, while holding back a wry smile, 'Thanks, Lola, I wasn't so sure about that last one.'

Lola flung her arms around Rico's neck and gave him a quick sloppy kiss, 'You'll love this one. It's *really* loud so you'll always hear when we're calling you.'

Rico shook his head indulgently and watched as she sped off to play with Agneta's grandson, from whom she was inseparable, her hair bouncing with wild and curly disarray around her shoulders.

Just then Gypsy appeared, wearing a short sundress that did nothing to conceal her gorgeous body and everything to send Rico's pulse-rate soaring. Her hair was only slightly less wild than their daughter's, with long tendrils curling over bare sun-kissed skin.

She led a small endearingly grumpy-looking boy by the hand; Zack had obviously woken prematurely from his nap, and Rico opened his arms so that he could clamber up and snuggle into his chest, promptly falling asleep again with a thumb stuck firmly into his mouth, exactly as his older sister had used to do.

Rico pulled Gypsy gently down beside him on the family lounger. She leant in to give him a long, lingering kiss. When they broke apart he caressed her jaw, rubbing her bottom lip with his thumb, and sighed with obvious but good-humoured frustration. The look that zinged between them said it all.

Gypsy smiled ruefully and put a hand on her swollen belly. 'I'd forgotten that I can never seem to nap when I'm pregnant…'

Rico smiled too, and growled softly, 'In which case we should aim for a nice early bedtime tonight…it's been far too long since I felt your naked body against mine, Mrs Christofides.'

Gypsy blushed to think of how they'd woken so entwined that morning. Rico had only had to make a subtle movement to bring them into more intimate contact. It had been slow and unbearably sensual. Full of love. She smiled. 'You're insatiable.'

'Only for you, *mi amor*.' Rico smiled, his eyes tender on his wife's face, revelling in the oceans of love that surrounded them. 'Only for you.'

The Call of
the Desert

ABBY GREEN

CHAPTER ONE

"THE Emir of Burquat. His Royal Highness Sheikh Kaden Bin Rashad al Abbas."

Kaden looked out over the thronged ballroom in London's exclusive Royal Archaeology Club. Everyone was staring at him and a hush had descended on the crowd, but that didn't bother Kaden. He was used to such attention.

He walked down the ornate marble steps, one hand in his trouser pocket, watching dispassionately as people were caught staring and turned away hurriedly again. Well, to be more accurate, the men turned away and the women's looks lingered—some blatantly so. Like that of the buxom waitress who was waiting at the bottom of the stairs to hand him a glass of champagne. She smiled coquettishly as he took the glass but Kaden had already looked away; she was far too young for his jaded heart and soul.

Ever since he'd been a teenager he'd been aware he possessed a certain power when it came to women. When he looked in the mirror, though, and saw his own harsh features staring back at him, he wondered cynically if all they felt was the seductive urge to wipe away that cynicism and replace it with something softer. He had been softer…once. But it was so long ago now that he could hardly remember what it had felt like. It was like a dream, and perhaps like all dreams it had never been real.

Just then a movement on the other side of the room caught his eye, and a glimpse of a shiny blonde head among all the darker ones had his insides contracting. *Still. Even now.* He cursed himself and welcomed the sight of the club's managing director hurrying towards him, wondering angrily why he hadn't yet mastered such arbitrarily reflexive responses to the memory of something that had only ever been as flimsy as a dream.

Julia Somerton's heart was palpitating, making her feel a little dizzy.

Kaden.

Here.

In the same room.

He'd descended the stairs and disappeared into the throng of people, despite his superior height. But that first image of him, appearing in the doorway like some sleek, dark-haired god, would be etched on her retina for ever. It was an image that was already carved indelibly onto her heart. The part of her heart that she couldn't erase him from, no matter how much she tried or how much time passed.

She'd noted several things in the space of that heart-stopping split second when she'd heard his name being called and had looked up. He was still as stupendously gorgeous as he'd been when she'd first met him. Tall, broad and dark, with the exotic appeal of someone not from these lands—someone who had been carved out of a much more arid and unforgiving place. He'd been

too far away for her to see him in any detail, but even
from where she'd stood she'd felt the impact of that black
gaze—eyes so dark you could lose yourself for ever. *And
hadn't she once?*

Some small, detached part of herself marvelled that
he could have such an effect on her after all this time.
Twelve long years. She was a divorcée now, a million
miles from the idealistic girl she'd once been. When
she'd known him.

The last time she'd seen Kaden she'd just turned
twenty—weeks before his own twentieth birthday.
Something she'd used to tease him mercilessly about:
being with an *older woman.*

Her heart clenched so violently that she put a hand to
her chest, and one of her companions said with concern,
"Julia, dear, are you all right? You've gone quite pale."

She shook her head, and placed her drink down on
a nearby table with a sweaty hand. Her voice came out
husky, rough, "It must be the heat… I'll just get some
air for a minute."

Blindly Julia made her way through the crowd, pushing, not looking left or right, heading for where patio
doors led out to a terrace which overlooked manicured
gardens. She only vaguely heard her colleague call after
her, "Don't go too far—you've got to say your piece
soon!"

When she finally reached the doors and stepped out,
she sucked in huge lungfuls of air. She felt shaky and
jelly-like—at a remove from everything. She recognised
shock. It was mid-August and late evening. The city air
was heavy and oppressively warm. The faintly metallic scent of a storm was in the atmosphere. Huge clouds
sat off in the distance, as if waiting for their cue to roll

in. The garden here was famous for its exotic species of plants which had been brought back by many an adventurer and nurtured over the years by the dedicated gardeners.

But Julia was blind to all that.

Her hands gripped the wall so hard her knuckles shone white in the gathering twilight. She was locked in a whirlpool of memories, so many memories, and they were as bright and as painfully bittersweet as if it had all happened yesterday.

Ridiculously tears pricked her eyes, and an awful sense of loss gripped her. Yet how could this be? She was a thirty-two-year-old woman. Past her prime, many people would say, or perhaps coming into it, others would maintain. She felt past her prime. The day she'd flown away from the Emirate of Burquat on the Arabian Peninsula something inside her had withered and died. And even though she'd got on with her studies and surpassed her own dreams to gain a master's degree and a doctorate, and had married and loved her husband in her own way, she'd never truly *felt* again. The reason for that was in the room behind her, a silent malevolent presence.

God, she'd loved him so much—

"Dr Somerton, it's time for your speech."

An urgent voice jarred her out of the memories. Dredging up strength from somewhere deep inside her, from a place she hadn't needed to visit in a long time, Julia steeled herself and turned around. She was going to have to stand up in front of all these people and speak for fifteen minutes, all the while knowing he was there, watching her.

Remembering?

Perhaps he wouldn't even remember... Perhaps he'd struggle to place her in his past. Her mouth became a bitter line. He'd certainly had enough women to make her blur into the crowd—not to mention a marriage of his own. She hated to admit that she was as aware of his exploits as the next person on the street who read the gossip rags on their lunchbreaks.

Maybe he'd wonder why she looked familiar. Acute pain gripped her and she repressed it brutally. Perhaps he wouldn't remember the long nights in the desert when it had felt as if they were the only two people in the world underneath a huge blanket of stars. Perhaps he wouldn't remember the beautiful poignancy of becoming each other's first lover and how their naïve lovemaking had quickly developed beyond naivetée to pure passion and an insatiable need for one another.

Perhaps he wouldn't remember when he'd said to her one night: "*I will love you always. No other woman could ever claim my heart the way you have.*"

And perhaps he wouldn't remember that awful day in the beautiful Royal Palace in Burquat when he'd become someone cold and distant and cruel.

Reassuring herself that a man like Kaden would have consigned her to the dust heap of his memories, and stifling the urge to run from the room, Julia pasted a smile on her face and followed her colleague back into the crowd, trying desperately to remember what on earth she was supposed to talk about.

"Ah, Sheikh Kaden, there you are. Dr Julia Somerton is just about to speak. I believe she used her research in Burquat for her masters degree. Perhaps you met her all those years ago? She's involved in fundraising now, for various worldwide archaeological projects."

Kaden looked at the red-faced man who'd forced his way through the crowd to come and join him, and made a non-committal response. The man was the managing director of the club, who had invited him with a view to wooing funds out of him. Kaden was trying to disguise the uncomfortable jolt of shock to hear the name *Julia*. Despite the fact that he'd never met another Julia in Burquat, he told himself that there might have been another student by that name and he wouldn't have necessarily been aware, considering his lack of interest in all things archaeological after *she'd* left.

This was his first foray back into that world and it would be ironic in the extreme if he was to meet *her*. She had been Julia Connors, not Somerton. Although, as an inner voice pointed out, she could be married by now. In fact, why wouldn't she be? *He* had been married, after all. At the memory of his marriage Kaden felt the usual cloud of black anger threaten to overwhelm him. He resolutely pushed it aside. He was not one to dwell on the past.

And yet one aspect of his past which had refused to dissolve into the mists of time was facing him right now. If it *was* her. Unaccountably his heart picked up pace.

A hush descended over the crowd. Kaden looked towards the front of the room and the world halted on its axis for a terrifying moment when he saw the slim woman in the black cocktail dress ascending the steps to the podium. *It was her*. Julia. In a split second he was transported back to the moment when he'd realised that, because of lust, he'd placed her on a pedestal that she had no right to grace. And only that realisation had stopped him making the biggest mistake of his life.

Shaking his mind free of the disturbingly vivid memory, Kaden narrowed his eyes on Julia. Her voice was husky; it had caught him from the first moment they'd met. She'd been wearing a T-shirt and dusty figure-hugging jeans. Her long hair had fallen in bright tendrils over her shoulders. A safari-style hat had shaded her face from the sun. Her figure had been lithe and so effortlessly sensual he'd lost the power of speech.

If anything she was more beautiful than that first day he'd seen her. Time had hollowed out her cheeks, adding an angularity that hadn't been there before. *She'd only been nineteen.* Her face had still held a slight hint of puppy-plumpness. As had her body. From what he could see now, she looked slimmer, with a hint of enticing cleavage just visible in the V of her dress. In fact there was a fragility about her that hadn't been there before.

She was a million miles from that first tantalising dusty image he held in his mind's eye; she was elegance personified now, with her long blonde hair pulled back into a low ponytail. The heavy side parting swept it across her forehead and down behind one ear. Her groomed appearance was doing little, though, to stop the torrent of carnal images flooding Kaden's mind— and in such lurid detail that his body started to harden in response.

He would have anticipated that she'd have no effect on him. Much like any ex-lover. But the opposite was true. This was inconceivable. He had to concede now, with extreme reluctance, that no woman since this woman had exerted such a sensual hold over him. He'd never again lost control as he had with her—every time.

And he'd never felt the same acrid punch of jealousy to his gut as when he'd seen her in another man's arms, with another man's mouth on hers, tasting her...feeling her soft curves pressed against him. The vividness of that emotion was dizzying in its freshness, and he fought to negate it, too stunned by its resurgence to look too closely into what it meant.

This woman had been a valuable lesson in never allowing his base nature to rule his head or his heart again. Yet the years of wielding that control felt very flimsy how he was faced with her again.

More than a little bewildered at this onslaught of memories, and irrationally angry that she was here to precipitate them, Kaden felt his whole body radiate displeasure. Just then a rumble of laughter trickled through the gathered crowd in reaction to something she'd said. Kaden's mouth tightened even more, and with that tension making his movements jerky he said something about getting some air and stalked towards the open patio doors.

As soon as Julia's speech was over he was going to get out of there and forget that he'd ever seen her again.

Julia stepped down off the dais. She'd faltered during her speech for long seconds when she'd noticed Kaden head and shoulders above the rest of the crowd, at the back of the room like a forbidding presence, those dark eyes boring through her. And then with an abrupt move he'd moved outside. Almost as if disgusted by something she'd said. It had taken all her powers of concentration to keep going, and she'd used up all her reserves.

To her abject relief she saw her boss at the fundraising foundation come towards her. He put a hand to her
elbow and for once she wasn't concerned about keeping distance between them. Ever since her divorce had
come through a year ago Nigel had been making his interest clear, despite Julia's clear lack of encouragement.
Tonight, though, she needed all the support she could
get. If she could just get through the rest of the relentless schmoozing and get out of there perhaps she could
pretend she'd never seen Kaden.

Nigel was babbling excitedly about something as he
steered her away, but she couldn't even hear him above
the din of chatter and the clink of glasses. People were
making the most of the *gratis* champagne reception.
Julia craved that sweet oblivion, but it was not to be.

With dread trickling into her veins and her belly
hollowing out, she could already see where they were
headed—towards someone at the back of the room, near
the terrace. Someone with his back to them: tall, broad
and powerful. Thick ebony-black hair curled a touch too
much over the collar of his jacket, exactly the way it had
when she'd first met him.

Like a recalcitrant child she tried to dig her heels into
the ground, but Nigel was blithely unaware, whispering
confidentially, "He's an emir, so I'm not sure how you
have to address him. Maybe call him Your Highness
just in case. It would be such a coup to interest him in
the foundation."

In that split second Julia had a flashback to when
she'd met Kaden for the first time. She'd only been working on the dig for a couple of weeks, had still been getting used to the intense heat, when a pair of shoes had
come into her line of vision. She'd barely looked up.

"*Don't* step there. Whoever you are. You're about to walk on top of a fossil that's probably in the region of three thousand years old."

The shoe had hovered in mid-air and come back down again in a safer spot, and a deep, lightly accented voice had drawled seductively, "Do you always greet people with such enthusiasm?"

Julia gritted her teeth. Since she'd arrived she'd been the object of intense male interest and speculation. She was under no illusions that it was most likely because she was blonde and the only female under fifty on the dig. "If you don't mind, I'm in the middle of something here."

The shoes didn't move and the voice came again, sounding much more arrogant and censorious. "I *do* mind, actually—I am the Crown Prince and you will acknowledge me when I speak to you."

She'd completely forgotten that the Emir was due to visit with some important guests that day—and *his son*. Dismay filling Julia, she put down her brush and finally looked up, and up, and up again, to see a tall, broad figure standing over her. The sun was in her eyes so all she could make out was his shape—which was formidable.

Taking off her gloves, she slowly stood, and came face to face with the most handsome man she'd ever seen in her life. Robes highlighted his awe-inspiring height and broad shoulders. He wore a turban, but that couldn't hide the jet-black hair curling down to his collar, or the square cut of his jaw. The most mesmerising dark eyes.

Feeling more than a little overwhelmed she took off her hat and held out her hand…

"And this is Dr Somerton, who you just heard. As our

funds manager she's been instrumental in making sure that funding reaches our digs all over the world."

Past merged into present and Julia found that she was holding out her hand in an automatic response to the introduction. She was now facing Kaden, and much as she'd have loved to avert her gaze he took up a lot of space, completely arresting in a dark suit with a snowy-white shirt open at the neck, making him stand out from the men in the crowd who were more formally dressed. He looked darker, and infinitely more dangerous than any other man there.

There was no such thing as sliding towards middle age with a receding hairline and expanding gut for him. He oozed virility, vitality, and a heady, earthy sexual magnetism far more powerful than she remembered. There was not a hint of softness about him, or his face. He was all lean angles. The blade of his slightly crooked nose highlighted a sense of danger and a man in his vigorous prime. She remembered the day he'd got that injury, while playing his country's brutal national game.

Her heart squeezed as she recalled that moment and saw the new harshness stamping the lines of his face. She wondered how long it had been there. Her eyes slid down helplessly…his mouth hadn't changed. It was as sensual as she remembered, with its full lower lip and the slightly thinner, albeit beautifully shaped upper lip. She'd used to love tracing that line with her finger. Heat flared in her belly. *And with her tongue.* It was a mouth which held within it the power to inspire a need in the most cynical of women to make this man *hers*.

The strength of that need washed through Julia, and dismay gripped her. She couldn't still want this man—not after all these years. Her hand hovered in mid-air as the moment stretched out between them. He was looking at her as intently as she was looking at him, but it was no consolation. There was no polite spark of recognition, only an extreme air of tension. He knew her, but clearly did not relish meeting her again.

Julia realised that just as his big hand enveloped her much smaller one, and a million and one sensations exploded throughout her body.

Far too innately civilised to be deliberately rude and ignore Julia's hand, as he perversely longed to do, Kaden reached out to take it. He instinctively gritted his jaw against the inevitable physical contact but it was no good. At the first touch of his fingers to that small, soft hand he wanted to slide his thumb with sensual intent along the gap between her thumb and forefinger in a lover's caress. He wanted to curl his fingers around her palm and feel every delicate bone.

He wanted to relearn this woman in an erotic way that was so forceful it set off a maelstrom of biblical proportions inside him. And somewhere in his head he wondered when had just shaking a woman's hand ever precipitated such an onslaught of need.

A voice answered him: about twelve years ago, in the searing heat of the afternoon sun amongst dusty relics, when this same woman had stood before him with a shy smile on her face, her hand in his. And, much to his chagrin, Kaden felt his intention to walk away and forget he'd seen her again dissolve in a rush of lust.

CHAPTER TWO

A MINOR earthquake was taking place within Julia's body, and Kaden seemed loath to let her hand go—about as reluctant as she was for him to let it go. The realisation shamed her, and yet to her horror she couldn't seem to muster up the energy to extricate her hand from his. She noticed the look in his eyes change to something ambiguous, and every cell in her blood jumped and fizzed in reaction.

An emotion which felt awfully poignant and *yearning* was threatening. She struggled to remember where she was, and with whom, but it was almost impossible. The reality that it was *Kaden* in front of her was too much to take in. All she could do was react.

As suddenly as Julia had registered the changed intensity in Kaden's gaze locked onto hers it was gone, and his eyes moved to take in their companions. Julia had forgotten all about them. Her hand was dropped as summarily as if he had flung it away from him, and a dark cloud of foreboding seemed to blot out the sultry evening just visible through the open patio doors. She shivered in response, and wanted to hug her arms around her body.

Nigel was saying nervously, "His Royal Highness the

Emir of Burquat," and Julia was wondering a little hysterically if she should be curtseying. She didn't trust her voice to speak and then Kaden's black gaze was back on her.

"Dr Somerton."

His voice was so achingly familiar that she longed to be able to hold onto something for balance, only dimly registering the cool tone.

A small anxious-looking man with a red face was beside Kaden. Julia recognised him as the director of the club. He was talking, but his voice seemed to be coming from far away,

"Perhaps you have met before, Doctor? When you were in Burquat during your studies?"

A sharp pain lanced Julia and she looked at Kaden, not sure what to say.

His mouth turned up in a parody of a smile and he drawled, "I seem to have some vague recollection. What year were you there?"

The slap of rejection was so strong it almost made Julia take a step back. The awful sense of isolation she'd felt when she'd left Burquat was as fresh now as twelve years ago. That this man could transport her so easily back to those painful emotions was devastating. Perhaps he could tell just how excruciating this was for her— hadn't she all but thrown herself at him that last day? Perhaps he thought he was sparing her some embarrassment now?

She forced an equally polite and distant smile to her lips. "It's so long ago now I can barely recall it myself."

She switched her brittle-feeling smile to the other men. "Gentlemen, if you don't need me for this discussion I'd appreciate it if you would excuse me. I just got back from New York this afternoon, and I'm afraid the jet lag is catching up with me."

"Your husband is waiting for you at home? Or perhaps he's here in the room?"

Shock at the bluntness of Kaden's question slammed into Julia. How dared he all but pretend not to know her and then ask such a pointedly personal question? Her jaw felt tight. "For your information, *Your Highness*, I am no longer married. My husband and I are divorced."

Kaden did not like the surge of emotion that ripped through him at her curt answer. He had had an image of her returning to a cosy home to be greeted by some faceless man and had felt a blackness descend over his vision, forcing him to ask the question. Even realising that, he couldn't stop himself asking, "So why are you still using your married name?"

Julia's face tightened. "I'm involved in various contracts and it's simply been easier to leave it for the moment. I have every intention of changing it back in the future."

It was as if Kaden was enclosed in a bubble with this woman. The other men went unnoticed, forgotten. Unbidden and unwelcome emotion was clouding everything.

At that moment Nigel, Julia's boss, moved perceptibly closer to her, taking her elbow in his hand, staking a very public claim.

Only moments ago she'd welcomed his support and his tacit interest as a barrier. Now Julia chafed and made a jerky move away, causing Nigel's hand to drop. She could feel his wounded look without even seeing it, and her head began to throb. The club's director who still stood beside Kaden, was looking a bit bewildered at the obvious tension in the air, which was making a lie of the fact that she and Kaden claimed to barely know one another.

She knew she'd only been introduced as a polite formality. She wasn't expected to take part in Nigel's wooing of new donors. Her job started when they had to decide how those funds would be best used. If she'd known for a second that Kaden was due to be here this evening, she would have made certain not to come.

Determined to succeed this time, Julia stepped away from the trio of men on very shaky legs. "Please, gentlemen—if you'll excuse me?"

Ignoring the dagger looks from Nigel, and the dark condemnation emanating from Kaden like a physical force, she turned on her heel and walked away. It seemed to take an age to get through the crowd. She was almost at the door when she felt a hand on her arm, but it didn't induce anything more than irritation and she reluctantly turned to face Nigel. His handsome face was red.

"Are you going to tell me what that was all about?"

Once again Julia pulled her arm free and kept walking. "It was about nothing, Nigel. I'm tired and I want to go home, that's all."

She hoped the panic she felt at being there for one second longer than was absolutely necessary didn't come through in her voice. She reached the cloakroom and handed in the ticket for her jacket, noticing a visible tremor in her hand.

"So you two obviously know each other, then? I'd have to be deaf, dumb and blind to fail to notice *that* atmosphere."

Julia sighed. "We knew each other a long time ago, Nigel." She turned and put on her jacket, which had just been handed to her, and pointed out gently, "Not that it's any of your business."

His face became mottled. "It *is* my business when the most potentially lucrative donor we've had in years could get scared off because he's had some kind of previous relationship with my funds manager."

Julia stopped and faced Nigel, forcing herself to stay civil. "I'm sure he's mature enough not to let a tiny incident like this change his mind about donating funds to research. Anyway, it's all the more reason for me to leave and stay out of your way."

She turned to go and Nigel caught her hand. Gritting her teeth at his persistence, Julia turned back, her stomach churning slightly at the sweaty grip of his hand—so far removed from the cool yet hot touch from Kaden.

He was conciliatory. "Look, I'm sorry, Julia. Forgive me? Let me take you out to dinner this week."

Julia fought back the urge to say yes, which would be the easy thing to do, to placate him. Seeing Kaden had upset any equilibrium she thought she might have attained since her divorce had become final. Since she had last seen *him*. And that knowledge was too frightening to take in fully.

She shook her head, "I'm sorry, Nigel. I have thought about it…and I'm just not ready for dating." She pulled her hand from his and backed away. "I'm really sorry. I'll see you tomorrow in the office." Already she could imagine his sulky mood at being turned down and dreaded it.

She turned and walked quickly to the door. Her heart was hammering, and all she wanted was to escape to the quiet solace of her house where she could get out of her tailored dress and curl up. She wanted to block out the evening's events and the fact that her past had rushed up to meet her with the force of a sledgehammer blow.

As soon as Julia had turned and walked away Kaden should have been putting her out of his mind and focusing on the business at hand, as he would have with any other ex-lover. But he wasn't. He found that the urge to go after her was nigh on impossible to resist. Especially when that obsequious man who'd had the temerity to put his hand on her had followed her like a besotted lap dog.

Kaden made his excuses to the still bewildered-looking director of the club and forged his way through the crowd, ignoring the not so hushed whispers as he passed people by. His blood was humming. He felt curiously euphoric, and also uncultivated—like a predator in the desert, an eagle soaring high who had spotted its prey and would not rest until it was caught.

It was an uncomfortable reminder of how he'd felt from the moment he'd first met Julia, when sanity had taken a hike and he'd given himself over to a dream as dangerous as any opiate could induce. But this feeling was too strong to deny or rationalise.

The fact that she represented a lapse in emotional control he'd never allowed again only caught up with him when he reached the lobby and saw it was empty.

She'd disappeared.

So what was this desolation that swept through him? And what was this rampant need clawing through him to find her again? He was done with Julia. He'd been done with her a long time ago.

Disgusted with himself for this lapse, Kaden called up his security, determined to get out of there and do what he'd set out to do all along: forget that he'd ever seen Julia Connors——he scowled, *Somerton*——again.

He had no desire to revisit a time when he'd come very close to letting his heart rule his head, forgetting all about duty and responsibility in the pursuit of personal fulfilment. He didn't have that luxury. He'd *never* had that luxury.

Julia could see the tube station entrance ahead of her, not far from the building she'd just left behind. The night-time London air was unbearably heavy around her now, making a light sweat break out over her skin and on the nape of her neck under her hair. Thunder rolled ominously in the distance. A storm had been threatening all evening, and if she'd been in better humour she might have appreciated the symbolism. The clouds that had been squatting in the distance were now firmly overhead—low, dark and menacing.

What was making the weather feel even more ominous was the fact that she'd been having disturbing dreams of Kaden lately. Maybe, she wondered a little hysterically, she was hallucinating?

Hesitating for a moment, Julia stopped and looked back. But the building just sat there, innocently benign, lights blazing from the windows, laughter trickling out into the quiet street from the party. She shuddered despite the heat. She wasn't going back now anyway. She couldn't face Nigel again. *Or* Kaden's coolly sardonic demeanour. As if nothing had ever happened between them.

Part of her longed to just jump in a cab, but her inherently frugal nature forbade it. Out of the corner of her eye she saw a sleek black shape slow to a crawl alongside her—just before she heard the accompanying low hum of a very expensive engine. At the same time as she turned automatically to look, lightning forked in the sky and the heavens opened. She was comprehensively drenched within seconds, but had become rooted to the spot.

Everything seemed to happen in slow motion as she registered the Royal Burquati flag on the bonnet of the car. She noticed the tinted windows, and the equally sleek accompanying Jeep, which had to be carrying the ubiquitous security team.

As she stood there getting soaked, unable to move, Julia was helplessly transported back to a moment in the hot, winding, ancient streets of Burquat City, when, breathless with laughter, her hand clamped in Kaden's, they'd escaped from his bodyguards into a private walled garden. There, he'd pushed her up against a wall, taken away the veil hiding her face, and kissed her for the first time.

It was only when the back door of the car opened near her and she saw the tall figure of Kaden emerge that reality rushed back. Along with it came her breath and her heartbeat, and the knowledge that she hadn't been hallucinating.

The rain seemed to bounce off him, spraying droplets into a halo around him. The sky was apocalyptic behind him. And still that rain was beating down.

Julia backed away, her eyes glued to him as if mesmerised.

"Julia. Let me give you a lift."

Her name on his tongue with that exotic accent did funny things to her insides. A strangled half-laugh came out of Julia's mouth. "A lift?" She shook her head, "I don't need a lift—I need to go home. I'll take the tube."

She dragged her gaze from his and finally managed to turn around. Only to feel her arm caught in a hard grip. Electric tingles shot up and down her arm and into her groin just as more lightning lit up the sky. She looked up at Kaden, who had come to stand in front of her. So close that she could see his jet-black hair plastered to his skull, that awesomely beautiful face. Those black eyes. Rain ran in rivulets down the lean planes, over hard cheekbones.

"What do you want, Kaden? Or should I address you by your full title?" Bitterness and something much scarier made her feel emotional. "You gave a very good impression back there of not knowing who I was. I'm surprised you even remember my name."

Through the driving rain she could see his jaw clench at that. His black gaze swept her up and down. Then his hand gentled on her arm, and perversely that made her feel even shakier. With something she couldn't decipher in his voice he said, "I remember your name, Julia." And then, with easy solicitude, "You're soaked through. And now I'm soaked. My apartment isn't far from here. Let me take you there so you can dry off."

Panic mixed with something much more hot and primal clutched Julia's gut. Go with Kaden to his apartment? To *dry off*? She remembered the way his look had changed earlier to something ambiguous. It was a long time since she'd felt that curl of hot desire in her abdomen, and to be reminded of how this man had been the only one ever to precipitate it was galling. And that he could still make it happen twelve years on was even more disturbing.

She shook her head and tried to extricate her arm. "No, thank you. I don't want to put you out of your way."

His jaw clenched again. "Do you really want to sit on a tube dripping wet and walk home like a drowned rat?"

Instantly she felt deflated. She could well imagine that she *did* resemble a drowned rat. Mascara must be running down her cheeks in dark rivers. He was just being polite—had probably seen her and hadn't wanted to appear rude by driving past. His convoy would have been far too conspicuous to go unnoticed.

"I can take a taxi if I need to. Why are you doing this?"

He shrugged minutely. "I wasn't expecting to see you…it's been a surprise."

She all but snorted. It certainly was. She had no doubt that he'd never expected to see her again in his lifetime. And thinking of that now—how close she'd come to never seeing him again—Julia felt an aching sense of loss grip her. And urgency. She wouldn't see Kaden after tonight. She knew that. This was a fluke, a monumental coincidence. He was just curious—perhaps intrigued.

He'd been her first lover. Her first love. *Her only love*?

Before she could quash that disturbing thought Kaden was manoeuvring her towards the open door of his car, as if some tacit acquiescence had passed between them. Julia felt weak for not protesting, but she knew in that moment that she didn't have the strength to just walk away. Because meeting him again *didn't* mean nothing to her.

He handed her into the plush interior of the luxury car and came around the other side. Once his large, rangy body was settled in the back seat alongside her he issued a terse command in Arabic, and the car pulled off so smoothly that Julia only knew they were moving because the tube station passed them in a blaze of refracted light through the driving rain.

Kaden sat back and looked over at Julia. He could see her long dark lashes. Her nose had the tiniest bump, which gave her profile an aquiline look, and her mouth…

He used to study this woman's mouth for hours. Obsessed with its shape, its full lower lip and the perfect curve of its bow-shaped upper lip. He'd once known this profile as well as his own. *Better*.

She wore a light jacket, but the rain had made her clothes heavy and the V in the neckline of the dress was being dragged downwards to reveal the pale swells of her breasts. He could see a tantalising hint of the black lace of her bra, and evidence of her agitation as her chest rose and fell with quick breaths.

Rage at his uncharacteristic lack of control rose high. He'd fully intended to leave and put her out of his mind, but then he'd seen her walking along the street, with that quick, efficient walk he remembered. Not artful or practised, but completely sensuous all the same. As if she was unconscious of how sexy she was. He'd forgotten that a woman could be unconsciously sexy. Before he'd known what he was doing, he'd found himself instructing his driver to stop the car.

Sexual awareness stunned him anew. It shouldn't be so overwhelmingly fresh. As if they'd hardly been apart. For a long time after she'd left Burquat Kaden had told himself that his inability to forget about her was because of the fact that she'd been his first lover, and that brought with it undeniable associations and indelible memories.

But he couldn't deny as he sat there now, with this carnal *heat* throbbing between them, that the pleasure they'd discovered together had been more than just the voluptuous delight of new lovers discovering unfamiliar terrain. It had been as intensely mind—blowing as anything he'd experienced since. And sitting beside Julia was effortlessly shattering any illusion he'd entertained that he'd been the one to control his response to women in the intervening years. They just hadn't been *her*. That knowledge was more than cataclysmic.

Julia could feel Kaden's eyes on her, but she was determined not to look at him. When they'd been together he'd always had a way of looking at her so intently...as if he wanted to devour her whole. It had thrilled her and scared her a little in equal measure. His intensity had been so dark and compelling. She'd felt the lash of that dark intensity when it had been turned against her.

If she turned and saw that look now...

She raised her hand to her neck in a nervous reflex and felt that it was bare. The wave of relief that coursed through her when she realised what she'd just done was nothing short of epic. She always wore a gold necklace with the detail of an intricate love knot at its centre. It had been bought from a stall in the souk in Burquat. But its main significance was that Kaden had bought it for her, and despite what had happened between them she still wore it every day—apart from when she was travelling, for fear of losing it.

The only reason she wasn't wearing it now was because she'd been in such a rush earlier, upon returning from the US, that she'd forgotten to put it back on. The knowledge burned within her, because she knew that it somehow symbolised her link to this man when no link existed any more. If he had seen the necklace— Her mind seized at the prospect. It would have been like wearing a badge saying *You still mean something to me.* And she was only realising herself, here and now, how shamefully true that was.

"We're here."

The car was drawing to a smooth halt outside an exclusive-looking building. A liveried doorman was hurrying over to open the car door, and before Julia knew it she was standing on the pavement watching as Kaden came to join her. The rain had become a light drizzle, and Julia shivered in clothes that felt uncomfortably damp against her skin, despite the heavy warmth of the night.

Kaden ushered Julia in through the open doors. The doorman bowed his head deferentially as they passed. Julia felt numb inside and out. Shock was spreading, turning her into some sort of automaton. Sleek doors were opening, and then they were standing in an opulently decorated lift. The doors closed again, and with a soft jolt they were ascending.

A sense of panic was rising as she stood in that confined space next to Kaden's formidable presence, but before she could do anything the door was opening again and Julia was being led straight from the lift into what had to be the penthouse apartment. It was an old building, but the apartment had obviously been refitted and it oozed sleek modernity with an antique twist. It was decorated in understated tones of cream and gold, effortlessly luxurious. The tall windows showcased the glittering city outside as Kaden led her into a huge reception room and turned to face her.

Julia looked away from the windows to catch Kaden's

dark gaze making a leisurely return up her body. Heat exploded in her belly, and when his eyes met hers again she found it hard to breathe.

He backed away to an open door on the other side of the room and said coolly, "There is a bedroom and *en suite* bathroom through here, if you want to freshen up and get dry."

Julia followed his tall form, feeling very bedraggled. She was aware of trailing water all over the luxurious carpet. He turned again at the open door, through which she could see a set of rooms—a smaller sitting room leading into a bedroom.

"I'll have your clothes attended to if you leave them in the sitting room."

Julia looked at him, and a curious kind of relief went through her. "You have a housekeeper here?"

Kaden shook his head, "No, but someone will attend to them, and I'll leave some dry clothes out for you."

How could she have forgotten the myriad silent servants who were always present to do the royal bidding, no matter what it was? Like erecting exotic Bedouin tents in the desert in a matter of hours, just for them. Her belly cramped. Still in a state of shock, she could only nod silently and watch as Kaden strode away and left her alone.

She walked through the opulent rooms until she came to the bedroom, where she carefully closed the door behind her, leaning back against it. She grimaced at herself. Kaden was hardly likely to bash the door down because he was so consumed with uncontrollable lust. She could well imagine that his tastes no longer ran to wet and bedraggled archaeologists.

Shaking her head, as if that might shake some sanity

back into it, she kicked off her shoes and pushed away from the door. She explored the bathroom, which held a glorious sunken bath and huge walk-in shower. She caught a glimpse of herself in the mirror and her eyes grew big. She did indeed look as if she'd been dragged through a hedge backwards and then hosed down with water. Her long blonde hair hung in rats' tails over her shoulders and was stuck to her head. Mascara had made huge dark smudges under her eyes.

With a scowl at herself, she peeled off her drenched clothes. She got a towel from the bathroom to protect the soft furnishings and left them in the outer sitting room, half terrified that Kaden would walk back through the door at any moment. She scuttled back through the bedroom into the bathroom. With a towel wrapped around her she gave a longing glance to the bath, but stepped into the shower instead. Taking a bath in Kaden's apartment felt far too decadent a thing to do.

As it was, just standing naked under the powerful hot spray of water felt illicit and wicked. To know that Kaden was mere feet away in another room...also naked under a hot shower... With a groan of disgust at her completely inappropriate imagination, Julia turned her face upwards. She resolved to get re-dressed in her wet clothes if she had to, and then get out of there as fast as she could.

Kaden had showered and changed into dry clothes, and now stood outside the rooms he'd shown Julia into. He dithered. He never dithered, but all he could see in his mind's eye was the seductive image of Julia standing before him in those wet clothes. She should have looked like a drowned rat, but she hadn't. That cool, classic

English beauty stood out a mile—along with the delicate curves of her breasts, waist and hips.

The burning desire he'd felt in the car hadn't abated
one bit, and normally when he was attracted to a woman
it was a straightforward affair. But this wasn't just some
random woman. This woman came with long silken ties
to the past. *To his heart.* He rejected that rogue thought
outright. She'd never affected his heart. He'd thought
she had...but it had been lust. Overwhelming, yes, but
just lust. Not love.

He'd learnt young not to trust romantic love. His father had married for love. But after his mother had died
in childbirth with his younger sister his father had silently communicated to him that love only brought pain.
It had been there in the way that his father had become a
shadow of his former self, wrapped up in grief and solitude. Kaden had always been made very aware that one
day he would rule his country, so he could never afford
to let such frivolous emotions overwhelm *him* the way
they'd taken over his father's life.

Kaden's father had married again, but this time
for all the *expected* reasons. Practicality and lineage.
Unfortunately his second wife had been cold and ma-
nipulative, further compounding Kaden's negative im-
pressions of marriage and love. Any halcyon memories
he might have had of his mother and father being happy
together had quickly faded into something that felt like
a wispy dream—unreal.

Yet when Kaden had met Julia he'd been seduced into
forgetting everything he'd learnt. Guilt weighed heavily
on him even now. And that sense of betrayal. If he hadn't
seen her with that other man...if he hadn't realised how
fickle she was...

Kaden cursed himself for this sudden introspection. In his hands he held some dry clothes. He knocked lightly and heard nothing. So he went in. The bedroom was dimly lit and the door to the bathroom was slightly open. As if in a trance he walked further into the bedroom and laid the dry clothes down on the bed. He'd picked up Julia's wet clothes on the way through. Her scent hit his nostrils now and his eyes closed. Still the same distinctive lavender scent. A dart of anger rose up, as if her scent was mocking him by not having changed.

Before his mind could become clouded with evocative memories a sound made him open his eyes to see Julia, framed in the doorway of the bathroom, with only a towel wrapped around her body and another towel turban—like on her head. Steam billowed out behind her, bringing with it that delicate scent.

Lust slammed into Kaden like a two-ton lorry. Right in his solar plexus. Long shapely legs were bare, so were pale shoulders and arms. Kaden cursed himself for bringing her here. The last thing he needed right now was to be reopening doors best left shut.

He said, with a cool bite in his voice, "I'll send these out to be dried." He indicated the clothes on the bed, "You can change into these for now. They should fit."

Julia's eyes, which had widened on seeing him, moved to the clothes on the bed. He saw her tense perceptibly. She shook her head, a flush coming into her cheeks, and put out a hand. "I'll change back into my own clothes and go home."

An image of her walking out through the door made Kaden's self-recrimination dissolve in an instant. He held the clothes well out of Julia's reach. "Don't be silly. You'll get pneumonia if you put these back on."

Julia's eyes narrowed and she stretched her hand out more. "Really—I don't mind. This wasn't a good idea. I should never have agreed to come here."

CHAPTER THREE

SILENCE thickened and grew between them. Julia couldn't fathom what was going on behind those darker than dark eyes. And then Kaden moved towards her and she stepped back. Her heart nearly jumped out of her chest.

He pointed out silkily, "But you did come. What are you afraid of, Julia? That you won't be able to control yourself around me?"

A few seconds ago she'd seen a look of something like cool distaste cross his face, and yet now he was acknowledging the heat between them. Baiting her. Her heart was thumping so hard she felt sure it would be evident through the towel wrapped around her.

A long buried sensation rushed through her like a tangible force—what it had felt like to have his naked body between her legs, thrusting into her with awesome strength.

For a moment she couldn't breathe, then she said threadily, "Just give me my clothes, Kaden. This really *isn't* a good idea."

But Kaden ignored her, was already stepping back and away, taking her clothes with him and leaving the fresh ones on the bed. She looked at them. Jeans and a delicate grey silk shirt. Rage filled her belly at being humiliated like this.

She indicated the clothes with a trembling hand. Too much emotion was coursing through her. More than she'd felt in years. "I won't wear your mistress's cast-offs. I'll walk out of here in this towel if I have to."

Kaden turned. He was silhouetted in the doorway, shoulders broad in a simple white shirt. Black trousers hugged his lean hips. Julia hadn't even noticed his still damp hair. She'd been so consumed by his overall presence.

He said, with a flash of fire in his eyes, "Be my guest, but there's really no need. Those clothes belong to Samia. You remember my younger sister? You're about the same size now. She's been living here for the last couple of years."

Immediately Julia felt petulant and exposed. She blushed. "Yes, I remember Samia." She'd always liked Kaden's next youngest sister, who had been bookish and painfully shy. Before she could say anything else, though, he was gone and the door had shut behind him.

Defeated, Julia contemplated the clothes. She took off the towel and put them on. There were even some knickers still in a plastic bag, and Julia could only figure that someone regularly stocked up Samia's wardrobe. The jeans were a little snug on her rear and thighs, and she felt extremely naked with no bra under the silk shirt. Her breasts weren't overly large, but they were too big for her to go bra-less and feel comfortable. There wasn't much she could do. It was either this or dress in the robe hanging off the back of the bathroom door. And she couldn't face Kaden in just a robe.

She went back into the bathroom and dried her hair

with the hairdryer. It dried a little frizzy, but there was not much she could do about that either. And, anyway, it wasn't as if she wanted to impress Kaden, was it? She scowled at the very thought.

Fresh resolve to insist on leaving fired her blood, and she picked up her shoes in one hand and took a deep breath before emerging from the suite, steeling herself to see Kaden again. When she did emerge though, it was to see him with his back to her at one of the main salon windows, looking out over the view. Something about his stance in that moment struck her as acutely lonely, but then he turned around and his sardonic visage made a mockery of her fanciful notion.

She hitched up her chin. "I'll get a taxi home. I can arrange to get my clothes from you another time."

Kaden's hand tightened reflexively on the glass he held. He should be saying *Yes, I'll call you a taxi*. He should be reminding himself that this was a very bad idea. But rational thought was very elusive as he looked at Julia.

Her hair drifted softly around her narrow shoulders. Like this, with the veneer of a successful, sophisticated woman stripped away, she might be nineteen again, and something inside him turned over. The grey silk shirt made the grey of her eyes look smoky and mysterious. He could remember thinking when he'd first met her that her eyes were a very icy light blue, but he had then realised that they were grey.

The silk shirt left little to the imagination. Her bare breasts pushed enticingly against the material, and under his gaze he could see her nipples harden to two thrusting points. His body responded forcibly. The jeans were too tight, but that only emphasized the curve of her hips and thighs. He wanted her to turn around so he could see her lush *derrière*. She'd always had a voluptuous bottom and generous breasts in contrast to her otherwise slender build.

Heat engulfed him, and he struggled for the first time in years to cling onto some control. Once again when it came to it…he couldn't let her go.

Julia was on fire under Kaden's very thorough inspection. "Please…" She wasn't even really aware of what she was saying, only that she wanted him to stop. "Don't look at me like that."

He smiled and went into seduction mode. "Like what? You're a beautiful woman, Julia. I'm sure you're used to having men's eyes on you."

Julia flushed at the slightly narrowed dark gaze, which hinted at steel underneath the apparent civility. The memory of what had happened just before she'd left Burquat flashed through her head and brought with it excoriating heat and guilt. And nausea… Kaden's eyes had been on her in her moment of humiliation. Even now she could remember the way that man had pulled her so close she'd felt as if she were suffocating, when all she'd wanted— She slammed the door on that memory.

She shook her head, "No, actually, I'm not. And this is not appropriate. I really should be leaving. So if you'll just call me a taxi…?"

Kaden smiled then, and it was the devil's smile. She sensed he'd come to some decision and it made her incredibly nervous.

"What's the rush? I'm sure you could do with a drink?"

Julia regarded this suddenly urbane pillar of solicitude suspiciously. Her shoes were unwieldy in her hand. She felt all at once awkward, hot, and yet pathetically reluctant to turn and never see Kaden again. That insidious yearning arose…the awareness that tonight was a bizarre coincidence. Fate. Surely the last time she would ever see him?

As much as she longed to get as far away as possible from this situation, and this man, a dangerous curiosity and a desire for him not to see how conflicted she was by this reunion made her shrug minutely and say grudgingly, "I suppose one drink wouldn't hurt. After all, it has been a long time."

He just looked at her. "Yes, it has." Hardly taking his eyes from hers, he indicated a bottle of cream liqueur on the sideboard and asked, "Do you still like this?"

Julia's belly swooped dangerously. He remembered her favourite drink? She'd only ever drunk it with him, and hadn't touched it in twelve years. She nodded dumbly and watched as his large, masculine yet graceful hands deftly poured the distinctive liquid. He replaced the bottle on the sideboard and then came and handed the delicately bulbous glass to Julia.

She took it, absurdly grateful that their fingers didn't touch. Bending her head, she took a sniff of the drink and then a quick sip, to disguise the flush she could feel rising when the smell precipitated a memory of drinking it with Kaden one magical night in his family's summer palace by the coast. It was the night they'd slept together for the first time.

For a second the full intensity of how much she'd loved him threatened to overwhelm her. And he'd casually poisoned those feelings and in one fell swoop destroyed her innocent idealism. Feeling tormented, and wondering if this avalanche of memories would ever go back into its box, she moved away from Kaden's tall, lean body, her eyes darting anywhere but to him.

She sensed him move behind her, and then he appeared in her peripheral vision.

"Please, won't you sit?"

So polite. As if nothing had happened. As if she hadn't given him her body, heart and soul.

Slamming another painful door in her mind, Julia said quickly, nervously, "Thank you."

She followed him, and when he sat on a plush couch, easily dominating it, she chose an armchair to the side, putting her shoes down beside her. She was as far away from him as she could get, legs together primly. She glanced at him to see a mocking look cross his face. She didn't care. This new Kaden intimidated her. There was nothing of the boy she'd known. They'd both just been teenagers after all…until he'd had to grow up overnight, after the death of his father.

Now he was a man—infinitely more commanding. She'd seen a glimpse of this more formidable Kaden the last time they'd spoken in Burquat, but that had been a mere precursor of the powerful man opposite her now.

Julia felt exposed in her bare feet and the flimsy shirt. It was too silky against her bare flesh. Her nipples were hard, tingling. She hadn't felt this effortlessly aroused once during her marriage, or since she'd been with Kaden, and the realisation made her feel even more exposed. She struggled to hang on to the fact that she was a successful and relatively sophisticated woman. She'd been married and divorced. She was no naïve virgin any more. She could handle this. She had to remember that, while he had devastated *her*, he'd been untouched after their relationship ended. She'd never forget how emotionless he'd been when they said goodbye. It was carved into her soul.

Remembering who the clothes belonged to gave her a moment of divine inspiration. With forced brightness she asked, "How *is* Samia? She must be at least twenty-four by now?"

Kaden observed Julia from under hooded lids. He was in no hurry to answer her question or engage in small talk. It was more than disconcerting how *right* it felt to have her here. And even more so to acknowledge that the vaguely unsettled feeling he'd been experiencing for what felt like years was dissipating.

She intrigued him more than he cared to admit. He might have imagined that by now she would be far more polished, would have cultivated the hard veneer he was used to in the kind of women he socialised with.

Curbing the urge to stand and pace out the intense conflict inside him as her vulnerability tugged at his jaded emotions, Kaden struggled to remain sitting and remember what she'd asked.

"Samia? She's twenty-five, and she's getting married at the end of this week. To the Sultan of Al-Omar. She's in B'harani for the preparations right now."

Julia's eyes widened, increasing Kaden's levels of inner tension and desire. He cursed silently. He couldn't stand up now even if he wanted to— not if he didn't want her to see exactly the effect she had on him. He vacillated between intense anger at himself for bringing her here at all, and the assertion that she would not be walking out through his front door any time soon.

Kaden was used to clear, concise thinking—not this churning maelstrom. It was too reminiscent of what had happened before. And yet even as he thought that the tantalising prospect came into his mind: why not take her again? Tonight? Why not exorcise this desire which mocked him with its presence?

"The Sultan of Al-Omar?" Julia shook her head, not liking the speculative gleam in Kaden's eyes. Blonde hair slipped over her shoulders. She tried to focus on stringing a sentence together. "Samia was so painfully shy. It must be difficult for her to take on such a public role?"

An irrational burst of guilt rushed through Kaden. He'd seen Samia recently, here in London before she'd left, and had felt somewhat reassured by her stoic calm in the face of her impending nuptials. But Julia was reminding him what a challenge this would be for his naturally introverted sister. And he was surprised that Julia remembered such a detail.

It made his voice harsh. "Samia is a woman now, with responsibilities to her country and her people. A marriage with Sultan Sadiq benefits both our countries."

"So it is an arranged marriage, then?"

Kaden nodded his head, not sure where the defensiveness he was feeling stemmed from. "Of course—just as my own marriage was arranged and just as my next marriage will be arranged." He quirked a brow. "I presume your marriage was a love match, and yet you did not fare any better if you too are divorced?"

Julia hid the dart of emotion at hearing him say he would marry again and avoided his eye. Had her marriage been a love match? In general terms, yes—it had. After all, she and John had married willingly, with no pressure on either side. But she knew in her heart of hearts that she hadn't truly loved John. And he'd known it too.

Something curdled in her belly at having to justify herself to this man who had haunted her for so long. She looked back at him as steadily as she could. "No, we didn't fare any better. However, I know plenty of arranged marriages work out very well, so I wish Samia all the best."

"Children?"

For a moment Julia didn't catch what Kaden had said it had been uttered so curtly. "Children?" she repeated, and he nodded.

Julia felt another kind of pain lance her. The memory of the look of shame on her husband's face, the way he had closed in on himself and started to retreat, which had marked the beginning of the end of their marriage.

She shook her head and said, a little defiantly, "Of course not. Do you think I would be here if I had?" And then she cursed herself inwardly. She didn't want Kaden analysing why she *had* come. "My husband—*ex*-husband—couldn't... We had difficulties... And you? Did you have children?"

That slightly mocking look crossed his face again, because she must know well that his status as a childless divorcee was common knowledge. But he just shook his head. "No, no children."

His mouth had become a bitter line, and Julia shivered minutely because it reminded her of how he'd morphed within days from an ardent lover into a cold stranger.

"My ex-wife's mother suffered a horrific and near-fatal childbirth and stuffed my wife's head with tales of horror and pain. As a result Amira developed a phobia about childbirth. It was so strong that when she did discover she was pregnant she went without my knowledge

to get a termination. Soon afterwards I started proceed-
ings to divorce."

Julia gave an audible gasp and Kaden saw her eyes
grow wide. He knew how it sounded—so stark. His jaw
was tight with tension. How on earth had he let those
words spill so blithely from his mouth? He'd just told
Julia something that only a handful of people knew.
The secret of his ex-wife's actions was something he
discussed with nobody. As were the painstaking efforts
he'd made to help her overcome that fear after the abor-
tion. But to no avail. Eventually it had been his wife who
had insisted they divorce, knowing that she could never
give him an heir. She hadn't been prepared to confront
her fears.

Kaden's somewhat brutal dismissal of a wife who
hadn't been able to perform her duty made a shiver run
through Julia. The man she'd known had been compas-
sionate, idealistic.

To divert attention away from the dismay she felt
at recognising just how much he'd changed, she said
quickly, "I thought divorce was illegal in Burquat?"

Kaden took a measured sip of his amber-coloured
drink. "It used to be. Things have changed a lot since
you were there. It's been slow but steady reform, undoing the more conservative laws of my father and his
forebears."

A rush of tenderness took Julia by surprise, coming
so soon after her feeling repelled by his treatment of his
wife. Kaden had always been so passionate about reform
for his country, and now he was doing it.

Terrified that he would see something of that emotion
rising up within her, Julia stood up jerkily and walked
over to the window, clutching her glass in her hand.

She took in the view. Kaden had told her about this apartment, right in the centre of London. Pain, bitter-sweet, rushed through her. He had once mentioned that she should move in here when she returned to college in London—so that he could make sure she was protected, and so she would be waiting for him when he came over. But those words had all been part of his seductive pat-ter. Meaningless. A wave of sadness gripped her.

She didn't hear Kaden move, and jumped when his deep voice came from her right, far too close. "Why did you divorce your husband, Julia?"

Because I never loved him the way I loved you. The words reverberated around her head. Never in a million years had she imagined she would be standing in a room listening to Kaden ask her that question.

Eventually, when she felt as if she had some measure of control, she glanced at him. He was standing with one shoulder propped nonchalantly against the wall, look-ing at her from under hooded lids. With one hand in his pocket, the glass held loosely in the other, he could have stepped straight out of a fashion magazine.

He looked dark and dangerous, and Julia gulped—because she felt that sense of danger reverberate within her and ignite a fire. She tried to ignore the sensation, telling herself it was overactive hormones mixed in with too many evocative memories and the loaded situation they were now in. She looked back out of the window with an effort. She felt hot and tingly all over, her belly heavy with desire.

"I…we just grew apart." She shook her head. "It seemed like a good idea, but it never really worked. And our difficulty with having children was the last straw. There wasn't enough to keep us together. I'm glad there were no children. It wouldn't have been the right environment to bring them into."

Julia had never told Kaden that she was adopted, or about her own visceral feelings on the subject of having children. She'd never told anyone. It was too bound up in painful emotions for her. And perhaps she hadn't told him for a reason—because on some level she'd been afraid of his judgement, and that what they shared hadn't been real. She'd been right to be afraid.

She was aware of tension emanating from Kaden and didn't want to look at him, afraid he might see the emotion she felt she couldn't hide. Her face always gave her away. He was the one who had told her that as he'd held her face in his hands one day...

Suddenly from out of the still ominously cloudy sky came a jagged flash of lightning. Julia jumped so violently that liquid sloshed out of her glass. Immediately shocked and embarrassed by her overreaction, she stepped back. "I'm sorry..."

Kaden was there in an instant. He took the glass out of her hand, placing it down on the table alongside his own. He was back in front of her before she could steel herself not to react. His dark eyes looked her up and down and then rested on her chest. As if mesmerised, Julia followed his gaze to see where some of the drink had landed on her shirt, right over one breast, and now the material was clinging to the rounded slope.

Panicky, Julia stepped back, "I'll get a cloth... I don't want Samia's shirt to get ruined."

A big hand snaked out and caught her upper arm. "Leave it."

Kaden's voice was unbearably harsh, and in that instant the air between became even heavier and more charged. As if the tension and atmosphere between them was directly affecting the weather, a huge booming roll of thunder sounded outside.

Julia flinched, eyes glued to Kaden's with some kind of sick fascination. Faintly she said, "I thought the storm was over."

With a move so smooth she didn't even feel it happening Kaden put his hands on her arms and pulled her closer. Their bodies were almost touching.

"I think the storm is just beginning."

For a second confusion made Julia's head foggy. She didn't seem to be able to separate out his words, or even understand what Kaden was saying. And then she realised, when she saw how hot his gaze had become and how it moved down to her mouth. Desire was stamped onto the stark lines of his face and Julia's heart beat fast in response. Because it was a look that had haunted her dreams for ever.

Desperately trying to fight the urge to succumb to the waves of need beating through her veins, she shook her head and tensed, trying to pull back out of Kaden's grip. His hands just tightened.

"Kaden, *no*. I shouldn't be here...we shouldn't have met again."

"But we did meet. And you're here now."

Julia asserted stiffly, "I didn't agree to come here for this."

Kaden shook his head, and a tiny harsh smile touched his mouth. "From the moment we stood in front of each other in that room earlier the possibility of *this* has existed."

Bitterness rang in Julia's voice. "Even when you pretended not to know me?"

More lightning flashed outside, quickly followed by the roll of thunder. The unmistakable sound of torrential rain started to lash against the window.

"Even then."

Nothing seemed to be throwing Kaden off. Had he somehow magically dimmed the lights in the room? Julia wondered frantically, feeling as though reality was slipping out of her grasp. The past was meshing into the present, and the future was fast becoming irrelevant.

Julia tried again. "The possibility of this stopped existing twelve years ago in Burquat—or have you forgotten when you informed me our *affair* was past its sell-by date?" Bitterness laced her voice, but she couldn't pretend it wasn't there, much as she would have loved to feign insouciance. The rawness of that day was vivid.

Kaden's hands were steady. "I don't wish to discuss the past, Julia. The past bears no relationship to this moment."

"How can you say that? The past is the reason I'm standing here now."

Kaden shook his head, eyes glowing with dark embers, effortlessly stoking Julia's desire higher and higher, despite what her head might be saying.

"I would have wanted you even if tonight was the first time we'd met."

His flattery did nothing for Julia's ego. The evidence of how unmoved he was by the past broke something apart inside her. Of course it had no effect on him now. Because he felt nothing for her—just as he'd never really felt anything for her.

Julia tensed as much as she could. She had to get out of there. Things were spiralling out of all control. "Well, the past might not be relevant to you, but it is to me, and I think this is a very bad idea."

Kaden's eyes flashed, showing Julia a glimpse of the emotion that thickened the atmosphere between them, no matter how he might deny it. "*This* is desire, pure and simple. We're two single consenting adults and I want you."

Julia looked up, helpless to pull away or articulate any kind of sane response. Which should be *no*. How was it possible that this desire hadn't abated one bit? That if anything it felt stronger? There were so many layers of meaning here, and Kaden wanted to ignore all of that. As if they had never met before.

He lifted a hand and slid it around the back of her neck, under the fall of her hair, and pulled her even closer. Huskily he said, "I didn't expect this. I didn't expect that if I ever saw you again I would feel this way. Perhaps this was meant to be...a chance encounter to burn ourselves free of this insatiable desire."

Insatiable desire. That was exactly how it felt—how it had always felt between them. Moments after making love Julia had always been ashamed of how quickly she'd craved Kaden's touch again, and only the fact that it had been mutual had stopped her shame from overwhelming her.

As he said, he hadn't expected to see her again. And she could well believe that he'd not expected to desire her again. But he did, and obviously resented it. Why wouldn't he? He'd turned his back on her, and he'd bedded plenty of women far more beautiful than Julia since then. It must be galling to meet your first lover and realise you still wanted her. That made Julia feel acutely vulnerable. But it was too late.

Kaden had pulled her even closer, and now her soft belly touched his hard-muscled form—far harder than she remembered—and his head was lowering to hers. She tried to stiffen, to register her rejection, but everything was blocked out when she felt the explosive touch of Kaden's mouth to hers. Did it coincide with another clap of thunder outside or was that in her head?

Her heart spasmed in her chest, as if given an electric shock, and as his mouth moved and fitted to hers like a missing jigsaw piece she fell down into a dark vortex of desire so intense that it obliterated any kind of rational thought. Her hands had gone automatically to his chest, but instead of pushing him away they clung. The feel of powerful muscles under his shirt was intoxicating.

Time stood still. Everything stood still except for their two hearts, beating fast. Blood was rushing through veins and arteries, pumping to parts of Julia's body that hadn't been stimulated in a long, long time.

Kaden was seduction incarnate. His hands moved over and down her back, cupping her bottom in the tight jeans, floating sensuously over the silk shirt. With an easy expertise he certainly hadn't displayed when she'd known him before he coaxed her mouth open and his tongue stroked along hers, making a faint mewl come from the back of her throat.

Through the heat haze in her head and her body Julia felt something urgent trying to get through to her. Kaden's touch was all at once achingly familiar, and yet so different from how she remembered. They'd been so young, and their passion had been raw and untutored. The man who held her in his arms now was not raw and untutored. He was a consummate seducer, well-practised in the art. His body was different too. Muscles were filled out and harder.

It was that realisation that finally broke the spell cast around Julia. Plus the fact that within a mere hour of meeting Kaden again she was kissing him like a sex—starved groupie.

Wrenching herself away in one abruptly violent move, Julia staggered backwards, looking at Kaden's flushed face and glittering eyes. "I don't know you. You're a stranger to me now. I don't do this... I don't make love to strangers."

Something dark crossed Kaden's handsome features. He drawled, "From what I recall, you found it remarkably easy to make love to relative strangers."

With the memory of that incident so vivid, Julia lashed out. "It was just a kiss, Kaden. A stupid kiss. It meant nothing... It was just—" She stopped abruptly. Had she really been about to blurt out that she'd only allowed that man to kiss her because she'd felt so desperately insecure after days of silence from Kaden? That she'd pathetically wanted to try and prove to herself that his touch alone couldn't be the only touch she'd ever crave?

She clamped her mouth shut, burning inside. This man would never know that her experiment had backfired spectacularly—on more levels than one.

She had to claw back some sense of sanity. Some sense of the independent woman she'd become. Her voice was shaky. "This is not a good idea, Kaden. The past is the past and we should not be revisiting it."

Kaden felt tight and hot inside. With ruthless effort he excised the image of her kissing that man from his mind. What on earth had prompted him to bring up that kiss?

The last thing he wanted was for Julia to know that he remembered the incident. And yet it was like the stain of a tattoo on his memory, the jealousy fresh.

She was avoiding Kaden's eye. He might have appreciated the dark humour of the situation if he'd been in a better mood: merely *kissing* her just now had had a more explosive effect on his libido than anything he'd shared with a woman in years. If ever. Her chest was rising and falling rapidly. Some more buttons had opened on her shirt, exposing the shadowy line of her cleavage, and his erection just got harder. If that was possible.

The fact that what she said was right irked him beyond belief. He knew with a soul-deep certainly that to explore this desire with *this* woman had danger written all over it. He had a sense of having escaped the fire years before, only to be standing right on its edge again.

But stronger than that was this life-force rushing through his veins, along with the very carnal urge to sate himself. It was heady, and it made him feel as if he was awakening from a long sleep. He could no more turn back from it than he could stop breathing. He struggled to control himself. The rawness of what he was feeling was rising up, and Kaden ruthlessly drove it down, back to depths he'd never plumbed and had no intention of doing so now.

He crossed the room to where Julia stood. She looked up. Those grey eyes were dark and troubled. A line of pink slashed each cheek, and her lips were full and tender-looking. In a completely instinctive gesture he reached out and tucked some hair behind her ear, only realising as he did it that he'd used to do that all the time. His jaw clenching hard was the only sign that he'd recognised this tell-tale gesture which was at such odds with the dark emotion seething through his gut. *Jealousy*. He had to distance himself from their past, focus on the present.

"If we had met at any other time we wouldn't have been available, and yet this desire would still have blown up. It would have made a mockery of the fact that twelve years had gone by. And of our marriages." He went on, his deep voice mesmerising, "But we're both free and single now, two consenting adults."

Julia knew she should run—and fast. Get away and pray to God that she never saw Kaden again. But her feet wouldn't move. The way he'd casually reached out to tuck her hair behind her ear had broken something apart inside her, bringing with it an onslaught of memories of so many moments when he'd done that. It had been the first physical gesture he'd made to her.

Fatefully, knowing that on some level she was making a momentous decision by *not* leaving, Julia couldn't seem to turn away. She felt curiously lethargic—as if she'd been running towards something for a long time, only to have finally reached her destination. She wanted this man with a hunger she'd known only once before... for *him*.

She'd fully expected that if they ever met again that he would act as dismissively as he had earlier...and yet here she was. He wasn't pretending not to know her now. He was looking at her as if she was the only woman on the planet. That elusive feeling of home and connection that she'd only ever found with him whispered to her like a siren song, calling her to seek it again.

Desperately she fought it—going that way again could only end in worse devastation. Clinging furiously to some last vestige of pride, to the illusion that she had control, she backed away. "Just because we've met again, it doesn't mean anything, Kaden. It doesn't mean that we have to end up…in bed."

For a long tense moment they just looked at each other, and then, after another ear-splitting crack of thunder, the electricity went off.

Julia gasped and Kaden cursed. "The storm must have outed the power. Wait here. I'll get some candles."

Julia felt Kaden move away from her and took a deep, shaky breath. The darkness seemed to envelop her in a cloak of collusion. It made her want to forget the outside world, forget to remember their history. To give in to what he was offering. She wanted him so badly she shook.

Desperately she tried to remember the awful excoriating pain of the moment when he'd coolly informed her that all they'd shared had been a summer fling, that he had a life of responsibilities that didn't include her. But it was like trying to hold onto a wispy cloud. All she knew was the exhilaration rushing through her blood, the heightened awareness of desire.

Through the silence of the apartment she heard a crash somewhere and a colourful curse. They were sounds that *should* have been restoring her sanity, making her more determined to leave. But instead they were only firing her desire. She heard a movement and saw flickering light. This was it.

Kaden came back into the room, and in the soft glow Julia could only look at him and marvel at the shadows which made his face seem even more mysterious, his eyes two dark pools. He put down the candle and came closer and closer, until his body was just inches away from hers. His heat enveloped her, along with his exotic masculine scent. It made her think of hot nights in the desert, and of even hotter things.

"Julia, I don't want to analyse why this has happened like this. I don't want to discuss the past... I just want you."

She looked up at Kaden. So many feelings were rushing through her like a torrent, but one above all others. She wanted him too. She'd dreamt for years of seeing him again. He'd cast her out without a moment's hesitation, and when she'd heard about his nuptials something in her had died. So she had given in and accepted John's proposal, believing it was futile to love a ghost.

But he wasn't a ghost any more. He was flesh and blood and standing right in front of her. And then he reached out a hand and cupped her jaw, his thumb stroking her cheek. She was undone. When he pulled her closer she didn't resist. Because she couldn't.

CHAPTER FOUR

KADEN found himself relishing the other-worldliness that enforced darkness imposed, surrounding them in this cocoon. Julia's eyes were huge, her breaths coming short and rapid, and as he lowered his head so that his mouth could drink from hers he felt an inalienable sense of rightness. It was too strong to deny or question or rail against. His mouth settled over Julia's, his arms pulled her close, and when he felt her breasts crushed against his chest he was lost.

The outside world—the lashing rain against the windows and the intermittent thunder and lightning—all faded into the background as flames of heat started licking around them.

After what seemed like an aeon had passed Kaden pulled back. Julia was stunned, her limbs jelly-like. Her mouth felt swollen and her heart was hammering as if she'd just run half a marathon. Her hands were around Kaden's neck, his breath was harsh, and she could feel the hard ridge of his erection against her belly.

He just said coarsely, "Julia."

She didn't stop him when he shifted slightly so that he could pick her up into his arms. "Take the candle," he instructed roughly.

Half in a daze, Julia looked down to see the flickering candle on a table. She reached down to pick it up in
its stand and then Kaden was striding out of the room,
the soft light guiding their way to a door which he all
but kicked open. In the shadowy half-light Julia could
pick out a huge bed and unmistakably masculine furnishings. Kaden's bedroom.

A sliver of sanity returned, and Kaden must have felt
her tense, because he looked down into her face and said
implacably, "There is no going back from here."

Her breath was suspended for a long moment, and
then the enormity of meeting Kaden again struck home.
How fleeting this night would be. The weight of her
yearning for this man was heavy on her shoulders, and
it was too strong to deny, much as the tiny sliver of sanity she had left might be urging her to. Slowly. Fatefully,
she shook her head. "I don't want to go back."

He carried her over to the chest of drawers, where she
put down the candle, then let her slide down his body,
his hands touching her from shoulder to waist to hip.
He pushed some of her hair back over one shoulder and
bent his head to her neck, pressing a kiss there. Julia's
head fell back. It was too heavy to hold up. Her blood
was hot as it pumped through her veins.

Kaden's fingers came to her shirt and he started to
undo the buttons in the slippery fabric. She shivered
slightly when the air whispered over her bare skin. Soon
her shirt hung open. Kaden drew back and stood to his
full height.

He was downright intimidating in the dusky light,
with no help from an obscured moon, but he was also
thrilling. He was a big man all over. Julia watched with
a drying mouth as he coolly started to open his own

buttons. Part of her wanted to be as bold as she'd once been and brush his hands aside so that she could do it. But this wasn't the past. She was more cautious now, no matter how time seemed to be blurring here tonight.

His shirt was open, and with an economy of movement he pulled it off, revealing his awe-inspiring chest. It was broad and tautly muscled, and he had filled out since she'd seen him last. Coarse dark hair covered his pectorals, leading downwards in a dark line to just above his belt.

A finger to her chin lifted her face back up and Julia flamed guiltily. She'd all but been licking her lips at the prospect of seeing him fully naked for the first time in years.

Instead of pushing her shirt off her shoulders and arms, Kaden's big hands came to her waist, spanning it easily. His action pushed the shirt off her breasts, revealing them to his incendiary gaze. She could see a pulse throb in his neck and her belly quivered. Hot, wet heat moistened her sex in readiness.

Kaden breathed out. "So beautiful…you're so damn beautiful."

He cupped one fleshy weight in his hand and a thumb moved back and forth rhythmically over the tight peak. Julia moaned, and didn't even realise she was pushing her breast into his hand to increase the friction.

With a languorous movement he brought his thumb to his mouth and sucked it deep, before moving it back and repeating the action, moistening the hard tip. Julia moaned even louder, her breath coming short and fast. Excitement was building, ratcheting her inner tension upwards.

"Kaden…please."

"Please what?" he asked, almost casually. "Do you want me to put my mouth on you? Do you want me to taste you?"

Julia was almost weeping. "Yes..."

Kaden's head came down and his mouth closed unerringly over her already deeply sensitised nipple. Silky hair brushed the hot skin of her breast, adding to the exquisite sensation. He sucked so hard that Julia cried out, her fingers arrowing through his hair, holding him in place. His other hand was moulding and cupping the flesh of her other breast, readying it too for his ministrations.

His mouth moved to the second peak and Julia's legs all but buckled. Ruthlessly, with an arm around her waist, Kaden clamped her to him, not letting her fall, all the while subjecting her to something on the knife-edge of pleasure and pain.

Julia was fast losing sight of any reality. She was made up of sensations, a slave to this man and his touch. He was so much more confident than she remembered. He knew exactly what to do, where she ached to be touched.

As abruptly as he'd started torturing her with his mouth he stood back again, and with his hands clamped on her waist he drew her into him with an urgency that sent blood rushing to her pelvis. His head bent, mouth finding hers, tongue delving deep and seeking hers. The friction of her sensitised breasts against his chest was delicious torture. Through the haze of desire and excitement Julia felt a wild surge of exhilaration at being with this man again. It was as if now she'd given in to it she could fully appreciate the experience.

Blindly obeying the deep call of her blood, Julia let

her hands seek and fumble with Kaden's belt and zip, undoing them with a feverish intensity. While their mouths still clung, Julia pushed his trousers down over his lean hips. She could feel Kaden step out of them and kick them away. And then her hands were on his boxers.

He drew back at that, and she could see his eyes glittering. Her breasts were heavy. Her blood was on fire. Not taking her eyes off his, she put her fingers between his hot skin and the material and pulled them down. It was only when they snagged that she looked. The bulge of his erection was formidable. Running a finger around the rim of his boxers, unaware of the look of torture on Kaden's face, Julia stopped just where she could feel the smooth head of him.

Slowly she pulled the boxers out, free of his erection, and then they too were slid down over his powerfully muscled thighs. It reminded Julia again of the national sport that Kaden so loved to play, which had broken his nose at least once. It had looked barbaric to her: men stripped to the waist, using a crude form of shortened hockey stick to whack a ball between two goals. Part of the play was to crash into one another and divert each other from the ball. It was visceral, exciting and undeniably violent. And Kaden excelled at it.

But now she couldn't take her eyes off his impressive erection, springing free from the cradle of black hair. Moisture beaded the tip enticingly, and she could feel her own body moisten in answer.

His voice broke the spell. "I'm feeling a little underdressed here."

Julia's wide gaze clashed with his as he pushed her shirt off her shoulders, down her arms, from where it slithered to the floor in a pool of grey silk. Then his efficient hands were on her jeans, flicking open the button and pulling down the zip. Julia barely had a chance to get her breath before she felt him tugging them down over her hips and thighs.

Any embarrassment because the jeans were too small was lost when she saw how his gaze roved hungrily over her body. She sucked in a shaky breath when he took her by the hand to lead her to the bed. The candlelight and the dark, ominous sky outside made everything seem even more unreal. But the heat between her and Kaden was very real.

As he pushed her back onto the bed she realised with an illicit thrill that his touch was all at once familiar and yet that of a stranger. He was truly a man now, and she sensed a hunger in him that hadn't been there before, an easy dominance.

He joined her on the cool sheets and all rational thought fled. Pulling her into his body, touching her chest to chest and down, he kissed her again, deeply, as if he couldn't get enough of kissing her. Julia sank back into the covers, relishing the latent strength in Kaden's powerful form. His hand smoothed its way down, over her chest and to her belly. Fingers seeking even further until they encountered her pants.

With a perfunctory movement they were dispatched, and Kaden pushed her thighs apart, his hand seeking between her legs to where her body told of its readiness for him.

One finger stroked in and out of her moist heat. Julia's hands gripped Kaden's shoulders. She couldn't breathe, and almost arched off the bed when one finger was joined by another one, opening her up, stretching her, preparing her for his own body. Julia's hand sought his erection and wrapped around it, squeezing and moving up and down—a silent plea for him to stop torturing her. She couldn't speak, couldn't articulate anything.

Kaden shifted and was moving down her body, pressing kisses along her belly until his mouth was at the juncture of her legs and his tongue was tasting her as he'd once shocked her by doing all those years ago. She gasped, but ruthlessly he held her thighs wide apart, baring her to his mouth and that wickedly stabbing tongue.

He reached one hand up to find her breast and rolled a nipple between his fingers. Without anything to cling onto, Julia felt her body tighten in a spasm of pleasure so intense she didn't even notice when Kaden moved again, so that his huge body now lay between her legs.

Shattered from the intensity of the strongest orgasm she could remember having, she could only lie there in a stupor as Kaden took himself in his hand and stroked the head of his erection back and forth against her moistened sex. Her body was already greedy for him, her muscles still clenching as if trying to suck him in. At some point he'd had the sense to don protection, and Julia was exceedingly grateful—because all concerns for practicalities had gone out of the window.

Torturously he let himself be sucked in slowly, sheathing the head in her heat before pulling out. Julia moaned softly, her eyes glued to Kaden's harsh face. He looked so stark, like a pagan god stripped bare of all civility. And then he leaned over her on both hands and with one cataclysmic thrust seated himself in her fully. All the way to the hilt. Julia gasped at his size, but the fleeting pain quickly morphed to an intense pleasure, as if her body recognised him and was rejoicing.

"You…" he said roughly. "You are the only one who has ever made me feel like this…"

Julia asked brokenly, "Like what?"

"Like I'm not even human any more."

And with that he started up a remorseless rhythm, stroking in and out, his thrusts so long and full that Julia pulled up her legs to allow him to slide even deeper. There had not been one second of hesitation on her part in allowing him into her body. It had taken her husband months to woo her, for her to trust him enough to sleep with him. She'd still been so shaken by what had happened in Burquat… But here with Kaden it felt so natural and right she couldn't fight it.

The tremors of her last orgasm were still dying away as new tremors started up, even more intense than the last time. Sweat beaded her brow and dampened her skin. And Kaden still moved between her legs and inside her, as if he wanted to wring out this pleasure for as long as possible. Julia knew she wouldn't last. Head flung back, she arched upwards and splintered all over again, just as Kaden's thrusts increased, and when the storm in her body abated he gave a guttural groan and sank over her, his huge body stilling.

During the night Julia woke briefly to see that the storm had finally died away. The candle had gone out and she was tucked against Kaden's chest, his arms tight around her like a vice. The moon peeked out from behind a cloud.

The storm outside might have abated, but another storm was starting up inside her.

What on earth had she done?

Her thoughts must have made her tense, because she

could feel Kaden stirring behind her. He shifted them so that she lay on her back, looking up into slumbrous long-lashed eyes. She felt extremely vulnerable. She'd never expected to see him again, much less—

"Kaden... I—"

But he cut her off by putting a finger over her mouth. He shook his head, a lock of silky black hair flopping over his forehead, making him look sexily dishevelled. "Don't say a word. I don't want to hear it."

He took her mouth with his, and within seconds the conflagration that had burnt them before was starting up again. Julia's mind was screaming at her to stop, but the call of her blood was too strong. Kaden didn't even move over her this time. He gently shifted her so that she was on her side and lifted up one of her legs, pulling it back over his thigh. She gasped out loud when she felt him surge up and into her from behind, his arm snaking around her midriff and holding her firm as he thrust upwards.

His other hand cupped a breast, trapping a nipple between his fingers, and Julia helplessly fell into the fire all over again.

When Julia woke next she knew it was morning. She could sense the bright sunlight on her face. She was replete and lethargic. And at peace. *At peace?* The words resounded in her head as she registered her nakedness and the pleasurable ache throughout her body.

Almost superstitiously, she didn't open her eyes. She didn't need to; the pictures forming behind her closed lids were too lurid. Images formed into a set of scenarios: seeing Kaden at the top of the stairs after he'd been announced at the club; standing in front of him and registering that sardonic coolness; the rain; coming back here; the lights going out…and then heat. Nothing but heat. Maybe it had all been a dream. God only knew she'd had a few like it…

"I can tell that you're going through exactly what I went through when I woke. And, yes, every second of it happened for real." The voice was dry, mocking, and not a dream.

Julia's eyes flew open and she squinted in the bright light. Mercifully the sheet was up over her breasts. She pulled it up higher and could see Kaden now, standing at the window, looking gorgeous and pristine in a dark suit, drinking nonchalantly from what looked like an espresso cup.

He gestured with his other hand to a small breakfast table. "There's coffee there for you too, and some orange juice and a croissant."

Her stomach churned. It was excruciating to be facing Kaden like this. She'd been so *easy*. She came up on one arm and bit her lip, looked down. Her eyes were watering, and she couldn't tell if it was from the bright sunlight or looking at Kaden. The storm from last night had well and truly passed, and already the bitter recrimination was starting.

What on earth had she been thinking? Had one thunderstorm rewired her entire brain?

He moved forward then, and put down his cup. He came closer to the bed. Julia sat up awkwardly. Kaden's eyes were very black and intense on her, and already she could feel the heat of renewed desire deep within her.

"I'm here until the end of the week, when I have to fly to Al-Omar for Samia's wedding. I'd like to see you again, Julia."

Julia didn't know what to make of the maelstrom that erupted inside her at his words. She'd been expecting him to tell her casually to let herself out of the apartment when she was ready. "You want to see me again?"

He shrugged, oozing insouciance and an ease with this morning after situation. Another indication of the urbane seducer he'd become. "I don't see why not. I think we have unfinished business…why not finish it?"

Julia's mouth twisted. "You mean have an affair for a few days and then walk away?"

His mouth thinned. "It doesn't have to be as crass as that. You can't deny the attraction is as strong as ever. Why not indulge it to its natural conclusion? I don't see it lasting for longer than a few days."

That warm spread of desire suddenly cooled. Julia sat up straighter, pulling the sheet around her carefully. She felt seriously dishevelled and at a disadvantage in front of Kaden like this. She attempted her haughtiest look. "I'm extremely busy this week. I don't know if I have time to fit in an…*affair*."

Kaden's face became mocking. "I don't plan on spending the *days* with you, Julia, I was thinking more along the lines of the evenings…and the nights."

Instantly she castigated herself. Of course he wasn't talking about having *conversations*. She stood up, clinging onto the sheet like a lifeline.

"It's a crazy idea, Kaden. Last night was…" She bit her lip. "It should never have happened."

He strolled closer, and Julia would have moved back if she could—but the bed was at the back of her legs. Up close to him in her bare feet, she was reminded of how huge he was—and how utterly gorgeous. Once again the juxtaposition between the boy and the man was overwhelming. But his hands were shoved deep in his pockets, and she sensed an underlying tension to his otherwise suave manner.

He took one hand out then, and touched his knuckles to her chin. She gritted her jaw against his touch. His dark eyes roved her face and she couldn't make out any emotion. It made her wonder at the depths this civility hid from her.

Steel ran through his voice, impacting her. "Well, it did happen, Julia. And it's going to happen again. I'll pick you up from your house this evening at seven."

And with that he stepped back and strolled away.

Julia's mouth opened and closed ineffectually. She couldn't get over his easy arrogance that she would just fall in with his wishes. "You..." she spluttered. "You can't just seriously think that I will—"

He turned at the door. "I don't think, Julia. I *know*." He arched a brow. "I believe you said you were busy this week? You'd better get a move on. You'll find your clothes hanging in the closet. Help yourself to whatever you need. One of my cars will be waiting outside. You will be taken wherever you wish to go."

Kaden turned and left the room, shutting the door behind him. He didn't like the way he'd just had to battle to control himself enough not to topple Julia back onto that bed and take her again. And again. She'd looked tousled and thoroughly bedded, and far too reminiscent of memories he'd long suppressed. And he was *still* ignoring the voice in his head urging him to walk away, to forget he'd seen her again. He *should* have been able to leave last night as a one-off, an aberration. But he couldn't do it.

He was well aware that he'd just acted like some medieval autocrat, but the truth was he hadn't wanted to give her a chance to argue with him. To have her tell him that she was refusing to see him again, or point out again that this shouldn't have happened. He might have appreciated the fact that this was the first time a woman was clearly less than eager to share his bed if he'd been able to think past the urgent lust he still felt.

Standing in front of Julia just now, he'd not been able to think beyond the immediate future. He'd had a vision of being in London for the next few days, and the thought of not seeing her again had been repugnant.

He tried to rationalise it now. Their desire was clearly far from sated, but he had no doubt a couple of nights would be more than enough to rid himself of this bizarre need to reconnect with an ex-lover. *An ex-lover who almost had you in such thrall that you forgot what your priorities were.*

Kaden scowled, but didn't stop. By the time he reached his waiting car his face was as dark as thunder, tension vibrating off him in waves.

Minutes later Julia was still standing looking at the closed door, clutching the rumpled sheet, her mouth half open. And to her utter chagrin she couldn't drum up anything other than intense excitement at the thought of seeing Kaden again. Even after he'd so arrogantly informed her that it would suit him to have an affair while he was in London, to fill his time. Pathetic.

Last night ran through her brain like a bad movie, and all she could remember was the wanton way she'd succumbed to his caresses over and over again. The way she'd sought him out, her hand wrapping around him, eager to seduce him.

She groaned out loud and finally stumbled towards the bathroom. That was nearly worse. His scent was heavy in the air, steam still evident from his recent shower. She could see that glorious body in her mind's eye—naked, with water sluicing down over taut, hard muscles and contours.

She tore off the sheet and turned on the shower, relishing the hot pounding spray, but try as she might she couldn't stop older memories flooding her brain, superseding the more recent and humiliating ones. Pandora's Box had been well and truly opened. All she could think of now were the awful last weeks and days in Burquat. Even under the hot spray, Julia shivered.

A few weeks before she'd been due to return to England to complete her studies, Julia and Kaden had returned from a trip to the desert where they'd celebrated her birthday. She'd been so in love with him, and she'd believed that he'd loved her too. He'd *told* her he loved her. So why wouldn't she have believed him?

But, as clear as if it was yesterday, she could remember watching him walk away from her when they got back to Burquat. For some reason she'd superstitiously wished for him to turn around and smile at her, but he hadn't. That image of his tall, rangy body walking away from her had proved to be an ominous sign. She'd not seen him again until shortly before she was due to leave Burquat.

That very night it had been announced that the Emir wasn't well, and so Kaden had in effect become acting ruler. Heartsore for Kaden, because she'd known he was close to his father even though he'd been a somewhat distant figure, she'd made attempts to see him. But she'd been turned back time and time again by stern-looking aides.

It was as if he'd been spirited away. Days had passed, Julia had made preparations to go home and there had still been no sign or word from Kaden. She'd put it down to his father's frailty and the huge responsibility he faced as the incumbent ruler. She'd never realised until then how different it would have been if he had already been ruler. Much to her shame, she hadn't been able to stop the feeling of insecurity growing when there was no word, even though she'd known it was selfish.

A few nights before she'd been due to leave, Julia had given in to the urging of some fellow archaeology students and gone out for a drink, telling herself it was futile to waste another evening pining for Kaden. She hadn't been used to drinking much normally, and all she could remember was standing up at one point and feeling very dizzy. One of her colleagues had taken her outside to get some air. And it was then that he had tried to kiss her.

At first Julia had rejected his advances, but he'd been persistent...and that awful insecurity had risen up. What if Kaden had finished with her without even telling her? What if he wasn't even going to say goodbye to her? Even stronger had been the rising sense of desperation to think that Kaden might be the only man who would ever make her feel whole, who would ever be able to awaken her sensuality. The thought of being beholden to one man who didn't want her terrified her. The way she'd come to depend on Kaden, to love him, had raised all her very private fears and vulnerabilities about being adopted...and rejection.

He *couldn't* be the only one who would ever make

her feel anything again, she'd determined. So she had allowed that man to kiss her—almost in an attempt to prove something to herself.

It had been an effort in futility from the first moment, making instant nausea rise.

And that was when she'd seen Kaden, across the dark street, in long robes and looking half wild, with stubble darkening his jaw. She'd been so shocked she hadn't been able to move, and then…too late…she'd started to struggle. Kaden had just looked at her with those dark implacable eyes, and then he'd turned and left.

The following day the death of Kaden's father had been announced.

Only by refusing to move from outside the state offices had Julia eventually been allowed to see Kaden before she left the country a few days later. She'd stepped into a huge, opulent office to see Kaden standing in the middle of the room, legs splayed, dressed in ceremonial robes, gorgeous and formidable. And like an utter stranger.

She'd been incredibly nervous. "Kaden… I…" She'd never found it hard to speak with him, not from the moment they'd first met, but suddenly she struggled to get two words out. "I'm so sorry about your father."

"Thank you." His voice was clipped. Curt.

"I…I've tried to see you before now, but you've been busy."

His mouth thinned. "From the looks of things you've been busy yourself."

Julia flushed brick red when she remembered her tangled emotions and what they'd led her to do. "What you saw the other night…it was nothing. I'd had a bit too much to drink and—"

Kaden lifted a hand, an expression of distaste etched on his face. "Please, spare me the sordid details. It does not interest me in the slightest how or when or where you made love to that man."

Julia protested. "We didn't make love. It was just a stupid kiss… It stopped almost as soon as it had started."

Kaden's voice was icy. "Like I said, I'm really not interested. Now, what was it you wanted to see me about? As you said yourself, I'm very busy."

Julia immediately felt ashamed. Kaden was grieving.

"I just…I wanted to give you my condolences personally and to say…goodbye. I'm leaving tomorrow."

A layer of shock was making her a little numb. Not so long ago this man had held her in his arms underneath a blanket of stars and said to her fervently, *"I love you. I won't ever love another woman again."*

Nausea surged, and Julia had to put her hands against the shower wall and breathe deep. She hadn't thought of that awful evening for a long time.

And yet it wouldn't go away, the memory as stubborn as a dark stain. She could remember feeling compelled to blurt out, "Kaden…why are you behaving like this?"

He'd arched a brow and crossed his arms. "Like what?"

"Like you hardly know me."

His face had been a mask of cool civility. "You think six months of a summer fling means that I *know* you?"

Julia could remember flinching so violently that she'd taken a step backwards. "I didn't think of it as a fling. I thought what we had was—"

He had slashed down a hand, stopping her words, his face suddenly fierce. "What we had was an affair, Julia. Nothing more and nothing less than what you were engaging in with that man the other night. You are not from this world." His mouth had curled up in an awful parody of a mocking smile, "You didn't seriously think that you would ever become a permanent part of it, did you?"

Of course she hadn't. But her conscience niggled her. Deep within her, in a very secret place, she'd harboured a dream that perhaps this was *it*. He'd even mentioned his London apartment. Bile rose as she acknowledged that perhaps all he'd meant by that was that he'd give her the role of convenient mistress.

Horror spread through her body as the awful reality sank in. It was written all over every rejecting and rigid line of his body. Everything she'd shared with Kaden had been a mere illusion. He'd been playing with her. A western student girl, here for a short while and then conveniently gone. Perfect for a summer fling. And now he was ruler, a million miles from the carefree young man she thought she'd known.

Shakily she said, "You didn't have to tell me you loved me. You could have spared yourself the platitudes. I didn't expect to hear them." And she hadn't. She truly hadn't. She knew she loved this man, but she hadn't expected him to love her back…and yet he had. Or so she'd been led to believe.

Kaden shrugged and looked at a cuff, as if it was infinitely more interesting than their conversation. He looked back at her with eyes so black they were dead. "I went as far as you did. Please don't insult my intelligence and tell me that you meant it when *you* said it. You can hardly claim you did when within days you were ready to drop your pants for another man."

Julia backed away again at his crude words, shaking

her head this time, eyes horrifically glued to Kaden. "I told you, it wasn't like that."

She realised in that moment that she'd not ever known this man. And with that came the insidious feeling of worthlessness she'd carried ever since she'd found out she was adopted and that her own birth mother had rejected her. She wasn't good enough for anyone. She never had been…

To this day Julia couldn't actually remember walking out of that room, or the night that had followed, or the journey to the airport next day. She only remembered being back in grey, drizzly autumnal England and feeling as though her insides had been ripped out and trampled on. The feeling of rejection was like a corrosive acid, eating away at her, and for a long time she hadn't trusted her own judgement when it came to men. She'd locked herself away in her studies.

Her husband John had managed to break through her wall of defences with his gentle, unassuming ways, but Julia could see now that she'd fallen for him precisely because he'd been everything Kaden was *not*.

When she thought of what had happened last night, and Kaden's cool assertion that he would see her later— exactly the way a man might talk to a mistress—nausea surged again, and this time Julia couldn't hold it down. She made it to the toilet in time and was violently ill. When she was able to, she stood and looked at herself in the mirror. She was deathly pale, eyes huge.

What cruel twist of fate had brought them together like this again?

And yet even now, with the memory of how brutally he'd rejected her still acrid like the bile in her throat, Julia felt a helpless weakness invade her. And, worse, that insidious yearning. Shakily she sat down on the closed toilet seat and vowed to herself that she would thwart Kaden's arrogant assumption that she would fall in with his plans. Because she didn't know if she could survive standing in front of him again when he was finished with her, and hearing him tell her it was over.

CHAPTER FIVE

KADEN sat in his car outside Julia's modest-sized town-house. He was oblivious to the fact that his stately vehicle looked ridiculously out of place in the leafy residential street. His mind and belly were churning and had been all day. Much to his intense chagrin he hadn't been able to concentrate on the business at hand at all, causing his staff to look worried. He was *never* distracted.

He'd struggled to find some sense of equilibrium. But equilibrium had taken a hike and in its place was an ever-present gnawing knowledge that he'd been here before. In this place, standing at the edge of an abyss. About to disappear.

Kaden's hand tightened to a fist on his thigh. He was not that young man any more. He'd lived and married and divorced. He'd had lovers—many lovers. And not one woman had come close to touching that part of him that he'd locked away years before. When Julia had turned and walked out of his study.

He shook his head to dislodge the memory, but it wouldn't budge. That last meeting was engraved in his mind like a tattoo. Julia's slate-grey eyes wide, her cheeks pale as she'd listened to what he'd said. The burning jealousy in his gut when he'd thought of her with that man. It had eclipsed even his grief at his father's death. The realisation that she was fallible, that she was like every other woman, had been the start of his cynicism.

Most mocking of all though—even now—was the memory of why he'd gone looking for her on that cataclysmic night of his father's death. Contrary to his father's repeated wishes, Kaden had insisted that he wanted Julia. He'd gone to find her, to explain his absence and also to tell her that he wanted her to be his queen some day. That he was prepared to let her finish her studies and get used to the idea and then make a choice. Fired up with love—*or so he'd thought*—he hadn't been prepared for seeing her entangled in that embrace, outside in the street, where anyone could have seen her. *His woman.*

He could remember feeling disembodied. He could remember the way something inside him had shrivelled up to nothing as he'd watched her finally notice him and start to struggle. In that moment whatever he'd felt for her had solidified to a hard black mass within him, and then it had been buried for good.

Only a scant hour later, when Kaden had sat by his dying father's bed and he had begged Kaden to "*think of your country, not yourself*", Kaden had finally seen the future clearly. And that future did not include Julia.

It had been a summer of madness. Of believing feelings existed just because they'd been each other's first lover. He'd come close to believing he loved her, but had realised just in time that he'd confused lust and sexual obsession with love.

As if waking from a dream, Kaden came back to the car, to the street in suburban London. He looked at the townhouse. Benign and peaceful. His blood thickened and grew hot. Inside that house was the woman who stood between him and his future. On some level he'd never really let her go, and the only way he could do that was to sate this beast inside him. Prove that it was lust once and for all. And this time when he said goodbye to her she would no longer have the power to make him wake, sweating, from vivid dreams, holding a hand to his chest to assuage the dull ache.

Julia felt as if she was thirteen all over again, with butterflies in her belly, flushing hot and cold every two seconds. She'd heard Kaden's car pull up and her nerves were wound taut waiting for the doorbell. What was he doing? she wondered for the umpteenth time, when he still didn't emerge from the huge car.

Then she imagined it pulling away again, and didn't like the feeling of panic *that* engendered. She'd vacillated all day over what to do, all the while knowing, to her ongoing sense of shame, that she'd somewhere along the way made up her mind that she wasn't strong enough to walk away from Kaden.

By the time she'd returned from work, with a splitting headache, she'd felt cranky enough with herself for being so weak that she'd decided she *wouldn't* give in so easily. She would greet Kaden in her running sweats and tell him she wasn't going anywhere. But then she'd had an image of him clicking his fingers, having food delivered to the house and staying all night. She couldn't forget the glint of determination in his eye that morning. And the thought of having him here in her private space for a whole night had been enough to galvanise her into getting dressed in a plain black dress and smart pumps.

The lesser of two evils was to let him take her out.

She'd thank him for dinner, tell him that there couldn't possibly be a repeat of last night, and that would be it. She'd never see him again. She was strong enough to do this.

She'd turned away from her furtive vigil at the window for a moment, so she nearly jumped out of her skin when the doorbell rang authoritatively. And all her previous thoughts were scrambled into a million pieces. Her hands were clammy. Her heart thumped. She walked to the front door and could see the looming tall, dark shape through the bubbled glass. She picked up her bag and cardigan and took a deep breath.

When she opened the door she wasn't prepared for the hit to her gut at seeing a stubble-jawed Kaden leaning nonchalantly against the porch wall, dominating the small space. He obviously hadn't shaved since that morning, and flames of heat licked through her blood. He was so intensely masculine. He was in the same suit—albeit with the tie gone and the top button of his shirt open.

His eyes were dark and swept her up and down as he straightened up. She tingled all over. Julia wished she'd put her hair up, it felt provocative now to have it down. Why had she left it down?

Kaden arched a brow. "Shall we?"

Julia sucked in a breath and finally managed to move. "Yes…" She pulled the front door behind her, absurdly glad that Kaden hadn't come inside, and fumbled with the keys as she locked it. Kaden was waiting by the door of the car and helped her in. His hand was hot on her bare elbow.

The car pulled off smoothly and Julia tried to quell her butterflies. Kaden's drawling and unmistakably amused voice came from her right.

"Are we going to a funeral?"

She looked at him and could see him staring pointedly at her admittedly rather boring dress. She fibbed. "I didn't have time to change after work."

His eyes rose to hers and he smiled. "Liar," he mocked softly.

Julia was transfixed by that smiling mouth, by the unbelievably sensuous and wicked lines. Her face flamed and her hand moved in that betraying reflex to her throat. She stopped herself just in time. She felt naked without his necklace. It was the first time she'd not worn it at home. Her hand dropped to her lap, and to hide her discomfiture she asked, "Where are we going?"

To her relief Kaden released her from his all too intent gaze and looked ahead. "We're going to the Cedar Rooms, in the Gormseby Hotel."

Julia was impressed. It was a plush new hotel that had opened in the past few months, and apparently there was already a year-long waiting list for the restaurant. Not for Kaden, though, she thought cynically. They'd be tripping over themselves to have him endorse their restaurant. Yet she was relieved at the idea of being in a public place, surrounded by people, as if that would somehow help her resist him and put up the fight she knew she must.

Kaden was struggling to hang on to his urbanity beside Julia. Her dress was ridiculously boring and plain, but it couldn't hide her effortless class, or those long shapely legs and the enticing swell of her bosom. Her hair was down, falling in long waves over her shoulders, and she wore a minimum of make-up. Once again he was struck that she could pass for years younger. And by how beautiful she was. She had the kind of classic beauty that just got better with age.

The minute she'd opened the front door her huge swirling grey eyes had sucked him into a vortex of need so strong that he'd felt his body responding right there. Much as it had in that crowded room last night. A response he'd never had to curb for any other woman, because he'd always been in strict control.

With Julia, though, his brain short-circuited every time he looked at her. It only fired up his assertion that this was just lust. With that in mind, and anticipating how urgent his desire would be by the time they got to dessert, he made a quick terse call in Arabic from his mobile phone.

By the time they were on their desserts Julia had given up trying to maintain any kind of coherent conversation. The opulent dining room was arranged in such a way that—far from being surrounded by the public—she and Kaden were practically in a private booth. And it was so dark that flickering candles sent long shadows across their faces. It was decadent, and not at all conducive to remaining clear-headed as she'd anticipated.

Their conversation had started out innocuously enough. Kaden had asked her about her career and why she'd taken the direction she had. She'd explained that her passion for fund distribution had grown when she'd seen so much misused funding over the years, and she'd seen it as the more stable end of archaeology, considering her future with a husband and family. To her surprise his eyes hadn't glazed over with boredom. He'd kept looking at her, though, as if he wanted to devour her. Desperately trying to ignore the way it made her feel, she'd asked him about Burquat.

It sounded like another country now—vastly different from the more rigidly conservative one she'd known. Once again she was filled with a rush of pride that his ambition was being realised.

Scrabbling around for anything else to talk about, to take the edge off how intimate it felt to be sitting here with him, Julia said, "I saw something in the papers about drilling your oil-fields. There seems to be great interest, considering the world's dwindling oil supplies."

"We're certainly on the brink of something huge. Sultan Sadiq of Al-Omar is going to help us drill the oil. He has the expertise."

"Is that part of the reason why he's marrying Samia?" Julia felt a pang of concern for Kaden's younger sister. From what she remembered of her she was no match for the renowned playboy Sultan.

Kaden's mouth tightened. "It's a factor, yes. Their marriage will be an important strategic alliance between both our countries."

Kaden sat back and cradled a bulbous glass of brandy. He looked at Julia from under hooded lids. She felt hunted.

"So…your boss—Nigel. Are you seeing him?"

Julia flushed, wondering what kind of woman Kaden had become used to socialising with, *sleeping* with. She swallowed. "No, I'm not." Not sure why she felt compelled to elaborate, she said, "He's asked me out, but I've said no."

"You've had no lovers since your husband?"

Julia flushed even hotter and glared at Kaden. "That's

none of your business. Would you mind if I asked *you* if you've had any lovers since your divorce?"

He was supremely relaxed, supremely confident. He smiled. "I have a healthy sex life. I enjoy women...and they enjoy what I can give them."

Julia snorted indelicately, her imagination shamefully providing her with an assortment of images of the sleek, soignée women she'd seen grace his arm over the years. "No doubt." And then something dark was rising up within her, and she said ascerbically, "I presume these women are left in no doubt as to the parameters of their relationship with you, much as you outlined to me this morning?"

Kaden's face darkened ominously. "I took your advice a long time ago. Women know exactly where they stand with me. I don't waste my breath on platitudes and empty promises."

For some perverse reason Julia felt inexplicably comforted. As if Kaden had just proved to her that no woman had managed to break through that wall of ice. And yet...how would *she* know? She was the last woman in the world he would confide in. And she was obviously the last woman in the world who could break through the icy reserve she'd seen that last evening in Burquat.

She realised then just how provocative the conversation was becoming, and put down her napkin. "I think I'm ready to go now."

Kaden rose smoothly to his feet and indicated for Julia to precede him out of the booth. With his head inclined solicitously he was urbanity incarnate, but Julia didn't trust it for a second. She knew the dark, seething passion that hummed between them was far from over.

When they reached the lobby Julia turned towards

the main door, her mind was whirring with ways to say goodbye to Kaden and insist on getting a taxi. At the same time her belly was clenching pathetically at the thought of never seeing him again. Kaden caught her hand and her mind blanked at the physical contact. She looked up at him, and that slow lick of desire coiled through her belly. She cursed it—and herself.

"I've booked a suite here for the night."

Julia straightened her spine and tried to block out the tantalising suggestion that they could be in bed within minutes. "If your aim is to make me feel like a high-class hooker then you're succeeding admirably."

Kaden cursed himself. Never before had he lacked finesse with a woman. He wanted Julia so badly he ached, and he'd booked the room because he'd known he wouldn't have the restraint to wait until he got back to his apartment or her house. But she was as stiff as a board and about as remote as the summit of Everest. He had a good idea that she had every intention of walking away from him. He didn't like the dart of panic he felt at acknowledging that.

Julia watched Kaden's face. It was expressionless except for his jaw clenching and his eyes flashing. A dart of panic rose; to willingly spend another night with this man was emotional suicide.

"Kaden, I don't know what you think you're doing, but I came here tonight to have dinner with you. I do not intend repeating what happened last night. There's no point. We have nothing to say to each other."

In a move so fast her head spun, he was right in front of her. He said roughly, "*We* may have nothing to say to each other, but our bodies have plenty to say."

He put his hands on her arms and pulled her close.

She sucked in a breath when she felt the burgeoning response of his body against her. Immediately there was an exultant rush of blood to her groin in answer. Any thoughts of emotional suicide were fading fast.

And it was then that she noticed they were standing in the middle of the lobby and attracting attention. How could they not? Kaden was six feet four at least, and one of the most recognisable men on the planet. Even if he wasn't, his sheer good looks would draw enough attention.

He intuited the direction of her thoughts, and his eyes glinted down at her. "I have no problem making love to you here and now, Julia."

To illustrate his point he pulled her in even tighter and brought his mouth down so close that she could feel his breath feather along her lips. Instinctively her mouth was already opening, seeking his.

He whispered, "We have unfinished business, Julia. Are you really ready to walk away from this? Because I'm not."

And with that he settled his mouth over hers, right in the middle of that exclusive lobby, in front of all those moneyed people. But for all Julia was aware they might have been in her house. What undid her completely was that his kiss was gentle and restrained, but she could feel the barely leashed passion behind it. If he'd been forceful it would have been easier to resist, but this kiss reminded her too much of the Kaden she'd once known...

His hands moved up to cradle her face, holding her in place while his tongue delved deep and stroked along hers, making her gasp with need.

Eventually he drew back and said, "The reason I booked the room was because I knew I wouldn't be able to wait until I got you home. Not because I wanted you to feel like a high-class call girl. Now, we can continue this where we stand, and give the guests the show of their lives, or we can go upstairs."

Julia's hands had crept up to cling onto Kaden's arms. She felt the muscles bunch and move and looked up into those dark eyes. She could feel herself falling down and down. There was no space between them. No space to think. She didn't have the strength to walk away. Not yet.

Hating herself, she said shakily, "OK. Upstairs."

With grim determination stamped all over his darkly gorgeous features, Kaden held her close and walked her across the lobby to the lifts. Her face flamed when she became aware of people's discreet scrutiny, and Julia realised that within the space of twenty-four hours her carefully ordered and structured life had come tumbling down around her ears—so much so that she didn't even recognise herself any more.

And the worst thing about this whole scenario: she was exhilarated in a way she hadn't felt in a long time.

For the second morning in a row Julia woke up in an unfamiliar room and bed. But this time there was no pristine Kaden in a suit, watching her as she woke. The bed beside her was empty, sheets well tousled. She knew instantly that she was alone, and didn't like the bereft feeling that took her by surprise. Their scent mingled with the air, along with the scent of sex. In a flash the previous night came back in glorious Technicolor.

They'd said not a word once they'd got to the room. They'd been naked and in bed within seconds, mutually combusting.

They'd made love for hours, insatiably. Hungering for one another only moments after each completion. Julia was exhausted, but she couldn't deny the illicit feeling of peace within her. She sighed deeply. She knew Kaden was going to Al-Omar the next day for Samia's wedding.

Then she spotted something out of the corner of her eye. She turned her head to see a folded piece of stiff hotel paper. She opened it up and read the arrogantly slashing handwriting: *I'll pick you up at your place, 7.30. K*

Julia sighed again. One more night in this strange week when everything felt out of kilter and off balance and slightly dream-like. She'd love to be able to send a terse note back with a curt dismissal, but if last night had proved anything it was that the fire had well and truly been stoked and she was too fatally weak to resist. All of the very good reasons she had for saying no—her very self-preservation, for a start—were awfully elusive at the prospect of seeing Kaden for a last time.

When the doorbell rang that evening Julia was flustered. She opened the door, and once again wasn't prepared for the effect of the reality of Kaden on her doorstep.

"Hi… Look, I've just got back from work." She indicated her uniform of trousers, shirt and flat shoes. "I need to shower and change. Today was busy, and then there was a problem with the tube line, and—" She stopped abruptly. She was babbling. As if he cared about the vagaries of public transport.

Kaden took a step inside her door before she knew what was happening, dwarfing her small hallway, and said easily, "We're in no rush. You get ready; I'll wait down here."

Julia gulped, and her hand went nervously to her

throat again. But of course the necklace wasn't there. Every morning she had to consciously remember not to put it on. Self-recrimination at her own weakness made her say curtly, "I won't be long. There's fresh coffee in the kitchen if you want to help yourself."

And with that she fled upstairs and locked herself into her *en suite* bedroom. Lord, she was in trouble.

Kaden prowled through the hallway. From what he could see it was a classic two-up-two-down house, with a bright airy kitchen extending at the back, which was obviously a modern addition. He hated this weakness he felt for the woman upstairs. Even now he wanted to follow her into the shower and embed himself in her tight heat.

Last night had been very far removed from the nights he'd shared with other women. He was always quickly sated and eager to see them leave, or leave himself. But it had only been as dawn was breaking and his body was too weak to continue that he'd finally fallen asleep.

When he'd woken a couple of hours later all he'd had to do was look at Julia's sleeping body to want to wake her and start all over again. Right now he didn't feel as if an entire month locked in a hotel room would be enough to rid him of this need.

His mind shied away from that realisation, and from more introspection. It was perhaps inevitable that his first lover should make a lasting impression, leave a mark on his soul. The chemistry between them had been intense from the moment they'd met over that fossil at the city dig. Kaden's mouth twisted. It had been as if he'd been infected with a fever, becoming so obsessed with Julia and having her that he hadn't been able to see anything else.

He hadn't even noticed his own father's growing frailty. Nor even listened to his father's pleas until they'd been uttered with his last breath.

With a curse he turned away from the view of the tiny but perfect garden. What was he doing here, in this small suburban house? His movements jerky, he found a cup and poured himself a strong black coffee, as if that might untangle the knots in his head and belly.

He wandered through to the bright and minimalist sitting-room. He wondered, with an acidic taste in his mouth, if this had been the marital home. He couldn't see any wedding photos anywhere, but stopped dead when he saw the panoramic photo hanging above the fireplace, his insides freezing in shock.

It was a familiar view—one of his favourites. A picture taken in the Burquati desert, with the stunning snow-capped Nazish mountain range in the distance. He had a vivid memory of the day Julia had taken this picture. His arms had been tight around her waist and she'd complained throatily, "I can't keep the camera steady if you hang onto me like you're drowning!"

And he'd said into her ear, overcome with emotion, "I'm drowning, all right. In love with you."

The shutter had clicked at that moment, and then she'd turned in his arms and—

"I'm sorry—I tried to be as quick as I could."

Kaden's hand gripped the coffee mug so tightly he had to consciously relax for fear of breaking it into pieces. He schooled his features so they were a bland mask which reflected nothing of his inner reaction to the memory sparked by the picture.

He turned around. Julia was wearing a dark grey silky dress that dipped down at the front to reveal her delicate collarbone and clung to the soft swells of her breasts, dropping in soft, unstructured folds to her knee. Her legs were bare and pale, and she wore high-heeled wedges. He dragged his eyes up to hers. She'd tied her hair back into a ponytail and it made her look ridiculously innocent and young.

Julia's body was reacting with irritating predictability to Kaden's searing look. When she'd walked in she'd noted with dismay that he'd spotted the photograph. It was one of her favourite possessions. Her husband John had used to complain about it, having taken an instant dislike to it, and she'd hidden it away during their marriage. It was almost as if he'd intuited that she'd lost her heart in that very desert. At that very moment.

Kaden indicated behind him now, without taking his dark eyes off hers. "The frame suits the photo. It turned out well."

She fixed a bright smile on her face, resolutely blocking out the memory of that day. "Yes, it did. I'm ready to go."

Kaden looked at her for a long moment and then threw back the rest of his coffee. He went into the kitchen, where he put the cup in the sink, rinsed it, and then came into the hall. Julia already had the door open, and allowed Kaden to precede her out so she could lock up.

Like the previous night, she asked him, once in the back of the car, "Where are we going?"

"I thought we'd go to my apartment this evening. I've arranged for a Burquati chef to cook dinner. I thought you might appreciate being reminded of some of our local dishes."

Sounding a little strangled, Julia answered, "That sounds nice."

* * *

And it was. Julia savoured every morsel of the delicious food. She'd always loved it. Balls of rice mixed with succulent pieces of lamb and fish. Tender chicken breasts marinaded for hours in spices. Fresh vegetables fried in tantalising Burquati oils. And decadent sweet pastries dripping with syrup for dessert, washed down with tart black coffee.

"You haven't lost your appetite."

Julia looked across the small intimate table at Kaden. He was lounging back in his chair like a sleek panther, in a dark shirt and black trousers. She felt hot, and her hand went in that telling gesture to her neck again. She dropped it quickly. "No. I've never lost my healthy appetite." She smiled ruefully and the action felt strange. She realized she hadn't smiled much in the past few days. "That's why I run six miles about three times a week—to be able to indulge the foodie within me."

Kaden's eyes roved over her. "You were definitely a little...plumper before."

There was a rough quality to his voice that resonated deep inside Julia. She could remember Kaden's hands squeezing her breasts together, lavishing attention on the voluptuous mounds.

"Puppy fat," she said, almost desperately.

Abruptly she stood up, agitated, and took her glass of wine to go and stand by the open doors of the dining room, which led out to an ornate terraced balcony overlooking the city. She needed air and space. He was too intense and brooding. The tension between them, all that was not being acknowledged about their past history, was nearly suffocating. And yet what was there to say? Julia certainly didn't need to hear Kaden elaborate again on why he'd been so keen to see the back of her...

She heard him move and come to stand beside her. She took a careful sip of wine, trying to be as nonchalant as possible, but already she was trembling with wanting him just to take her in his arms and make her forget everything. One last night and then she would put him out of her mind for good.

"I want you to come to Al-Omar with me for Samia's wedding."

Julia's head whipped round so fast she felt dizzy for a moment. "What?" she squeaked, "You want me to come…as your date?"

He was looking impossibly grim, which made Julia believe that she hadn't just had an aural hallucination. He nodded. "It'll be over by Sunday."

Julia felt bewildered. She hadn't prepared emotionally for anything beyond this night. "But…why?"

Kaden's jaw tightened. He wasn't sure, but he was damn hopeful it would mean the end of his burning need to take this woman every time he looked at her. And that it would make all the old memories recede to a place where they would have no hold over him any more. That it would bring him to a place where he could get on with his life and not be haunted by her and the nebulous feeling of something having gone very wrong twelve years before.

He shrugged. "I thought you might enjoy meeting Samia again."

Julia looked at Kaden warily. His expression gave nothing away, but there was a starkness to the lines of his face, a hunger. She recognised it because she felt it too. The thought of *this*—whatever it was between them—lasting for another few days out of time was all at once heady and terrifying.

She'd once longed for him to come after her, to tell her he'd made a mistake. That he *did* love her. But he hadn't. Now he wanted to spend more time with her. Perhaps this was as close as she would ever get to closure? This man had haunted her for too long.

She stared down at her wine glass as if the ruby liquid held all the answers. "I don't know, Kaden..." She looked back up. "I don't know if it's such a good idea."

Kaden sneaked a hand out and around the back of her neck. Gently he urged her closer to him, as if he could tell that her words were a pathetic attempt to pretend she didn't want this.

"This is desire—karma—unfinished business. Call it what you will, but whatever it is it's powerful. And it's not over."

Kaden's hand was massaging the back of her neck now, and Julia felt like purring and turning her face into his palm. She gritted her jaw. "I have to work tomorrow. I can't just up and leave the country. I'll...have to think about it."

His eyes flashed. Clearly he was unused to anything less than immediate acquiescence. "You can do whatever you want, Julia. You're beholden to none. But while you're thinking about it, think about *this*."

This was Kaden removing the wine glass from her hand and pulling her into him so tightly that she could feel every hard ridge of muscle and the powerful thrust of his thighs and manhood. Cradling her face in his hands, he swooped—and obliterated every thought in her head with his kiss.

CHAPTER SIX

"WOULD you like some champagne, Dr Somerton?"

Julia looked at the impeccably made-up Burquati air hostess and decided she could so with a little fortitude. She smiled tightly. "Yes, please."

The woman expertly filled a real crystal flute with champagne, and then passed a glass of what looked like brandy to Kaden, who sat across the aisle of his own private jet.

It was dark outside. It would take roughly six hours to get to B'harani, the capital of Al-Omar. They'd been scheduled to leave that afternoon, but Kaden had been held up with business matters—hence their overnight flight.

Julia's brain was already slipping helplessly back into the well-worn groove that it had trod all day. *Why* had she decided to come? A flush went through her body when she remembered back to that morning, as dawn had been breaking. She'd been exhausted. Kaden had been ruthless and remorseless all night. Each orgasm had felt like another brick dismantled in the wall of her defences.

Kaden had hovered over her and asked throatily, "So, will you come to Al-Omar with me?"

Julia had sensed in him a tiny moment of such fleeting vulnerability that she must have imagined it, but it had got to her, stripping away any remaining defences. Stripping away her automatic response to say no and do the right thing, the logical thing. Lying there naked, she'd been at his mercy. To her ongoing shame, she'd just nodded her head weakly, reminding herself that this was finite and soon she would be back to normal, hopefully a little freer of painful memories.

"You don't need to look like you're about to walk the plank. You're going to be a guest at the society wedding of the year."

Julia clutched the glass tightly in her hand now and looked at Kaden. Since she'd got into his car just a couple of hours ago outside her house he'd been on the phone. And he'd been engrossed in his laptop since boarding the flight. But now he was looking at her.

Unbidden, the words tumbled out. "Why are you doing this? Why are we here?" *Why have you come back into my life to tear me open all over again? And, worse, why am I allowing it to happen?*

It was as if she had to hear him reiterate the reasons why she was being so stupid. Kaden's dark eyes held hers for a long moment and then dropped in a leisurely appraisal of her body. Julia was modestly dressed: a plain shirt tucked into high-waisted flared trousers. Her hair was coiled back into a chignon. It should have felt like armour, but it didn't. Kaden's laser-like gaze had the power to make her feel naked.

His eyes met hers again. "We are doing this to sate the desire between us. We're two consenting adults taking pleasure in one another. Nothing more, nothing less."

Julia swallowed painfully. "There's more to it than

that, Kaden. We have a past together. Something you seem determined to ignore."

Kaden turned more fully in his seat, and Julia felt threatened when she saw how cynicism stamped the lines of his face. And something else—something much darker. Anger.

"I fail to see what talking about the past will serve. We had an affair aeons ago. We're different people now. The only constant is that we still want each other."

Affair. Julia cursed herself for opening her mouth. Kaden was right. What on earth could they possibly have to talk about? She was humiliatingly aware that she wanted him to tell her that he hadn't meant to reject her so brutally. She didn't feel like a different person. She felt as if she was twenty all over again and nothing had changed.

Incredibly brittle, and angry for having exposed herself like this, she forced a smile. "You're right. I'm tired. It's been a long day."

Kaden frowned now, and his eyes went to her throat. "Why do you keep doing that? Touching your neck as if you're looking for something?"

Julia gulped, and realised that once again in an unconsciously nervous gesture her hand had sought out the comforting touch of her necklace. Panic flared. She wasn't wearing it, but she'd broken her own rule and brought it with her, like some kind of talisman. She blushed. "It's just a habit…a necklace I used to wear. I lost it some time ago and I haven't got used to it being gone yet."

His eyes narrowed on her and, feeling panicky, Julia put down her glass and started to recline her chair. "I think I'll try to get some sleep."

Kaden felt the bitter sting of a memory, and with it an emotion he refused to acknowledge. It was too piercing. He'd once given Julia a necklace, but he had no doubt that wasn't the necklace she referred to. It was probably some delicate diamond thing her husband had bought her.

The one he'd given her would be long gone. What woman would hold on to a cheap gold necklace bought in a marketplace on a whim because he'd felt that the knot in the design symbolised the intricacies of his emotions for his lover? His lover. Julia. Then and now.

He cursed himself and turned away to look out at the inky blackness. He should have walked away from her in London this morning and come to Al-Omar to make a fresh start. He needed to look for a new bride to take him into the next phase of his life. He needed to create the family legacy he'd promised his father, and an economically and politically stable country. It was all within his grasp finally, after long years of work and struggle and one disastrous marriage.

He glanced back to Julia's curved waist and hips and his blood grew hot. He still wanted her, though. She was unfinished business. His hands clenched. He couldn't take one step into the future while this hunger raged within him and it *would* be sated. It had to be.

Arriving in B'harani as dawn broke was breathtaking. The gleaming city was bathed in a pinky pearlescent light. It was festooned with flags and decorations, and streets were cordoned off for the first wedding procession, which would take place later that day.

Kaden had barely shared one word with Julia as they'd sped through the streets to the imposing Hussein Castle.

There, they'd been shown to their opulent suite, and Kaden had excused himself to go and see his sister.

Now Julia was alone in the room, gritty-eyed with tiredness and a little numb at acknowledging that she was back on the Arabian Peninsula with Kaden. She succumbed to the lure of a shower and afterwards put on a luxurious towelling robe. The massive bed dressed in white Egyptian cotton was beckoning, and she lay down with the intention of having a quick nap.

When she woke, some time later, the sun was high outside and she felt very disoriented when she saw Kaden emerge from the bathroom with a tiny towel slung around his hips. He was rubbing his hair with another towel, and he was a picture of dark olive-skinned virility, muscles bunching and gleaming.

Julia sat up awkwardly. "Why didn't you wake me?"

He cast her a quick glance. "You were exhausted. There's nothing much happening till this evening anyway. The civil ceremony took place this morning, and Sultan Sadiq and Samia are doing a procession through the streets this afternoon. This evening will be the formal start of the celebrations, with more over the next two days. On Sunday they will marry again in a more western style."

"Wow," breathed Julia, while trying to ignore the sight of Kaden's half naked body, "That sounds complicated."

Kaden smiled tightly, seemingly unaware of his state of undress. He flung aside the towel he'd been drying his hair with, leaving it sexily dishevelled. "Yes, quite. In Burquat things are much more straightforward. We just have a wedding ceremony in front of our elders at dawn and then a huge ceremonial banquet which lasts all day."

Against her best effort to focus on what he was saying, Julia couldn't stop her gaze from dropping down Kaden's exquisitely muscled chest. He really had the most amazing body—huge but leanly muscled. The towel around his hips looked very precarious, and as she watched, wide-eyed, she could see the distinctive bulge grow visibly bigger.

Her cheeks flamed and her gaze jumped up to meet Kaden's much more mocking one. His hand whipped aside the towel and it fell to the floor along with the other one. Gulping, she watched as he walked to the bed. He lay alongside her and pushed aside the robe, baring her breasts to his gaze. Once again Julia was a little stunned at this much more sexually confident Kaden and how intoxicating he was.

Weakly, she tried to protest, "What if someone comes in?"

"They won't," he growled, and bent his head to surround one tight nipple with hot, wet, sucking heat.

Julia moaned and collapsed back completely. Kaden's other hand slid down her belly, undoing the tie on the robe as he dipped lower and between her legs, to where she was already indecently wet and ready.

He removed the robe and within seconds she was naked too, with Kaden's body settled between her legs, his shoulders huge above her. She could feel him flex the taut muscles of his behind and widened her legs, inviting him into more intimate contact. When he thrust into her Julia had to close her eyes, because she was terrified he would see the emotion boiling in her chest. As he started up with a delicious rhythm Julia desperately assured herself that this was just about sex, not emotion. She didn't love him any more. She couldn't… Because if she did, the emotional carnage was too scary to contemplate.

Later that evening Julia paced the sitting room, barely aware of the gorgeous cream and gold furnishings, carpet so thick her heels sank into it.

She'd been whisked off that afternoon to be pampered in readiness for the banquet—something she hadn't expected. And while there she'd had a selection of outfits for her to pick from. Too unsure to know whether or not she could refuse, she'd chosen the simplest gown. Deep green in colour, it was halter-necked, with a daringly low-cut back. She'd been returned to the suite and now, made-up and with her hair in an elaborate chignon, she felt like a veritable fashion doll.

And there was no sign of Kaden. Julia paced some more. Being dressed up like this made her intensely uncomfortable. She'd caught a glimpse of herself in the mirror and for a moment hadn't even recognised the image reflected back. Her eyes were huge and smoky grey, lashes long and very black. Her cheeks had two spots of red that had more to do with her emotions than with artifice.

The door suddenly clicked, and Julia whirled around to see Kaden striding in, adjusting a cufflink on his shirt. The breath literally left her throat for a moment. It was the first time she'd ever seen him in a tuxedo and he looked…stunning. It nearly made her forget why she was so incensed, but then he looked at her with that irritating non-expression. The irrational feeling of anger surged back.

She gestured to the dress. "I agreed to come with you to a wedding. I'm not your mistress, Kaden, and I don't appreciate being treated like one."

He put his hands in his pockets and looked her up and down, and then, as if he hadn't even heard her, he said, "I've never seen you look so beautiful."

To Julia's abject horror her mind emptied and she stood there, stupidly, as Kaden's black gaze fused with hers. She read the heat in its glowing depths. She'd always veered more towards being a tomboy, and had truly never felt especially *beautiful*. But now, here in this room, she did.

It made the bright spark of anger fade away, and she felt silly for her outburst. Of course Kaden didn't see her as his mistress. She couldn't be further removed from the kind of women he sought out.

She half gestured to the dress, avoiding Kaden's eye. "I didn't mean to sound ungrateful. It's a lovely dress, and the attention…wasn't all bad." She looked back up. "But I don't want you to get the wrong idea. I don't expect or even want this kind of treatment. I'm not like your other women. This…what's happening here…is not the same…"

He took his hands out of his pockets and came close. Julia stood her ground, but it was hard. Black eyes glittered down into hers. A muscle throbbed in his jaw and she saw how tightly Kaden was reining in some explosive emotion.

"No, you're not like my other women. You're completely different. Don't think I'm not aware of that. Now, let's go or we'll be late."

After a tense moment she finally moved. Kaden stood back and allowed Julia to precede him out of the room.

Feeling off-centre, he didn't touch her as they walked down the long corridor. She wasn't and hadn't ever been like any other woman he'd been with. It was only now that he was noticing the disturbing tendency he'd always had to judge the women he encountered against his first lover—noticing the faint disappointment he always felt when they proved themselves time and time again to be utterly different. Materialistic. Avaricious. *Less.*

He was used to being ecstatically received whenever he indulged a woman, and wondered if this was some ploy or game Julia was playing—affecting uninterest. But with a sinking feeling he knew it wasn't. Years ago she'd have laughed in his face if he'd so much as attempted to get her into a couture dress. She'd been happy in dusty jeans and shirts. That crazy safari sunhat.

There'd only been one moment when she'd worn a dress. When he'd presented her with a cream concoction of delicate lace and silk that he'd seen in a shop window and hadn't been able to resist. As dresses went, it hadn't been sophisticated at all, but Julia had put it on and paraded in front of him as shyly as a new bride. It had been the first and only time she'd worn a dress, and that had been the night that he'd realised just how deeply—Kaden shut the door on that unwanted thought that had come out of nowhere. His insides clenched so hard he could feel them cramp.

Breathing deep, he brought his focus back to the here and now. To the woman by his side who was blissfully unaware of his wayward thoughts. He was vitally aware of the smooth curve of Julia's bare back in the dress. The pale luminescence of her skin. And the vulnerable part of her neck, which was revealed thanks to her upswept hair.

The dim hum of the conversation of hundreds of people reached them as they rounded a corner. Kaden took Julia's arm in his hand and felt her tension. Good. He wanted her to be tense. And unsettled. And all the things he was. They walked across a wide open-air courtyard and pristine Hussein servants dressed all in white opened huge doors into the glorious main ballroom.

Julia had been in plenty of stately homes and castles on her travels, but this took her breath away. She'd never seen such opulence and wealth. The huge ballroom was astounding, with an enormous domed ceiling covered in murals, and immense columns which opened out onto the warm, evocatively dusky night.

Waiting to greet them were the Sultan and his new bride—Kaden's sister Samia. As they approached, Julia saw Samia's face light up at seeing Kaden. She'd blossomed from a painfully shy teenager into a beauty with great poise. She'd always had a strong bond with her older brother, being his only full sibling, daughter of their father's first beloved wife. Their father had married again, and Julia remembered Kaden's stepmother as a cold, disapproving woman. She'd gone on to have three daughters of her own, but no sons which, Kaden had once told Julia, made her extremely bitter and jealous of Kaden and Samia. Certainly Julia could remember avoiding her malevolent presence at all costs.

Samia transferred her look to her then, and Julia attempted a weak smile. Samia looked at her with a mixture of bewilderment and hostility. It confused Julia, because she'd imagined that Kaden's younger sister would barely remember her.

But she didn't have time to analyse it. Kaden gripped

her hand, and after a few perfunctory words dragged her into the throng. Still shaken by Samia's reaction, Julia asked, "Why did Samia look at me like that? I'm surprised she even recognised me."

Kaden sent her a dark glance that was impossible to comprehend and didn't answer. Instead he took two glasses of champagne from a passing waiter and handed her one. Raising his glass in a mocking salute, he said, "Here's to us."

He clinked his glass to Julia's and drank deeply. She couldn't stop an awful hollow feeing from spreading through her whole body. She sensed that he was regretting having brought her here. No doubt he would prefer the balm of a woman well versed in the ways of being a compliant and beautiful mistress. Suitably appreciative of all he had to offer. All Julia wanted to do was to get out of there and curl up somewhere comforting and safe.

Several people lined up then, to talk to Kaden, and Julia became little more than an accessory while they fawned and complimented him on the news that the vast Burquati oil fields were to be drilled. Once again Julia had a sense of how much had changed for Kaden since she'd known him.

Before long the crowd were trickling into another huge banquet room for dinner, and she and Kaden followed. He was deep in conversation with another man, speaking French.

During the interminable dinner Julia caught Samia's eyes a few times, and still couldn't understand the accusing look. Kaden was resolutely turned away from her, talking to the person on his other side, which left Julia trying to conduct a very awkward conversation with the man on her left, who was infinitely more interested in her cleavage and had not a word of English.

Kaden was acutely aware of Julia, and how close her thigh was to his under the table. He had to clench his fist to stop himself from reaching out and touching it, resting his hand at the apex of her thighs, where he could feel her heat.

He felt constricted. His chest was tight. It had been ever since he'd seen Samia's reaction to Julia. Samia was the chink in his armour. She was the only one who knew the dark place he'd gone to when Julia had left Burquat. It made him intensely uncomfortable to remember it. He reassured himself now, as he had then, that it had only been because he'd physically ached for her, his lust unquenched.

He knew he shouldn't be ignoring Julia like this. It was unconscionably rude. But he was actually afraid that if she looked at him she'd see something that he couldn't guard in his eyes. Samia's reaction had been like rubbing sandpaper over a wound, surprising in its vividness.

Assuring himself that it was nothing—just another trick of the mind where Julia was concerned—Kaden finally gave up trying to pretend to be interested in what his companion was saying, made an excuse, and resolutely ignored Samia's pointed looks in his direction. They were like little lashes of a whip.

He turned to Julia and could see from the line of her back that she was tense, that her jaw was gritted. Instinctively he put his hand around the back of her neck, and felt her tense even more in reaction. He moved his fingers in a massaging movement and she started to relax. Kaden had to hold back a smile at the way he sensed she resented it.

Immediately a sense of calm and peace washed over Kaden, and for once he didn't castigate himself or deny it. He gave himself up to it. The rawness subsided.

After what felt like an interminable moment Julia finally turned to look at him, and as his gaze met hers his body responded with predictable swiftness.

"Kaden...?"

He looked at her, and in that moment some indecipherable communication seemed to flow between them. Her eyes were huge, swirling with emotion, and Kaden couldn't find the will to disguise his own response. The room faded and the din of conversation became silent.

Julia wanted to ask Kaden to stop looking at her like that...as if they were nineteen again and he wanted to discover the secrets of her soul. But she couldn't open her mouth. She didn't want to break the moment.

The clatter of coffee and liqueurs being served finally seemed to break through the trancelike state, and in an abrupt move Kaden took his hand off her neck, reached for her hand and stood up.

Julia gasped and looked around. A couple of people had started to drift away from the table, but many still sat. Kaden tugged at her and she had no choice but to stand. People were looking.

"Kaden...what are you doing? It's not over yet."

His eyes were so black Julia felt as if she might drown in them for ever.

"It is for us. I can't sit beside you for another minute and not touch you."

And with that he pulled her in his wake as he strode away from the table. Before she knew what was happening they were outside the ballroom. She could barely catch her breath, and when she stumbled a little he turned and lifted her into his arms.

"Kaden!" she spluttered, as they passed servants who looked away diplomatically, as if they were used to seeing such occurrences all the time.

She couldn't deny the thrill of excitement firing up her blood. Kaden was acting like a marauding pirate. He carried her all the way back through a labyrinthine set of corridors to their room, and only once inside the door, which he kicked shut with his foot, did he let her down. He wasn't even breathing heavily. But Julia was, after being carried so close to his hard-muscled chest.

In the bedroom, he let her down on shaky legs. He pushed her up against the firmly shut door, crowding her against it and saying, "We'll have to endure enough pomp and ceremony over the next two days, but every spare minute will be spent in this room. *That's* the focus of this weekend."

The sheer carnality stamped on his face and the hint of desperation in his voice stopped Julia from thinking too deeply about the hurt that lanced her—as if for a moment there, when he'd been looking at her at the table, she'd got lost in a fantasy of things being different.

And then his urgency flowed through to her—the realisation that even now time was slipping out of their hands. Overcome with an emotion she refused to look at, she took his face in her hands and for the first time felt somewhat in control. Kaden was right. Focus on the now, the physical. Not on the past. Or on a future that would never exist.

"Well, what are you waiting for, then?" And she kissed him.

* * *

Some hours later, Kaden was standing by the open French doors of the bedroom. B'harani lay before him like a twinkling carpet of gems. Soaring minarets nestled alongside modern buildings, and he knew that this was what he wanted to create in Burquat too. He'd already started, but he had a long way to go.

He sighed deeply and glanced back at the woman asleep in the bed amongst tumbled sheets. She was on her back, the sheet barely covering her sex, breasts bare, arms flung out, cheeks flushed. Even now his body hardened in helpless response. He grimaced. He'd taken her up against the door, her legs wrapped around his waist, with no more finesse than a rutting animal. And yet she'd met him every step of the way, her body accepting him and spurring him to heights he'd not attained in years.

Since her.

It all came back to her—as if some sort of circle was in effect, bringing them helplessly back to the beginning and onwards like an unstoppable force.

Julia woke slowly, through layers and layers of sleep and delicious lethargy. With an effort she opened her eyes and saw the tall, formidable shape of Kaden leaning against the open doors which led out to a private terrace. He was looking at her steadily, no expression on his face.

Helpless emotion bubbled up within her—especially when she saw the vast star-filled Arabian sky behind him. She had so much she wanted to say, but the past was all around her, in her. The lines were blurring ominously.

Instinctively she put out a hand and said huskily, "Kaden…"

For a long moment he just stood there, arms crossed, trousers slung low on narrow hips, top button open. He was so beautiful. And then he gritted out, "Damn you, Julia."

He strode back into the room, all but ripped off his clothes and came down over her like an avenging dark angel. All the inarticulate words she wanted to say were stifled by Kaden's expert touch and quickly forgotten.

When Julia woke on Sunday morning she ached all over. But it was delicious. Kaden was not there, and she found a note on his pillow to inform her that he'd gone riding.

When she thought of how Samia had been looking at her for the past two days she felt guilty, and she had no idea why.

The previous day, evening and night had passed in a dizzying array of events and functions all leading up to the grand ceremony today, which would be held in front of hundreds of guests and the media.

With a sigh Julia got up, went to the bathroom and stepped into the shower. Once finished, and dressed in a robe with a towel around her damp hair, she stepped out onto the open terrace to see that breakfast had been left for her on a table. She grimaced at the dewy fresh rose in an exquisite glass vase. That was a touch Kaden wouldn't welcome.

All that existed between her and Kaden was this intense heat. They couldn't even seem to hold a coherent conversation before things became physical. And she didn't doubt that was exactly how Kaden wanted it.

Julia assured herself stoutly that that was just fine. She picked up a croissant and walked to the wall, from where she could see the stunning city of B'harani spread out before her.

Her heart swelled—not for this city in particular, but for this part of the world. If any city held her heart it was Burquat, high on its huge hill, with its ancient, dusty winding streets and mysterious souks. But the air here was similar, and the heat…

She heard a sound behind her and turned to see Kaden standing at the doors. Her heart leapt. He was dressed in faded jeans which clung to powerful thighs and a sweaty polo shirt, boots to his knees. Damp hair stuck to his forehead.

As she watched, he started to pull off his shirt with such sexy grace that she dropped the croissant and didn't even notice. How could she feel so wanton and hot, mere hours after—?

Kaden threw down his top and came to Julia, hemming her in against the wall with his arms. His mouth found and nuzzled her neck. He smelled of sweat and musk and sex.

Julia groaned and said, half despairingly, "Kaden…"

He pulled one shoulder of her robe down and kissed her damp skin. "You missed a bit here…I think we need to remedy that."

With that awesome strength he picked her up, and within minutes they were naked and in the shower.

Much later, when the daylight was tipping into dusk outside, Julia woke from a fitful sleep. She felt disorientated and a little dizzy, even though she was lying down. Flashes of the day came into her head: the lavish wedding ceremony in the ornate ceremonial hall, Samia looking pale and so young, her husband tall and dark and austere, reminding Julia of Kaden.

And then, after a token appearance at the celebration, Kaden pulling her away, bringing her back here, where once again passion had overtaken everything. Her body was still sensitive, so she couldn't have slept for long.

She heard a noise and turned her head to see Kaden sitting at a table in the corner of the palatial room, with his slim laptop open in front of him. That lock of hair was over his forehead, and he sipped from a cup of what she guessed was coffee.

There was something so domestic about the scene that Julia's heart lurched painfully. And she knew right then with painful clarity that she had to be one to walk away this time. She couldn't bear to stand before Kaden again and have him tell her it was over.

As if he could hear her thinking, he looked over. He was already half dressed, in black pants and a white shirt. His look was cool enough to make her shiver slightly, and he glanced at his watch. "We have to be ready in half an hour for the final banquet."

Julia shot up in the bed, clutching the sheet. "You should have woken me." With dismay she thought of her dress for this evening that was already in the wardrobe. It was another couture gown, and she was going to require time to repair the damage and restore herself to something approximating normality. If she could ever feel normal again.

Feeling absurdly grumpy, Julia marched into the bathroom and locked the door behind her.

Kaden sat back in the chair and frowned, looking at the tangled sheets of the bed. The truth was he'd felt so comfortable here in the room, with Julia sleeping in the bed just feet away, that he'd forgotten all about waking her. His skin prickled at that. He'd felt that way before… with her, but never with another woman. Even with his own wife he'd insisted on separate bedrooms and living quarters. He knew now that if the situation had been reversed and he'd been married to Julia it would have been anathema not to share space with her.

If he'd married Julia.

That all too disturbing thought drove him up out of his chair and to the phone. He picked it up and gave instructions to the person on the other end.

When Julia emerged from the bathroom there was a pretty young girl dressed all in white waiting for her. She said shyly, "My name is Nita. I'm here to help you get changed."

Too bemused even to wonder where Kaden had disappeared to, Julia let Nita help her, and within half an hour she was dressed and ready again. At precisely that moment Kaden reappeared at the bedroom door, resplendent in another tuxedo. He held out his arm for Julia, who took it silently.

This time her dress was a deep purple colour. A tightly ruched strapless bodice gave way to swirling floor-length silk which was covered in tiny crystals. The effect was like a shimmering cloud as Julia walked alongside Kaden.

She could feel the ever-present tension in his form beside her, and marvelled at the irony of the whole situation. She was arguably living every little girl's fantasy, here in this fairytale castle, yet with the bleakest of adult twists.

She had to end this tonight—before he did. Before he could see how helplessly entangled she'd already become again.

A few hours later, when the crowd had watched Sultan Sadiq lead his new wife from the ceremonial ballroom, Julia was exhausted, and more than relieved when Kaden took her hand to lead her from the room. Her traitorous blood was humming in anticipation as they neared the bedroom. But she forced ice into her veins.

When they reached the room she extricated her hand and went and stood apart from him. He was surveying her warily, and she realised just how little they'd really communicated all weekend—as if he had been deliberately trying to avoid any conversation or any kind of intimacy beyond sex. It galvanised her.

She hitched up her chin. "The couple I was talking to earlier are leaving Burquat tonight, on a private flight back to England. They've offered me a seat on the plane if I'm ready to go in an hour."

Julia was vaguely aware of tension coming into Kaden's form. "You can't wait until tomorrow morning, when I am going to take you home?"

She shook her head, almost dizzy with relief that she was taking control of things. That Kaden wasn't coming closer, scrambling her brain. "There's no need. I need to get back. I've got work this week. I've got a life, Kaden. I think it's best if we just say this is over, here and now. What's the point in dragging it out?"

Kaden was seeing a red mist over his vision. So many conflicting things were hitting him at once. No woman had ever walked away from him, for one thing. But a dented ego had never been his concern. It was Julia, standing there so poised and cool, as if ice wouldn't melt in her mouth. When only hours before she'd been raking his back with her nails and sobbing for him to release her from exquisite pleasure.

Jerkily Julia moved to the drawers and picked up what looked like a jewellery box. She was already gathering her things to start packing. Filled with something that felt scarily close to panic, Kaden took a step forward and noticed how skittishly she moved back. Her face had an incredibly vulnerable expression but he blocked it out, and it was only then that he noticed—at the same time as she did—that some jewellery had fallen from the box after her skittish move.

He watched as she bent to pick up the trinkets and then, as if in slow motion, something gold fell back to the floor. Before he even knew what he was doing he'd stepped forward and picked the piece up.

Julia stood up. Her heart had stopped beating. It was like watching a car crash in slow motion. Kaden straightened. The distinctive gold chain with its detail of a love-knot looked ridiculously delicate in his huge hand. He didn't even look at her.

"You still have it."

Julia didn't have the strength to berate herself for having brought it. She swallowed and said, far more huskily than she would have liked, "Yes, I still have it."

Even now her fingers itched to touch the tell—tale spot where it usually sat, and she clenched her hand into a fist. Kaden looked at her and his face was unreadable, those black eyes like fathomless wells.

"You always touch your throat…" He reached out his other hand and touched the base of her neck with a long finger. "Just here…"

Julia gulped, and could see his eyes track the movement. With dread in her veins and a tide of crimson rising upwards she could only stand still as Kaden carefully stepped closer and opened the necklace, placing it around her neck and closing it as deftly as he had the day he'd bought it for her.

She felt the weight of the knot settle into its familiar place, just below the hollow at her throat. Kaden took his hands away, but didn't move back. Julia couldn't meet his eyes. Mortified and horrifically exposed.

Kaden looked at it for a long moment, and then he stepped back. When she raised her eyes to his they were blacker than she'd ever seen them. His face was set in stark lines. "If you're sure you want to go home now, I'll see that Nita comes to help you."

Julia shook her head, feeling numb. She wasn't sure how to take Kaden's abrupt *volte face*, when moments ago he'd looked as if he was about to tip her back onto the bed and persuade her to stay in a very carnal way. Now he looked positively repulsed. It had to be the necklace. He was horrified that she still had it, and what that might mean. Memories, the sting of rejection—all rushed back.

"It's fine. I don't need help."

Kaden saw Julia's mouth move but didn't really hear what she was saying. All he could hear was a dull roaring in his head, the precursor to a pounding headache. And all he could see was that necklace. It seemed to be mocking him. He could still feel its imprint on his hand.

A tightness was spreading in his chest. He had to get out of there *now*. He backed away from Julia. Gathering force within him was the overwhelming sensation of sliding down a slippery slope with nothing to hold onto.

Julia watched the play of indecipherable expressions cross Kaden's face. She felt like going over and thumping him. She wanted to wring some sort of response out of him... But then she felt deflated. How could she wring a response out of someone who had no feelings?

She swallowed painfully. "I... It's been—"

She stopped as he cut her off. "Yes," he agreed grimly. "It has. Goodbye, Julia."

And with that he turned and was gone, and all Julia's flimsy control shattered at her feet—because she felt as if she'd just been rejected all over again.

Less than an hour later Kaden was in his own private plane, heading back to Burquat. He'd actually had a meeting lined up the following morning, with some of Sultan Sadiq's mining advisors, but had postponed it. The fact was he'd felt an overwhelming need to get as far away from B'harani as possible, as quickly as possible.

He looked down at his hand. It was actually shaking. All he could see, though, was that necklace, sitting in his hand, and then around Julia's neck. It was obviously the necklace she went to touch all the time. It hung in exactly that spot, and when he'd put it on she'd looked *guilty*.

The question was too incendiary to contemplate, but he couldn't help it: who would keep and wear a cheap gold necklace for twelve years? It was the only piece of jewellery, apart from his ex-wife's wedding rings, that he'd ever given to a woman, and he remembered the moment as if it was yesterday.

Kaden's mind shut down... He couldn't handle the implications of this.

He watched the B'harani desert roll out below him,

and instead of feeling a sense of peace he felt incredibly restless. His hands clenched to fists on his thighs, he didn't even see the air hostess take one look at his face and beat a hasty retreat.

Kaden assured himself that for the first time since he'd met Julia he was finally doing the right thing. Leaving her behind in his past. Where she belonged.

CHAPTER SEVEN

"You are definitely pregnant, Julia. And if the dates you've told me are correct I'd say you're almost three months gone—at the end of your first trimester."

Julia's kindly maternal doctor looked at her over her half-moon glasses,

"Why didn't you come to me sooner? You must have suspected something, and we both know your periods are like clockwork."

Julia barely heard her. Shock was like a wall between her and the words. Of course she'd suspected something for the last two months, but she'd buried her head in the sand and told herself that fate couldn't be so cruel—not after years of trying for a baby with her husband. Hence the reason why her doctor knew her so well.

But then the problem hadn't been on her side. It had been her husband's.

The doctor was looking at Julia expectantly, and she forced herself to focus. "I just... I couldn't believe what it might be."

Her doctor smiled wryly. "Well it's a baby, due in about six months if all goes well." She continued gently, "I take it that as you're divorced the father is...?"

"Not my ex-husband, no." Julia bit her lip. "The father

is someone I once knew, long ago. We met again recently…"

"Are you going to tell him?"

Julia looked at her friend. "To be honest? I don't know
yet…what I'm going to do."

The doctor's manner became more brisk. "Well, look,
first things first. I'll book you in for a scan, just to make
sure everything is progressing normally, and then we
can take it from there— OK?"

One month later

Kaden paced in his office. The ever-present simmering
emotions he'd been suppressing for about four months
were threatening to erupt. Julia was here. Outside his
office. Right now. She'd been waiting for over an hour.
He would never normally keep anyone waiting that long
but it was *Julia*, and she was here.

He ran a hand through his hair impatiently. What the
hell did she want? His heart beat fast. Did she want to
continue the affair? Had she spent the last months waking in the middle of the night too? Aching all over? He
felt clammy. Would she be wearing that necklace?

He clenched a fist. Dammit. He'd hoped that by now
he'd have chosen a wife and be in the middle of wedding
preparations, but despite his aides' best efforts every
potential candidate he'd met had had something wrong
with her. One was too forward, another too meek, too
sullen, too avaricious, too fake… The list was endless.

And now he couldn't ignore the fact that Julia
Somerton had come to Burquat, going unnoticed on the
flight lists because of her married name. In Burquat all

repeat visitors were noted. She'd made her way to the castle and now she was sitting outside his door.

His internal phone rang and he stalked to his desk to pick it up. His secretary said, "Sire, I'm sorry to bother you, but Dr Somerton is still here. I think you should see her now. I'm a little concerned—"

Kaden cut her off abruptly, "Send her in."

Julia finally got the nod from Kaden's secretary, who was dressed not in traditional garb, as everyone used to be when she'd been here last, but in a smart trouser suit, with a fashionable scarf covering her hair. She'd been solicitous and charming to Julia, but Julia had noticed her frequent and concerned looks and wondered if she really looked so tired and dusty.

Her flight from London had left at the crack of dawn, and the journey from Burquat airport in a bone-rattling taxi with no air-conditioning had left her feeling bruised and battered. Thankfully, though, the incessant morning sickness she'd been suffering from had finally abated in the last month, and she felt strong enough to make the journey. Physically at least. Mentally and emotionally was another story altogether.

She knew that she'd lost weight, thanks to the more or less constant morning sickness, and she was pale. She couldn't even drum up the energy to care too much. She wasn't coming here to seduce Kaden. When he'd said that clipped and cold goodbye in B'harani after seeing the necklace it couldn't have been more obvious that he'd been horrified. She'd watched his physical reaction and known that any desire had died a death there and then.

Julia stopped herself from touching her neck now, and reminded herself that the necklace was safely back in the UK. She stood up and walked to the door. The secretary had told her to leave her suitcase by her desk. Julia hadn't even booked into a hotel yet, but she'd worry about that after.

The door swung open and she took a deep breath and stepped into Kaden's office. The early evening sunlight was in her face, so as the door shut behind her all she could see was the formidable outline of Kaden's shape.

She put a hand up to shade her eyes and tried to ignore the wave of *déjà-vu* that almost threatened to knock her out. The last time she'd been in this room—

"To what do I owe the pleasure, Julia?"

So cool.

Julia forced herself to breathe deep and focus on getting the words out. "I came because I have to tell you something."

Kaden finally stepped forward and blocked the light, so now Julia could see him. She felt her breath stop at being faced with his sheer male beauty again. And also because he had a beard—albeit a small one. His hair was longer too. He looked altogether wild and untamed in traditional robes, and her heart took up an unsteady rhythm.

Stupidly she asked, "Why do you have a beard?"

He put up a hand to touch it, almost as if he'd forgotten about it, and bit out, "I've spent the last ten days in the desert, meeting Bedouin leaders and councils. It's a custom among them to let their beards grow, so whenever I go I do the same. I haven't had time to shave yet. I just got back this morning."

Julia found this unexpected image of him so compelling that her throat dried. He was intensely masculine anyway, but like this... Her blood grew hot even as she looked at him. And he was looking at *her* as if she'd just slithered out from under a rock.

He quirked a brow. "Surely you haven't come all this way to question me on my shaving habits?"

A wave of weakness came over her then, and Julia realised she hadn't eaten since a soggy breakfast on the plane—hours ago. She cursed herself. She had to be more careful. But in fact, whether fatigue or hunger, whatever it was created a welcome cushion of numbness around her.

She looked at Kaden again and willed herself to be strong, straightening her spine. "No, I've come for another reason. The truth is that I have some news, and it affects both of us." She continued in a rush, before she could lose her nerve. "I'm pregnant, Kaden. With your baby... Well, actually, the thing is, it's not just one baby. If it was I might not have come all this way. But you see, I'm almost four months pregnant with twins...and the thought of two babies was a bit much to deal with on my own...and I know I could have rung, but I tried a few times...but that's when you must have been away in the desert and I didn't want to leave a message..."

Kaden lifted a hand. He'd gone very still and pale beneath his tan. "Pregnant? Twins?"

Julia nodded, hating herself for babbling like that. She'd wanted to be ultra-calm and collected, but now she was in front of Kaden she felt as if she was nineteen again. She wanted to run into his chest and have him hold her—but that scenario was about as likely as a sudden snow shower inside the palace.

"You look like you've *lost* weight—not as if you're pregnant." He sounded almost accusing.

Julia stifled a slightly hysterical laugh when she

thought of the sizeable bump under her loose top. She was already wearing stretch-waisted jeans.

His hand dropped. His eyes narrowed. He looked even wilder now. "And you say these babies are mine?"

At that insulting insinuation Julia actually swayed on her feet. Kaden came around his desk so fast it made her feel even dizzier. She put out a hand, as if that could stop him.

"Do you really think I came all this way for the good of my health? Just to pass off some other man's babies as yours?" Her voice rang with bitterness. "Believe me, I've been actuely aware of the awful irony of this situation for months of sleepless nights now. One baby I could have coped with. I wasn't even sure if I was going to tell you. But two babies…"

Kaden's eyes raked her from head to toe. His lip practically curled. "I used protection."

Julia's chin went up. "There is a failure rate, and clearly it failed."

The enormity of what Julia was saying, and to whom hit her then like a ton weight. Two babies. Who would be unwanted and unloved by their father. It was so much the opposite of what she'd once dreamt of with this man that the pain lanced her like a sharp knife right through the heart.

Everything was becoming indistinct and awfully blurry. That numbness was spreading. But in the face of his overwhelmingly hostile response Julia had to assert her independence. She had a horror of him assuming she'd come for a hand-out.

Faintly, Julia tried to force oxygen to her brain and to be articulate. "These are your babies, Kaden, whether you like it or not. And now that I've told you I'll leave.

I don't expect anything from you. I just wanted you to know that they exist...or will exist in about five months, all being well."

She turned on her heel, but it seemed to take an awful long time—as if everything had gone into slow motion. And then, instead of getting closer to the door, she seemed to be moving further and further away. With a cry of dismay as black edges appeared on her peripheral vision, Julia felt herself falling down and down. Only faintly did she hear a stricken "*Julia!*" and feel something warm and strong cushion her back before the blackness sucked her down completely.

"Why is she taking so long to come round?" Kaden asked the wizened palace doctor impatiently. He didn't like the metallic taste of fear in his mouth. "Shouldn't we go straight to the hospital? I told you she's pregnant."

The doctor was unflappable and kept his fingers on Julia's wrist, checking her pulse. Kaden had laid her down on the couch in his office before bellowing for his secretary to call Dr Assan. She'd been so limp and lifeless, her cheeks paler than he'd ever seen, dark bruises under her eyes.

And he'd kept her waiting all that time—after a long journey. She was pregnant. His conscience stung him hard.

Dr Assan looked at Kaden pacing near to him. "We're just waiting for the paramedics to come and then she will be taken to the hospital for a full examination. But as far as I can tell she is fine—probably just tired and dehydrated. You said she flew from England today?"

"Yes—yes, I did," Kaden agreed irritably. He was used to things happening quickly, and even though it was only a couple of minutes since she'd collapsed time seemed to have slowed down to the pace of a snail.

With a granite-like weight in his chest, he cursed himself for lashing out just now and insinuating that he might not be the father. Of *course* he believed her when she said the babies were his. She'd looked shell-shocked, not avaricious. He knew with a bone-deep certainty that she wasn't mercenary enough to make a false claim of paternity.

In five months' time he would have a ready-made family.

The thought was overwhelming.

Just then a knock came to the door, and in the flurry of activity Kaden concentrated on what they were doing to Julia. When they produced a stretcher to carry her out to the ambulance Kaden reacted to a surge of something primal, and waded in and picked her up into his arms himself, ignoring the paramedics.

Dr Assan motioned for them to follow Kaden as he strode out with Julia in his arms. Kaden was oblivious to the sea of people hurrying after him. He was only aware of the swell of Julia's pregnant belly against his chest, and something powerful rose up within him. His gut clenched tight. In his arms Julia stirred, but he didn't even break his stride as he looked down to see those pools of grey on him. Dazed and confused.

For a moment he forgot everything and reacted only to those eyes, and to the sensation of relief rushing through him. "Don't worry, you're safe, and I'm going to take care of you."

Julia was warm and secure in a dark place. But someone kept prodding her and shining a light in her eyes.

Instinctively she moved away from the light, but it kept following her until eventually she opened her eyes, and then it blinded her. She squeezed her eyes shut again, but heard a kindly voice saying, "Julia, you need to wake up now. You've given us all quite a fright."

In her hazy consciousness she heard an echo of Kaden's voice. *Don't worry...I'm going to take care of you...*

Without really knowing where she was or what was happening, she spoke from a place of urgent instinctive need, "Kaden...where is Kaden?"

A moment of silence, and then she felt his presence. A hand on hers. The relief was overwhelming. "I'm right here."

And at his touch and his voice it all came back. She wasn't nineteen any more. She was thirty-two, and pregnant with his babies. And he didn't want her—or them. Instantly she was cold and wide awake. Her eyes opened to see Kaden towering over her where she lay in a hospital bed, austere and remote in his robes and with that beard. She pulled her hand away, knowing that he must be hating her so much right now.

She looked to the man who had to be the doctor. "What happened?"

"You're severely dehydrated and fatigued. You'll need to be supervised on a drip for at least twenty-four hours. But apart from that everything is fine, and your babies are fine too. You just need rest and sustenance."

Julia immediately put a hand to the swell of her stomach and felt Kaden take a step back from the bed. She couldn't bear to look at him and see the censure in his eyes. The disgust he must feel that she was here, with this unwelcome news. The last woman in the world he would have picked to be the mother of his children.

She wondered again if she should have come, and her own doctor's words came back to her. "Julia, twins are a monumental task for anyone to take on board. You should not do this by yourself. You *must* include the father."

Kaden's doctor patted her hand and said, "I'll leave you alone now to rest."

He left the room and the silence was oppressive. Kaden walked around so that he was in Julia's line of vision. She felt acutely vulnerable, lying on the bed in a hospital robe.

"Where are my things?" she asked, as if that would postpone the painful conversation that was due.

"Your bag is still with my secretary and your clothes are here."

Julia bit her lip. "I can't believe I collapsed like that. I had no idea—"

He exploded. "How could you not have known you were so weak and dehydrated? For God's sake, you're pregnant. Are you not taking care of yourself?"

Julia could actually feel any colour she'd regained drain from her face. She'd known Kaden must be angry, but to see it like this....

He cursed and ran a hand through his unkempt hair. Somehow it only had the effect of making him look even more gorgeous. His black eyes came back to her, and to Julia's utter shock he looked contrite.

"I'm sorry. I had no right to speak to you like that. This has all been a bit of a shock...to say the least."

Julia's heart thumped. "I'm sorry that I couldn't warn you first. It just seemed too huge to send via text..." She blushed. "I don't even have your mobile number...and I didn't think it appropriate to leave a message with your aides."

His eyes narrowed on her face. "You said if it hadn't been twins you might not have told me?"

Julia avoided his eye guiltily, fingers plucking at the bedspread. "I don't know what I would have done, to be honest. It was pretty clear at our last meeting that neither one of us wanted to see each other again."

His mouth tightened. "Yes...but once a baby is involved...he or she...they are my heirs. Part of the royal Burquati dynasty. If you had kept my child from me I would never have forgiven you."

Julia looked at him, curling inwards at his censure. "I'm sure I would have told you about the baby, even though I know a lasting reminder of our...our meeting again was the last thing you wanted or expected."

Kaden's eyes flashed. For a long moment he didn't speak, and then he said, "That's beside the point now. We'll just have to make this work."

Julia's eyes narrowed on Kaden as a shiver of foreboding went down her spin. "What do you mean?"

"What I mean, Julia, is that we will be getting married. As soon as possible."

Kaden hadn't even realised he was thinking of such a thing until the words came out of his mouth, but to his utter surprise he felt a wave of equanimity wash over him for the first time in months.

Julia just looked at Kaden where he stood at the foot of the bed. Dominating. Powerful. Implacable. Inevitability and a sense of fatalism made her feel even weaker even as she protested shakily, "Don't be ridiculous, Kaden. We don't have to get married just because I'm having your baby."

He folded his arms, and corrected her. "*Babies*. And, yes, we do."

"But…" Julia's mind was feeling foggy again. She was glad she was lying down. "The people won't accept me as your wife…"

His mouth tightened. "They're conservative. It might take a while for them to accept you, but they will have no choice. You will be my sheikha—the mother of my children."

Julia wondered how it could be possible for her to feel dizzy when she was lying down, but the room was spinning and those black edges were creeping back. She heard Kaden swear again, and he moved towards her, but by the time he'd reached her she'd slipped back down into the comforting numbness of the black place.

One week later

"You are much improved, my dear. You should get out and enjoy some of the sunshine. Sit in the garden, breathe the fresh air. I'll go and get Jasmine to come and help you."

Julia smiled at the kindly Dr Assan and watched him leave. He'd been on standby since she'd returned to the palace from the hospital nearly four days before, and had been checking up on her at regular intervals.

For the last few days all she'd done was eat and sleep. And tried to block out Kaden's proposal—if she could even call it that. He hadn't mentioned it again. He'd come in and out of her bedroom and not said much at all, usually just looked at her broodingly.

Julia sighed deeply now and sat up. Her room was stupendously luxurious. Kaden had obviously had the palace redecorated in the intervening years, because before it had always had a very rustic and ascetic feel. Now, though, it might have come straight from the pages of an interior design magazine.

It hadn't completely lost that rustic feel. For instance it didn't share the de luxe opulence of the Hussein Castle in B'harani. But it was just as impressive. The palace itself looked as if it had been carved out of the hill it stood on, soaring majestically over the small city. Vast courtyards opened out into colourful gardens, where peacocks picked their way over glittering mosaics.

The interior stone floors were minimalist, but covered in the most exquisitely ornate rugs. The walls were largely bare, apart from the occasional silk wall hanging or flaming lantern. Windows were huge and open, with elaborate arches framing stunning views of the city.

Julia had a suite of rooms comprising a bedroom, bathroom and sitting room. With every mod-con and audio visual requirement cleverly tucked away so as not to ruin the authentic feel.

Outside the French doors of her sitting room lay a private courtyard filled with flowers. There was a pond, and a low wall which overlooked the ancient hilly city. In the near distance could be seen the blue line of the Persian Gulf. Seagulls wheeled over head, and the scent of the sea was never far away.

Julia felt incredibly emotional whenever she looked out over the city. From the moment she'd first come to Burquat the country and its people had resonated deep within her. She felt at home here. Or she had until that night—

"Dr Somerton? I'll help you get ready to go outside."

Julia glanced around from where she'd been sitting on the edge of the bed to see Jasmine, the pretty young girl who'd been helping her every day. She knew she'd only worry Dr Assan if she didn't go out, and she craved some air, so she smiled and let Jasmine help her.

Clothes had materialised one morning—beautiful kaftans and loose-fitting trousers to wear underneath—and Jasmine laid out a set now, in dark blue. They were comfortable and easy to wear in the heat—especially now that her bump seemed to be growing bigger by the day. It was as if her coming to Burquat had precipitated a growth spurt.

The palace had many gardens, but Julia's favourite so far was the orchard garden, filled with fruit-bearing trees. Branches were laden with plums and figs, and a river ran through the bottom of the garden, out of the palace grounds and down into the city. It was peaceful and idyllic.

Jasmine left her alone to walk there after showing her where a table and chair had been set up for her to rest in the shade. Julia couldn't believe how kind everyone was being to her. Certainly the oppressive atmosphere she remembered from Kaden's father's time had lifted, and she had to wonder if that was because Kaden's stepmother had also died, and some of the older, more austere aides were no longer part of Kaden's retinue.

She sat down and took a sip of fresh iced lemonade, savouring the tart, refreshing bite.

"I hope you don't mind if I join you."

It wasn't a question. Julia looked up to see Kaden standing nearby, and her belly automatically clenched. He'd shaved off his beard and had a haircut, but he looked no less wild or uncultivated despite the custom-made suit he now wore. He alternated between western and traditional dress easily.

She shook her head. As if by magic a man appeared with another chair, and through the trees some distance away Julia could see a man in a suit with an earpiece, watching over his precious Emir.

He sat down, his huge body dwarfing the chair, and helped himself to some lemonade. "You're looking much better."

Julia fought not to blush under Kaden's assessing gaze as it swept down over her body, and wished she'd put her hair up and some make—up on. Then she remembered how quick he'd been to let her go in B'harani and looked away, afraid he might see something of her emotions. Once again she felt humiliated heat rise at remembering that he'd seen the necklace.

"I'm feeling much better, thank you. All of your staff have been so kind. I should be well enough to return home soon. I'll have to organise a plane ticket back to the UK."

He shook his head. "You're not going home, Julia. I'm already arranging to have your belongings packed up and sent here. We can rent out your house in London while you decide what you want to do with it."

Julia looked at Kaden and her mouth opened. Nothing came out.

He leaned forward, his face grim. "We are getting married, Julia. Next week. Your life is here now—with me."

Panic bloomed in her gut, but it had more to do with the prospect of a lifetime facing Kaden's cool censure than the prospect of a lifetime as his wife. "You can't keep me here if I decide I want to go home. That would be kidnap."

"It won't be kidnap because you'll be staying of your own free will. You know it's the right thing to do."

Julia reacted. "Is it really the right thing to agree to a marriage just for convenience's sake?" She laughed a little wildly. "I've already been through one unhappy marriage. I'm not about to jump head-first into another one."

Kaden was intent, his face stark. "This isn't about just you—or me. It's about the two babies you are carrying. And it's about the fact that everyone knows you're here and that we were once lovers. The news of your pregnancy will soon filter out, and I want us to be married before that happens. For your sake and our babies' sakes as much as mine."

Our babies. Her eyes were wide. She felt control of her own existence slipping out of her grasp. She knew she must have gone pale again, but at least she felt stronger now.

As much as she didn't want to admit it, his words resonated within her on a practical level—bringing up two children on her own would be next to impossible with no familial support to speak of. Both her adoptive parents had died some years previously. Her divorce had wiped out any savings and a meagre inheritance. How could she afford childcare for two children unless she worked like a demon? And what kind of a life would that be for her children?

But Kaden's words also impacted on her at a much deeper and more visceral level. Growing up knowing she was adopted had bred within Julia an abiding need to create her own family. To have children and give them the assurance of their lineage and background that she'd never had. Her adoptive parents had loved her, of course… But she'd never really got over the stain of being unwanted by her birth mother and father. Irrationally she felt it was a reflection on *her*, something *she'd* done. And she had carried it down through the years to make what had happened with Kaden so much more devastating. But he was the last person she could confide in about this…

The haunting call of the *muezzin* started up in the city nearby and it tugged on her heart. She'd once fantasised about living here for ever with Kaden, but this was like a nightmare version of that dream.

As if sensing her turmoil, Kaden came out of his chair and down on one knee beside Julia. He took her hand in his. For a hysterical moment she thought he was going to propose to her, but then he said, "You said it yourself when you came here—two babies change everything. I won't allow them to be brought up on another continent when their heritage is here, in this country. It's *two* babies, Julia. How can you even hope to cope with that on your own? They deserve to have two parents, a secure home and grounding. I can provide that. They will have roles to fulfil in this country—one of them will be the next Emir, or Queen of Burquat. Who knows? They might even rule together…"

Julia moved back in her seat. The thought of him seeing how his touch affected her was terrifying. "They also deserve to have two parents who love one another."

Kaden's face became cynical as he dropped her hand and spat out, "*Love*? You speak of fairytales that don't exist. We will make this work, Julia, because we have to. We don't need love."

She saw the conflict in his eyes and on his face. His mouth was a thin line.

He stood up, instantly tall and intimidating. "I'll do whatever I have to to make this work. You know this is the only way. I will be a good husband to you, Julia. I will support you and respect you." A flash of heat sparked between them. "And I will be faithful to you."

A week later Julia looked at herself in the floor-length mirror in her dressing room. The dawn light hadn't even broken outside yet. According to Burquati tradition, they would exchange vows and rings in a simple civil ceremony as dawn broke.

At any other time Julia would have found the prospect impossibly romantic. As it was all she could think about was Kaden's grim avowal: "*I'll do whatever I have to to make this work.*"

She was wearing an ivory gown, long-sleeved and modest, but it clung to every curve and moved sinuously when she walked. Thankfully the heavy material skimmed over her bump, so it wasn't too glaringly obvious. A lace veil was pinned low on the back of her head, and Jasmine had coiled her hair into a loose chignon. She wore pearl drop earrings, and Kaden had presented her with a stunning princess cut diamond ring set in old gold the day before, telling her it had been his mother's engagement ring, to be kept for his own bride.

The thought of wearing a ring that his first wife had also worn made her feel sullied somehow, but she hadn't had the nerve to say anything to a closed-off and taciturn Kaden. It couldn't be clearer that he was viewing this marriage as a kind of penance.

If she was stronger… Julia sighed. It was more than

strength she needed to resist the will of Kaden. And deep within her she had to admit to a feeling of security at knowing that at least her babies would live lives free of shadows and doubts. She wasn't even going to admit to another much more personal and illicit feeling…of peace. Julia quickly diverted her thoughts away from *that* dangerous area.

She thought of the whirlwind it had been since she'd tacitly agreed to this marriage. And of the very muted fanfare that had greeted the public announcement a few days ago. At dinner on the evening their nuptials had been announced, Julia had voiced her building concern to Kaden; the reality of what might be expected of her had started sinking in. "Wasn't your mother half-English? The people will be used to a foreign Sheikha, won't they?"

Kaden had avoided Julia's eye, and that had made her instantly nervous. "Unfortunately the track record of Sheikhas here hasn't been good since my mother died. Both my wife and my stepmother never really connected with the people. As for my mother… They accepted her, yes…after a rocky start. The truth is that my father went against his own father's wishes to marry for love. The only reason he was allowed to marry my mother was because she came from a lineage on her father's side that went back as far as our own."

He'd looked at her then, with a carefully veiled expression. "It took the people some time to accept her, but they did, and when she died they were just as devastated as my father. He never came to terms with her death during Samia's childbirth. It changed him…made him withdraw and become more cynical… He blamed himself for having pursued his own selfish desires in bringing her here."

Julia had protested. "But it was just an awful tragedy."

Kaden had abruptly changed the conversation then.

Julia had hardly slept since that night, more and more aware of how hard it was likely to be for her to be accepted by the Burquati people, and wondering how far Kaden was prepared to test his people's limits of acceptance to keep his heirs safe—and here.

CHAPTER EIGHT

KADEN paced back and forth in the huge ceremonial ballroom of the palace. He was dressed in the royal Burquati military uniform. His chief aides and the officiator for the wedding ceremony waited patiently. He looked out of the window for the umpteenth time and saw the faint pink trails in the clear sky that heralded the dawn breaking. The thought of how delicate Julia had looked at dinner the previous evening. She'd hardly said a word, and her eyes had been huge, full of shadows, with the faintest purple smudges underneath.

He bit back a curse, hating the urgency rushing through his blood that had nothing to do with protocol and much to do with his disturbing need to see Julia.

He hadn't felt like this on his first wedding day. He'd been battling an almost dread feeling of suffocation that day. But since his marriage had ended he'd put that down to a presentiment of what had happened with his wife, and nothing to do with the lingering memory of another woman.

A sound came from the other end of the room and Kaden turned. His mind was emptied of all thought. Julia was a vision in ivory edged with pale gold as she walked towards him, with Jasmine holding her dress behind her. Her face was obscured by a long veil, and his eyes dropped to where the swell of her belly told the story of why they were getting married.

Something so fierce and primal gripped him in that moment that he had to clench his jaw and fists to stop shaking with it as Julia came to a stop just inches away. She was looking down, and Kaden longed to tell everyone to leave so that he could pull back the veil and tip her face up to his.

Instead he reached for her hand and lifted it up, bringing it to his mouth. Her head lifted and he could see the shape of her face, the flash of grey eyes, as he kissed her palm. Her perfume was soft and delicate, winding around him like a silken tie, bringing with it evocative memories and whispers of the past.

In that moment he hated her for coming back into his life, for reawakening a part of himself that he'd thought buried for ever. The only part of him that had ever been vulnerable, and the only part of him that had believed a different future was possible for him. It hadn't been.

With Julia's hand still in his he turned to the officiator and said curtly, "Let's get started."

What felt like aeons later Julia was sitting beside Kaden at the massive dining table and her face felt as if it was frozen in a rictus grin. Her heart hurt. From the moment Kaden had said, *"Let's get started"* earlier, he'd been curt to the point of dismissal.

She dreaded to think what the photographs would look like—Kaden tall and stern, and her like a rabbit in the headlights. Only a few of months ago she'd been independent and strong, living her life, and now she'd morphed into someone she barely recognised. All because of this man coming back into her life like a tornado.

A small voice mocked her: *she'd been with him every step of the way.*

Julia straightened her spine. She wasn't going to let Kaden ignore her like this. She turned towards him, where he sat beside her. He was looking out over the sea of some five hundred guests with a brooding expression. She knew none of them except for his three youngest sisters, who had travelled from their schools and colleges for the weekend. Samia and her husband had been unable to attend, and Julia had felt a little relieved, not sure if she could take Samia's hostility again.

"Kaden?"

He turned, and Julia sucked in a shocked breath when she saw the look of pure bleakness on his face. But in an instant it was gone, and replaced with something she thought she'd never see again. *Heat.* He took one of her hands and brought it to his mouth. His touch sent her pulse skyrocketing and a flood of heat between her legs.

She tried to pull her hand back, seriously confused, forgetting what she'd wanted to say in the first place. "Kaden…?"

"Yes, *habiba*?

She felt very shaky all of a sudden. "Why are you looking at me like that?"

He arched a brow. "Is this not how a man is supposed to look at his wife?"

Feeling sickened, Julia wrenched her hand free from his. He was faking it. Of course. In front of his guests.

Julia muttered something about the bathroom and got up, barely noticing Kaden's frowning look as she hurried away, head down.

Kaden watched Julia walk away, eyes glued to the graceful lines of her body in the stunning dress. The veil was long gone, and her hair was coiled at the nape of her neck. She was like a warmly glowing pearl against this backdrop. And for a moment, before she'd called him, he'd been drawn back into the memory of their time in the desert just before everything had changed.

He'd once dreamed of exactly this moment—having Julia by his side as his Queen, his heart full to bursting with pride and love... And then she'd called his name and he'd realised that it wasn't like the dream. That dream had existed in the mind of a foolishly romantic young man who hadn't known any better. *This* was reality, and reality was a long way from any dream.

Cursing himself, he could still feel desire like a tight coil in his body. A desire he'd curbed for too long. Kaden threw down his napkin and stood up. They'd had speeches and ceremonial toasts. Everyone now expected the Emir to take his leave with his wife. Striding out of the room, servants scurrying in his wake, Kaden felt his blood growing hotter by the second.

Julia had made her way out of the crowded room feeling stifled and extremely emotional. Jasmine had appeared as if from nowhere to guide her back to her rooms. She still didn't even know her own way around the palace!

When Jasmine showed her into the suite it took a minute before she realised that the distinctively masculine furnishings weren't familiar. She turned to Jasmine, who was waiting patiently for instructions.

"These aren't my rooms."

Jasmine inclined her head deferentially. "Sheikh

Kaden told me to move your things in here. You will be sharing his rooms from now on."

Julia's heart fluttered in her chest. She wasn't sure what Kaden was playing at, but she told Jasmine she wouldn't need her further. When the girl had left, emotion started rising again, and blindly Julia made her way out to Kaden's outdoor terrace. Much grander than her own.

It was dusk, and the call of an exotic bird pierced the air as Julia gripped the wall and looked out over Burquat. She could see people coming and going about their business far below, a line of blue which indicated the sea. She smelled the tang of salty air.

And all Julia could think of was how far Kaden was willing to go to make sure everyone believed he desired his wife, and how the immense crowd of guests had looked at her warily, with few smiles. An overwhelming feeling of aloneness washed over her. She put a hand to her bump and thought of her babies. *They* would be protected from this awful feeling of isolation. But she couldn't help, for one weak and self—indulgent moment, feeling sorry for herself. And she couldn't help the tears springing into her eyes and overflowing.

Kaden came into his rooms silently, and immediately saw Julia standing outside. The line of her back looked incredibly slim and tense, and the coil of her hair was shining in the dusky light. A curious feeling of peace mixed with desire rushed through his veins.

He moved forward and saw that Julia heard him. She tensed even more, and didn't turn around. Irritation prickled over his skin. "Julia?"

Julia was frantically swallowing and trying to blink back tears, her cheeks stinging. The thought of Kaden witnessing her turmoil was too much, but she heard him come closer, and then his hands came onto her shoulders and he was turning her around.

She looked down in a desperate bid to hide, but he tipped her chin up. She looked at him almost defiantly through the sheen of tears. He frowned, eyes roving over her face. "You're crying."

Kaden was not prepared for the blow he felt to his solar plexus. Julia's face was pale and blotchy, wet with tears. Eyes swimming, dark pools of grey. Her mouth trembling.

"It's nothing," she said huskily, lifting a hand to wipe at her cheek.

Kaden took her hand away and cupped her face. His chest felt so constricted he could hardly breathe. His thumbs wiped away the lingering tears.

"What is it?"

Julia bit her lip, clearly fighting for control. "It's just all…a bit much. Finding out about my pregnancy, coming here…my life changing overnight."

A solid mass of something dark settled into Kaden's chest. Clearly this was not what she'd envisaged for herself. He felt the sting of guilt. He'd seduced her. And changed their lives.

"Julia…you will not want for anything ever again. You or our babies. You can be happy here."

She gave a half-strangled laugh. "When your people look at me as if I'm about to do something scandalous?"

He grimaced. "They just need time, that's all. There's been so much change in Burquat…my divorce…"

Julia was finding it hard to breathe with Kaden so close and holding her face. She couldn't bear for him to see her desire on top of this. She tried to pull his hands down but they were immovable. She looked into his eyes. "Kaden…it's OK. You don't have to pretend here. No one is watching. And I don't expect to share your rooms. I'll go back to my own."

"Pretend what?"

Julia avoided his gaze. "Pretend to…want me."

Kaden frowned. Pretend to want her? Could she not feel how on fire he was for her? And then the notion that perhaps she didn't want *him* sent something cold to his gut. He moved his hands and took her wrists. He could feel the hammering of her pulse. A sigh of relief went through him.

"Julia, look at me."

With obvious reluctance she lifted her head. Her eyes were clear now, but no less troubled.

"What on earth made you think that I didn't want you?"

Now she frowned, a flush coming into her cheeks. "That last night in B'harani…you were so quick to leave…" She stopped when she thought of his reaction to the necklace, and then said hurriedly, "Not that I wanted it to go on. I was happy for it to be over. But I just thought…"

"That I didn't desire you any more?"

She nodded, and Kaden moved close to her again, lifting her hands and trapping them against his chest, where she would feel the thundering beat of his heart. Standing so close to her like this was exquisite torture. A deep contentment flowed through him that he wasn't even aware of. He thought of the necklace then, of how seeing it had made him feel. But instead of dousing his desire, or making him want to flee, it actually made him feel even hotter.

Julia's cheeks flushed even more when Kaden moved so close that his erection pressed against her lower belly. Sensation exploded behind his eyes, through his body, and he had to bite back a groan. He said throatily, "Does that feel like the response of a man who doesn't desire you?"

He marvelled. How could she not know? He felt as if every time he looked at her she must see the extent of his hunger. She was so different from any other woman he'd known. He'd almost forgotten that a woman like her could exist, and had a fleeting image of how bleak his life would have been if he'd not met her again.

Julia's eyes dropped to Kaden's mouth. She was transfixed. Almost without realising what she was doing, she extricated her hand from his grip and reached up to trace the sensuous line of his lips.

Kaden's hand went around the back of her neck, under the heavy fall of her hair, massaging the tender skin and muscles. His other hand was on her waist, big and possessive. Her breathing was already coming quickly, and she was telling herself to try and stay clear...but it was impossible.

Kaden dropped his head to hers. They were so close now that his breath feathered along her mouth. "I've never wanted another woman the way I want you."

Julia looked into his eyes and saw the flame in their depths. She reached up and pressed her mouth to his softly, chastely. For a moment he did nothing, and then with an urgency that made her blood exult in her veins he brought her even closer and fused his mouth to hers, opening her up to him so that his tongue could explore and seek a deeper intimacy.

Julia's hands and arms wound around Kaden's neck,

fingers tangling in the silky hair brushing his collar. She could feel the swell of her belly pressing into him, the stab of his erection against her, and something deeply feminine and primal burned within her. This was *her* man.

Perhaps their desire was the one pure, true thing between them? Perhaps they could build on this? Perhaps one day the fact that he'd rejected her once would fade away?

All of these thoughts and other incoherent ones raced through her head in time with her heart, but she just wanted to lose herself in the release only he could give.

He drew back and took in a deep, ragged breath, eyes looking wild. Julia's mouth was burning.

"Wait... I want you so badly, Julia... But can we? I mean, is it safe?"

For a moment she didn't understand what he was saying, and then she felt him place a hand to her belly. Something inside her melted even more. Blushing, because she was aware of the rampant need inside her, she said, "Dr Assan told me that it would be OK if we wanted to...you know..."

Kaden clamped her face in his hands and said, "Thank God."

And then they were kissing again, and that helpless emotion was bubbling up within Julia. There was a desperation about their kiss, as if they'd been separated for years. As if something had broken open.

He broke the kiss only to lift her up into his arms and carry her into the dimly lit bedroom, with its huge king-size bed. Julia kept her eyes on Kaden, as if to look away might break the spell.

With a kind of reverence Kaden divested Julia of her

jewellery and started to take off her clothes, undoing her dress at the back so that it fell open and then down to the floor in a pool of silk and satin at her feet, heavy under its own weight.

She stood in her underwear with her head tipped forward as Kaden took the pins out of her hair so that it tumbled around her shoulders. She could feel him open her bra, and shivered deliciously when his finger traced the line of her spine all the way down to her buttocks. Her breasts were heavy, nipples tight and tingling.

Gently he turned her to face him again, and pulled the open bra down her arms and off. She felt self-conscious for a moment, aware of her bigger breasts and her rounded belly. But under Kaden's hot gaze all trepidation fled. He cupped her breasts, eyes dark and molten as he moved his thumbs over the taut peaks. They were more sensitive now, and Julia groaned softly. Her hands were shaking with need as she reached out to take off Kaden's jacket and shirt. The buttons were elaborate and proved too much for her clumsy ministrations.

Kaden took her hands away and she watched, dry-mouthed, as bit by bit his glorious torso was revealed. Stepping close, she pressed a kiss to one flat nipple, tugging gently with her teeth and then smoothing it with her tongue. Kaden's hand speared her hair, holding her head. Julia exulted in his rough breathing, in the way his chest filled to suck in more air.

Her hands had found his belt and buckle. Urgently she opened them and pushed his trousers and briefs down to the floor, freeing his impressive erection. Drawing back for a moment, she looked down, feeling dizzy with desire. She reached out a hand and touched him, stroking the hard length, feeling the decadent slide of silky skin over steel.

"Julia…"

Kaden sounded hoarse. Julia acted on pure instinct and bent her knees until she knelt before him on the floor. Still holding him, she took the tip of him into her mouth, tongue swirling around him. Fresh heat flooded through her at doing something so wanton, and she only dimly heard Kaden say harshly, "Stop… *God*, Julia, if you keep doing that I won't—"

She felt Kaden gently pull her head away. She looked up, and the feral, almost fierce expression on his face reminded her of a wild and beautiful animal. He pulled her to her feet. "You don't know what you do to me. I won't last…and I want you too much. I need to be inside you. *Now*."

Within what felt like seconds they were on Kaden's bed, with not a stitch of clothing between them. Kaden's hands smoothed down over Julia's curves, her belly. She reached for him. "Kaden, I need you."

His hand dipped between her legs, feeling for himself that she was ready, and if Julia hadn't been so turned on she would have been embarrassed by the triumphant glitter in Kaden's eyes.

He settled his lean hips between her legs, one hand on her thigh, pushing it wider, careful not to rest his weight on her belly. Julia arched her back, nipples scraping against his chest.

And then, just when she was about to plead and beg, she felt him slide into her, inch by delicious inch, filling her and stretching her. Eyes wide, she looked at him as he started to thrust, taking them higher and higher.

Time was transcended. All that existed was this blissful union. And Julia was borne aloft on a wave of ecstasy so overpowering that it seemed to go on for ever, her whole body pulsing and clenching for long seconds even after Kaden's seed had spilled deep inside her. After a timeless moment he extricated himself and pulled her tight into his chest, arms wrapped around her. Julia wondered for one lucid moment before she fell asleep if this was a dream.

Kaden lay awake beside Julia. His heartbeat was still erratic, and a light sweat sheened his skin. Julia was curled into his chest, bottom tucked close into the cradle of his thighs. Already he was growing hard at the feel of her lush behind. Once again he was struck with the immutable truth that no other woman had this effect on him after making love. He felt all at once invincible, and yet more vulnerable than he'd ever felt.

One hand was on Julia's belly, his fingers spread across the firm swell. He put the feelings welling up inside him down to knowing that she was pregnant— with *his* babies, his seed. Undoubtedly that was what had imbued their lovemaking with a heightened intensity.

But as Kaden finally let sleep claim him his overriding feeling wasn't one of peace at being able to put the experience into a box. It was the same disconcerting one he'd had in B'harani, when he'd seen Julia wearing that necklace. He felt as if he was sliding down that slippery slope again, with nothing to hold onto, and there was a great black yawning abyss at the bottom, waiting to suck him down.

A few hours later, as dawn broke outside, Kaden woke sweating and clammy, his heart racing. He'd just had a vivid dream of nightmare proportions. He'd been surrounded by a crowd of faceless people and held back by hundreds of hands as he was forced to watch Julia make love to another man. He'd wanted to rip that man limb from limb. He felt nauseous even now, as it came back in lurid detail.

He looked to where Julia lay sleeping on her side on the other side of the bed and felt all at once like holding her close and running fast in the opposite direction.

Two weeks after that cataclysmic wedding night Julia was wondering if it had been a dream. It *felt* like a dream, because they hadn't made love since then. Kaden had been cool the following morning at breakfast, while Julia had felt as if she'd survived an earthquake.

He'd informed her, while barely meeting her eyes, "Unfortunately local elections are coming up this week, which means that we'll have to postpone a honeymoon."

Julia's insides had curdled in the face of this remote man. How could she have been seduced so easily into thinking she'd seen something of the young man she'd fallen in love with?

"That's fine with me," she'd answered stiffly. "I hadn't expected anything else."

And then he'd said, "I've arranged for you to have lessons in Burquati history and royal protocol. You'll be well prepared for any public engagements. I should be able to accompany you until you get your bearings. The lessons will give you a broad overview of everything you need to know, and some tuition in our language."

Now Kaden shifted on the other side of the dinner table, and Julia glanced up guiltily to see him assessing her. His eyes dropped to her hand.

"Why aren't you wearing your engagement ring?"

Julia looked at the plain gold wedding band on her finger and flushed. "I was afraid I might lose it."

She saw his sceptical look, and then felt a surge of adrenalin. The fact that he'd clearly been avoiding coming to bed until she was asleep for the past two weeks, while she lay there aching for him to touch her, was inciting hot anger.

She lifted her chin. "The truth is that I don't like the idea of wearing a ring that was given to your first wife."

"Why would you feel that?"

She frowned. "You said that it was your mother's ring, which was to be given to the woman you married... I just assumed—"

He cut her off. "I gave Amira a different ring—one that she kept when we were divorced..." His mouth tightened, "I believe it fetched a nice price at auction in London a few months ago. Clearly her generous divorce settlement is fast running out."

Julia was disconcerted, her anger fading. "Why didn't you give your mother's ring to her?"

Kaden looked at Julia, and those big grey eyes threatened him on so many levels. He shrugged nonchalantly, very aware that this was exposing him. He hadn't given the ring to Amira because it hadn't felt right. And yet with Julia there'd been no hesitation.

"It didn't suit her colouring. It meant nothing significant."

Julia was stung. Well, she'd got her answer. He'd given it to *her* because it suited her colouring. The fact that she hungered so desperately for him mocked her, when she knew more certainly than ever that the only reason she was here at all was because of the heirs she carried. He couldn't even bring himself to make love to her again.

Wanting to disguise how hurt and vulnerable that made her feel, she said, "How do I know that once I have these babies you won't try to extricate yourself from *me*? You cast your first wife out just because she couldn't give you an heir. Obviously you weren't committed enough to pursue other options. Perhaps it's just the heirs you care about? Maybe a wife is superfluous to your needs?"

Kaden's mouth tightened with anger. "For your information, I did all I could to make my marriage work. Amira was the one who insisted on a divorce, because she knew she could never give me an heir. She wouldn't even discuss options. And I'm still paying for ongoing treatment to get her over her phobia."

Julia felt deflated when she thought of the fact that if his wife had been more amenable they might still be married. Cheeks flaming, she said, "I'm sorry. I had no right to assume I knew what had happened. It must have been…very painful."

Kaden emitted a curt laugh. "I wasn't in love with her, Julia. It was an arranged marriage." His voice sounded surprisingly bitter. "She had the right lineage."

Julia glanced at him, pushing down the lancing pain at this evidence of his cynicism. "And now you've got the heirs, but a wife with all the wrong lineage."

He just looked at her with those black eyes, and for the first time Julia felt something rising up within her— something she couldn't keep suppressing.

She fiddled with her napkin and avoided Kaden's eye. "Speaking of lineage, there's something you should probably know." She rushed on before she could lose her nerve. "I'm adopted, Kaden. I was adopted at birth. I know who my birth mother is, but she doesn't want to know me. For all I know she could even be dead by now."

Julia was breathing fast, aghast that she'd just blurted out the stain on her soul like that.

Kaden said carefully, "Why did you never tell me this before?"

Julia shrugged minutely, still avoiding his eye. "I don't talk about it—ever."

"Why not? It's not a bad thing. Plenty of people are adopted. I would have considered adoption myself if Amira had been open to the idea."

Shock at Kaden's easy acceptance made her look up. His eyes were dark, assessing. Not cold and judgemental. Julia felt as if she was being drawn into those eyes. His reaction was loosening something that had always felt tight inside her.

"From the day my parents told me I was adopted, when I turned thirteen, I always felt...*less*." She grimaced. "My parents went out of their way to assure me they loved me, but to know that someone else had had you first...and let you go because they didn't want you..." Even now Julia shivered.

"What about your father? You say your birth mother didn't want to know you?"

"The records from the agency showed that my parents hadn't been married. I found out that my father had emigrated to Australia almost immediately after my birth. He was too far away to trace, so I focused on my mother. I was too impatient to write, so not long before I came here to work on the dig I tracked down her phone number and called her..."

Julia smiled tremulously. "She knew exactly who I was. It was as if she'd been waiting for my call." Her smile faded. "But then she just said, '*Don't call here again. I don't want to have anything to do with you. I gave you up once and it's done*'."

The pain in Julia's heart was acute. She only realised she was crying silent tears when Kaden took her hand across the table, enveloping her in warmth.

"It sounds to me as if giving you up was an incredibly traumatic experience for her. Perhaps it's something she simply couldn't deal with."

Julia brushed away the tears and attempted a smile. "I know… I saw a counsellor attached to the adoption agency before I contacted her, so I was warned about the reaction I might get. But somehow I'd hoped for the kind of thing you see in the movies—the great reunion. Stupid…"

Kaden was shaking his head, his hand tightening on hers. "Not stupid at all. It's very human. I'm sorry, Julia…really sorry you went through that. I can't imagine what it's like to grow up not knowing where you've come from."

Feeling very exposed and brittle at Kaden's sensitivity, Julia pulled her hand back from his and put it on her belly, saying lightly, "At least these little ones won't ever have to face that."

Kaden was grim. "No, they won't."

The evidence of Kaden's grimness made Julia's emotions see-saw all over the place. She desperately wanted him to hold her…to make love to her and help her forget her pain which was far too close to the surface. But he hadn't touched her in two weeks, and wasn't likely to any time soon.

In a bid to escape before he could see the extent of how this affected her, she stood up. "I'm quite tired this evening... If you'll excuse me...?"

Kaden stood too. "Don't forget about the visit to the new hospital wing tomorrow."

"Oh..."

Julia *had* forgotten about her first public function tomorrow. She was due to cut the ribbon on a new wing of the national hospital. Immediately her concerns about going out in public rose up.

Kaden said, "I'll be with you tomorrow. All you'll have to do is smile and wave. They won't expect any more. They'll just want to see you."

Julia turned to walk away from the table, but Kaden caught her wrist. She looked back. She could feel her pulse throbbing against his hand and flushed.

She took her wrist from his grip. After everything she'd just shared, the deep vulnerability she felt was acute enough to be a physical ache within her. She forced a smile. "I'll be fine. I'm looking forward to it."

She left the room, feeling Kaden's black eyes boring into her back.

Kaden waved away the staff that came in to clear the plates from the private and intimate dining room not far from their suite of rooms. He needed to be alone, to digest everything Julia had just told him. Suddenly restless, he stood up, his long robes falling around him.

He paced back and forth, as if that might dampen the ever-present burn of desire, made worse now after feeling Julia's hectic pulse. It was all jumbled up in his head: his need to lose himself in her body; his equal need to keep his distance; the almost overwhelming need to protect her from ever being hurt again as she so evidently had been by her birth mother.

Julia had looked so vulnerable just now, and he hated the thought of exposing her to the crowds tomorrow. But he couldn't avoid it. He felt inordinately protective, but told himself it was a natural response because she was pregnant, and not because of what she'd revealed about her birth.

He'd had no clue about her adoption. From what she'd told him about herself years before he'd guessed she came from a solidly middle class background. When she hadn't talked about family too much he'd just put it down to English reticence. The fact that she'd made that painful contact with her birth mother just before she'd come to Burquat was uncomfortable for him to dwell on.

For a second Kaden had a glimpse into how rudderless *he* might have felt if he hadn't grown up knowing exactly where he'd come from. The sliver of isolation that washed through him at contemplating that scenario made him want to call Julia back, so that he could hold her close and never let her go again.

He immediately rejected that urge. His hand clenched to a fist. *This* was what he'd been avoiding ever since their wedding night. This rising tide of emotions that he refused to look at or acknowledge. The depth of passion on that night had stunned him. And that awful dream... which had obviously been precipitated by sleeping with Julia. Perhaps here in Burquat the memories were too close to avoid.

The truth was that when Julia touched him he became something else—someone else. It was too reminiscent of how she'd made him feel before. He'd never forget that struggle with his father before he'd died. His total absorption in himself and meeting his own needs…and then the awful shock of seeing her with that man, the excoriating jealousy. Realising how much he'd lost sight of himself and who he was, who he had to be. Exactly what his father had warned him against.

Kaden strode over to the drinks cabinet, poured himself a measure of neat whisky and knocked it back. The burn made him reach for another one, as if that might douse the unquenchable desire, the tangled knot of feelings his wife so effortlessly evoked. He'd told himself that when he'd met her again in London he'd just wanted to bed her. And when she'd arrived to tell him about her pregnancy he'd thought only of the babies.

Now those assertions rang like the hollow untruths they were. Since he'd seen Julia again things had gone a lot deeper than he liked to admit.

The truth was, it was easier to avoid Julia and any chance of intimacy than face her and those grey eyes which made him feel as if he was coming apart at the seams every time he looked at her. Now more so than ever.

CHAPTER NINE

JULIA was trembling with nerves by the time they pulled up in Kaden's chauffeur-driven state car outside the hospital the following morning. She was dressed in a silvery grey long tunic, with matching pants underneath and a shawl to match. Her hair was tied back in a loose low bun, make-up and jewellery discreet. The tunic hid her pregnancy quite well—they'd agreed to wait another few days before making the announcement.

She took a deep shaky breath at the sight of the crowds amassed behind cordons, and then felt her hand being taken in a strong, warm grip. She almost closed her eyes for a second at the wave of longing that went through her. She turned to look at Kaden. His eyes were intent, compelling.

"I'll be right by your side. Just be yourself. They won't be able to help but respond to you."

"But I'm not a public person, Kaden… I've given speeches to rooms full of archaeologists, but never anything like this. They'll expect me to be something I'm not."

Something fierce crossed Kaden's face and he said, "They will accept you, Julia, because you're my wife and I've chosen you."

Julia felt sad, and pulled her hand away. She bit back the words trembling on her tongue. *You wouldn't have chosen me if you'd had a choice.*

Kaden's door was opened then, and with a last look he got out. The crowd went wild. He wore long cream robes and a traditional headdress. Julia's heart clenched amidst her trepidation. He reminded her so much in that moment of the young man she'd first met.

He was coming round the car. He'd instructed the driver to let him open her door. And then he was there, against the bright searing sun, holding out a hand. Julia took a deep breath and stepped out, clutching Kaden's hand. The roar of the crowd dipped ominously.

Security guards shadowed them as they walked towards the hospital. Julia tried to smile, but the crowd was blurring into a sea of faces that all looked suspiciously unfriendly. She was reminded of the aides who had surrounded Kaden after his father's death, when she hadn't been able to get close to him. She stumbled slightly and his arm came around her waist.

"OK?"

She looked up. "Yes, fine."

She drew on all her reserves as they got to the top of the steps and were greeted by officials from the hospital. They were exceedingly polite, but with a definite reserve. Kaden gave a short heartfelt speech about the new unit, which was specifically for heart disease, and then they turned towards the huge ribbon over the main doors.

Julia was handed a pair of scissors and cut it. Everyone clapped and cheered, but she couldn't help but notice the reticence of the crowd ever since she'd appeared at Kaden's side.

After being shown around inside by the doctors and officials they re-emerged, and Kaden led her towards the crowds. He said, "We'll do a short walkabout. It's expected."

Urged forward, Julia went towards a little girl, who pushed forward shyly to hold out some flowers. She bent down and took them, saying thank you in their native language. But Julia noticed the mother pull the child back, her lips pursed in disapproval, eyes dark and hard.

Another woman who held a baby visibly turned away, and adjusted a shawl over the baby's face so that Julia couldn't see it. As if to protect it from her gaze. Amongst her shock at the people's obvious rejection of her Julia felt a welling desire to have them look at her with open faces and smiles. She realised that she desperately wanted to be able to connect with them.

Kaden was taking her hand and pulling her back to the car. When they got in Julia was a little shell-shocked.

Kaden was grim as the car pulled away. "I'm sorry about that. They're wary after Amira and my stepmother...they'll come round."

"It's OK," Julia replied faintly, feeling more hurt than she'd thought possible. She'd not even known till then how important the Burquati people's opinion of her was. "I can understand that they wanted to see you with someone more suitable."

Kaden was silent beside her, and Julia didn't want to look at him and see disappointment in his second wife etched into his face.

When they got back to the palace Kaden stopped Julia and said, "I've got to go into the desert for a couple of days to meet with the newly elected Bedouin council."

Julia looked at him against the backdrop of the magnificent central courtyard and felt a hollowness echoing through her. This was how it would be between them. Distance and polite civility.

She nodded. "Fine. I'll see you in a couple of days. I've got lessons to get on with in the meantime."

Julia turned away, and Kaden had an irrational urge to grab her back, throw her into the car and drive them far away. He wanted to be going into the desert with *her*, the way they'd used to. Sneaking off like fugitives, spending nights in a hastily erected tent under the stars. No thought in the world beyond exploring each other and sating mutual desire. And talking for hours.

An ache welled up inside him, and this time he couldn't ignore it. He had a sudden overwhelming need for those memories not to be tainted by what had happened twelve years before. For Julia to look at him the way she'd used to, with such open love and warmth. But the reality was clear. If Julia had ever had any feelings for him they were long gone. She was bound to him for ever, and she couldn't help but hate him for that. He'd seen the way that woman in the crowd had shielded her baby from Julia, as if she were some sort of witch. And Julia had just smiled.

With a jerky move, Kaden got back into the car which would take him to a helicopter to fly him into the desert. In that moment he'd never felt such bleakness surround him, and pain for subjecting Julia to the cold disapproval of his people when he knew just how deep her vulnerability went.

As Kaden flew over the desert a short time later the helicopter dipped abruptly for a moment in an air pocket. The pilot apologised and Kaden smiled tightly.

That physical sensation mirrored exactly how he felt emotionally, and it wasn't comfortable.

Julia spent the next two days working hard with her own secretary to encourage meetings with locals. She was determined to do what she could to bridge the gap, and wanted to avoid having any free time to brood about Kaden and the distance between them. She had to admit, though, that talking to him about her adoption had been cathartic. Thoughts of it and her birth mother no longer came with the heavy oppressive weight they'd used to.

To her delight she'd managed to set up a few coffee morning events at the palace, to meet with local women's groups and dicuss various issues. Julia had always had an interest in the more anthropological end of archaeology, so the prospect of meeting Burquati people and coming to learn their customs excited her.

She was in the middle of her first coffee morning when she saw Kaden again, and she nearly dropped her cup. He stood in the doorway, tall and gorgeous in long robes, jaw dark with stubble. He'd obviously just returned. She could swear her heart physically clenched as she saw him again.

All the women immediately bowed and went silent.

He inclined his head. "I'll leave you to it. I'm sure you're discussing far more important things than I will be at my cabinet meeting later."

He smiled, but to Julia it looked slightly strained. His eyes skated over her, giving her no more nor less attention than the other women. The awful yearning for him to acknowledge her with more than that inclusive glance nearly overwhelmed her, and she had to shove the hurt down deep.

He left, and after a moment of pregnant silence the women started chattering in a mixture of English and Burquati. Julia had been struggling to connect with the women, who'd seemed very suspicious, but suddenly they were all smiles and laughs.

Her secretary smiled at her sympathetically, misreading her anguish. "Don't worry. It'll just take some time."

Julia smiled wanly and went to join in again, feeling prickly because, if truth be told, she was jealous of these women. Kaden could come and charm them so effortlessly when he couldn't even be bothered to touch her any more!

Julia was lying in bed that night, unable to sleep. Kaden hadn't returned to their suite all evening, and she'd eaten dinner alone. She knew she couldn't continue like this, with Kaden holding her at arm's length and looking at her as if she might explode at any moment like a ticking bomb.

When she heard his familiar step she tensed. He came into the moonlit room, treading quietly.

Julia came up on one elbow and said huskily, "I'm awake."

He stopped, and all she could see in the gloom was his huge shape. Predictably, despite her tangled head and emotions, her body reacted to the sight of him. Softening, melting.

She sat up and pulled her knees towards her to try and hide her agitation. "Why didn't you come to dinner?"

Kaden started to disrobe. Julia could see gleaming flesh revealed bit by bit, and her belly clenched helplessly with desire.

His voice was cool. "I got held up with a phone call

to Sadiq, discussing the oil wells. They're expecting a baby too. Not long after us."

"Oh…" Julia didn't know what to say. Kaden seemed to be determined to avoid any further discussion.

He came to the bed and lifted back the covers, getting in and lying down. Tension vibrated between them like a tangible thing.

Julia turned to face him, feeling her hair slip over her shoulders. "Kaden…we need to talk. It's obvious that this isn't working out."

Kaden didn't like the flare of panic. He'd been reacting all day to the gut-wrenchingly urgent need he'd had to see Julia immediately on his return from the desert. And then, when he had seen her, the relief had sent him away again just as quickly, for fear she'd read something into his reaction that he didn't want her to see.

He felt as if he was clinging onto the last link that was rooting him in reality. That was rooting him in what he knew and had accepted for twelve long years. His distance from Julia for the past couple of days had restored some clarity, some perspective, and a sense that perhaps he wasn't going mad… Except earlier, and now, it was back with a vengeance. Any illusion of control gone.

His whole body was rigid against the effortless pull of Julia beside him. Her soft scent was like a siren's call to his blood. He turned his head and saw her outline: the slim shoulders, the curve of her breasts, the swell of her belly under the soft cotton of her vest. She wore vests and shorts to bed, attire he'd never seen another woman wear, and yet it inflamed him more than the slinkiest negligée he'd ever seen.

He turned away from temptation and forced out, "What isn't working out?"

His clear reluctance to talk made the tiny flame of hope Julia had harboured that they might discuss this fade away. She was overwhelmed for a moment by the sense of futility, and lay down too. She said in a small voice, "Nothing. It doesn't matter."

For a moment there was nothing but thick silence, and then, in a move so fast she gasped, Kaden was looming over her, eyes like black pools. "Tell me, Julia. What were you going to say?"

He was fierce, when only moments before his rigid control had been palpable. She smelt the slightest hint of whisky on his breath, and somehow suspecting that he was in some sort of turmoil too made her feel simultaneously tender and combative. And something in her exulted that he was finally reacting.

Before she could say anything, though, something in the atmosphere shifted and his fingers touched her throat. He said huskily, "You're wearing the necklace."

Julia froze all over, going clammy. Some of her things had arrived from London earlier and she'd found the necklace. She'd put it on, feeling some silly need to connect with something she'd always found comforting. She'd fully intended to take it off.

She immediately sought to protect herself from his scrutiny and drew back minutely. "It's OK. You don't have to get the wrong idea…"

His voice was a lot harsher than a moment ago. "What does it mean, Julia? Why have you kept it all this time?"

Julia knocked his hand away and scrambled inelegantly out of the bed, feeling far too vulnerable lying so close to a naked Kaden.

She lashed out in her own anger for exposing herself like this and in anger at Kaden for questioning her.

"I just saw it and put it on. It doesn't mean anything. It certainly doesn't mean that I don't know what this marriage is about. It's about the fact that I'm pregnant with your precious heirs—nothing more, nothing less."

Kaden uncoiled his big body from the bed and walked around to Julia. Acting on the irrational panic rising within her that she was about to come apart completely, Julia reached up and grabbed the necklace with her hand. She yanked at it, breaking the delicate chain instantly, and flung it aside onto the ground.

Inside she was weeping. Outwardly she hitched up her chin. "See? It means *nothing.*"

Kaden looked at where she'd thrown the necklace and then back to her. The air crackled between them. In an abrupt move he pulled her into his body and said fiercely, "You don't have to resort to dramatics to make your point. I get the message. From now on there will be no doubt as to what this marriage is about."

Julia closed her eyes as Kaden's mouth fused to hers, his arms like a vice around her. Their bodies strained together. Tears burned the backs of her eyes, but she would not let Kaden see the helpless emotion. It was hot and overflowing, but as Kaden lowered her onto the bed and came down over her she shut her mind to all the mocking voices which told her that she was fooling no one but herself.

The following day Kaden was standing alone on an open terrace in the palace. He'd been having a meeting with an architect about the palace's preservation, but the architect had long gone. The city of Burquat was laid out before him. Cranes dotted the skyline—evidence of much necessary modernisation.

Kaden didn't see the view, though. His thoughts were inward. He smiled grimly to himself. He'd been right to fear touching Julia again. It was as if he'd known it would be the final catalyst in his coming undone. His own useless defence system had crashed and burned spectacularly last night, like a row of elaborate dominoes falling down with one small nudge.

Julia had only had to wear that necklace for him to see clearly for the first time in years.

His jaw tightened. Even then he hadn't been able to give in, still fighting right to the end... He'd had to make her say it, make her tell him how she really felt. As if he needed the concrete proof of her words and to feel the pain that came with them. Because he knew he deserved it. Perhaps that was what he'd been protecting himself against all along—the truth of *her* feelings. Not just his own.

He'd held something very precious a long time ago, and he'd broken it for ever. Kaden looked down and opened his fist to reveal the necklace, its chain in two pieces.

CHAPTER TEN

JULIA was in their private dining room, where Kaden had said he'd meet her for lunch. She was standing at the open French doors but seeing nothing of the glorious view. A couple of weeks had passed since that night. When Julia had woken the morning after she'd been alone. She'd immediately got up to look for the necklace but hadn't found it. Her sense of loss was profound, but she was too nervous to mention it to anyone or ask for help in searching for it. The last thing she wanted was for Kaden to know she was scrabbling around looking for it at any given opportunity.

She'd had to realise with a heavy heart that perhaps she needed to be rid of it because it symbolised something she'd never really had or would have—Kaden's love.

Kaden hadn't avoided her at night since then. They'd made love. And yet his touch was more…reticent. As if he was scared he'd hurt her. It seemed to compound the yawning chasm growing between them, so much worse than before.

How could they have gone three steps forward only to go about a hundred back?

"I'm sorry to have kept you waiting."

Julia whirled around to see Kaden in the doorway. Even though he'd left their bed only hours before, she blushed. She schooled her reaction and walked to the table. Just as she put out a hand to touch her chair she felt a kick in her womb, forcible enough to make her gasp and touch her bump, which was now big enough to be obvious to everyone.

Instantly Kaden was at her side, holding her arm. "What is it?"

As much in reaction to his touch as the kick, Julia said shakily, "I'm fine…it was just a kick—the first real kick I've felt."

Another one came then, and she couldn't stop a smile spreading across her face. Feeling the babies move was dissolving any inhibitions. She reached instinctively for Kaden's hand and brought it to her belly, pressing it down, praying that they would kick again. She looked at Kaden, and as always the ever-present awareness seemed to hum between them.

When the seconds stretched and there were no more kicks Julia flushed. She felt exposed. Kaden was too close, looking at her too assessingly. She pulled his hand away,

"They've stopped…"

Instantly the connection was broken, and Kaden stalked to the other side of the table and sat down. Staff appeared as if by magic and served them. Their conversation was stilted, centring around a charity fête that Julia was due to attend that afternoon.

When they'd finished eating Julia wiped her mouth, preparing to go.

Kaden said, "You don't have to go to the fête this afternoon if you don't want to. Unfortunately I can't get out of my meeting with the foreign minister. He's due to fly to the US tomorrow."

Julia smiled tightly. "It'll be fine. I need to get used to going to these things on my own sooner or later."

Kaden leaned forward and took her hand in his. Julia's eyes widened.

"I know this is hard for you, but already I can see a difference in people's attitudes. You're winning them round." He grimaced then. "I'm sorry that you have to go through this when you'd never have willingly signed up for this life."

Julia's face burned. Little did he know that she'd often dreamt of being by his side.

She took back her hand and pushed back her chair. "The car will be waiting."

Kaden watched her leave the room and cursed himself. He clenched his fist and just stopped himself from bringing it crashing down on the table. He kept thinking about the moment after their wedding, when he'd found her sobbing her heart out. Guilt burned in his gut, compounded now by the way he'd felt when he'd seen that beatific smile lighting up her face. He'd felt jealous that something else could make her happy. Jealous of his own babies!

The moment hadn't lasted long before she'd withdrawn again to that cool, polite distance which only dissolved when they were in bed.

He didn't need to be reminded that Julia hadn't smiled like that once since she'd met him again. As if he didn't know why. She was stuck in a marriage of convenience with a man who had brutally rejected her when she'd been at her most vulnerable just to protect his own cowardly heart. Julia was humbling him every day with her innate grace and stoic acceptance of a difficult situation. Of a life she didn't want.

Kaden knew that he had to be fully honest with her. She deserved to know everything. Later, he vowed. When she got home he would tell her. *Everything.* And whatever her reaction was...he would have to deal with it.

Two hours later Kaden was sitting at his desk listening to his minister for foreign affairs talk, but not taking anything in. He was wondering where Julia was now. Had she reached the fête? Was she feeling awkward? Was she smiling in that slightly fixed way which signi-fied she was shy or uncomfortable? His gut clenched at the thought of anyone being rude or unfriendly to her.

Only last week he'd watched her host another of her coffee mornings, this time outside in the palace grounds. He'd been inordinately proud of the way she'd listened to people, really devoting her time to them. A million miles away from his ex-wife and stepmother who had both been brought up specially schooled to be in this world.

"Sire?"

They'd announced the news of Julia's pregnancy a few days ago, now that she was showing more obviously, and he was hoping it would have an effect on people's interaction with her. Surely the prospect of—?

"Sire!"

"Hmm?" Kaden looked at his minister, a little dazed for a moment, and then saw that his secretary was also in the room. He frowned. He hadn't even noticed her come in. "Yes, Sara?"

He only noticed then that she was deathly pale and

trembling. The hair went up on the back of his neck for no reason.

"Sire, I'm sorry to disturb you, but I've just heard— there's been a terrible multi-vehicle accident on the main freeway to Kazat, where the fête is. We've been trying to call your wife and the driver, but there's no response from them or the bodyguards. We don't have news yet as the emergency services haven't reached them."

Kaden heard her words and tried to react, to move. But it was as if his limbs were instantly weighted down with wet cement. He couldn't get up. He could feel his blood draining south and put his hands on his desk to hold on to something.

His secretary started crying and the foreign minister stood up. "Sire, I'll get your car immediately."

Kaden stood up then, even though he couldn't feel his own legs, and said with an icy calm which belied the roaring in his brain, "Not the car. Too slow. Get the helicopter ready and make sure there's a doctor and a paramedic on board. *Now.*"

What felt like aeons later, but what was in fact only thirty minutes, Kaden's helicopter pilot was setting down in a clearing beside the freeway. All Kaden could see was a tangled mass of vehicles, a school bus on its side, with steam billowing out of its engine, and lines of cars blocking the freeway.

The flashing lights of the first emergency vehicles were evident, and there were people blackened from smoke and fire rushing everywhere. And amongst all that twisted metal and heat was Julia. Kaden's mind shut down and he went into autopilot. He simply could not contemplate anything beyond the next few seconds.

The blast of heat nearly pushed him backwards

when he got out of the chopper, but Kaden ignored it and waded straight into the carnage. He shouted at the young, scared-looking doctor with him, "Stay beside me!"

All around them people were wandering around looking dazed, with blood running down their faces, holding hands and arms. But to Kaden's initial and fleeting relief there seemed no serious-looking injuries. He focused on the school bus on its side, and as he went towards it, acting on instinct, he finally saw the Royal car. It was skewed at an angle near the bus, ploughed into the steel girder which ran down the middle of the highway, and near it, on its roof, was the security Jeep.

Kaden's heart stopped. He ran towards the car, and when he got there, his lungs burning, ducked his head into the back seat. It was empty. He felt sick when he saw the trail of blood that led out of the car.

He stood up. *"Julia!"*

Nothing. Panic at full throttle now, he went towards the other side of the school bus and stopped dead in his tracks, a mixture of overwhelming relief and incoherent rage making him dizzy. Julia was handing a small child to her driver, who was in turn handing it to someone else. Adults who looked like teachers were standing in groups with other children, crying. Julia's kaftan was ripped and bloody.

He went towards her and she saw him. "Oh, Kaden—thank God! Please…you have to help us. There are still some children trapped inside, and the engine is leaking petrol."

She looked half crazed, which he could see was due to shock and adrenalin, and in the periphery of his vision he could see people standing with phones, taking videos and photos. Very deliberately he put his hands on Julia's arms and bodily moved her out of harm's way. He looked at the doctor and said, "She's over five months pregnant. If anything happens to her you'll be held personally responsible."

Julia protested. "But, Kaden, there are still children—"

He cut her off. "*You* stay here. *I* will go and get the children. If you move one inch, Julia, so help me God I will lock you in the palace for the rest of your life."

Through a haze of shock and panic Julia could only feel limp with relief as she watched Kaden stride back to the bus, climb up, and reach in to help pull the children out. Within minutes they were all accounted for, and Julia had already instructed the now terrified-looking doctor to go and help the injured children instead of babysitting her. She was helping too, ripping material off her dress to tie around bleeding arms and legs.

She felt herself being lifted upwards and was turned into Kaden's chest. His eyes burned down into hers. "Are you OK? Are you in pain anywhere?"

Julia shook her head. Some of the shock was starting to wear off, so she was aware of how deranged Kaden looked. She put it down to the accident. "I'm fine. We need to help these people…"

But her words were muffled against Kaden's chest as he pulled her into him and hugged her so tightly that she couldn't breathe. Eventually he pulled back. "We're getting out of here right now. I need to get you to the hospital."

Julia protested. "I'm fine—what about all these people? The children? They need help more than me!"

But Kaden wasn't listening. She could see an emer-

gency medical plane circling overhead, and more choppers landing. The scene was swarming with emergency
staff now, and the young doctor was busy.

When she still resisted, Kaden uttered an oath and
turned and picked her up into his arms. Julia opened her
mouth, but closed it again at the stern set of his features.
He looked as if he was going to murder someone, and
she felt a pang when she recalled what he'd said to the
doctor. *"She's over five months pregnant..."* He must be
livid with her for putting their babies at risk.

She was in the chopper and secured within minutes,
and then they were lifting up and away from the mayhem. Julia was comforted to see that the emergency vehicles were already speeding back towards the city, and
other choppers were loading up with patients.

Kaden couldn't speak because of the noise but Julia
was glad. She wasn't looking forward to what he had to
say.

"Kaden, why don't you just spit it out? You're giving me
a headache, pacing around like a bear with a sore head."

He stopped and glared at her, his jeans and shirt
ripped and dusty. "You're a national hero. Do you know
that? With one fell swoop the entire nation is in love with
you."

"What do you mean?" Julia was confused.

Kaden picked up the remote and turned on the TV. A
rolling news channel was showing images of the crash,
and then it zoomed in on Julia, where she was handing
a small child to someone.

She glanced at Kaden. He'd gone grey.

He switched the TV off and muttered thickly, "I can't
even watch that."

Tears stung Julia's eyes. "I'm sorry, but I couldn't just ignore what was happening. I know these babies are important to you, but surely your own people are important too?"

He just looked at her. "What are you talking about?"

Julia put her hand on her bump. She'd just had a scan with Dr Assan and been reassured that all was fine. "The babies. I presume that's why you're so angry with me... for putting them in danger?"

Kaden raked a hand through his hair and ground out, "I'm not angry with you for putting the babies in danger. I'm *livid* with you for putting *yourself* in such danger."

He came close before Julia could fully take in his words and sat down, pulling a chair close to the bed and taking her hands in his with a tight grip. "Do you have any idea what I went through before I got to you?"

Julia shook her head slowly. An ominous fluttering feeling was starting up in her chest.

"I think I aged about fifty years, and made blood promises to several gods. So if some strange-looking person turns up and demands our firstborn baby don't be surprised."

"Kaden..." Julia was feeling more shaky now than when she'd been at the crash. "What are you talking about? You're not making sense." And yet at the same time he was making a kind of sense she didn't want to think about.

"What I'm talking about, *habiba*, is the fact that for the longest thirty minutes of my life I didn't want to go on living if anything had happened to you."

Feeling suspiciously emotional, and very vulnerable, Julia couldn't take her eyes off Kaden.

He continued. "I was going to talk to you this evening when you got back…I don't want to tire you now…"

Concern was etched onto his face, and Julia said fiercely, "I'm fine. Talk."

Kaden looked down, and then back up at Julia. "I'm not sure where to start… There's so much I have to say… But I think first I need to tell you the one truth that is more important than anything."

Julia held her breath as Kaden gripped her hand tighter.

"I want you to know that I'm not saying this now because of the crash, or because of the after effects of adrenalin and shock. I had arranged for us to go to the summer palace this evening, for a belated honeymoon. You can ask Sara. She was organising it."

"Kaden…" Julia said weakly. She couldn't look away from the dark intensity of his eyes.

He took a deep, audibly shaky breath. "I love you, Julia. Mind, body, heart and soul. And I always have. From the moment we met in the middle of that dig. I did a wonderful job of convincing myself twelve years ago that I hadn't ever loved you, but as soon as I saw you again the game was up…and eventually I had to stop lying to myself."

Julia looked at Kaden in shock. She could hear her heart thumping. Her mouth opened.

Kaden shook his head and said, "Don't say any-thing—not yet. Let me finish."

Julia couldn't have spoken, even if she'd wanted to. Her mouth closed. She could feel the babies moving in her belly, but that was secondary to what was happen-ing right now.

"The day you left twelve years ago was possibly the

worst day of my life." He winced. "Barring today's events. I felt as if I was being torn in two—like Jekyll and Hyde. For a long time I blamed the grief I felt on my father's death—and that was there, yes. But a larger part of my grief was for you. There's something I have to explain. When we returned from that last trip to the desert I went to my father. I told him that I was going to ask you to marry me. All I could think about was you—you filled up my heart and soul like nothing I'd ever imagined, and I couldn't imagine not being with you for ever."

Julia could feel herself go pale as she remembered that heady time. And then her confusion when Kaden had abandoned her. She shook her head. "But why did you not come to see me? Tell me this…?"

Kaden's jaw clenched. "Because that night my father had his first heart attack. Only those closest to him knew how serious it was. We sent out the news that he wasn't well, but we hid the gravity of the situation for fear of panicking the people. I became acting ruler overnight. I was constantly surrounded by aides. I couldn't move two steps without being questioned or followed. And I suspect that after what I'd told my father he instructed his aides to keep an eye on me and not let me near you.

"I think he saw history repeating itself. His second wife had been a bad choice, unpopular with the people. He knew how important it would be for me to marry well and create a stable base, and here I was declaring my intention to ask *you* to marry me and to hell with the consequences."

Kaden sighed. "I stuck to my guns. I was still deter-mined to ask you to marry me. I decided that while you were finishing your studies I'd give you the time to think about whether or not you really wanted this life…"

Julia felt tears prickle at the back of her eyes. She knew how she would have answered that.

Kaden's voice was gruff. "The first chance I had I got away on my own and went to find you. One of your tutors told me you were all out that night in a bar…"

Julia squeezed Kaden's hand, willing him to believe her. "You have to know what you saw meant nothing…it was just a stupid kiss. It was over the moment it started. I was feeling insecure because I hadn't heard from you, and I think I wanted to assure myself that you couldn't be the only man who could make me feel. I was afraid we were over and I'd never see you again."

To Julia's intense relief Kaden picked up her hand and kissed her palm. "I know that now…and I can see how vulnerable you must have felt—especially so soon after that blow from your birth mother…" He grimaced. "I, however, was blindingly jealous and hot-headed. It felt like the ultimate betrayal. Especially when I'd been pining for you for what felt like endless nights, dreaming of proposing to you even if it meant going against my father's wishes. And then to see you in another man's arms…it was too much. The jealousy was overwhelming. I'd been brought up to view romantic love suspiciously. My father became a shadow of himself after my mother died, and he never stopped telling me that my duty was first and foremost to my country. He was most likely trying to protect me…but when I felt so betrayed by you it only seemed to confirm his words. I convinced myself that it wasn't love I felt. It was lust. Because then it wouldn't hurt so much."

Kaden shook his head. "I returned to the palace and

that night my father had his final heart attack. I got to him just before he slipped away, and his last words to me were pleas to remember that I was responsible for a country now, and had to look beyond my own personal fulfilment. By then I was more than ready to listen to him."

"Oh, Kaden...I had no idea." Pain cut through Julia as she saw how the sequence of events had played out with a kind of sickening synchronicity.

Kaden let her hands go and stood up, pacing away from Julia, self-disgust evident in every jerky movement. He turned round and looked haunted. "When you came to me before you left and tried to explain you got the full lash of my guilt and jealousy. I couldn't be rational. All I could see was you and that man. It haunted me even when we met again. The depth of the feelings I had for you always scared me a little, and I never resolved them years ago. I buried them, and that's why it took me so long to come to my senses..."

Julia felt incredibly sad. "We were so young, Kaden. Maybe we were just too young to cope with those feelings."

Kaden raked a hand through his hair. "That's why Samia looked at you with such hostility at her wedding. She was protecting me because she was the only one who saw the dark place I went to after you left. I never explained anything to her, so she assumed you'd broken my heart. When in fact I did a pretty good job of breaking yours."

"And your own..." Julia bit her lip to try and keep a lid on the overwhelming feelings within her. Tears blurred her vision, and despite her best efforts a sob broke free.

Kaden was standing apart, hands clenched at his sides, looking tortured.

She shook her head. "I just…I can't believe you're saying all this…" Another sob came out and she put a hand to her mouth. Tears were flowing freely down her face now.

Kaden clearly wanted to comfort her, but was holding back because he didn't know if she wanted him. "God, Julia…I'm so sorry. What I've done is—"

"Kaden, don't say anything else. Just hold me, please."

Julia wasn't even sure if her words had been entirely coherent, but Kaden moved forward jerkily, and after a moment he was sitting on the bed and enveloping her in his strong embrace.

Julia's hands were clenched against his chest. She couldn't stop crying, and kept thinking of all those wasted years and pain. Ineffectually she hit at his chest, and he tensed and pulled her even closer, as if to absorb her turmoil. Eventually he drew back and looked down, his face in agony. Seeing that made something dissolve inside Julia.

"Don't let me go, Kaden…"

He shook his head and said fiercely, "Never. I'll never let you go ever again."

When the paroxysm of emotion had abated Julia pulled back in the circle of his arms and said shakily, "I've always loved you. I never stopped. You and no one else. From the moment I saw you again in London all the feelings rushed back as if we'd never even been separated."

Kaden shook his head, clearly incredulous. "How can you? After everything… You don't have to say this…

You don't want to be here. You've been forced into this life."

Julia touched his face and smiled tremulously. "I wouldn't want to be anywhere else in the world. I was resigned to my fate, loving you while knowing you'd never love me back."

Kaden's eyes shone suspiciously. "Oh, my love…that's what *I* expected. I love you so much that if anything had happened to you today…"

He went pale again, and the full enormity of what Kaden had gone through hit Julia when she thought of how *she* would have felt if their places had been switched.

Fervently she said, "Let's go home, Kaden. I want to go home with you and start living the rest of our lives together. I don't want to waste another moment."

EPILOGUE

Seven months later

JULIA and Kaden were hosting a christening for their twins and for Samia and Sadiq's baby son, who was just a few weeks younger than the twins. The ceremony had finished in the ancient chapel in the grounds of the archaeological dig site. Julia was standing with Samia now, and they were watching Kaden cradle his dark-haired baby daughter Rihana with all the dexterity of a natural. His brother-in-law Sadiq was holding his son Zaki with similar proficiency.

Samia and Julia's first proper meeting had been awkward, but as soon as Kaden had set Samia straight she'd rounded on him and castigated him for letting her think the worst of Julia for years. Now they were fast becoming good friends.

"No doubt they're discussing the merits of eco-friendly nappies," Samia said dryly.

Julia snorted. "Kaden nearly fainted earlier when he smelt Tariq's morning deposit."

Samia giggled and linked arms with Julia. They'd just been made godmothers to each other's babies. "Come on—let me introduce you properly to Iseult and

Jamilah. You'll love them. Jamilah, the dark-haired one, is Salman's wife. She's got an inner beauty to match her outer beauty, which makes it annoyingly hard to hate her."

Julia chuckled. She'd only been briefly introduced to Sheikh Nadim of Merkazad and his stunningly pretty red-haired wife, and his brother Salman and *his* wife Jamilah. Both couples also had babies, who were crawling or toddling around, being chased by one or other of their parents.

Just as they approached the other women, though, Kaden cut in and handed Rihana to Samia. "Here you go, Auntie. I'm stealing my wife for a minute."

Samia took her baby niece eagerly. "Be careful—you might not get her back. And I think Tariq has already been stolen by Dr Assan."

They'd made Dr Assan their son's godfather, and he was showing him off like a proud grandfather.

Kaden took Julia's hand and led her out through a side door. He was dressed in gold and cream ceremonial robes, and Julia wore a cream silk dress. She let herself be led by Kaden through the shade of the old trees to the other side of the dig, feeling absurdly happy and content.

Kaden glanced back and smiled. "What are you looking so smug about?"

Julia smiled mysteriously, her heart full. "Oh, nothing much."

Kaden growled. "I'll make you tell me later, but first…"

They'd reached the corner, and Julia recognised the spot where they'd first met. Kaden brought her over to the ancient wall, and it took a moment before she could see what he was directing her attention to. A new stone had been placed amongst the older ones, and it held within it a fossil and an inscription.

She gasped and looked at him. "That's not the same fossil—?"

He smiled. "Read the writing."

She did. The inscription simply read: *For my wife and only love, Julia. You hold my heart and soul, as I will hold yours, for ever. Kaden*

It also had the date of the day they'd met. She looked at Kaden, feeling suspiciously teary, and saw that he was holding out his palm. She looked down and saw a familiar chain of gold. Her necklace. She picked it up reverently.

He sounded gruff. "I got it mended after that night."

Julia's eyes had filled with proper tears now, and Kaden said mock sternly, with his hands cupping her face and jaw, "I won't have tears marking this spot."

Julia smiled through the tears. "Kiss me, then, and make me happy."

"That," Kaden said, with love in his eyes and on his face, "I can most definitely do."

And so they kissed, for a long time, on the exact spot where they'd first met almost thirteen years before.

* * * * *

The Legend of
de Marco

ABBY GREEN

This is especially for Haze. You're a doll.
Thanks for being my friend since we were spotty
teenagers with dodgy hairstyles.
Point Break for ever! x

CHAPTER ONE

ROCCO DE MARCO felt contentment ease into his bones as he took in his surroundings. He was in a beautiful room in a world-renowned museum, right in the heart of cosmopolitan London. It had been designed by a famous French Art Deco designer in the 1920s and drew afficionados from all over the world to see its spectacular stained-glass windows.

The crowd was equally exclusive: high-ranking politicians, erudite commentators, A-list celebrities and billionaire philanthropists who controlled the world's stockmarkets with a flick of a finger or the raising of a brow. *He* was in the latter category, and at the age of thirty-two was surrounded by hushed and awed speculation as to how he'd achieved his untouchable status in such a short space of time.

At that moment he caught the eye of a tall, elegant, patrician blonde across the room. Her glossy hair was pulled back into a classic chignon, and her haughty blue gaze warmed under his look. He did notice, however, that not a tinge of *real* colour came into those carefully rouged cheeks. She was dressed head-to-toe in shimmering black, and he knew that she was as hard as the diamonds at her throat and ears. She smiled and raised her glass to him in a small but significant gesture.

A sense of triumph snaked through Rocco as he raised

his glass in a mirror salute. The prospect of wooing the immaculately bred and oh, so proper Ms Honora Winthrop flowed like delicious nectar through his veins. His gut clenched hard. This moment was *it*. He was finally standing at the pinnacle of everything he'd fought so hard for. Never had he dared to imagine that he would be in such a position—hosting a crowd such as this, contemplating becoming an indelible part of it.

He was finally standing far enough above and away from the degradation of his young life in the slums of a poor Italian city where he'd been little more than a feral child. With no way out. He'd been spat upon in the street by his own father and he'd watched his half-sisters walk past him without a single glance at their own flesh and blood. But he *had* clawed his way out, with guts and determination and his infamous intelligence. And to this day no one knew of his past.

He put his empty glass on the tray of an attentive hovering waiter and declined another one. Keeping his wits about him was as ingrained in him as a tattoo on his skin. For a second he thought of the crude tattoo he'd borne for years, until he'd had it removed. It was one of the first things he'd done on his arrival in London almost fifteen years ago, and his skin prickled now at the uncomfortable reminder.

He shrugged it off and went to stake his claim on Ms Honora Winthrop. For a brief second a sense of claustrophobia rose but he clamped down on the sensation. He was where he wanted to be, where he'd fought to be.

Composing himself, and irritated that he felt the need to do so, he found his eye snagged and caught by a lone figure. A female figure. He could see immediately that she was not half as polished or alluring as the other women in the room. Her dress was ill-fitting and her hair was a long, wild tangle of vibrant red. It suggested that there was something untamed about her, and it called to him on some deep level.

Rocco's mind emptied of its original purpose. He couldn't look away from the enigmatic stranger.

Before he had even registered his intent he'd veered off course and was moving in her direction...

Gracie O'Brien was trying to look nonchalant. As if she was used to being a guest at glittering functions in London's most prestigious venues. When in fact she was more used to being a waitress...in far less salubrious surroundings. The kind of places where men habitually pinched her bottom and said crude things about her lack of ample assets.

She gritted her jaw unconsciously, acknowledging that in today's economic climate a hard-won yet paltry art degree didn't count for much. She had a dream. But unfortunately to finance her dream she needed to work and to eat and survive. And the only jobs available to her right now were on the menial end of the scale.

She mentally shook herself out of the uncharacteristic introspection. She could handle the menial end of the scale. She couldn't handle *this*. She was clutching her bag to her belly. *Where had Steven gone?* She'd only come tonight as a favour to him. Her mouth compressed. Tension gnawed at her in this kind of surroundings—along with the habitual anxiety she felt for Steven.

Gracie forced herself to relax. This annual charity benefit thrown by the company her brother now worked for signified a huge turning point in his life—which had to explain his moody humour and nerves lately. That was all it was. She had to stop worrying about him. They were twenty-four now, and she couldn't go on feeling responsible for him just because she'd taken on that role from as far back as she could remember, when she'd been the one who had inevitably stood between him and some bully. She still bore scars of the scrapes she'd been in, protecting her little brother—younger by twenty fraught minutes.

Their mother, before she'd abandoned them, had never let Gracie forget that her beloved son had almost died, while Gracie had had the temerity to flourish with rude health. Her mother's parting words to Gracie had been, *'I'd take him with me and leave you behind if I could— he's the one I wanted. But he's too attached to you and I can't deal with a screaming brat.'*

Gracie pushed down the surge of emotion she felt whenever she thought of that dark day, and sighed when she finally caught sight of her brother in the distance. Her heart swelled in her chest with love for him. Despite their abandonment, and so much that had happened since then, they'd always looked out for one another. Steven's inherent weakness had meant that even Gracie's strength hadn't saved him for a few dark years, but now he was back on track.

Her brother had implored her earlier, 'Please, Gracie… I really want you there with me. They're all going to have their wives with them. I need to fit in. Do you know what a coup it is to get a job with De Marco International…?'

He'd gone on to wax lyrical once again about the god-like Rocco de Marco. So much so that Gracie had relented just to make him stop rhapsodising about this person who couldn't possibly be human because he sounded so perfect.

She'd also relented because she'd seen how anxious he was, and she knew how hard he'd worked for this chance. Long hours in prison, studying and sitting his A-levels so that he could get into college as soon as he got out. The constant fear that he would relapse back into his old drug-addicted ways. But he hadn't. Finally his uniquely raw talent and intellect was being used.

He was talking to another man. To look at Steven across the room, no one would even think he was related to Gracie. Steven was tall, and as skinny as a rake. Gracie was five foot five and her almost boyish figure caused her no end of dismay. Her brother was blond, pale and blue-eyed. She was red-haired, freckled and brown-eyed, taking after their feckless Irish father. Another reason why her mother had hated her.

She grimaced now, when her dress slipped half an inch further down her chest, exposing even more of her less than impressive cleavage. She'd seen it in a charity shop earlier and hadn't tried it on. *Big mistake*, Gracie grumbled to herself. The dress was at least two sizes too big and trailed around her feet like her nan's dresses had when she'd been a child playing dress-up.

She gave up hope that Steven was coming to look for her, figuring he was too busy, and turned her back on the crowd to hitch up her dress. She faced a buffet table groaning under the weight of platters of deliciously delicate canapés and an idea struck her.

Happily engrossed in her task a few minutes later, she froze when a deep and sexily accented voice drawled from nearby, 'The food won't disappear, you know... Most of the people in this room haven't eaten in years.'

The cynical observation went over Gracie's head. She flushed guiltily, her fingers tightening around the canapé she'd just wrapped in a napkin to put in her bag along with the three others she'd already carefully wrapped up. She glanced to her left, where the voice had come from, and had to lift her eyes up from a snowy-white broad chest, past a black bow tie and up to the most arrestingly gorgeous vision of masculinity she'd ever seen in her life.

The canapé dropped unnoticed from her hand into her open bag. She was utterly gobsmacked and transfixed. Dark eyes glittered out from a face so savagely beautiful that Gracie felt ridiculously like bowing, or doing something equally subservient. And she was *not* a subservient person. Sexual charisma oozed from every unashamedly masculine molecule.

'I…' She couldn't even speak. Silence stretched between them.

One ebony brow went up. 'You…?'

His mouth quirked, and that made things worse because it drew her attention there, and she found herself becoming even more mesmerised by the decadently sexy shape of his lips. There was something so provocatively sensual about his mouth. As if its true purpose was for kissing and only kissing. Anything else would be a waste.

Her face flaming now, because she was not used to thinking about kissing men within seconds of meeting them, Gracie dragged her gaze back up to those black eyes. She was aware that he was tall and almost intimidatingly broad. But it was actually hard to process the reality that the rest of him was equally gorgeous. His hair was thick and black, with one lock curling on his forehead. It gave him a devilish air that only enhanced the strong features which held a slightly haughty regard.

He carried an unmistakable air of propriety, his hands in his pockets with easy insouciance, and that realisation finally managed to dissolve Gracie's paralysis. She contracted inwards, lowered her eyes. 'The food isn't for me… It's for…' She searched wildly for some excuse for her gauche actions and thought belatedly of what Steven would say if she was thrown out for this. Maybe she'd read this man all wrong? She glanced up again and asked suspiciously, 'Are you Security?'

Even as the words left her mouth, and there was a clearly incredulous split second before he threw his head back to laugh throatily, she knew she shouldn't have said anything. This man was no mere security guard.

The sting of embarrassment, the knowledge that she was utterly out of her depth in these surroundings, made Gracie retort sharply, 'There's no need to get hysterical about it. How am I meant to know who you are?'

The man stopped laughing, but his eyes glittered with wicked amusement—further raising Gracie's ire. She knew that she was reacting to the very peculiar effect he was having on her body. She'd never felt like this before. Her skin was sensitive, with goosebumps popping up despite the heat of the room. Her senses were heightened. She could hear her heart thumping and she felt hot—as if her insides were being slowly set on fire.

'You don't know who I am?'

Blatant disbelief was etched into the man's perfect features. Gracie amended that thought. They weren't actually perfect. His nose looked slightly misaligned, as if it had been broken. And there were tiny scars across one cheek. Another faint scar ran from his jaw to his temple on the other side of his face.

She shivered slightly, as if she'd recognised something about this man on a very deep and primal level. As if they shared something. Which was ridiculous. The only thing she shared with a man like this was the air they were currently breathing. His question and his incredulity brought her back to earth.

She hitched up her chin. 'Well, I'm not psychic, and you're not wearing a name tag, so how on earth *should* I know who you are?'

That gorgeous mouth closed and firmed, as if he was trying to keep in a laugh. Absurdly Gracie felt like smacking him and had to curb the flash of he renowned temper, which unfortunately *did* match her hair.

'Who are you, then, if you're so important that everyone should know you?'

He shook his head, any trace of humour suddenly gone. Gracie shivered again, but this time it was because she saw another facet of this fascinating specimen of maleness. Strange how in the space of just mere seconds she felt as if she was seeing hidden layers and depths in a complete stranger. Now he had a speculative gleam in his eyes. She sensed strongly that behind the easy charm lurked something much less benevolent—something dark and calculating.

'Why don't you tell me who *you* are?'

Gracie opened her mouth, but just then a man materialised between them and directed himself to the tall man/god, completely ignoring Gracie as if she was some random nobody—which, she needed no reminding, she was. But also as if he was used to inserting himself between women and this man—which was extremely irritating.

'Mr de Marco, they're ready for you to give your speech.'

Shock slammed into her. *Mr de Marco?* This man she'd just been ogling was Rocco de Marco? From the way Steven had described him and his achievements she'd imagined someone much older. And quite possibly short and fat, with a cigar. Not this dynamic, virile man. She guessed him to be early thirties at the most.

The obsequious man who'd interrupted them melted away, and Rocco de Marco stepped closer to Gracie. Immediately his scent hit her, and it was musky and disturbingly masculine. He put out his hand and, still in shock, she lifted hers to let him take it. His eyes never leaving hers, he bent down and pressed a kiss to the back of her small, pale and freckled hand. Inwardly, even as her blood leapt to his touch, she cringed at how work-rough her hands must feel.

He stood again and let her hand go. He wasn't speculative any more. He was all hot and seductive. 'Don't go anywhere, now, will you? You still haven't told me who you are…'

And then after a searing look he turned and strode away into the throng. It was only then that Gracie breathed again. Unable to stop herself, she took in the sheer masculine majesty of his physique. He stood head and shoulders above most of the crowd, who were parting like a veritable Red Sea to let him through. A broad back tapered down to narrow hips and long legs. Physical perfection.

He was Rocco de Marco. Legendary financier and billionaire. Some people called him a genius. Wildly her glance searched for and found Steven, who was looking raptly to where Rocco now stood on a dais, commanding the packed ballroom.

Without even knowing quite why it was so important to get out of there, Gracie just knew she had to leave. The thought of facing that man again was frankly overwhelming. Her utter gaucheness screamed at her. The rough skin on her hands itched. Not one person in that room could be unaware of who he was. Except her. The sheer class of these people struck home—hard. The jewels the women wore were *real*, not like her cheap plastic baubles. She didn't belong here.

She thought of how the most important man in the room had witnessed her filching canapés from the buffet, and when she had a scary vision of being introduced to him by Steven she blanched. Steven would be mortified if Rocco de Marco mentioned it. He might even get into trouble.

That well ingrained sense of responsibility kicked in and Gracie did the only thing she could do. She ran.

Rocco de Marco regarded the profile about him in the newspaper's financial supplement with a disdainful twist of his lips. A cartoon depiction of his face made his features markedly more masculine and dark. A dart of satisfaction ran through him, however, when his eye went to the picture which had been taken of him with the glacially beautiful Honora Winthrop. He knew without arrogance that they looked good together—dark against pale. It had been taken at the De Marco Benefit in the London Museum the week before. The night he'd embarked on his campaign to seduce his way into respectable society for ever.

His smile turned hard at the thought of how eager Ms Winthrop had been to get into his bed. But so far he'd resisted her lures. He'd made the decision that night that the endgame would be to make her his wife, and in pursuing that aim he wouldn't allow sex to cloud the issue. His smile faded when he conceded that it hadn't taken much effort on his part to resist her.

As if to taunt him, the image of a petite, sparky redhead inserted itself mischievously into his mind's eye. It was so vivid that it drove him up and out of his chair. He stood at the vast window of his office which overlooked London. The view went as unnoticed as the paper which had fallen to the floor with his abrupt move. Rocco's jaw clenched in utter rejection of that image and memory. And the extremely uncomfortable reminder that after his speech he'd not gone straight to Honora Winthrop's side but to look for the nameless stranger—only to find that she'd disappeared.

He could still remember his shock and surprise. No one—especially not a woman—walked away from him.

He didn't relish the fact that not once before in the fifteen years since he'd left Italy had he ever deviated from his well-laid plans—not even for a beautiful woman. She hadn't even been that beautiful. But she'd been *something*. She'd exerted some kind of visceral pull on him the moment he'd seen her across the room.

For that entire evening he hadn't quite been able to stop his reflex to look for her. It burned him to acknowledge that he was still thinking of those few seconds of what should have been an unremarkable meeting. Especially when he was on track to achieving the stamp of respectability which would forever put him in a sphere far, far away from his past.

In an uncharacteristic gesture of fatigue Rocco rubbed the back of his neck. He put his momentary introspection down to the recent security breach in his company. It had been quickly discovered and sealed off, but had made Rocco realise how dangerously complacent he was becoming.

He'd hired Steven Murray a month ago—as much on a gut instinct as anything else, which was not normal practice for him. But he'd been unusually impressed with the young man's raw eagerness and undoubted intellect, and something about the man had connected with Rocco on a deep level. So, despite the worryingly vague CV, Rocco had given him a chance.

Only to be rewarded just this past week by the same man transferring one million euros to an unlocatable account and disappearing into thin air. The party last week had been a high point—and now this. It was like a punch in the face to Rocco. A sharp reminder that he could never let his guard down for a second.

His skin went clammy when he thought of how the people he sought so desperately to be his peers would turn their backs on him in a second if he revealed himself to be vulnerable in any way. And if that happened how quickly Honora Winthrop's gaze would turn disdainful if he even dared ask for her hand in marriage.

For so long now he'd been in absolute control, and suddenly he was chatting up random women in ill-fitting dresses and hiring people on gut instinct. He was in danger of jeopardising everything he'd worked so hard to attain. He was courted and fêted now because wealth made him powerful. It would be social acceptance that would secure his position for ever.

This chink in his otherwise solid armour made him wary. People were already curious about his past. He didn't want to give the hungry English tabloids any excuses to dig even further.

The fact that his security team had failed to find Steven Murray yet was like an irritating splinter stuck in Rocco's foot. He would not rest until the man had been found and questioned. And punished.

With a grimace at his own moody thoughts, Rocco turned from the view and picked up his jacket to leave his glass-walled office. Dusk was enveloping the city outside and the offices surrounding him were empty. It was usually his favourite time to work—when everyone had left. He liked the enveloping silence. It comforted him; it was so far removed from the constant cacaphony of his youth.

Just as he was almost out of his office the phone rang. Rocco turned back and picked it up. He heard what the person on the other end said and his whole body tautened. He bit out his words. 'Send her up to me.'

Tension kept Rocco's body tight as he walked to his lift and watched the numbers ascend. Someone was here asking for Steven Murray. There was a pause when the lift stopped, and in the split second before the doors opened

Rocco had a prickling sensation of something momentous about to happen.

The doors opened to reveal the petite form of a woman dressed in a grey T-shirt, faded jeans, and what looked like a cardigan tied around her waist. Her form was lithe and compact, with small pert breasts pushing against the fabric of her top. A heavy coil of red hair lay over one shoulder, reaching almost to those breasts. Her face was pale and heart-shaped, her freckles stood out, and her eyes were huge and brown, flecked with gold and green.

Instant recognition, shock, and something much hotter slammed into Rocco as he reached in and clamped his hands around slim arms almost as if he had to touch her before doing anything else.

He breathed out incredulously. *'You!'*

CHAPTER TWO

'You…' Gracie echoed faintly, still reeling after the lift doors had opened to reveal…*him*. In a haze she asked, 'What are you doing here?'

Rocco de Marco's hands pulled her from the lift, forcing her legs to move and she heard the faint swish of the doors closing again behind her. Her heart was thumping, and shock choked her at being faced with this man again.

His hands were on her arms like vices. 'I own this building,' he ground out, dark eyes blazing down into hers. 'I think the more pertinent question is this: why are *you* here, looking for Steven Murray?'

Dimly Gracie realised that he recognised her from that night they'd met a week ago. But there was no comfort in that. Adrenalin was pumping through her at seeing Rocco de Marco again, but from one look at his face she could take a wild guess and assume Steven was far away from this place. And in big trouble.

She couldn't speak. She could only look up into the most arrestingly handsome features she'd ever seen for the second time in just over a week.

His grip tightened. '*Why* are you here?'

Gracie shook her head, as if that might force oxygen to her malfunctioning brain. 'I just… I thought he might be here. I wanted to find him.'

Rocco's mouth tightened into a flat line. 'I think it's safe to assume that Steven Murray is in any number of locations now—none of which are close to here if he's got half a brain cell. He's done what most criminals do: they go underground.'

Gracie's heart stuttered at hearing her own fears so baldly spoken, but her innate protectiveness surged upwards even as her conscience protested. 'He's not a criminal.'

One of Rocco's brows arched up. 'No? Then what would *you* call stealing a million euros?'

If Rocco de Marco hadn't been holding her arms then Gracie would have fallen down. *A million euros?*

'What is he to you? Your lover?' He almost spat the words out.

Gracie shook her head and tried to back away—a futile exercise while he still held her arms. Paramount was the need to protect Steven at all costs as she tried to assimilate this mind-boggling information.

'I'm just worried about him. I thought he might be here.'

De Marco all but snorted. 'He's hardly likely to return to the scene of the crime. I don't think he's stupid enough to try and steal another million from the same source.'

Gracie felt trapped and claustrophobic, but fire surged up. 'He's not stupid!'

With a desperate wrench to get away that had more to do with this man's intensely physical effect on her than anything else, Gracie finally freed herself from his hands and whirled around, wildly searching for escape. She spotted emergency doors in the distance and sprinted, hearing a faint curse behind her. Just as her hands were about to touch the bar her shoulders were caught and she was twirled around, landing with a heavy thud against the doors. Rocco de Marco was glaring down into her face, hands either side of her head, effectively trapping her.

On some rational level Gracie knew she shouldn't have run, but the shock of hearing what her brother had done was too much. She realised now that she'd just made herself look as guilty as Steven.

As if reading her mind, Rocco de Marco breathed out and said in a chilling voice, 'You're obviously in this too—up to your pretty neck. The question is: why did you come back here? It must have been to get something important.'

She shook her head, her anger fading as fast as it had risen and leaving her feeling sick. 'Mr de Marco, I swear I'm not involved. I'm just worried. I came because I thought Steven might be here. I don't know anything.'

His face grew even harder and it sent a shiver through Gracie.

'You knew who I was last week when we met.'

It wasn't a question. She shook her head again. There was a quivery feeling in her belly at the thought of that meeting now. 'No…I didn't. I had no idea. Until that man came and used your name.'

As if not even listening to her, Rocco de Marco said, 'You were there with Murray as his accomplice. You and he cooked the whole thing up.'

Gracie just shook her head. It was throbbing with a mixture of anxiety and lingering shock. Rocco de Marco's focus seemed to come back to her, and with something that sounded like a snarl he stood up straight and took her arm, ignoring her wince. He was frogmarching her back to the lift and Gracie panicked, having visions of police waiting for her downstairs.

She started to struggle. 'Wait… Look, please, Mr de Marco, I can explain…'

He cast her a dark look as he punched a button on the lift. 'That's exactly what you're going to do.'

Fear and trepidation silenced Gracie as he pushed her into the lift ahead of him, yet kept a hold on her arm, and pressed another button once they were in. Silence, thick and tense, swirled around them, and Gracie cursed herself for coming here in the first place.

Standing next to him in the lift, she had a very real and physical sense of the disparity in their sizes. Her head barely grazed the top of his arm. His tautly muscled strength radiated outwards, enveloping her in heat. Gone was any trace of the man who had oozed warmth and seduction the night they'd met. Evidently if you moved within his rarefied milieu you were accorded his attention. A few steps out of it, however, and it was an entirely different story.

Gracie did not need this situation to demonstrate to her that someone like Rocco de Marco would look right through her if he saw her in her natural habitat. Her stomach twisted. She'd faced down many opponents over the years with plucky resilience, but for the first time she recognised someone who was immovable. And more powerful than anyone she'd ever encountered.

Oh, Steven, she groaned inwardly. *Why did you do this?*

He'd rung her earlier, and she could still taste the acrid fear in her mouth when he'd said, 'Gracie, don't ask any questions—just listen. Something has happened. Something really bad. I'm in serious trouble so I have to go away...'

She'd heard indistinct noises in the background, and Steven had sounded distracted.

'Look, I'm going away and don't know when I'll be able to get in touch again. So don't try and call, okay? I'll e-mail or something when I can...'

Gracie had clutched the phone with sweaty hands. 'Steven, wait—what is it? Maybe it's something I can help you with…?'

Her heart had nearly broken when he'd said, 'No. I won't keep doing this to you. You've done enough. It's not your problem, it's mine—'

Gracie had cut in, with fear constricting her voice. 'Is it…drugs again?'

Steven had laughed, and it had sounded a little hysterical. 'No…it's not drugs, Gracie. To be honest, it might be better if it was. It's work… Something to do with work.'

Before she'd been able to ask him anything else he'd said goodbye and cut her off. She'd kept calling his phone but it had only answered with an automated message to say that it was out of service. With a sick feeling she could well imagine he'd chucked his phone. She'd gone round to the small, spartan bedsit that he'd been so proud of and found it trashed, his stuff everywhere. No sign of him. And then she'd remembered him mentioning work and so she'd come here, to De Marco International, to see if by some miracle he was sitting in his office.

But she hadn't even got that far. The minute she'd seen Rocco de Marco's face she'd known her brother was in serious trouble.

Gracie was so preoccupied that it was a moment before she realised they'd ascended and she was being walked out of the elevator and into what looked like a penthouse apartment. The stunning dusky views over London added a surreal touch to the events unfolding.

A huge full moon was rising in the beautiful bruise-coloured sky, but it went unnoticed as Rocco let her go and moved about, switching on lights which sent out pools of inviting warmth. Gracie shivered and rubbed her arms.

The rush of adrenalin and shock had dissipated, leaving her feeling drained.

She looked around and was surprised to notice that the penthouse, for all its modernity, exuded warmth and an understated opulence. The parquet floor added an antique feel, and the heavy dark furniture stood out against the more industrial architecture, somehow working despite the apparent incongruity. Huge oriental rugs softened the austere lines.

If she hadn't been in such dire straits the artist in her would have longed to explore this tantalising glimpse into Rocco de Marco. Her eyes snagged on his powerful form as he bent and stretched. Her insides twisted and tightened—who was she kidding? Her interest in this man stemmed from a much more carnal place than an interest in aesthetics.

Rocco rounded on the petite woman who now stood in his apartment and curbed his physical response to that pale freckled skin and the wild russet hair which still trailed over one shoulder to rest on the curve of one small breast. The wild look in her eyes just before she'd sprinted away from him downstairs was burnt into his memory. It had touched something deep inside him. A memory. And he'd lost precious seconds while he'd been distracted.

She was nothing like the soignée beauties he usually favoured. Women renowned for their breeding, looks, intellect and discretion. Women who wouldn't have allowed him to lay a finger on them if they knew what kind of world he'd been born into.

Anger at his own indiscriminate response and something much deeper—a dark emotion which seethed in his gut as he thought of her as Steven Murray's lover—made him say harshly, 'You will tell me everything. Right here and now.'

When she flinched minutely, as if he'd struck her, he ruthlessly clamped down on the spike of remorse. She looked very pale and vulnerable all of a sudden. Rocco chastised himself. She was no quivering female. There was an inherent strength about her that warned of a toughness only bred from the streets. He recognised it well, and he didn't like to be reminded of it.

He dragged out a nearby chair and all but pushed her into it. Her small heart-shaped face was turned up to him and his insides tightened. *Dio*, but she was temptation incarnate with those huge brown eyes and those soft pink lips. Displaying a kind of artful innocence. His instinctive reversion to Italian even in his head just for that moment surprised him. He'd spent long years doing his best to erase any trace of his heritage. His accent was the one thing that proved as stubborn as a stain, reminding him every time he opened his mouth of his past. But he'd learnt to embrace that constant reminder.

There was a long, tense silence, and Rocco tried to figure out what was going on behind her wide eyes. And then she looked as if she was steeling herself for a blow. 'What did you mean when you said Steven stole a million euros?'

Rocco opened his mouth and was about to answer when he stopped. Incredulous, he said, 'You have the temerity to *still* pretend ignorance?'

He saw her small hands clench to fists on her lap. He remembered how spiky she'd been with him that night at the benefit, and how intrigued he'd been by her. He remembered kissing her hand, the feel of slightly rough palms which had been so at odds with the soft skin of the women he was used to, and how it had sent a dark thrill though him. She must have known exactly who he'd been and *they* must have been laughing at him all week. He burned inside. He hadn't felt so uselessly humiliated in years.

She'd seen him in a weak moment and he didn't like it. At all. He hadn't been weak since he'd left Italy far behind him, with its stench-filled slums and the humiliation he'd endured. Thinking of that restored Rocco's fast unravelling sense of control. With icy clarity he said, 'Who are you, and how do you know Steven?'

Gracie glared balefully at Rocco de Marco. He had the uncanny ability to make her feel as if you had no option but to comply with his demands. The man was like a laser.

'Well?'

The word throbbed with clear frustration and irritation. He was standing in front of her, hands on hips. His shoulders were broad under the white shirt, tapering down to lean hips. In the dim light he was like some beautiful dark lord. Heavy black brows over deepset pools of black. High cheekbones. A strong nose with that slight misalignment. And those lips…full and sensual. The lock of hair she remembered still curled on his forehead, but even that didn't soften the taut energy directed her way.

Half without thinking Gracie said, 'I'm Gracie. Gracie O'Brien.'

His mouth took on a disdainful curve. 'And? Your relationship to Steven Murray?'

Gracie swallowed. She was afraid if Rocco de Marco knew she and Steven were related he would expect her to know where he was for sure. She could feel the blush rising even as she formulated the words. She'd never been able to lie to save her life. 'He's…he's an old friend.'

Rocco's eyes went to her mouth and he said mockingly, with a chill kind of menace, 'Liar.'

Gracie shook her head. Protecting her twin brother was

so ingrained she couldn't fight it. And didn't want to. He'd protected her over the years as much as she'd protected him. Just in a different way. 'That's all he is. An old friend. We go back…a long way.'

Rocco's mouth twisted and disgust etched his features into a grimace. 'You go back to a double bed in a squat somewhere.'

Gracie paled at the very thought. Bile rose. She shook her head more strongly. 'No. *No.*' She stopped short of saying *That's disgusting*, and closed her mouth. 'Really… it's not like that.' She'd half risen out of the chair and her hand was out, as if that could reinforce her words. She sat back down abruptly.

Rocco folded his arms across his chest, but that only brought her attention to the awesome strength in his arms, the bunched muscles. She felt curiously light-headed all of a sudden, but put it down to the fact that she hadn't eaten all day.

'I'll tell you what it's *like*, shall I?' Rocco didn't wait for her to answer. 'You're Steven Murray's accomplice, and both of you were stupid enough to think that you could come back to the scene of the crime to recover something important. What was it?' he continued. 'A flash drive? That's the only thing small enough to have escaped our searches.'

Before she knew what was happening Rocco was right in front of her, hauling her out of the chair. Amidst her confusion and shock Gracie was aware of the fact that his touch on her arms was light, almost gentle this time. The contrast of that touch to the fierce energy crackling around them made her even more confused. But he was squatting at her feet now, running big hands up her legs.

It took a second for the fact to register that he was frisking her. His hands were now creeping up the insides of her

legs. She reacted violently, jerking away, hands slapping
everywhere, catching Rocco's silky head. He cursed and
stood up, catching hold of her arms again with his hands.
This time he wasn't gentle.

'You little wildcat. Hold still.'

Holding her captive with one hand, he quickly delved
into her pockets with his free one and turned them out.
The speed with which he moved made Gracie feel dizzy.
Soon she was standing there with the linings of pockets
sticking out and the disconcerting feeling of his hands
probing close to her skin.

This time when she jerked back he let go, and she almost stumbled. She felt violated—but not in the way she
should have. It was in some illicitly thrilling way.

'You...' she spluttered. 'I'd prefer to be dragged down
to the police station than have your hands mauling me.' A
sudden realisation sliced through the frantic pulse in her
blood and she asked faintly, '*Have* you called the police?'

Rocco stood back. His face was flushed. With anger,
Gracie had to assume, not liking the way her blood pooled
heavily between her legs even as she struggled to concentrate. He had gone very still.

He shook his head and with clear reluctance admitted,
'I haven't called the police because I don't want the news
that I employed a rogue trader to get out. It could ruin my
reputation. Image and trust are everything in this game.
If my clients knew I'd jeopardised their precious invest-
ments I'd be finished within days as rumour and innuendo
spread.'

For a second Gracie felt nothing but abject relief flowing
into her veins, but the cruel smile on Rocco's face made
her blood run cold again.

'Don't assume for one second that not calling the police
gives your lover a reprieve. Do you think an overworked

police force or a fraud squad can be bothered looking for one man?' He shook his head and crossed his arms. 'I have people looking for Steven right now, and they have infinitely more sophisticated resources at their disposal. It's only a matter of time.'

Fear constricted Gracie. 'What'll happen to him?'

Rocco's face was hard. '*After* he's returned every cent of the money? Then I will blacklist him from every financial institution in the world and hand him over to the fraud squad whilst protecting my own anonymity. He could be looking at ten years in jail. I have used my own money to bridge the gap caused by his stolen funds. He owes me personally now.'

Gracie felt weak. She groped to find the chair behind her and sat down heavily. Her brother would never survive another day in jail. He'd told her fervently when he'd got out that he would prefer to die than end up there again.

Rocco frowned. For the first time this evening he could swear the woman in front of him wasn't acting. She looked like a car crash victim. He had to resist the urge to ask if she wanted a drink.

She was looking at the ground. Not at him. Rocco wanted to go to her and tip her chin up. He didn't like how disconcerted he felt not being able to look into her eyes. And then she did look up, and her eyes were like two huge dark pools, made even darker against the sudden pallor of her skin.

She opened her mouth. He could see her throat work. She shook her head and finally said, 'I can't… I can't lie to you. This is too serious. I haven't told you the truth about Steven.'

Rocco felt the hardness return. He ruthlessly pushed down the weakness which had invaded him for a moment.

'I'm getting bored waiting for it. You have one minute to speak or I *will* hand you over to the police as an accomplice and deal with the consequences.'

Gracie's head was too tangled up with fear and shock for her even to try and persist in making Rocco de Marco believe she wasn't related to Steven. His casual mention of jail had decimated her defences completely. Any faint hope she'd been clinging onto that there must be some kind of mistake had also gone. Gracie knew with a defeated feeling that Steven wouldn't have run if it wasn't true. He must have been trying to play for stakes way outside his league. Was that why he'd gone for the job in the first—?

'*Gracie!*'

Her feverish thoughts stuttered to a stop and she looked up at Rocco. Her name on his lips did funny things to her insides. For a moment she'd forgotten she was under his intense scrutiny. Illicit heat snaked through her abdomen, and in the midst of her turmoil she couldn't believe he was affecting her so easily.

Taking a deep breath, she stood up, her legs wobbling slightly. 'Steven is not my lover and I'm not his accomplice… He's my brother.'

'*Go on.*'

Rocco's voice could have sliced through steel. He'd crossed his arms again and her gaze skittered over those bunched muscles.

Gracie shrugged minutely, unaware of how huge her eyes looked in her small face.

'That's it. He's my brother and I'm worried about him. I was looking for him.' She wasn't sure why, but she didn't want to let Rocco know that he was her *twin* brother. That information suddenly felt very intimate.

Rocco's jaw clenched, and then he said slowly, 'You

expect me to believe that? After everything I've just witnessed and after I saw you at the benefit last week? You were both cooking up this plan together.'

Gracie shook her head. 'No. It wasn't like that, I swear. I only went with Steven because—' She stopped. She couldn't explain about her brother's inherent insecurity and how badly he needed to fit in. And also she'd realised now why he'd been so abnormally anxious for the past few weeks—way more than she would have expected for new job nerves. She felt sick.

Rocco filled in the silence, 'Because you and he had a grand plan to do some inside trading and make yourselves a million euros without anyone noticing.' He emitted a curt laugh. 'For God's sake, you couldn't even help yourself stealing food from the buffet!'

Gracie flushed bright red. 'I took that food for my next-door neighbour. She's old and Polish, and always talks about when she used to be rich and go to balls in Poland. I thought they would be a nice treat for her.'

This time Rocco did laugh out loud, head thrown back, exposing his strong throat. Gracie burned with humiliation, her disadvantaged upbringing stinging like an invisible tattoo on her skin.

Rocco finally stopped laughing and speared her with those dark eyes again. Gracie fought not to let him see how much he affected her. It scared her, because ever since her mother had left them, and then their nan had turned her back on them, leaving them to the mercy of Social Services, Gracie had allowed very few people close enough to affect her—apart from her brother.

Becoming slightly desperate, she flung out a hand. 'I barely passed my O-level Maths. I wouldn't know a stock from a share if it jumped up and bit me. Steven is the smart one.'

'And yet,' Rocco went on with relentless precision, 'you were with him last week, flaunting yourself in front of me. You *knew* who I was.'

Gracie sucked in an outraged breath that had a lot to do with the memory of how transfixed she'd been by him that night. 'I was *not* flaunting myself. *You* came over to *me.*'

At this Rocco de Marco flushed a dull red, and for the first time Gracie had a sense that she'd gained a point. But any sign of discomfiture was quickly erased and his face became a bland mask again. Bland, but simmering—if that was possible.

Quickly, before he could launch another attack, Gracie admitted reluctantly, 'I was with Steven because he was self-conscious about going alone.'

Rocco's lip curled. 'I have yet to believe that you are even Steven Murray's sister. Why does he have a different surname?'

Gracie shifted uncomfortably and knew she must look pathetically guilty. She looked down. 'Because...because he fell out with our father and took our mother's maiden name.' It wasn't entirely untrue.

'Not to mention the fact that you look nothing like him.'

Gracie looked up to see Rocco's dark gaze travelling up her body, over her chest to her face. She could feel the heat rising. 'No,' she snapped. 'I know I look nothing like him. But not all—' She stopped abruptly, realising she'd been about to say *twins*. She amended it. 'Not all families resemble each other. He looks like my mother and I look like my father.'

She crossed her arms too, feeling ridiculously defensive, and knew it was only because for her whole life she'd wondered if she'd looked more like their mother would she have loved her the way she'd loved Steven? Would she have stayed?

The fact that she'd eventually abandoned them both was little comfort and a constant source of guilt for Gracie. She could still remember the long nights of hugging her brother as he'd cried himself to sleep, wondering where their mother had gone.

For a long time she'd felt it had been *her* fault, because her mother hadn't wanted her. It was only with age and maturity that she'd realised their mother had had no intention of ever taking Steven—too wrapped up in her own problems and her own dismal world.

After a long moment of glaring at Rocco, Gracie could feel herself sway. Her vision blurred slightly at the edges. Just as she was inwardly cursing her own weakness Rocco emitted something unintelligible and came towards her, putting a big hand on one arm. She stiffened at his touch, hating the incendiary effect he had on her, but at the same time aware of how close she was to collapsing. Like some Victorian heroine in a swoon. *Pathetic.*

She tried to pull away, but to no avail.

Rocco said, from far too close, 'When was the last time you ate, you silly woman?'

This time she did pull free, and glared at him again. 'I'm *not* a silly woman. I've just been…worried. I didn't think about eating.'

That black gaze swept up and down again and his lip curled. 'You don't seem to think about eating a lot.'

He strode away from her and Gracie watched him, half mesmerised by his sheer athletic grace. He flung over his shoulder. 'There are some instant meals in the fridge. Follow me.'

Gracie felt seriously woozy now. Rocco de Marco was offering her *food*?

She tore her gaze away from six feet four of hard-muscled alpha male and looked to the apartment entrance, beyond which lay the private lift doors. Suddenly the distance to freedom seemed tantalisingly close.

As if he'd read her mind Rocco materialised again a few feet away, with hands on his hips, and said softly, 'Don't even think about it. You wouldn't make it to the next floor before you were returned.'

Her heart stammered as she looked at him. 'But...I didn't see anyone.'

Rocco winked at her, but there was no humour on his face. 'Haven't you watched any Italian movies? My men are everywhere.'

Gracie tried to reassure herself that he was just joking, but she had the very real sense that if she did try to leave some faceless person *would* materialise and frogmarch her back to Rocco. She knew enough from the streets to know when someone meant business. And Rocco de Marco meant business. She was as captive as if he'd tied her to a chair.

He turned to walk away again and with the utmost reluctance, and yet an illicit excitement fizzing in her blood, she followed him.

It was only when Rocco was pressing the button on the microwave oven that a cold wave of realisation washed over him. What was he *doing*? Feeding the enemy? All because for a moment she'd looked as if she might faint at his feet? Her face had been so pale that it had sent a shard of panic through him, and as much as he wanted to deny it he had to admit that her shock had been almost palpable. And yet every instinct he possessed counselled him not to trust his judgement in this. He'd learnt early how women could manipulate. He'd seen his mother manipulate her way through life right up until she died.

Closing his eyes for a moment, Rocco willed the image away. His hands clenched on the countertop as he heard Gracie come into the kitchen behind him. Why the hell was he even thinking of that now?

He schooled his features and turned around. Something suspiciously like relief went through him when he saw that her cheeks were a bit pinker. Her big eyes were darting around the vast room and he welcomed the surge of cynicism. No doubt she was already calculating the worth of everything. That was what he would have done. Years ago. Before figuring out what he could take.

The microwave pinged and he turned to take out the ready meal, finding a plate and some cutlery. He all but threw it down in front of her, then gestured to a stool and growled out, 'You're my only link to Steven Murray, and if you're going to lead me to him then I don't want you fainting away.'

Her eyes flashed at that, and her mouth tightened as if she was about to refuse the food. A shaft of desire he couldn't control made Rocco clench his hands to fists. He hated her for his arbitrary response.

'Go on. Eat.'

CHAPTER THREE

GRACIE chafed at Rocco de Marco's high-handedness. She hitched up her chin and tried to ignore the tantalising smell of food. Even that alone was making her feel weak again with hunger.

'Are you going to leave it in front of me until I eat it? Like an autocratic parent?'

Rocco leaned forward on the other side of the counter and Gracie fought not to move back. 'I'm no parent and I'm no autocrat. Just eat.'

Gracie looked down to escape that blistering gaze and saw creamy mashed potato and what looked like succulent beef pieces in a stew of vegetables. This was no standard ready meal—this was from a fancy deli. Her stomach rumbled and she went puce.

Defiant to the end, even as she gave in and pulled back the covering she said waspishly, 'I might have been vegetarian, you know.'

She heard a noise that sounded slightly strangled, but wouldn't look at Rocco for fear of what she might see. She started transferring the food onto the plate, hating being under his watch but too hungry to stop.

After a moment he said, with over-studied politeness, 'Forgive me for not checking with you first.'

She cast him a quick glance and something in her belly

swooped. He'd been laughing at her. She hurriedly looked away again and concentrated on the food. Once the first succulent morsel of beef hit her mouth she was lost, and devoured the lot like a pauper who hadn't eaten in weeks.

From out of nowhere a napkin and a glass of water materialised. Gracie wiped her mouth and took a long drink of water. Only then did she dare to look at Rocco again. He was staring at her, transfixed. She immediately felt self-conscious and wiped her mouth again. 'What? Have I got food somewhere?'

He shook his head. His voice sounded rough. 'When was the last time you ate?'

For a moment Gracie couldn't actually recall. She fidgeted with the plate and mumbled, 'Yesterday...lunchtime.' But in fact she knew she hadn't really eaten properly in days.

'Where do you live?'

Gracie met Rocco's dark and hard gaze. Something in his demeanour had changed. He was back into questioning mode. And then the full reality of her situation flooded back. She flushed and avoided his eyes. She felt like such a pathetic failure at that moment.

'Gracie...' he said warningly, and her insides flipped again at the way he said her name. It felt incredibly intimate.

She looked at him and squared her shoulders. She couldn't go any lower in his estimation, and perhaps if he knew just how harmless she was he'd let her go?

'I lived in Bethnal Green until this morning. But I lost my job two days ago and they wouldn't give me my wages. I couldn't give my landlord the full rent today, so he suggested I make it up to him in other ways.'

Gracie shuddered reflexively when she remembered his sweaty face, grabbing hands and acrid breath. Before she knew it Rocco had moved. She felt her right hand being picked up and he was inspecting the grazed and reddened knuckles. She'd forgotten, and winced slightly because they were still tender.

He speared her with a glance, 'You hit him?'

She shrugged slightly, more mortified than ever now. She hated her instinct to fight. She'd had it ever since someone had picked on Steven when they'd been tiny. 'He was backing me into a corner. I couldn't get out.'

Still holding her hand, Rocco said grimly, 'I suppose I should consider myself lucky you didn't aim a swing at me too.'

Gracie looked up at his hard jaw and figured she would have broken her hand if she had. He was standing very close now, still cradling her hand. Her belly clenched and a coil of something hot seemed to stretch from her breasts right down to between her legs. And as if on cue she felt a throb, a pulse coming to life.

She pulled her hand away and started babbling. 'I left my cases at Victoria train station in the left luggage. I should go and get them and find somewhere for the night.'

She was off the stool and backing away now, as if she'd forgotten for a moment why she was there in the first place, suddenly terrified at the weak longing that had sprung up inside her when Rocco had held her hand.

He continued to just look at her with his arms folded. 'I told you before that you won't make it to the next floor if you try to leave.'

Panic rose up, constricting Gracie's voice. 'You can't keep me here. That would be kidnap. I only came to Steven's office to try and find him. That's *all*. I really don't have an ulterior motive. I didn't take anything and I didn't know about the money.'

Rocco looked at the woman in front of him. Strange

how his entire world had contracted down to her since he'd seen her in the lift. For a second that knowledge threatened to blast something open inside him, but Rocco reminded himself that she was providing him with the key to finding the culprit who'd had the temerity to think he could take advantage of him.

That was why he hadn't thought about anything else.

It had nothing to do with the fact that just a moment ago, when he'd held her hand in his and seen her bruised knuckles, he'd felt rage within him at the thought of some faceless man threatening her.

To divert his mind away from those provocative thoughts, he asked, 'Why did you lose your job?'

He could see her hands ball into fists. She was like a glorious feline animal, bristling and lashing out in defence, and a curious weakness invaded his chest. When he'd watched her eating ravenously he'd been mesmerised—first of all because he wasn't used to seeing women eat like that, and also because it had reminded him of *him*. He would never forget what it was to be hungry.

'I had issues with some of the customers.'

Rocco arched a brow and welcomed being forced to refocus on the present. 'Customers?'

She flushed pink. 'I worked in a bar in a less than salubrious part of town.' And then she said in a rush, 'Just temporarily.'

Again Rocco felt a kind of rage growing within him—not at her, but *for* her. He could well imagine men finding her feisty allure something to challenge and harness. She was proving to be altogether far more of an enigma than she'd appeared that night just a week ago.

Out of nowhere, immediate and incendiary, Rocco had the desire to see her tamed and acquiescent, and he wanted to be the one to tame her. Sheer shock at the strength of that desire made Rocco blanch for a moment. Women like her should hold no appeal for him. It felt like a self-betrayal. Before she could see anything of his loss of composure, and wondering if he'd lost his mind completely, he strode forward and stopped in front of her, as if to prove to himself that he *could* stand in front of her and restrain himself from tipping her over his shoulder like some caveman. The surreal circumstances of their meeting and her connection to Steven Murray was causing this completely uncharacteristic response, that was all.

As implacable as a stone wall, he told her now, 'You're not leaving this apartment until your brother—' He broke off and swore for a moment. 'If he even *is* your brother, is found and brought to task for his actions. Now, give me the ticket for your bags and I'll have them picked up.'

Scant minutes later Gracie found herself being shown into a sumptuously decorated guest bedroom. She still wasn't entirely sure how she'd allowed herself to be bulldozed into submission, but on some very secret level she felt so tired. For the first time in her life she was being subservient to someone else and she couldn't drum up the energy to fight it. She had no one to turn to and nowhere to go—literally. An uncharacteristic wave of loneliness washed over her.

'There's a bathroom through there, with a robe and toiletries. When your bags come I'll bring them to you.'

Gracie looked around with wide eyes gritty with fatigue. Rocco was striding towards the door and she envied his seemingly unstoppable force. If she'd known there was a chance she might bump into him again there was no way she would have ever attempted to go to her brother's office. She sighed. Too late for regrets now.

Rocco turned at the door, filling it with his broad frame. 'We'll discuss where we go from here in the morning.'

Some sliver of fight sparked within her. 'You'll let me walk out of this apartment. Because if you don't—'

He cut her off. 'You'll what? Call the police?' He shook his head and smiled with insufferable coolness. 'No, I don't think so. I'm sure you don't want the police sniffing around your brother any more than I want the news leaked that I employed an inside trader.'

Silence grew and thickened between them. What could she say to refute that? He was absolutely right, and for deeper reasons than he even knew.

He inclined his head in a false gesture of civility. 'Until the morning, Miss O'Brien.'

The door closed softly behind him and Gracie almost expected to hear a key turning in the lock, but she heard nothing. Experimenting, she went to the door and opened it softly. She nearly jumped three feet in the air when she saw Rocco lounging against the wall outside.

'Don't make me lock the door, because I will.'

Wanting to avoid any further questioning or scrutiny Gracie closed the door again hurriedly. She moved like an automaton to the window and looked out over the spectacular view, seeing nothing but her inward turmoil.

It had always been her and Steven—even when their mother had still been with them. And then when their nan had taken them in until she'd declared she couldn't handle two children and had given them over to Social Services.

Their bond had been forged early, when their mercurial mother had cossetted Steven and treated Gracie harshly. One evening, when Gracie had been sent to bed with no dinner for some minor misdemeanour, Steven had crawled in beside her with some food which he'd hidden for her. They'd been four years old.

Steven had always been a target for bullies with his weedy, sickly frame and his thick glasses, so Gracie had

got used to stepping in with raised fists. He'd been preter-
naturally bright, and Gracie knew now if they'd grown up
in different circumstances he might well have been nurtured as a genius student. As it was he'd constantly been
ahead of his classmates, and yet had patiently and labori-
ously helped Gracie through the torture of maths and sci-
ence.

It was thanks to him she'd managed to scrape enough
marks in her exams for art college. Even whilst he'd been
in the midst of drug addiction and had given up studying himself he'd still been advanced enough to help her.
Her belly clenched now when she thought of how Steven
had protected her from far worse things than inexplicable
maths.

She leant her forehead against the cool glass, and even
though her mind was churning with sick worry for her
brother she couldn't get another face out of her head. A
dark, compelling face with eyes so intense she shivered
even now. And she couldn't stop a wave of heat from
spreading outwards from her core, threatening the cool
distance she'd protected herself with for so long.

Rocco looked at the two battered bags that had been delivered a short time before. One was a backpack and the
other an old-fashioned suitcase. The kind you might see in
a movie from the 1940s about immigrants leaving Europe
for America. She'd left her flat with just *these*? Rocco was
used to women travelling with an entire set of matching
luggage, complete with personally monogrammed initials.
But then he didn't need reminding that *this* woman was
a world away from the ones he knew. He shook his head
and picked up the bags. He'd long ago given up on the notion of sleeping tonight.

Opening the door to the guest bedroom silently, Rocco

half expected to see Gracie standing on the other side, as obstinate and defiant as ever, but she wasn't. In the gloom his eyes quickly picked out a shape on the bed. Standing still for a moment, he registered she was fast asleep.

Putting down the bags, he felt compelled to go closer. Gracie was lying on top of the covers in a white robe. She was curled up in the foetal position, legs tucked under themselves, hands under her chin. Her hair flowed out around her head like something out of a Pre-Raphaelite painting, the curls long and wild.

Everything in him went still when her head moved and she said brokenly, *'No, Steven...you can't...please...'*

That brought Rocco down to earth with a bang. Once again it was as if she'd exerted some kind of spell over him, making him forget for a moment who she was and why she was here. She was a thieving, lying nobody and her brother had had the temerity to think he could abuse Rocco de Marco's trust.

Rocco stepped back and away from the curled-up shape on the bed, and ruthlessly clamped down on any tendrils of concern or unwelcome desire. He vowed there and then that he would not let her go until he was satisfied that she *and* Steven Murray had been brought to justice.

When Gracie woke in the morning she had the awful sensation of not knowing where she was or what day it was. Her surroundings were completely unfamiliar and scarily luxurious. She was lying on top of a massive bed, in a robe. Slowly, it all came back. Leaving her awful damp flat after nearly being mauled by her landlord, getting that worrying phone call from Steven, and then coming to his office to see if he might be there.

And then she remembered coming face to face with Rocco de Marco. Gracie groaned and put a pillow over her face. *Rocco de Marco*. Her stomach cramped at the vivid memory of his hands around her arms, the way they'd felt when he'd frisked her. The intense excitement in her blood at seeing him again.

Groaning even more, she sat up and saw that the curtains were still open. She now had the most jaw-dropping views out over London, with the Thames snaking like a brown coil through the grey and steel buildings.

She turned away from the view and something caught her eye. She saw her two battered bags just inside the bedroom door. Her face grew hot when she thought of Rocco coming in while she lay sleeping.

Feeling seriously at a disadvantage, Gracie scrambled out of bed and dragged the bags over. She pulled out some jeans and a T-shirt and found her sneakers. After washing her face she dragged her hair back into a knot at the back of her head and left the room.

The entire apartment was still and quiet. Gracie checked her watch. It was still early. Maybe Rocco wasn't up yet? But even as she thought that she got to the doorway of the enormous kitchen and saw him sitting at a large chrome kitchen table. Her heart stopped. He was reading the distinctively pink *Financial Times*. His hair was damp and slicked back from that strong profile. Skin gleaming dark olive in the morning light. Immaculately dressed in a light blue shirt and royal blue tie.

And then he looked up, after taking a lazy sip from a small cup which should have looked ridiculous in his huge hand but didn't. 'Good morning.'

'Good morning,' she echoed faintly, for all the world as if she'd been some benign overnight guest and not one step away from being locked in her room.

Rocco gestured with a hand to the kitchen. 'I'm afraid

you'll have to help yourself. I'm currently without a house-keeper.'

Gracie tore her eyes away from his raw masculine appeal and helped herself to some coffee and toast, which was already laid out. She hated that her hands were shaking. Very little had ever intimidated her, but this did.

She stood awkwardly at the huge island in the middle of the room until Rocco said, a little impatiently, 'Come and sit down. I won't bite.'

Gracie gritted her teeth and reluctantly picked up her coffee and plate and sat down at the other end of the table. She didn't miss his sardonic look. She felt very pale and washed out next to his vibrant masculinity.

She swallowed her toast with an effort and wiped away some crumbs, studiously avoiding Rocco's eyes, and nearly jumped out of her skin when he said, 'I spent a little time investigating your brother last night, and the full picture is very interesting.'

Gracie went cold inside and put down her cup. Frantically she rewound events in her head and froze. She'd told Rocco Steven's real name by revealing her own. She looked at him with wide eyes.

Rocco looked almost bored, but she could sense the underlying anger as tangibly as if he'd started shouting. 'He's got quite an impressive rap sheet. Three years in jail for carrying Class A drugs. Not to mention the fact that he forged papers to get a job in my company so we couldn't find out about his past. His crimes are mounting, Gracie.'

Feeling desperate, Gracie blurted out, 'He's not like that. He really was trying to make a fresh start, to use his intelligence and turn his life around. He did a degree. There has to be some good reason for what he's done—he wouldn't have risked jail again.'

Rocco was impossibly grim. 'I think a lot of people

would agree that a million euros provides quite a good reason.'

Gracie sagged back into her chair and looked down at her pale hands. They were trembling and she clasped them together. Hot tears pricked at the back of her eyes. Rocco's mention of the astronomical sum of money struck hard. She'd almost forgotten about it with everything else that had happened. How could Steven ever come back from this? He'd spend his whole life paying it back. And that was if he was lucky enough to get the chance.

She heard Rocco sigh but couldn't look up, terrified he'd see her emotion. He said with palpable reluctance, 'Nevertheless, I don't think you're about to phone him and tell him to give himself up?'

Willing the emotion down, Gracie looked up. Huskily she admitted, 'I did speak to him yesterday, but he wouldn't tell me where he was, or where he was going, and when I tried to call him back his phone was switched off. I think he's thrown it away.' She omitted to mention that he'd said he'd try to contact her when he could. Gracie vowed then that if that happened she'd tell Steven to stay away and never come back...

Rocco stood up and held out a hand. 'Give me your phone.'

Gracie's mouth opened and closed. Feeling bullish now, she said, 'Why?'

Rocco's mouth tightened. 'Because I don't believe you. Because I think you'll make every attempt to get in touch with your brother and warn him to stay away. And because if he does try and contact you then we'll have him.'

Gracie crossed her arms.

They glared at each other for long seconds and then Rocco bit out with evident distaste, 'Don't make me search you again.'

Something pierced Gracie at the thought of how he'd touched her the night before and how it had obviously repulsed him. In a bid to cover up her emotion she stood up, knowing that he would just find her phone anyway.

She stalked out of the kitchen and retrieved her phone from her bag and brought it back to Rocco, handing it over with a baleful glare. 'He won't call me again. He knows he's in trouble.'

Rocco pocketed the phone and then said casually, 'I have a proposition for you.'

Gracie blinked. She was fairly certain that any proposition from him would be more like a royal decree. Unconsciously she took a step back and could breathe easier. She missed the way Rocco's eyes flashed at her movement.

'I don't have a housekeeper at the moment. I need one.' He flicked a faintly contemptuous glance up and down Gracie's casual clothes. 'I don't see how you could mess up such a basic job. You wouldn't even have to cook. I have a chef who prepares food when I need it. You'd just have to clean and manage the apartment. Deliveries, etc.'

Gracie was struggling to take this in. 'You're...offering me a job?'

Rocco grimaced slightly. 'Well, it's not so much a job as something to keep you busy while you're here. Because you're not leaving my sight until we have your brother.'

Gracie's heart palpitated in her chest at the thought of spending more time with this man. She crossed her arms. 'You can't do this. It's outrageous. You can't just keep me prisoner.'

Rocco arched a mocking brow. 'You have nowhere to go and no job. You've got a grand total of fifty pounds. You're hardly in a position to assert your independence or freedom. I think you'll find I'm doing you a favour—which you certainly don't deserve.'

Gracie gasped. 'You looked through my things.'

Rocco shrugged slightly. 'Of course I did.'

Gracie felt ashamed to have her pitiful amount of money laid out between them like this. She actually had slightly more than that in a bank account, but it was paltry. Since she'd finished her art degree she'd been struggling just to survive, never mind follow her dreams and ambitions. Rocco de Marco had most likely never even known what it was like to have to eke out a living.

Forcing herself to not crumble, she said caustically, 'So you're offering me this *job* out of the goodness of your heart?'

He smiled, but it was completely without humour. 'Something like that, yes. You're really in no position to argue, Gracie. You and your brother have got yourselves into this situation. Look at it this way: you're worth a million euros of collateral until your brother turns up.'

Her mind frantically searched for a way out, but right then she couldn't see one. She was well and truly trapped. As much as *she* was the link to Steven for this man, *he* was her last tangible link to Steven. And there was no way she was going to leave her brother to face this man's wrath alone when they did find him.

Gracie straightened her spine and drew herself up, determined to regain some measure of control amidst this awful powerlessness. 'If I'm going to be your housekeeper then I want the same amount that I was being paid in the bar. I have to keep my student loan repayments up.'

Rocco crushed down his surprise at her visible decision to stay without a fight and tried to ignore the prickling of his conscience. If she was guilty wouldn't she be doing her best to persuade him to let her go so she could meet her brother? And, also, why would she have been stupid enough to come where Steven worked? Rocco crushed the questions. She was up to something—probably just acting this way so that he *would* doubt her guilt.

Curious despite himself, he asked tightly how much she'd been paid and waited for her to triple the amount, which he had no intention of paying. Not with a million euros missing.

Gracie mentioned a figure and Rocco had to stop his shock from registering on his face. Her expression was so guileless and innocently defiant that he found himself inexplicably agreeing to pay her the pathetic sum, and had to wonder if that was even the minimum wage.

Gracie watched as Rocco pulled pen and paper out of a drawer and scrawled a couple of numbers and names on it before putting it into her numb hand.

'That's my executive assistant's number if you need to get me. I'll be in meetings all day on the other side of the city. You can use the phones in the apartment.' His eyes flashed. 'Needless to say, any calls to your brother will be recorded. I've also written down my old housekeeper's number, so you can call to consult with her on what I'll expect.'

Gracie looked down at the paper and then heard his mocking voice.

'My main head of security is positioned right outside this apartment and he can see every movement in and out of the building. If you attempt to leave you'll merely be brought back.'

She looked back and held up the paper, muttering caustically, 'You mean I don't have a direct line to God?'

Rocco smiled and it was wicked, making Gracie's heart-rate and body temperature soar.

'I reserve my private number for people I wish to speak to—not miscreants and thieves.'

His words had an instant effect on Gracie, causing a hot flush of anger to rise when she thought of the long struggle she and her brother had faced to drag themselves out of their adverse circumstances. 'You know nothing about me. *Nothing.*'

His eyes turned cool. 'I know all I need to know. Keep out of trouble until I see you again.'

Gracie watched as he turned and strode away, and shamingly her anger drained away as she found herself wondering what kind of person someone like Rocco would want to give his private number to and speak with in low, intimate tones.

Anger at her wayward imagination made her call defiantly after him, 'Don't think you can get away with this. You're nothing but an...autocratic megalomaniac.'

Rocco turned around and Gracie's heart stuttered to a halt when she saw the anger on his face. Fear gripped her, but it was fear because of her helpless physical response to him. This awful weak yearning he effortlessly precipitated.

'If you're so concerned then by all means call the police. And while you're onto them you can fill them in on your brother's recent activities. I'm sure they'll be delighted to hear about his progress in the real world since prison.'

Gracie gulped. She felt sick. 'You know I can't do that.'

In that moment Gracie could see the long lineage of aristocratic forebears stamped onto Rocco's arrogant features. He had her all boxed up and judged and right where he wanted her.

'Well, then, you'd better get acquainted with this apartment—because it's your home for the forseeable future.'

After he'd walked out Gracie tried hard to drum up

anger or even hatred, but to her intense chagrin all she could seem to think of was the way he'd insisted on feeding her the previous evening.

CHAPTER FOUR

ROCCO sat in the back of his chauffeur-driven car. The London traffic was at a standstill. He could sense the tension in his driver and leaned forward to say, 'Don't sweat it, Emilio. I'm not too bothered about time.'

The driver's shoulders visibly slumped a little. 'Thanks, Boss.'

It was only when Rocco sat back again and flicked the switch to raise the privacy window that he went very still. He never usually went out of his way to put people ease. He thrived on knowing that people never knew what to expect from him, or which way he'd jump. He was never rude to employees. He was scrupulously fair and polite. But he knew he possessed that edge. People were never entirely comfortable around him.

Except for Gracie O'Brien. She wasn't comfortable around him either, but she stood up to him like no one else ever had.

With the utmost reluctance Rocco had to concede that there was a strong possibility she wasn't lying when she said that she'd had nothing to do with her brother's plans. She'd looked far too shocked the previous evening when he'd mentioned jail, and if she'd known what he'd done she'd have to have been aware that jail was an option. Plus there was the fact she'd come to the offices in the first place.

Nevertheless, he'd learnt a lesson about trusting his instincts when it had come to her brother, so he'd be a fool to trust her for a second. Even if everything else had checked out once she'd told him who her brother was.

His security contacts had access to confidential information. She was listed as his sister, no criminal record—unlike her brother. No other siblings. No mention of parents. A grandmother appeared to have brought them up briefly and then Social Services had taken over. They'd come from one of the roughest parts of London, and without even knowing the details Rocco could close his eyes and imagine the scene. Disadvantaged areas were the same the world over.

Going through her pitiful personal possessions, he'd come across a file full of sketches and text. It looked like a mock-up of a children's book and he had to admit it was surprisingly good.

He'd also come across a photo of what had to be her and her brother when they were kids. She'd been freckle-faced, with a huge gap-toothed grin, red hair in pigtails, her arm tight around her smaller brother, who had looked skinny and nervous, shy behind thick glasses.

Rocco felt his chest grow tight. His fists clenched. He would *not* let those huge brown eyes get to him. Or her apparent vulnerability. She was as tough as nails. Clearly out to protect her brother at all costs, whatever her involvement. He'd never really known what that kind of loyalty was like and didn't like the sensation of envy which lanced him. It was further evidence of their bond, and he would watch her like a hawk until her brother resurfaced.

Rocco would not admit on any level that this desire to keep her close had anything to do with her enigmatic personality or her physical appeal. This was about seeing justice meted out. That was all. One million euros of it.

It was only when he looked at the leafy suburbs passing by outside the car that Rocco realised he hadn't thought of Honora Winthrop once. Determined not to let the arrival of Gracie O'Brien derail his life any more than she already had, Rocco made a call and ignored the sense of claustrophobia that spiked when Honora Winthrop answered her phone.

Gracie woke from a fitful sleep at five the next morning. She was still disorientated at first, and a familiar knot came into her belly when she realised where she was. A grey dawn light was breaking over London. Her mind went over the previous day and evening. Thankfully she'd been in bed by the time Rocco had come home, and she'd only heard faint sounds as he'd moved around.

He'd made a curt phone call late in the evening to inform her that he'd be dining out and she'd made a face at the phone, hating herself for wondering who he was dining with. After Rocco had left the apartment that previous morning Gracie had looked wistfully at the apartment door and had even opened it—only to find a large atrium outside and a huge barrel of a man sitting at a desk which seemed to have a dozen monitors.

He'd stood up to an alarming height and asked easily, 'Need to go somewhere, Ms O'Brien?'

Gracie had shook her head. 'I was just having a look around.'

Perfectly friendly, the man-giant had said, 'I'm George, and I'm here to take you wherever you want to go, so if you need anything just shout.'

Gracie had mumbled something incoherent. Evidently George was also there to make sure she didn't go anywhere without him as her close companion. Exactly as Rocco had warned. She'd gone back into the apartment and made a phone call to the last housekeeper, who sounded like a pleasant older woman. She'd cheerfully outlined for Gracie the list of chores Mr de Marco would expect to be done.

Gracie had stood in Rocco's bedroom and looked at the tousled sheets. His unmistakable scent had hung tantalisingly in the air. Musky and male. The indentation caused by his body had been evident, and Gracie had gone hot when she'd found herself wondering if he slept naked.

Feeling hot all over again, thinking of that bed and those sheets, Gracie registered that she was thirsty and got up. She stumbled out of the room, still foggy with sleep.

She was only belatedly aware that the kitchen light was on when she walked in and had to squint her eyes against it. When she saw a big dark shape move she screamed, suddenly wide awake.

Eyes huge, she took in the sight that greeted her. Rocco de Marco was standing in the kitchen, bare-chested and in nothing but a low-slung and very precarious-looking towel, which hugged his hips and barely covered his thighs.

A million things hit Gracie at once, along with a shot of pure adrenalin: he must have just showered as his hair was still damp; his skin gleamed olive in the light; his chest was broad and leanly muscled with a light covering of crisp dark hair that tapered down to that towel in a tantalising silky line.

He was more beautiful than any man had a right to be.

Realising all of those things, and also that she was looking at Rocco as if she'd never seen a man before, she tore her gaze away and blurted out, 'You're meant to be asleep.'

'Well,' he pointed out dryly, 'I'm not. I always get up around now.'

Gracie refused to look at him, hovering in the doorway.

Her heart was still hammering from the shock. 'Shouldn't you…put on some clothes or something?'

Again with that dry voice he pointed out, 'You're equally undressed. I might ask the same of you but I'm not sure I want to.'

At that Gracie looked at him, and felt scorching heat climb up her chest to her face. Rocco's gaze was dark and lazy, taking in her bare legs, the T-shirt which came to the top of her thighs, and then moving back up to her face. Gracie knew she must look a sight, with her hair all over the place and wild. She couldn't for a moment dwell on the fact that she might have seen a predatory gleam in *his* eyes. She could remember the distaste on his face when he'd stood back from frisking her.

Her throat was so dry, but she fought the urge to swallow. It made her voice sound rough. 'I just wanted to get some water.'

Rocco gestured with a hand. 'By all means. Never let it be said that I deny my prisoners the basics.'

That sardonic delivery restored some of Gracie's composure and she willed herself to move forward to the shelves. Very aware of her bare feet and Rocco's lazy gaze, she ignored him and reached up to get a glass on a shelf far too close to him for comfort. And then…couldn't reach it. Not even on tiptoes. She was very aware of her T-shirt riding up over her bottom and cursed silently, thinking of her very worn plain white knickers.

Suddenly a wave of heat emanated from behind her, along with a distinctive scent, and a very muscled brown arm was reaching up past her to pluck a glass down. His front was almost touching her back. Gracie knew if she stepped back she'd walk right into him, and felt weak at the strength of longing that rushed through her to know what it would feel like to have his arms wrap around her.

But then he put the glass down on the counter beside her with a clatter and moved away, taking that heat with him. Gracie gripped the glass and slowly turned around. For a big man he moved incredibly silently and gracefully. He was already on the other side of the kitchen island, sipping from a mug, regarding her as coolly as ever.

Gracie felt as if she was wading through treacle just getting to the sink to pour the water. The air had become dense with some kind of tension that was completely alien to her. She felt as if it was coiling deep within her, making her feel alternately light-headed and shaky.

'There's bottled water in the fridge.'

Gracie filled the glass and cursed herself for not going that route in the first place. 'Tap water is fine. Bottled water is a waste of money.' She turned around with her glass clutched in both hands like a shield.

Rocco raised a brow. 'Now you're an environmentalist?'

Pride stiffened Gracie's backbone. 'I do care about the environment, as it happens.'

Before he could question her again, or make some acerbic comment, he put his cup down. 'If you'll excuse me I've got a busy day ahead.'

He moved towards the door with all the lethal grace of a jungle cat, and yet looked as suave as if he was fully dressed. Gracie's eyes felt burnt just from looking at all that bared skin and taut musculature.

He turned at the door and said with a definite glint in his eye, 'Remind me to show you how to do hospital corners. That's how I prefer my bed to be made in the future.'

She looked at the empty door after he'd disappeared and it took a few seconds for his words to register. When they did, she wanted to throw the glass into the empty space he'd left behind. The arrogant so and so. She clamped her lips tight together. She would *not* let him get to her. She repeated this to herself as she went back to her bedroom, feeling very skittish.

Rocco stood under the punishing spray of a cold shower just a few moments later. Damn that woman. When she'd appeared in the doorway in nothing but that flimsy T-shirt and bare legs he'd blinked because he'd thought she was an apparition. He'd only just had a shower which he'd had to turn to cold because he'd woken from lurid dreams of stripping Gracie O'Brien bare and laying her out on his bed in all her pale glory.

When he'd realised she wasn't an apparition the blood had rushed south and hardened his body with an embarrassingly immediate effect. Thankfully she'd been so shocked to see him he didn't think she'd noticed.

He'd been unable to compose himself, as if confronted with a naked woman for the first time. He cursed volubly. What was it about her that turned him on so effortlessly? She was wild and untamed. As unsophisticated as you could get. Freckles, for crying out loud. All over. All down her legs and arms. And, he imagined, on her breasts, which would be so pale against his skin...

He cursed again when he thought of her stretching up to get that glass. His eyes had been glued to her smooth pale thighs and the pert curve of her bottom, that tantalising glimpse of white cotton. Never had such an unsexy fabric looked so sensual. Like a fool he'd moved closer, ostensibly to help her reach the glass, only to come so close that he had been able to smell the surprisingly sweet and clean scent of her shampoo. No perfume, just something faint, like wild flowers. More subtle and alluring than he would have imagined possible.

Her hair had brushed his bare chest and the nearly overwhelming urge to press close and slide his hands up and under that shirt, around to cup her breasts and feel their weight and firmness, had had him jumping back and away like a scalded cat to the other side of the kitchen.

Rocco shut off the shower and stepped out for the second time in the space of half an hour. He vowed at that moment to do everything in his power to find Steven Murray, so that he could draw a line under this incident once and for all and get this woman out of his head.

For two days Gracie managed to avoid Rocco by making sure she was up after him in the mornings and in bed before he came back to the apartment at night. Luckily, he seemed to be busy. She was congratulating herself on having evaded him for the third morning in a row when he suddenly emerged from the study in the apartment, issuing a string of expletives, looking seriously disgruntled. And absolutely gorgeous in faded jeans and a T-shirt.

Gracie couldn't avoid bumping straight into him, and sprang back as if burnt, heat washing through her body like a tidal wave. She went hot and cold all at once. She could smell his scent on the air, musky and masculine. He glowered at her from his superior height and Gracie fought the urge to apologise.

To fill the silence and deflect him from her embarrassment she blurted out, 'What are you doing here?'

Looking seriously disgruntled now, he said, 'Sometimes I work from this office—if that's all right with you?'

A little redundantly she found herself asking, 'Is there something wrong?'

Rocco's dark gaze swept over her and Gracie burnt up even more.

'My chef has just rung to say he's ill, and his replacement is busy. I have someone coming for dinner this evening and I didn't want to go out, but now it looks as though I'll have to.' Rocco chafed at having to look at the reasons why he *didn't* relish being seen out in public with Honora Winthrop, when just a few days ago he would have welcomed the prospect. The woman standing in front of him, who'd been avoiding him zealously for the past two days, was far too close to those reasons for comfort.

Something pierced Gracie's insides as she wondered churlishly if this dinner was a date. His mistress, perhaps? Again, almost without thinking, she found herself saying, 'I can cook if you like?'

Rocco smiled mockingly. 'You? Cook?'

His obvious incredulity combined with her recent disturbing flash of something which felt awfully like jealousy made her say waspishly, 'I can do better than baked beans and toast, if that's what your tastes run to.'

His eyes darkened at that, and dropped again in a leisurely appraisal, as if he was contemplating his tastes running to *her*. Gracie squirmed. He was just playing with her.

She drew back and stepped away, feeling seriously prickly, cursing herself and her mouth. 'Look, forget I said anything. It was a stupid idea.'

She was almost past him when he caught her arm and stopped her. His entire hand wrapped around her bicep. The breath stopped in her throat and she swallowed painfully. Slowly, she turned and looked up. His expression was contemplative, and he didn't let her go.

'Can you really cook?'

Gracie nodded, and fought the urge to tug her arm free. She didn't want him to see that he affected her. 'If you give me a list of what you want I'll do my best. How many is it for?'

A shadow crossed his face. He dropped her arm abruptly, as if he'd just realised he was still holding it.

'Two.'

That curious pain lanced Gracie again. She crossed her arms. 'I can manage two.'

He just looked at her for a long silent moment, until Gracie felt like screaming with tension, and then he nodded slowly. 'Okay, then. I'll give you the list and we'll eat at eight—after champagne and canapés.'

Later that morning Gracie and George were returning to Rocco's building after a visit to the shops. Rocco had issued her with a credit card and a list of dietary requirements not long after their exchange outside his study.

She'd scanned it and said faintly, 'I'm not sure I can get mercury-free fish from Hawaii at such short notice. Is there anything you're *not* allergic to?'

Rocco had grimaced faintly. 'They're not my requirements. I can eat anything. They're my guest's.'

'Oh.' Gracie hadn't asked who his guest was. She'd just put the piece of paper down and smiled sweetly. 'I'll do my best to work within these narrow parameters.'

To her shock Rocco had looked as if he was holding back a laugh and she'd felt weak inside. But then the look had faded, and he'd just made some inarticulate sound and said, 'Fine. See what you can do.'

It was only as she and George were about to enter the private entrance which led up to Rocco's apartment that Gracie noticed the newspaper headline on the news kisok near them. Her feet stopped in their tracks when she read: *'De Marco to wed society beauty Honora Winthrop...'*

George saw her captivated by the headline and informed her, 'That's the boss's latest companion.'

'You mean his fiancée,' Gracie corrected faintly. She didn't know why, but she suddenly felt flat.

George murmured something else that Gracie didn't hear, and then he was ushering her back into the building as the first few drops of a summer shower started to fall.

At the same moment on a floor high above them, back in his glass-walled office, Rocco was looking at the same headline. This was it. Another milestone moment on the way to securing his position in society. And yet the moment was curiously hollow and empty. He felt constricted, and he loosened his tie and opened the top button of his shirt without even being aware he was doing it.

All he could think about was Gracie's face that morning, when she'd commented about the absurd menu requirements for dinner. He'd wanted to burst out laughing, sharing her moment of incredulity.

No one made him laugh.

It had taken all his control not to pull her up into his arms and plunder that soft pink mouth. To make her close those far too wary brown eyes. To forget everything but *him*.

She'd taken him by surprise, offering to cook dinner. In truth he almost hadn't even registered what she'd said at first, he'd been so busy drinking her in. Not seeing her for the past two days had begun to seriously irritate him, and he'd only realised then that his decision to work from his study had stemmed in part from the fact she wouldn't be able to avoid him in the apartment.

His thwarted desire to see her had also been at the root of his irrational anger over the mere unavailability of his chefs, which would never normally have caused him to flip out.

He could still feel the electrifying sensation of her petite form crashing into him. Arousal had been immediate and burning. His skin had prickled with desire as she'd stood there with that determined chin tilted, daring him to let her cook dinner when he'd been sceptical.

Something outside caught his eye then, and across the expanse of his office space he saw that his private lift was in use, the light ascending. It was probably just George or one of the other bodyguards, but even so his skin tingled. *It could be Gracie.* Before he knew what he was doing he had dumped the paper and was out of his chair, striding to the lift.

Gracie was standing beside George in the lift, still trying to figure out why the news that Rocco was engaged could be affecting her so much. She hardly knew the man, so how on earth could she be feeling…betrayed? He at worst hated her, and at best felt nothing for her. And yet she couldn't help feeling that something intangible had drawn them together besides her brother. She couldn't forget the heated intensity in his eyes the night they'd met.

Or earlier…in the apartment.

Gracie frowned, feeling seriously confused. The lift came to a halt too soon and she looked at George, who just shrugged. They weren't at the penthouse level yet. The doors opened to reveal Rocco standing there, hands on hips. Jacket off, tie loose and top button open. Immediately Gracie's throat went dry and her heart beat faster.

'We were just shopping for dinner,' she blurted out. Why did she feel so guilty when he must know exactly where they'd been?

Rocco looked at George and took Gracie's bags out of her hands, handing them to the huge man whose hands were already full. 'Gracie will be up shortly. I have something to discuss with her first.'

Rocco led the way through a labyrinth of glass-walled offices and Gracie followed reluctantly, still feeling a little raw. She couldn't believe now that she'd ever had the temerity to think she could just waltz into this building to see if Steven might be here. That night felt like an age ago.

Rocco was holding open the door to his office, waiting for her to precede him. Somehow that small chivalrous gesture made her feel even more vulnerable. Once she'd walked in she went into attack mode to disguise her feelings, turning to face him as he shut the door.

'If you're going to have a go at me just because we went to the shops then—'

Rocco put up a hand. 'Have I said a word?'

Gracie shut her mouth and shook her head. She felt very shabby next to Rocco. He'd changed since this morning into a suit. Gracie watched warily as he went around his desk and sat down. And then she took in the full majesty of the awe-inspiring view.

Momentarily distracted despite herself, she went towards the window. 'Do you always have the best views?'

Rocco's voice was cynical. 'Of course. Don't you know that people are judged by how high they are and how far they can see?'

For some reason his words made Gracie feel sad for him. She ran a hand over the back of the sleekly modern chair that faced his desk and returned her gaze to him. 'I wonder when it becomes impossible to be too high, or see too far.'

The weight of silence that stretched between them became almost unbearable and Gracie looked away, feeling embarrassed. Where had *that* little philosophical observation come from?

To avoid Rocco's black gaze she took in the sleek furnishings and modern art that hung suspended on steel wires against the clear windows. Other staff, undoubtedly the best at what they did, were visible through the glass walls of their own offices nearby, but no one was looking up. They were all too busy. Making millions for Rocco and his clients, Gracie surmised grimly. Her brother had been one of those employees and yet he'd stolen from the people who trusted Rocco with their money. Her insides twisted.

She looked back to Rocco and didn't want him to guess the direction of her thoughts. She hunted for something—anything—to say. 'Don't you mind?'

'Mind what?'

Gracie gestured with a hand. 'That everyone can see you? You've no privacy?'

'This office is soundproofed, so no one can hear my private conversations. And this way I can see everyone.'

Gracie looked at him and his face was a bland mask, no expression. It made her feel prickly, wanting a reaction. 'You mean, that way you can control everything.'

Rocco shrugged minutely. 'I couldn't control your brother's scheming to swindle money from me and my clients.'

Gracie looked down and clasped her hands together. He'd just articulated her own thoughts. She heard Rocco move and glanced up to see him standing at his window with his back to her, hands in his pockets. For a moment his powerful physique looked completely incongruous against the cityscape, as if he should be outside, battling something elemental and natural.

He turned then, so abruptly that he caught her staring, and Gracie blushed.

'I hope you're not lying about your ability to cook dinner. I won't stand for any attempt at insolence, Gracie. Tonight is important to me.'

Pain lanced Gracie and she spoke before she could censor herself. 'Because you're entertaining your fiancée?'

Rocco frowned. 'How do you know about that?'

If she could have swallowed her own tongue she would have, but she said miserably, 'I saw a headline outside.'

For a long moment Rocco just looked at her, and then said, 'She is not my fiancée yet. Not that it's any business of yours.'

Gracie remembered what he'd said before she'd opened her big mouth and said rebelliously, 'If I did serve up fish fingers you'd have no one to blame but yourself.'

Once again she had the curious feeling that he was holding back a laugh, but then he glowered at her. 'Don't even think about it.'

'Was that all?'

He nodded curtly, and before Gracie did or said something she'd really regret she turned and fled.

Rocco watched Gracie's slim back retreating through his offices. He didn't miss the fact that she caught the eye of more than one male employee, or that it made his insides tighten. How did she have the singular ability to constantly make him veer off course and gravitate towards her?

Her observation about his offices being too transparent had never been made before—by anyone. He felt inordinately exposed, because only he knew that his preoccupation with being able to see all around him came from his early days and the constant need to watch his back. It was also why he surrounded himself with people when he knew most others in his position preferred solitude. On some level, because he'd grown up surrounded by so many, it was one thing he hadn't been able to let go of, and she'd effortlessly spotted it. Albeit without understanding it.

Most people assumed it was an aesthetic thing. But it was as if she'd *known* there was more to it. And then that comment about always striving to be at the highest point. Literally.

She disappeared into the elevator and Rocco sat down and swung his chair around to the view, so no one could see him. For the first time he actually did resent the lack of privacy. He rested his elbows on the armrests of his chair and his chin on steepled fingers. In that moment a very illicit and long-buried feeling of rebellion stirred his blood.

Mid-afternoon that day, Gracie was neck-deep in preparing her menu for the evening. She was hot and sweaty when George appeared in the kitchen, holding out a big white box.

'For you, from the boss.'

Gracie wiped her hands on her apron and took it. Her silly heart started to thump. Some rogue part of her brain seemed to run away with itself and she couldn't help imagining a beautiful chiffon dress in delicate shades of pink. And for a moment she couldn't help fantasising that dinner this evening was for *her* and Rocco.

She laid the box on the table and opened it up with unsteady hands. It only took a few seconds for those traitorous images to crumble to dust. She reached in and pulled out a black pinafore dress and a white apron. Sheer tights and plain black court shoes. A note fell out too. The arrogant scrawl said, *'Please wear this later. R.'*

Gracie alternately felt like laughing and crying. She'd never before allowed herself to daydream such fantasies even for a moment. Her life had been about gritty reality from day one. She'd had one boyfriend and he'd never given her anything—not even a birthday card. And suddenly she was indulging in Cinderella-esque dreams?

Disgusted with herself, Gracie stuffed the dress back into the box, childishly hoping it would get creased. She returned to her preparations and took a deep breath, curbing the desire to walk down to Rocco's gleaming office and tip the sauce she'd been preparing over his smarmy head.

CHAPTER FIVE

PACING in his drawing room that evening, Rocco couldn't remember the last time he'd been so tense. He'd come back to the apartment about thirty minutes before and had headed for the kitchen—only to find the door locked. He'd knocked on the door, to hear Gracie call from inside, 'Go away. I'm busy.'

He'd called through the door, 'I hope you have everything in hand.'

'Oh, don't worry,' she'd sung out sweetly. 'I do. The fish fingers are almost done.'

Rocco had bitten back the urge to demand she open up immediately. He'd never been kept so consistently in an uncomfortable state of arousal in his life, and it had nothing to do with the woman due to walk in the door at any moment and everything to do with the woman a few feet away, behind the closed kitchen door. The woman related to the man who had set out to destroy his reputation and steal from him. The woman to whom he'd all but handed a sterling opportunity to humiliate him this evening.

A discreet knock on the door at that moment heralded his security man showing Honora Winthrop into the drawing room. The door opened to reveal the icy beauty looking predictably stunning in a black silk draped dress which managed the amazing feat of being completely modest while at the same time daringly see-through.

The immediately negative effect on Rocco's libido was almost comical. She was effectively better than a cold shower. But, with smooth smile in place, Rocco went forward to greet her, pushing aside all visions of a red-haired temptress.

Gracie heard the voices outside in the drawing room and took a deep shaky breath. Much to her chagrin, the dress Rocco had sent was not creased. It was also about a size too small, proving to be a very snug fit around her breasts, bottom and thighs. At first she'd cursed him for doing it on purpose, but then had had to figure that it was far more likely to be because he had no interest in her body, therefore why would be have any notion, or care, what size she was?

She smoothed the small frilled white apron and tried once again to pull the dress down a little further to her knee. She tidied her hair, which she'd pulled back into a high bun, and picked up the tray that held two ice-misted glasses of champagne and a couple of small plates with crushed olive *vol-au-vents* and crab canapés.

When she walked into the room the voices died away. Gracie was burningly aware of two sets of eyes, one of which was dark and lingered, the other which glanced away again almost immediately. *It must be the woman from the paper.* Gracie was peripherally aware of a statuesque blonde beauty standing near Rocco at the window.

He surprised her by coming forward and taking the tray out of her hands. 'Thank you, Gracie. We'll eat in twenty minutes.'

She released the tray and tried to read the ambiguous look in his eyes, but couldn't. So she turned and forced herself to walk away, when all she wanted to do was run. Back in the kitchen she laid her face against the door for a moment. She was shaking. Thankfully Rocco hadn't expected her to hand out the drinks and canapés. She would have expected that he'd make the most of a moment like that and it was disconcerting that he hadn't.

Pushing herself off the door, she went to finalise preparations for the starter and forced from her head images of Rocco and that woman toasting each other with the sparkling drink.

Rocco couldn't get the image of Gracie walking into the drawing room out of his head. He felt as if it would be seared there for ever. Clearly the uniform he'd organised had come in a size too small. It was plastered to her petite lithe body, showing off the curves that were normally hidden. A button strained across her chest. The dress's hem rested teasingly above her knee, revealing pale and slender legs. It was more like a French maid's outfit for a hen night than the sophisticated serving dress he'd expected. And he had no one to blame but himself.

'Rocco?'

Rocco broke out of his trance and looked at the woman beside him, one finely drawn eyebrow arched above perfectly made-up blue eyes.

He smiled tightly. 'Forgive me…'

Gracie had just served the starter, and put her ear to the door to try and hear the conversation, or any observation about the food: She heard Rocco's low voice, and then an irritating tinkling laugh followed by, *'Oh, Rocco, you're terrible!'*

Gracie's face burned. She felt paranoid, as if Rocco might come back through the door and hold up his plate with its linguine and truffle starter and say, *Seriously? You thought this would be suitable?*

But he didn't appear. So Gracie got on with the main course.

After a suitable amount of time she went in to check the wine levels and saw that Rocco had finished his starter but Ms Winthrop's was half eaten. The woman barely glanced at Gracie, just pushed her plate slightly towards the edge of the table, clearly indicating that she was finished.

Gracie curbed her tongue when she got a warning glance from Rocco, and replenished the wine and took the plates away, also curbing a cheeky urge to curtsey.

When she brought in the main course Gracie couldn't help the dart of satisfaction at seeing Rocco's eyes widen. The smell of the guinea fowl *cacciatore* was impressively aromatic. She deftly served them both, and left again. She was starting to get seriously annoyed with Rocco's date's complete lack of acknowledgment. At least in the bar where she'd worked—as rough as it had been—people looked you in the eye and not through you.

She started clearing up, valiantly ignoring the hum of voices and trying not to imagine what they might be talking about. Wedding plans? Gracie slapped down the tea-towel at the spiking of irrational jealousy.

Any kind of feelings for Rocco de Marco beyond antipathy and extreme wariness were so patently futile that—

Gracie heard a noise and whirled around to see George coming in through the other kitchen door, which opened out to the entrance hall. She'd given him an early supper of the same food she was serving Rocco and his guest because he'd finished his shift.

He had a big grin on his face and patted his enormous belly. 'That was the singularly most amazing meal I've ever eaten.'

Gracie grinned. 'Really? Oh, George, thank you!' And she jumped up to give him a quick impetuous kiss, as much for his human affection and their growing friendship as anything else. Just then the other door opened and Gracie sprang back, cheeks burning.

Rocco stood there, looking like thunder, with his napkin in his hand. 'If you're quite ready? We've finished in here.'

George scuttled out as fast as he could for such a huge man, and Gracie leapt to attention, feeling absurdly guilty for no reason. Rocco stayed at the door, forcing her to go past him, and when her hip came into contact with his body she had to stop herself from flinching away. Even that small contact with his tall, hard-muscled body was seismic to her system. She cleared away the plates, glad for the first time that evening that the cold-looking blonde beauty wasn't looking at her.

When she'd composed herself as much as she could, she went back in with the lemon torte dessert and coffee. Ms Winthrop was saying, 'Darling, how on earth did you entice Louis away from the Four Seasons? Roberto must be simply livid! That meal was divine.'

A dart of satisfaction went through Gracie as she put down the tray on the nearby serving table. In the silence that followed she found she was holding her breath, waiting to see what Rocco would say. As the seconds ticked past it became incredibly important.

She was picking up the dessert plates and feeling sick inside when he cleared his throat. 'Actually, Louis was indisposed this evening. So Gracie here, who is my temporary housekeeper, prepared our meal.'

Gracie walked over and put down the plates. She felt a little light-headed for a moment. She couldn't believe Rocco had actually credited her. For the first time all evening the blonde shot her a narrow-eyed and very assessing glance.

'Oh…how quaint.'

The words dripped with condescension.

That glance had obviously taken in a multitude of facts, because she looked back to Rocco and said, very deliberately, 'I wasn't going to say anything, but I thought perhaps Louis was on an off-night or had sent one of his sous-chefs. The guinea fowl *did* taste slightly odd. I do hope she knew what she was doing, I have an important family function tomorrow. I can't afford to be ill.'

Gracie was rooted to the spot for a long moment. She couldn't believe that this woman was picking apart her efforts as if she wasn't even there. She registered a quick glance from Rocco, but was too stunned to look at him. She whirled around and escaped back to the kitchen, hearing his low tones as she went, but unable to make out the words.

Gracie was shaking—first of all with shock that Rocco had spoken up for her. She'd fully expected him to humiliate her by denying her contribution, but he'd sounded almost *proud*. And then shock morphed to anger at that woman's downright rudeness.

She heard a laugh coming from the drawing room—*her* irritating laugh. To Gracie's abject horror emotion surged, making hot tears prick at the back of her eyes as she looked at the chaos spread around the kitchen, the fruits of her hard labours.

She wasn't sure what had happened, but at some point she'd started cooking for *Rocco*. George had told her where he was from in Italy, and that had informed her choices. Even whilst hating herself for her weakness, she'd wanted to impress him. Perhaps she'd hoped he would see that she wasn't just some nobody who had nothing to offer except for a tenuous link to her brother?

She heard a door slam and flinched. No doubt that was Rocco and his date leaving for an exclusive club in town. Gracie wiped at her cheeks and set about cleaning up through a blur of tears.

She didn't hear the door open, so when she heard a soft, 'Gracie,' from behind her she dropped a pan on the marble floor.

Gracie whirled around, too startled to remember how she must look. Her eyes cleared but her cheeks still stung. Rocco was standing there, his jacket removed and his tie undone and loose as if he'd yanked at it impatiently. The top button of his shirt was open and his hair was dishevelled.

Gracie took all this in in a split second. 'I heard the front door,' she said dumbly, wondering if he was some kind of mirage. 'I thought you'd left.'

Rocco shook his head. His hands were deep in his pockets and even now Gracie had to fight the impulse to let her gaze drop.

His voice was tight. 'Miss Winthrop has gone home, and she won't be back. I must apologise for her rudeness. She refused to come in here and do it herself.'

Gracie's mouth opened and closed like a fish. 'You asked her to come in here? And apologise?'

Rocco nodded curtly. 'I shouldn't have even had to ask. She had no right to talk to you like that. And she was wrong. You served up an amazing meal.' He shook his head slightly. 'I had no idea you could cook like that.'

Half dazed, Gracie said, 'One of my foster parents trained in Paris as a chef in the sixties. She ended up working as a cook in a school kitchen when she came back to England because no one would hire a female chef.' Gracie shrugged. 'I'm not that proficient, really... I picked up some basics and I like cooking.'

Rocco stepped further into the kitchen and Gracie gulped. He looked so *intent*. She moved back a step and her foot knocked the pan on the floor. She looked down to see that some sauce had leaked out and automatically bent down to get it. Suddenly Rocco was there, taking her arm and helping her up, taking the pan out of her hand.

He led her away from the spill. 'No,' he said, his accent thick. 'Someone else will clean it up.'

Gracie just looked up at him. He was too close all of a sudden, his sheer physical presence more than overwhelming, and she was horribly aware of her red eyes. She hated that she had been so upset and was terrified Rocco would see it.

'You don't have to apologise. She's the one who was rude.'

'But I put you in that position. I let her speak to you like that.'

Gracie couldn't keep the hurt from her voice. 'Yes,' she said, 'you did. I thought you did it on purpose. To get some pleasure out of seeing me squirm. Seeing me out of my depth.'

Rocco shook his head, and the look on his face made tendrils of heat coil up inside her—along with panic. She didn't know if she could control her response when Rocco stood this close to her, touching her. And that awful uncontrollable emotion was rising again, that sense of how vulnerable she'd felt this evening. She hadn't felt a need to impress someone for a long time—if ever.

Gracie spoke with a rush. 'She looked through me, and then she looked at me as if I was dirt, as if she couldn't believe that I'd actually handled her food.'

'I'm sorry,' he said.

Confusion warred alongside the panic within Gracie. She didn't know what Rocco was trying to do to her. He was looking at her so intensely. 'Stop saying that. You're not sorry at all.'

Tears were blurring her vision again, and Gracie fought not to let them fall, blinking rapidly. He'd reduced her to a snivelling wreck—why wasn't he walking away? Anger at her response, and at him for precipitating it, made her lash out as she tried to extricate her arm from his grip.

'Do you know what it's like to be looked through? As if you don't exist? Do you have any idea how that feels? I am *someone*, Rocco. I am a person with hopes and dreams and feelings. I'm not a bad person, despite what you might think. When someone looks through you like you're invisible—'

'Gracie...'

Rocco had taken both her arms in his hands now. He was standing right in front of her, gripping her tight. She sucked in a shaky breath.

He spoke again. 'I know...I know what it's like.'

Faint scorn laced Gracie's voice. 'How can *you* know? You have no idea what I'm talking about.'

His hands gripped tighter. There was a white line of tension around his mouth and his eyes were blazing. 'I *know*.'

His hands gentled then, and Gracie stared up, dumbfounded. One hand came up to her chin and with his thumb and forefinger he tipped her face up higher, so she couldn't escape his gaze.

'I see you.'

Emotions were roiling in Gracie's belly. She felt hot all over. Confusion warred with the anger inside her, and she shook her head. 'You don't... You can't. I'm nothing to you.'

Fiercely, he shook his head. 'No. You are *not* nothing.'

Gracie was dimly aware that in their backward-forward dance they had now moved into a more dimly lit corner of the kitchen by the window seat. She could feel her hair unravelling. The entire world might have stopped turning in that moment and she wouldn't have noticed. All she could see were the black depths of Rocco's eyes and she was drowning. She had to fight the pull of the strongest tide she'd ever felt.

'Rocco...' Her voice was shaky. 'What are you doing? Why are you here?'

Her lower arms were between them, as if she was still valiantly making the effort to pull free from Rocco's hands. But his hands had gentled, and yet Gracie couldn't move back or break free. Some fatal lethargy had invaded her bones and her blood. He pulled her in closer.

He didn't speak for a long moment, and then it was as if the words were being pulled out from deep inside him. 'I want you. I am here because I want *you*. This whole evening, this past week, ever since I met you...I've wanted you. Not her. She guessed how I felt. That's why she was so cruel.'

Gracie shook her head even as molten heat seemed to bloom down low between her legs. She'd never felt so *hot*. And so out of her depth. She'd truly believed that her guilty little secret of obsessing about Rocco would never be noticed. Or reciprocated.

Gracie shook her head again, more forcefully this time. 'No. You're bored...or trying to make her jealous or something. I'm just convenient.'

Rocco grimaced then. 'You're definitely not convenient. And I am not bored. I don't care if she *is* jealous, because it's over and I'm never going to see her again.'

Gracie reeled. The full magnitude of what he was saying started to sink in. He'd had a fight with his fiancée over *her*? And he'd chosen *her*?

'But...you had a relationship. You were going to marry her.'

Rocco went still for a second as the enormity of her words sank in. He had just ended his relationship with Honora Winthrop, and in doing so his grand plans to marry her. He'd done it because he wanted to sleep with Gracie O'Brien more urgently than he'd ever wanted anything in his life. More than the social acceptance he'd hungered for for so long? He didn't even want to answer that.

In some rational part of his brain that was still functioning Rocco knew very well that if he ran after Honora Winthrop and caught her just as she reached home he might salvage something.

And like a slow-dawning yet cataclysmic realisation he knew he didn't want to. The feeling of claustrophobia that had been dogging him for weeks had lifted.

Rocco shook his head. 'We didn't have a relationship— not really. What we had was an understanding that a more permanent relationship would be mutually beneficial on many levels.'

'But that's...so cold.'

Rocco shrugged and said cynically, 'That's life. I hadn't yet asked her to marry me, and I haven't been sleeping with her.'

Gracie was trying to take it all in. She knew that Rocco wouldn't feel he had to hand her platitudes to get her into bed. She believed that he hadn't cared for that woman, and that he hadn't slept with her. He was too powerful to care about lying. She knew he wouldn't shy away from hurting her with the truth if he *had* slept with that woman.

Her head started to throb. She couldn't take any more in. She didn't want to hear anything else. Rocco pulled her even closer. She felt as if she was on a train with only one destination and there was no way she could get off now. Unconsciously she'd gone up on tiptoe, her body knowing what it wanted even before she did.

His head lowered towards hers, that beautiful mouth came closer and closer, and Gracie's eyelids fluttered closed just as darkness and heat swept over her mouth and settled there like a brand.

At first the kiss was like falling into a whirlpool. Instinctively Gracie reached out to hold onto Rocco's shirt because she couldn't feel her legs any more. And then an urgency gripped them both, as if the first taste was merely a civilised veneer. Rocco's hands went to Gracie's face. She was being backed against a wall, or some sort of solid surface, and Gracie leaned back and let it support her weight.

Rocco's mouth was hard, and yet his lips were soft, pressing, tasting, coaxing. She felt the slide of his tongue against the closed seam of her lips and her hands clenched tighter as her mouth opened up to Rocco. The kiss deepened. His chest pressed hard against her, crushing her hands between them. But Gracie didn't care. She revelled in Rocco's big hands holding her face just so he could plunder her mouth.

Gracie was falling, slipping and sliding into another dimension. Rocco's scent intoxicated her. His tongue stroked along hers in a wicked caress. Teeth nipped at her lower lip, only to soothe it in the same moment. It was tart and sweet all at once. It was all-consuming, like jumping right into the middle of a fire.

He took his mouth away and amidst the fiery excitement pressed a kiss to the corner of her mouth—an incongruously gentle gesture. Gracie opened heavy eyelids. Her mouth felt bruised, swollen. She wouldn't be surprised if the world had moved on a couple of decades since they'd started kissing. She felt that altered.

She looked straight up into the dark molten pools of Rocco's eyes. This close she could see flecks of gold. His cheeks were flushed.

Feeling bewildered, she asked shakily, 'What is this?'

Rocco took down his hands from her face and caught some of her hair, wrapping it around a finger, looking at the fiery gold strands.

'This…' his gaze came back up '…is called chemistry—except I've never felt it like this before.'

Gracie shook her head. 'I've never felt this before either.'

Rocco's hand moved slowly up over Gracie's hip to her waist, and then under one arm to rest where her breast curved out. With a lazy smile Rocco moved his hand so it cupped her breast, the thumb moving back and forth over the taut peak which tightened even more underneath the stiff material of her dress. Her breath hitched.

'This,' Rocco continued, 'is what started between us the night we met.'

Gracie's eyes searched Rocco's for sincerity. So he'd felt it too. This extraordinary connection. Like a livewire coming to life the moment she'd looked at him. This had nothing to do with her brother. This had existed between them before they'd even known who the other was.

Suddenly a desperate urgency Gracie had never felt before rushed through her body. She needed to connect on a base level with this man right now. She lifted her hands from between them and caught his head, his hair soft and silky between her fingers. Inexorably she brought his head down to hers and pressed her mouth to his. He took her cue and both hands moved to grip her waist tightly as his mouth opened and his natural dominance took over.

Tongues met and clashed furiously. Gracie arched herself into the hard wall of his chest, crushing her breasts to him, desperately seeking to assuage the ache building throughout her whole body and between her legs. Their hips were tight together. Gracie could feel the long ridge of his arousal and instinctively opened her legs to increase the contact and friction.

She was barely aware of Rocco tugging the tiny apron free and moving his hands to the buttons of her dress, ripping them apart. Cool air touched her heated skin and she craved to be free of her constricting garments, nearly sobbing out loud when she felt Rocco's big hands pull the top of the dress apart to bare her breasts to his gaze. She vaguely heard material rip.

He drew back from the kiss and looked down, breathing harshly. Gracie was dizzy, heart racing like an express train. She couldn't get enough oxygen to her brain. Rocco's eyes were feverish. As much as he could he pushed the shoulders of her dress down, baring even more of her breasts. The pale skin was framed by a black bra, not racy in the slightest. But Gracie was beyond caring. She needed this man's touch, his mouth...

As if reading her mind, Rocco pulled down one cup, forcing her plump breast to spring free. As if hypnotised, Rocco cupped and caressed her breast, a thumb stroking the peak back and forth. Gracie bit her lip to stop herself from begging.

Excitement zinged through her veins when his dark head lowered and finally the wet sucking heat of his mouth surrounded that taut peak. His tongue rolled around it, sucking it into even more tightness. Gracie's head fell back against the wall, the pain unnoticed in the haze of pleasure infusing her body. Her hips were squirming, undulating against Rocco's, her legs had parted even more and his erection was long and hard and thick against her sensitive sex.

Gracie wanted to see him unclothed and started searching for his shirt, clumsy hands fumbling with his buttons. He took his mouth away from her breast and stood up.

Rocco's head was consumed by fire. A fire of lust and desire and need too great to deny. Gracie was half slumped against the wall behind her. His hips grinding into hers was probably the only thing still keeping her standing. Her mouth was dark pink and swollen. Eyes huge with pupils so dilated they looked black.

Her fast breaths made her pale breasts rise and fall enticingly. She had small tight pink nipples, surrounded by slightly darker areolae and freckles. Rocco felt a sense of inevitability sink into his bones. This woman was *his*.

He knew he couldn't rationalise that assertion now. He could only act on the singularly strongest driving force of his life: to have her and make her his.

With impatience making his usually graceful movements jerky, Rocco opened his shirt, buttons popping off around them. He looked at Gracie's half-open dress. It had to come off over her head. He brought his hands to the thin material and ripped it all the way to the hem. His blood was pumping now. Her dress gaped open down to her thighs, giving a glimpse of black panties.

He felt feral. He felt wild. He'd never felt like this with another woman.

He looked at Gracie and forced himself to grind out, 'We're doing this right here, right now. Unless you say no. You have about ten seconds to decide.'

CHAPTER SIX

GRACIE looked up at Rocco, towering above her, making her feel impossibly small and delicate. The sheer stark hunger stamped onto his features was awesome and almost frightening. But she wasn't frightened. She hadn't even blinked when he'd ripped her dress open like some kind of animal. It had excited her.

She shook her head and reached out a hand to his belt. 'Don't stop.'

He seemed to wait for an infinitesimal moment, as if testing her resolve, and then with a guttural sound he took off his shirt and started to push Gracie's dress down her arms until it was off completely. Her bra came off too, so now she was naked except for her knickers. She felt vulnerable for a moment, until Rocco started undoing his belt and trousers. And then heat took over again.

She greedily took in his amazing physique. Taut muscles and gleaming skin. Springy dark hair on his chest that arrowed down into that tantalising line which was revealed as his trousers slid down over powerful thighs. He wore snug fitting briefs that were tented over his erection. Gracie's eyes went wide.

But then Rocco reached for her and she looked up, her gaze clashing with his. It was as if they were in the eye of the storm. Suddenly everything took on a languorous feel. His hands tangled in her hair, tumbling it from its bun completely. His mouth found hers, kissing her, rediscovering her taste with his tongue. And then it moved down, over her shoulder and to her breasts, which felt full and aching. Both hands cupped her breasts and he fed one hard peak and then the other into his mouth, teeth nipping gently, making Gracie cry out.

The urgency didn't take long to build again. Gracie was straining against Rocco, her back arched, hips moving impatiently. One of his hands moved around her rib cage and down her back, under her knickers to cup the cheek of her bottom, squeezing it harshly, making her nerve-points tighten and tingle.

His mouth moved back up to find hers, and he pulled her close making his chest hairs scrape against moist, sensitised nipples. Gracie was clutching at his shoulders, incapable of doing anything but succumbing to this onslaught on her senses. His hand moved from her bottom, tugging her panties down slightly, and around to the apex of her legs, between their bodies.

Gracie held her breath as his long fingers explored the damp curls surrounding her sex. Her hands gripped his wide shoulders as a finger delved deeper into the secret folds where she ached. He found the most intimate part of her and rubbed back and forth. Gracie started to shake.

Rocco's finger thrust deep inside, the invasion all at once shocking and cataclysmic. Gracie came in a rush, her body convulsing around Rocco's hand. The sudden tide of pleasure was so intense that tears leaked from her eyes, her whole body held taut for a long moment.

When it was over Rocco slowly withdrew his hand. Gracie felt shell-shocked, numb, with little fires of sensation racing over her skin. She'd never experienced anything like that. All she could remember of her few sexual experiences was how she'd never found any kind of satisfaction. She'd thought sex was overrated. She couldn't believe she'd just—

Suddenly she was being lifted. Rocco said roughly, 'Put your legs around my waist.'

Dumbly, she did so, wrapping them around him, feet locked together over his buttocks, arms around his neck. He walked them over to the huge table where they usually ate breakfast. Holding her securely with one strong arm, he used his other one to sweep the detritus on the table to the floor. Cookery books landed with dull thuds and a cup fell and smashed. Rocco laid her on her back, the apex of her thighs tight against his waist. She could feel his erection nudging her bottom and her sated body started to hum again.

Rocco gently disengaged her legs, all the time staring down at her if mesmerised by her. He hooked his hands into his briefs and with a quick downward movement tugged them off. Gracie looked down to see the full extent of his erection. It had felt big. But it looked massive. Shivers of fear at his size mixed with excitement went through her like electric rivers of shock.

His hands were on her panties, tugging them down. Gracie lifted her hips silently. Their eyes met. She saw Rocco's gaze go to the golden-red curls between her legs. His chest expanded and his eyes grew even darker. And then he was pushing her legs apart with those big hands and his head was going down...

Her heart stopped. He wasn't—no one had ever before—

And then she felt his breath cool against her hot skin, and her hands clenched into fists when she felt the first sweep of his tongue down her moist cleft. A shudder of pure ecstasy went through her as his tongue dipped and swirled and teased her. She could feel herself tensing again, the imminent onset of pleasure very obvious, and suddenly she couldn't bear for him to see how easily he could make her orgasm and lose control as she already had.

She tried to bring her thighs together, hands searching for his head, pulling on his hair before it was too late. She could already feel her muscles clenching and unclenching in preparation.

'No...*stop*...it's too much.'

Rocco finally seemed to hear her and came up over her like some kind of avenging dark angel. His body was tall and lean, and so powerful he took her breath away, making her forget everything else.

She was vaguely aware of him donning a protective sheath, and then with his hand between them and an intense look on his face she could feel the wide blunt head of him seek entrance at her moist core.

The intrusion made her suck her breath in. She looked down at their bodies to see the pale skin of her thighs tight against his hips. He was slowly and inexorably sinking into her, pushing and stretching her body. The full feeling was almost excruciating, and she put a hand out as if to stop him, but it came into contact with his tight abdomen muscles, damp with sweat, and fresh heat flooded her, easing his passage into her body.

After an infinitesimal moment, he was in all the way. She could feel his body snug against hers. She felt impossibly impaled, but even as she thought that awareness sank in and tiny tremors of pleasure pulsed through her. Almost slowly, Rocco started to move out again, and those pleasurable tremors increased, making Gracie arch her back towards him.

He bent his head and took one rosy nipple into his mouth, suckling fiercely as he began the inexorable ride back into her body. This time the ease of movement was markedly different. Gracie's muscles clenched around him, as if loath to let him go.

Any hint of restraint was a thin veneer, hiding their increasing urgency. Gracie locked her legs around Rocco's hips, forcing him even closer. His strokes became more urgent, harder and deeper. Gracie could feel the rush of pleasure coming towards her. As she began to lose herself in the flooding warmth of her second orgasm in the space of minutes she could see the intensity of Rocco's expression. He was holding back until she came. An extraordinary tenderness overwhelmed her just as the most powerful euphoric bliss broke her in two. What she'd felt before had been a mere precursor to this ecstasy.

Rocco pounded into her body. Her muscles clenched around his thick shaft as he too finally gave in and allowed his body to succumb to his own climax.

Finally a brief calm seemed to descend, and the only sound that could be heard was their ragged breathing. Gracie became aware of her legs locked around Rocco's waist, his damp chest crushing her pleasurably to the cool hard surface of the table.

Registering that was like a cold douche of water.

She tensed all over. She was naked, on her back with her legs clamped around Rocco's hips, in the harsh glow of the kitchen lights. And Rocco de Marco was between her legs, her body still holding his in an intimate embrace.

Before that reality could intrude too much Rocco raised himself off her and looked down, his hair flopping sexily over his forehead. Gracie could feel him inside her, and unbelievably he was still slightly hard.

As if reading the direction of her thoughts he smiled tightly. 'If we don't move, I think there's going to be a repeat performance very soon.'

He drew back and disengaged from her body. Immediately Gracie felt bereft and very naked. Until Rocco scooped her up into his arms and walked out of the kitchen, carefully avoiding the destruction they'd left on the floor, and through the silent apartment to his bedroom. He deposited her on the bed as gently as if she were made of china and went into the bathroom. She heard the sound of a shower running.

Rocco came back out and scooped her up again, as if she weighed no more than a bag of sugar, and within seconds she was gasping on wobbly legs under a powerfully warm spray. Rocco was soaping his hands and running them all over her body, washing her, and Gracie gave up trying to rationalise this and stood silently while Rocco thoroughly soaped her whole body.

When his hand slipped between her legs she widened slumberous eyes and her breath hitched. He was so virile and gorgeous, hair plastered to his skull, water running in rivulets down his face and over hard chest muscles. And those wicked long fingers were stroking between her legs, making her moan softly.

With a rueful smile Rocco took his hand away and shook his head. 'I think you need a break before we indulge again.'

Again. Gracie grew hot just thinking of all that passionate intensity *again*. She didn't know if she could cope.

Rocco was pouring shampoo into his hand and turning her around so that he could wash her hair. She was glad not to be the focus of that black gaze for a moment.

After a few seconds she heard him say behind her, 'You weren't a virgin?'

Gracie grew tense. She shook her head and said huskily, 'No. I've had sex before…'

Familiar pain gripped her when she thought of the boy

she'd trusted enough to sleep with her at her last foster home. She'd been just eighteen, so young and vulnerable. Steven had been in jail and she'd been desperately lonely. But as soon as he'd slept with her he'd dumped her, telling her that no one wanted to go out with a slag.

He'd spread the word among their peers and Gracie had been branded an easy lay, which had been so far from the truth that she hadn't trusted anyone since then. She'd escaped to college soon after, and had kept herself to herself.

Yet within days of meeting Rocco de Marco she was allowing him to seduce her on a kitchen table as if she'd done it all her life.

'But it's been a while?'

His voice cut off her tumultuous thoughts. Gracie was mortified. Had it been that obvious? She nodded her head quickly. Rocco stepped up close behind her then, and she went properly weak at the knees feeling that powerfully muscular body along the length of hers, his recovered erection between them. She fought not to move her hips against him as wantonly as she wanted to, awfully conscious of her vulnerability.

His arms came under her arms and his hands cupped her soapy breasts, trapping her nipples. His head came down and he said softly, 'You were so tight around me. I liked it.'

Gracie's feeling of vulnerability dissolved when she remembered how he'd felt when he'd thrust into her that first moment. She turned in his arms and looked up shyly. 'I liked it too...'

He just looked at her for a long moment, while the water beat down around them, and then he moved her so that she stood under the spray, to rinse all the shampoo and soap from her hair and body. His touch was no longer seductive, it was brisk.

Then he flipped off the shower and grabbed two towels, enveloping her in one. He handed her out of the shower first, and then stepped out too. It was as if a cold wind had sprung up between them and Gracie felt on edge. Had she said something wrong? Been too easy? How could she explain to him that it felt as if on some level she'd known him for ever—as if her body knew exactly how to be with him? How to pleasure him? That she wasn't like this normally?

She'd had no idea desire could consume her like a forest fire raging through dry wood. She watched as he turned away from her to rub himself dry roughly. Even now her eyes couldn't help devouring him, lingering on the way his muscles bunched and stretched.

Hesitantly she forced herself to ask, 'Are you…is everything okay?'

His hands stopped in their movement. And then he said gruffly, without looking at her, 'Why wouldn't it be?'

He sounded so remote and harsh that Gracie took a step back, clutching the towel to her. 'If you regret what just happened—'

He whirled around fast and snaked the towel around his hips. He glared at her. 'Why on earth would I regret it? It's the best sex I've ever had.'

Gracie blanched and then felt hot. His use of the word *sex* scored at her insides like a knife. 'Well, you don't have to sound so angry about it. It doesn't have to happen again.'

If anything that made him look even fiercer. He stepped close to her, jaw tight. 'That was not a one-off. It will be happening again, and it'll keep happening until we burn ourselves free of this insanity.'

Familiar fire rose within Gracie at his temper and his autocratic tone. She straightened her shoulders. 'Well, for your information, I think I've had enough. I don't need to burn myself free of *anything*. This was a really bad idea.'

Gracie grabbed the towel around her and went to step around Rocco to leave the bathroom, but he halted her progress with his hands on her shoulders. She glared at him as fiercely as he was glaring at her. The air crackled around them.

'Where do you think you're going?'

Gracie tossed her head, 'Oh, so now I'm a prisoner of this room? Not just your apartment?'

'Damn it, woman,' Rocco growled, and hauled her close. Before she knew what was happening he was kissing her, forcing her head back, mouth crushing hers. Defiant to the end she kept her mouth closed and stayed stiff. Until she started to feel dizzy and had to breathe in.

Rocco seized his moment and his tongue invaded her mouth with shockingly hot intimacy. He pulled her hips into his at the same time and she could feel the resurgence of his desire. Suddenly she was back in that mad vortex, with need clawing through her worse than before. Because now she'd tasted Rocco, felt the full force of him...and of course she couldn't turn her back on this any more than he could. Her bones turned to liquid and her tongue duelled with his, their mouths tight together as if in danger of being ripped apart at any moment.

He tore his mouth away after long, dizzying seconds and said gutturally, 'I won't take you like an animal again.'

He bent down and lifted her into his arms, strode back into the bedroom. He put her down on the bed and stripped the towel from around his waist. Gracie's eyes were glued to him as he came down over her, twitching her towel aside so he could feast his eyes on her body, laid out for him. He reminded her of some mythical pagan god. She'd sensed a raw wildness in him the night she'd met him, but the reality of it was intoxicating.

He trailed the back of his hand from the valley of her

breasts to the juncture of her thighs. She squirmed and bit her lip even as she wanted to have the strength to grab his hand and throw it aside, to tell him that she wouldn't succumb to him again.

He pushed her thighs apart with one hand and pressed his palm against her. He looked deep into her eyes, 'You're mine, Gracie O'Brien, and I'm going to make you mine over and over again—until you don't even know who you are any more.'

'I'm going to make you mine over and over again—until you don't even know who you are any more.'

Rocco was standing at the window of his bedroom with his back to the view of a faint pink dawn breaking over London's skyline. His arms were crossed and he was looking warily at the woman sleeping in his bed, as if she might jump out at any moment and grab him. He felt as if he'd just been catapulted back into reality after a psychedelic mind-altering experience.

Those words were reverberating in his head. When he'd said them to her he'd meant that he wanted to make her forget her own name because she'd made him forget…*everything*. Who he was. What he was. *Why* he was.

It had only been in the shower, as she'd looked up at him with those dark serious eyes, that the first sliver of sanity had returned—and with it the awful, excoriating realisation that he'd exposed himself comprehensively.

Acute vulnerability of a kind he hadn't felt in years— so long ago that he'd hardly recognised it—had burnt him up inside and he'd lashed out. But Gracie had stood up to him, like she had from day one, and he'd soon been fired up all over again, that feeling of vulnerability dissolving like a mist to be replaced with sheer lust.

Last night had proved to him that for all his hard-won

control and precious rationale he couldn't keep from acting on base desire. Once he'd touched Gracie there had been no going back. He grimaced. There had been no going back from the moment he'd seen her standing in that elevator, looking so pale and anxious.

And from the moment she'd walked into the drawing room in that provocative uniform Rocco had bitterly regretted that Honora Winthrop was there. If he'd ever needed a stark comparison between two women they'd unwittingly provided it. As the evening had unfolded, and Gracie had served them exquisite dish after exquisite dish, Rocco had become more and more entranced. More and more surprised that she wasn't using the opportunity to humiliate him. And more and more certain that he wanted her.

He'd battled an increasing need to *see* her. He'd suffered through the courses, tuning out Honora Winthrop's cut-glass tones, and come to life each time Gracie came back into the room, eyes devouring her, painfully aware of his state of arousal—for *her*.

He'd become so impatient at one stage that he'd gone looking for her himself, only to see her stretching up to kiss his own security man sweetly on the cheek. He'd looked as if he'd just received a bonus. The jealousy had been swift and shocking. He'd wanted to fire George on the spot and shake Gracie until she rattled.

When Honora had made those snide comments about the food Rocco had had to restrain himself from reaching across the table and pushing her sanctimoniously perfect face into her dessert. As soon as Gracie had walked out of the room he'd stood up and told Honora coolly, 'This evening is over. Thank you for coming, but I think we both know that this won't go any further.'

She had stood up too, quiveringly angry. She'd spat at

him, 'It's over because you want that tart of a housekeeper? Is *that* why you've refused to sleep with me?' Before he could answer she'd said, 'You don't get it, do you? You can have me and still have *her*. That's how it's done. I would only expect discretion. You can sleep with who you want while we maintain the façade of a happy marriage.'

She had articulated exactly what he'd set out to achieve by wooing her into marriage, and suddenly Rocco had recoiled from her words as if they were poisonous. Tight-lipped, he'd said, 'Get out. I've changed my mind.'

Honora had just shaken her head, eyes as cold as ice and full of malicious pity. 'You won't get another chance like this.'

He'd all but snarled at her, 'I'll make my chances—just as I've always done. Now, what I'd like you to do first is apologise to Gracie for your rudeness and then leave.'

She'd thrown her head back and laughed. And then she'd walked out, slamming the door behind her.

Now, in the early-morning light, Rocco could hardly believe that he'd so spectacularly ruined his reputation in one fell swoop. He knew someone like Honora Winthrop would waste no time in spreading the word, along with half a dozen untruths, so that her own reputation wasn't damaged. He wouldn't get so close to a society darling again for a long time. They were a closely knit clique. And yet he couldn't seem to drum up any urgency to want to rectify the situation. Not when he was looking at the woman on the bed, sprawled in voluptuous abandon, with the marks of their passionate lovemaking on her delicately pale skin.

Wild red curls and waves rippled around her head across the stark white pillow. One long curl twisted enticingly down over her breast, kissing the tempting curve. Rocco's body was already hard. All it took was a look, or the memory of what it was like to surge into her tight, hot embrace.

He couldn't remember if he'd ever been with a lover so responsive and generous. He prided himself on being a virile, sensual man, and he enjoyed sex, but his experiences in recent years had all been…restrained. He'd found it easy not to lose control.

But all that had changed with Gracie. He cringed inwardly now to remember how he'd swept the things off the table in the kitchen so that he could take her there, as if he was some out of control rutting animal. And yet… she'd loved it. She'd splintered apart around him like his most secret erotic fantasy.

It was as if he'd been merely existing for a long time, and something or *someone* had woken him from a trance. Colours were more vivid, sounds sharper. Something fundamental in his beliefs about this woman had shifted last night when he'd seen how hard she'd worked to put together that beautiful meal. And when he'd seen the genuine hurt in her eyes at how she'd been spoken to. The fierce pride in her expression.

She'd spent the bare minimum on his credit card for the food. George had handed it back to him with an explicit look when he'd come back to the apartment before dinner, as if to say, *See? She's not like the rest.* And the assertion struck Rocco again that she didn't have anything to do with her brother's machinations. Even so—the voice of reason intruded—she was loyal to her brother, and that alone meant he couldn't fully trust her.

Rocco could feel the dominant part of himself that had struggled for so long to survive and attain his position try to assert itself. How could he be jeopardising so much, so easily, just for a woman? All his life he'd wanted to distance himself from drama and passion. Chaos and violence. The life he lived now was the absolute antithesis of that. And he was considering diving back into it with Gracie?

Yet surely all was not lost? He could have Gracie O'Brien, and when this desire burnt itself out—as it always did—he would gather around the structures of his life again and ensure his precious status once more.

He smiled cynically. Despite Honora Winthrop's dire warning, he knew money could buy anything, and ultimately one of those women wouldn't be able to resist if he wanted to enter into their protected society via marriage. Ever since that day in Italy when he'd been spat at and ignored by his own blood family in the street, and he'd watched them walk away, immune and protected by their status, he'd craved that protection. That security. And he could not lose sight of that now, when he had it in the palm of his hand.

He could have it all, including Gracie, and he intended to.

Rocco walked back over to the bed and sat down, smiling when he saw a small frown pleat the smooth skin between her eyes. Her mouth was in a delicious moue, still a little swollen. He bent and pressed a kiss there and her eyes opened.

He drew back for a moment, to see her looking at him with those wide, serious and wary eyes. Then she just said, 'Hi,' with a husky voice.

It was so simple and lacking in artifice that something turned over in Rocco's chest. All his recent assertions suddenly felt very flimsy, and to avoid looking at *why* he just bent his head and kissed Gracie until she was breathless and arching her body into him and he lost himself in the bliss of her again.

When Gracie woke she blinked and squinted against the sun streaming into the bedroom. *Rocco's bedroom.* As realisation sank in she squeezed her eyes tightly shut and groaned softly. And then she registered that she was naked and half uncovered. She scrabbled around for the sheet and pulled it right up over herself, and then peeped out to look around the room, trying to ignore the ache between her legs and in every muscle of her body.

The room was empty. All was still and quiet. She looked at the bedside clock and saw that it was one pm. With a squeal she sat up. And then lay back down again when she felt dizzy. Images started to flood her head. The endless night of being entangled with Rocco. His powerful body surging into hers over and over again, until she'd been weeping from an overdose of pleasure.

And then that morning, as dawn had broken outside, she'd woken to find him sitting there, just looking at her with such an intense expression, eyes dark. And he'd kissed her, and it had started all over again. Her body had been sensitive, but Gracie had loved the feel of Rocco moving so urgently within her.

But now when she moved a leg she winced. Sitting up again, Gracie cautiously got out of the bed, hugging the sheet around her, and went into the bathroom. Rocco's used towels lay on the floor and over the sink. His distinctive smell made her reel with a fresh onslaught of memories.

Gracie's brain shied away from trying to figure out how she could have given herself so freely to someone like him. He not only didn't trust her—he was a world away from her world. She came from an ugly council estate surrounded by grim flats and few opportunities. He came from a country steeped in beauty and undoubtedly from a lineage in which he could list his ancestors back as far as Caesar.

Gracie couldn't shower in his bathroom now. Not with his scent so fresh and mocking. She got to his bedroom door still with the sheet clasped around her and opened it quietly, half terrified she'd see him on the other side. No one was there. Gracie hurried back to her own room and shut and locked the door behind her.

And then she dived into her shower and scrubbed herself until her skin felt raw and sore muscles finally relaxed back to some semblance of normality. When she got out she dressed in loose pants and a shirt, as covered up as she could be. She tied her hair back into a ponytail.

When she opened her bedroom door she heard a noise coming from the kitchen and heat flooded her face when she thought of the carnage they'd left behind them. Her dress ripped open from neck to hem! Her discarded knickers!

Gracie imagined huge George in the middle of it, looking around with a scandalised expression, and with her face flaming she rushed to the kitchen. But the sight that greeted her was so unexpected that she stumbled to a halt. A small woman was mopping the floor, and the kitchen reflected nothing of the previous day or evening. Everything was tidied away, and fresh flowers stood on the table where Rocco and she had—

'You must be Gracie.'

Gracie looked stupidly at the middle-aged woman who was smiling and coming towards her with an outstretched hand.

Numbly Gracie shook her hand and nodded. 'Yes…I'm Gracie. I'm sorry, but…who are you?'

The woman smiled broadly. 'I'm Mrs Jones. I've been retained by Mr de Marco as his new housekeeper subject to a month's trial period.' She leaned on her mop and said conspiratorially, 'I've only just started back working full-time now that the kids are in college, so I don't know how it'll suit, but he seems nice…'

Gracie thought a little hysterically how *nice* didn't do him justice, and just looked at the woman who was chattering away as if nothing was wrong. If this woman was now the housekeeper, then what on earth was she?

'Are you all right, love?'

Gracie's focus came back to the housekeeper. Vaguely she nodded. 'Is George outside?'

The woman's eyes grew round. 'Is he the big man?'

Gracie nodded again and backed away, saying something about it being nice to meet her. She went out of the apartment to see George calmly reading a paper. He looked up and smiled. Gracie looked at him suspiciously. He didn't appear to be traumatised by anything he'd seen. Perhaps he'd not been into the kitchen?

She took a shaky breath. 'Do you know where Mr de Marco is?'

George frowned. 'He should be in his office. He went there a couple of hours ago, just after the new housekeeper arrived.'

Gracie nodded and made for the lift. She stopped when George called her name gently and turned around to follow his gaze—which was on her feet. Her *bare* feet. Smiling weakly, she went back inside to get some shoes.

Rocco was standing at his window. He ran a hand around the back of his neck. He couldn't ignore the steady hum of pleasure in his body, as if he'd just gorged on a feast. He grimaced. He *had*. A feast of Gracie.

His skin tightened imperceptibly and he stilled. He recognised instantly when the energy around the office changed. Slowly he turned around to see a pale-looking Gracie, covered from neck to toe in loose drab clothes, heading for his office. Her hair was tied back, making her look young. His gaze narrowed on her and with fatal predictability his body reacted. He regretted the countless glass windows and lack of privacy even more. And then his conscience struck him as he had a lurid image of what he'd like to do to her in his office. Gracie must be sore. She was so much smaller than him and she'd been so tight...

And yet she'd met him head-on every time, until exhaustion had finally claimed them both.

Gracie was almost at the door, her dark eyes on him with unwavering intensity in an unsmiling face. This was so far removed from any other morning-after situation he'd been in it was almost funny. But Rocco wasn't laughing when she walked in.

CHAPTER SEVEN

'WHAT'S going on?' Gracie's arms were folded, as if that could help protect her from the sheer animal appeal of the man standing just a few feet away. Her body was betraying her, going into full on readiness mode. Nipples peaking, stomach tightening, and down below, between her legs…

'What are you talking about?'

Gracie willed her body to calm down and said tightly, 'I met the *new* housekeeper. So what does that make me?'

Rocco's hands were in his pockets. He wasn't wearing a jacket, just a shirt and tie, and he looked magnificent with the sun streaming in behind him, highlighting the broadness of his physique. His shirt was so finely made that she could see the dark hue of his skin and the delineated muscles.

He came around his desk then and perched on the corner, hands still in his pockets. For a moment Gracie had a rush of imagining that he had done that to stop himself from reaching for her, and cursed her runaway imagination.

'I hired Mrs Jones because I don't want you doing any more housework.'

Gracie injected false brightness into her voice. 'So I'm free to go?'

He shook his head, a glint in his eye. 'Not a chance.

You've never been less free.' There was a thrilling edge to his voice that made Gracie shiver and feel intense self-disgust at the same time.

'So...what? I've been promoted? To your bed?' She tried to make herself sound disgusted and scathing, but the words came out breathy.

A tiny smile turned up the corner of Rocco's mouth. 'Yes, you've been promoted to my bed. I like the sound of that.'

Feeling incredibly crabby all of a sudden, Gracie blurted out, 'Well, I don't. I'm not just a convenient plaything, you know.'

His mouth quirked. 'I am well aware of that. You're like a very volatile explosive substance mixed with the charm of a kitten and the claws of a big cat.'

Gracie blinked at him and said truthfully, 'I don't know if that's a compliment or an insult.'

'Oh, it's a compliment, believe me.' He stood up and came closer. Gracie's breath hitched. He cast a quick expressive glance either side of his office. 'You were right, you know...about the glass. It's so that I can see everyone at all times. It makes me nervous not to know who's coming or what's happening. But for once I wish I had blinds—or tinted windows.'

Gracie's throat went dry. She was mesmerised by the look in his eyes.

His voice was low and intimate, distracting Gracie from dwelling on his enigmatic words or their meaning. 'I'd lock the door so that I could take your hand and lead you over to the sofa. I'd pull you down and take off your top so that I could touch and taste your breasts. Then I would move my hand down, underneath the flimsy elastic of your trousers to your knickers. I would keep going until I could feel your soft curls. I wonder if they're already moistened—'

'Stop it!' Gracie all but hissed, arms clenched so tight across her chest that it was hard to breathe. She was sweating now, her heart beating rapidly, and down below... Lord, she wanted Rocco to pick her up and spread her across his desk the way he had in the kitchen last night.

She cast a quick mortified glance left and right. All she saw were bent industrious heads. She looked back to Rocco and felt dizzy. To anyone observing from the outside all they'd see was Rocco with his hands in his pockets, talking to the strange nondescript girl who'd suddenly started working for him.

But then Gracie looked down on an impulse and saw where his trousers were barely confining the truth of their conversation. She went puce.

In some pathetic effort to redirect the conversation she avoided Rocco's eye and asked, 'The kitchen...this morning...did Mrs Jones...?'

She couldn't finish—too mortified when she could see the carnage in her mind's eye again. She felt a finger come to her chin and Rocco tipped her face up. He'd moved closer, and she could smell heat and sex and lust. Her belly clenched tight with anticipation.

He shook his head. 'No. I cleared it up.'

Relief flooded Gracie even as she registered surprise. She said faintly, 'Somehow I can't see that happening.'

Rocco let her chin go and smiled dryly. 'I can pick things off the floor, you know. I'm not completely helpless.'

Gracie shivered. He wasn't helpless at all. He was like some magnificent urban animal. And then she thought of him picking up her knickers, and that dress that he'd ripped apart with his bare hands. With a muffled groan Gracie turned away to leave. Her head was churning, trying to make sense of where she stood now with Steven and everything, but she couldn't think when she was within three feet of this man.

She stopped when she heard Rocco say from behind her, 'Wait.'

Reluctantly she turned around again. He was standing behind his desk. She breathed a little easier.

'Do you have an up-to-date passport?'

She nodded, wondering where this was going.

'Good. In that case we're leaving this afternoon for Thailand for two days, and from there we'll go to New York for a couple of days.'

Gracie could hardly believe her ears. She shook her head slightly. 'Thailand?'

'It's a country in South-East Asia.'

'I know that,' she said impatiently, too afraid to believe this for a second. It had to be a joke. 'But…why?'

'Because I have to go on business and I want you to come with me.'

Her heart was thumping like a piston. 'As…what, exactly?'

He put his hands on his desk, spread wide. A feral look was in his eye and he smiled the smile of a consummate seducer. 'As my lover, of course.'

Gracie was still in a mild state of shock hours later, when she was in the back of Rocco's car with his long legs spread out beside her. She was clutching her passport in her hands and staring out of the window as London whizzed past and they entered countryside. Rocco's jet was at a private airfield. *Private jet.* Gracie felt a bubble of hysteria rising.

Suddenly her passport was taken out of her hands. Her head snapped around. 'Hey!'

She'd been avoiding looking at Rocco since he'd arrived back at the apartment to pick her up. He'd given her a scathing look up and down and muttered something about suitable clothes before making a call on his phone. Then he'd hustled her out of the apartment, leaving George behind, and into his car. And now he was perusing her passport. He looked up with an arched brow. 'You haven't travelled much?'

Gracie grabbed for her passport but Rocco held it aloft, and the motion of the car made her land awkwardly against his rock-hard torso. Cheeks flaming, Gracie scrabbled back, but Rocco snaked out an arm and captured her, holding her against him easily. Her breasts were crushed against him and her nipples were already peaking into tight stinging points.

Their faces were so close that Gracie could feel his warm breath. Her gaze slid to his mouth. She ached to touch it, to trace it with her finger. To feel the cushiony firmness.

Rocco's arm moved up and his hand speared into her hair, cradling the back of her head. 'Gracie...' he said roughly.

She ached for him to kiss her. The tension had been spiralling through her since she'd woken that morning, aching for him to touch her again. And she'd been in a state of near arousal since his provocative words in his office.

It was a few moments before either one of them heard the discreet knocking on the window beside Rocco. Gracie sprang apart from him, mortified by how ready she was for him to make love to her in the back of a car.

Gracie scrambled out, all but landing on the tarmac in an undignified heap. Rocco just looked at her with a bemused expression and Gracie scowled at him. She didn't need to suffer his look to know that he must be bemused by this attraction.

He set out across the tarmac to the plane, which was

glinting in the setting evening sun. Gracie stumbled slightly and Rocco stopped and held out a hand. She'd expected him to walk autocratically ahead of her, not even checking to see if she followed, and she looked at his hand for a long moment and then put her hand in his. His much bigger hand curled around hers, and her belly was swooping dangerously all the way to the plane with their fingers entwined.

For some reason, and she hated to admit this to herself, the moment felt significant.

Rocco looked at Gracie, sitting in a plush seat across the aisle from him. She was staring out of the window, fascinated, as if she'd never seen an airport before. He shook his head. This was a novelty for him: to be with a woman who didn't feel as if she had to give him her undivided attention and who also didn't seem to care one bit for the fact that she wore no make-up and such unflattering garments in front of her lover.

The few occasions he had ever taken a woman away with him for whatever reason had been like military operations, with an extra vehicle just to carry their luggage. He'd put up with it because he'd assured himself this was his world now, but he had to admit that it had always disgusted him a little bit.

He was getting irritated now by Gracie's extreme absorption in everything around her. The plane was starting to taxi down the runway and he spotted her open belt. That irritation laced his voice as he called to her, and something inside him clenched when he saw her flinch minutely before she turned her face to him.

He gestured to her lap. She looked down dumbly.

'Your safety belt.'

'Oh.' She found the two ends and clumsily tried to put them together.

Rocco had a flash of realisation when he remembered her brand spanking new passport. That something inside him clenched even tighter as he leaned across and made quick work of securing her belt, tightening it.

'I could have done it.'

Rocco sat back and looked at her. *Now* she was looking at him. 'You've never been on a plane before, have you?'

She flushed under his gaze. He could see her warring with the desire to blurt out, *Of course I have!* But after a moment she just shook her head, lips tight together. She was embarrassed, and Rocco's belly tightened with some nameless emotion.

He asked roughly, 'So why the brand-new passport? Were you planning on going somewhere?'

The second after he'd asked the question a cold trickle of realisation wound its way down his spine. His desire to trust her mocked him. How could he have been so stupid? Before Gracie could answer he laughed out loud. '*Dio.* Of course you were! You must have been planning a nice long overseas trip with your brother and the million euros he'd creamed off my clients.'

The mushy feelings Gracie had been feeling ever since Rocco had taken her hand dissolved. To think that she'd actually been about to tell him the real reason that she possessed a new passport! She cringed now at how he would have laughed at her.

Instead she tossed her head and smiled, drawing herself back deep inside and hating him for giving her such an amazing experience with one hand and then tainting it with the other.

'That's exactly it. We were thinking Australia, actually. A totally new and fresh start. Is that what you want to hear, Rocco? Because I can tell you what you want to hear until I'm blue in the face but it won't change the fact that it's not the truth.'

With that, she turned back to the window, drawing in a shaky breath. His inability to trust had taken her by surprise. It was as if once again she'd forgotten what lay between them. The inherent distrust and enmity. The waiting game until Steven came forward.

Steven. Abject guilt lanced her like a physical pain. How could she have not even thought about her brother? A lurid image from the previous night answered her question. She had no way of knowing now where he was or how he was, and for the first time she actually wanted Rocco's men to find him. Because at least that way she'd know he was safe and could then fight to protect him from Rocco's wrath. Also…Rocco would have no more reason to keep her as some sort of insurance. Because that was all this was to him: an indulgence, a convenient slaking of mutual desire.

As Gracie stared stonily out of the window, her hands clamping the armrests with a fear she refused to show at her very first take-off, she vowed not to let Rocco de Marco get under her skin, where he could do serious damage like all the other people in her life who'd hurt her. One by one they'd all left their indelible marks: her father, whom she barely remembered, her mother, grandmother, first boyfriend. She'd been abandoned or rejected by each and every one of them eventually. Steven was the only constant she'd ever known, and he needed her to be strong so that she could defend him again.

Ultimately Gracie could trust no one but herself, and the sooner she remembered that and stopped feeling things for Rocco de Marco that should never be given life the better.

* * *

An hour later Rocco sighed with frustration, spearing his hands through his hair. The tension between him and Gracie was thick enough to cut. And he couldn't stop feeling as if he'd done her some grievous injury. She was turned so resolutely towards the window that she was going to get a damned crick in her neck!

'Gracie…'

There was no reaction.

Rocco wasn't even sure what he wanted to say. Sorry? How could he be wanting to say sorry and believe in her innocence when he had every reason to believe that she would be firmly on the side of her brother? He'd seen the photo of them as kids; they were as thick as thieves. Why else would she have a brand-new passport…?

He looked more closely at Gracie now and saw that she was breathing steadily. But she looked extremely uncomfortable. Because she was hell-bent on avoiding him? Her words came back to him accusingly: *'I can tell you what you want to hear until I'm blue in the face but it won't change the fact that it's not the truth.'* Cursing softly, he put aside the papers that he'd been failing miserably to concentrate on anyway and got out of his seat.

He bent over Gracie to see her pale cheeks. She was asleep. Lashes, long and dark, highlighted the translucence of her skin. And everything in him stilled when he saw the distinctive salty track of a tear down one cheek. His belly clenched hard. *She'd been crying.*

Cursing more volubly now, Rocco undid Gracie's belt and scooped her up out of the chair. She came awake groggily in his arms as he made his way down the centre of the plane, moving against his chest, making his blood go hot when he felt her soft breasts.

'Shh, you fell asleep. I'm just going to make you more comfortable.'

Gracie was too sleepy to come out of it completely. And she didn't want to—not when she felt so secure and safe with Rocco's arms around her. She knew she should be fighting *something*, but she couldn't drum up the energy to figure out what, exactly, and she didn't want to look at why she felt the remnants of anger at Rocco.

She felt herself being lowered down onto a soft surface, and then something deliciously silky being lifted over her. Her shoes were being removed. And then the bed dipped and she felt the slightest touch to her forehead. So light she wasn't even sure if it was a kiss.

Much later Gracie woke up, completely disorientated, with a strange sound in her ears. She slowly came round and realised the sound was the relentless hum of the plane. She looked around the dimly lit room, her mouth opening. She was in a *bedroom*, on a *plane*.

She put back the cover and padded over to one of the porthole windows and looked out. She could see bright sunlight, the curvature of the earth, and down far below majestic white-capped mountains. She'd never seen anything so spectacular.

She stood up and stretched, and tried to piece together how she'd come to be lying in the bed. She remembered being in Rocco's arms. And a kiss? She frowned. Perhaps it had just been a dream?

Her hurt at his blatant mistrust seemed to have faded. Logically Gracie knew that there was no way he'd ever really trust her. Her brother was missing with a million euros and she looked guilty as hell because she'd gone looking for him. And she insisted on defending him when even she had to concede that he had to be guilty.

She shut off her brain from wishing things could be different and explored the bedroom. She found an *en suite* bathroom, complete with fluffy towels and a bath and shower. Stocked to the brim with toiletries. Feeling sticky and gritty, she took the opportunity and stripped down to step into a steaming shower. She couldn't get her head around the fact that she was having a shower thousands of feet in the air and smiled gleefully, choosing for a blissful moment to forget what lay beyond the doors.

When she emerged back into the bedroom with a towel wrapped around her body she spotted numerous shopping bags and boxes. Unable to help investigating, she saw that they were all women's clothes. *For her?*

She quickly dressed, in her own jeans and a fresh shirt from her own suitcase, and went to find Rocco. When she opened the door, though, the plane was quiet and still dimly lit. There'd only been one flight attendant when they'd embarked—a man—and Gracie imagined he must be sleeping somewhere too.

She couldn't see Rocco's head, and crept up the aisle—only to come to a halt when she could see that his seat was back as far as it would go and he was asleep. Guilt spiked her, because he couldn't be as comfortable as she'd been in the bed.

One arm was flung up; the other rested over his chest. He looked so much younger that she sat down on the arm of the seat opposite and let her eyes rove over his face. He looked so much more approachable when in repose, and she had a sudden aching desire to know what it would be like to see him really relaxed, without that brooding intensity or that constant sardonic smile.

Suddenly he shifted and Gracie sprang up, aghast at the thought of being found staring at him like some lovestruck groupie. She was glancing left and right before she looked down again and saw him coming awake. Still managing to look gorgeous and not half as bleary as she felt.

'I'm sorry. I didn't meant to wake you.' To Gracie's surprise Rocco looked uncharacteristically disorientated. She was so used to seeing him in full control at all times this was like seeing a chink in his armour, and it made her heart turn over. And then she remembered his caustic comments and felt hurt all over again.

Before she could do anything, though, he'd recovered his composure with lightning speed and reached out to catch her wrist, pulling her off balance so she fell on top of him. She squealed and landed breathless on his wide chest. He had his hands on her waist and they were burrowing under her shirt to find her skin. His eyes were dark and heavy-lidded from sleep.

Gracie squirmed and felt heat rush to every extremity. 'Rocco...stop.' The words came out breathy and carried absolutely no conviction whatsoever. Her hurt at his suspicion of her was draining away. She was officially weak and shallow.

And then his hands did stop. He looked at her for a long moment and asked in a rough-sounding voice, 'So why *do* you have a brand-new passport, then?'

Gracie held her breath for a long moment, eyes searching his face for some sign he wasn't taking her seriously. She let out her breath and said a little shakily, 'You'll laugh at me.'

'Try me.'

Gracie tried to pull back but Rocco only snaked his hands tighter around her, so that she was all but welded to his chest and her bottom sat snugly in his lap. How was she supposed to concentrate when she could feel him hardening against her?

She looked down, avoiding his eyes, as if that could help her concentrate, and played with a button on his shirt. She took a breath.

'The reason I have a brand-new passport is because ever since I was little I always wanted to travel. I got a passport as soon as I could, even though I had no intention of going anywhere, and it was renewed just recently. I just liked the idea of having one, so I'd be ready to leave at a moment's notice...it seemed romantic to me—like there was this world of opportunity I could explore some day.' Gracie snuck a quick glance at Rocco and couldn't decipher his stony expression. She'd never felt so exposed, and looked down again. 'It's silly, I know...'

Rocco battled hard against the maelstrom inside him. Either Gracie was the best actress on the planet...or she was telling the truth. She couldn't even look him in the eye and his heart twisted. He knew what she was talking about, because the moment he'd taken his first passport in his hand he too had felt that sense of opportunity open up before him. He'd left Italy and never looked back.

He put a hand to her chin and tipped her face up to his, valiantly trying to screen the emotion he felt with the only weapon in his possession. Passion. Softly, though, before he gave in to it weakly, he just said, 'Okay.'

Gracie looked at him. 'Okay?'

Gruffly now, he said, 'I believe you.'

Gracie's heart felt as if it was expanding in her chest. All her hurt and anger dissolved and silently she cursed Rocco, perversely knowing that if he'd insisted on not believing her she would find it so much easier to deal with him.

He stood up then, taking her with him in his arms, and she squealed again. As he brought her towards the bedroom and her skin prickled with anticipation, she said breathlessly, 'Where are we going?'

'To join the mile-high club.'

Gracie's insides liquified. '*Rocco*...we can't...'

But her plaintive plea was cut off by the closing door, and when Rocco put her down and put his hands around her face and kissed her senseless she couldn't think of one reason why they couldn't.

An hour later Gracie was draped over Rocco's big body, legs either side of his hips. Their breathing was still erratic, hearts thumping hard. She'd hoped that making love wouldn't be as intense as the first time, but it had been even more intense. Because now her body knew the pleasure he could give her.

She was a mere novice when it came to sex, but in the space of twenty-four hours she felt as if she'd been spoilt for life. She knew instinctively that no other man could affect her like Rocco did. Lightning didn't strike twice. Her heart twisted ominously when she considered that the experience for him must be so much more banal.

Her hand was on his shoulder, and as she moved it down she felt some puckered skin. She lifted her head to look and saw some kind of scar. She'd never noticed it before. She touched it with a finger, tracing the outline, and could feel Rocco tense.

'What's this?' she asked.

His chest moved. 'I fell off my bike when I was a child.'

Gracie looked at him suspiciously. His eyes were still closed and she'd bet money that that was a lie. It had come out far too glibly. But why would he lie?

Knowing that he would be as likely to open up to her as he would to forgive Steven for his crime, she veered away from danger and said instead, 'When I woke up first we were flying over snow-capped mountains. What were they?'

'It was most likely the Himalayas.'

'Wow…' Gracie breathed. Feeling a little emotional, she said, 'I can't believe I might have been looking at Everest.'

Rocco shrugged minutely and said, 'Could have been.'

He opened sleepy eyes and his vaguely bored tone affected Gracie. She half slithered, half climbed off his body and looked at him 'You don't have a clue how privileged you are, do you? Is it really so easy to take everything for granted?'

She stood up from the bed, self-conscious in her nudity, and looked around for her clothes. But her wrist was grabbed and she was pulled back down. Rocco's eyes were dark and unreadable.

'I don't take it for granted,' he bit out. 'Not one second of it.'

The quality of his voice made Gracie go still. She'd touched a nerve, and she was reminded of that cataclysmic night in the kitchen when he'd told her he knew what it was like to not be noticed.

'It's just…it doesn't seem that way. You have the best of everything. Expect the best without question.'

'Because I can. Because I've earned it. What do you care anyway?'

What do you care? That question sent shards of fear through her. Why did it matter so much? Gracie looked at him and tried in vain to read his expression. He was so closed. She cared because she just *knew* there was something more to this man than the surface desire to be successful and surround himself with the trappings of the truly rich. There was a darker vein. She'd always sensed it.

There was a long, enigmatic silence and Gracie held her breath. For a moment she felt sure that Rocco was going to say something, but then he moved his hand from around her wrist, up her arm and around her neck to pull her down. He pressed a kiss to her mouth, making her open up to him.

After an intoxicating few seconds Gracie could feel herself tumbling headlong back towards ecstasy. It was like standing on the edge of a huge chasm with nothing to hold onto when she started to fall. She was terrified Rocco would see how much control over her he had.

She pulled back and he smiled at her lazily, his hand making circles on her back. He was turning on the charm, and she cursed him because it worked. When he smiled like that all she wanted to do was purr like a kitten.

Clearly he was avoiding any more probing questions.

She pulled away more forcefully this time and sat up. 'I'm going to take a shower.'

She stood up and walked over to the bathroom with as much insouciance as she could muster, desperately aware of Rocco's eyes burning into her back.

As soon as Gracie had disappeared into the bathroom the smile slid from Rocco's face. He lay back in the bed, his whole body tense, hands clenched to fists over the sheet which barely covered him. He cursed himself and called himself all sorts of names. Gracie had a unique ability to push his buttons and he couldn't help lashing out. He'd nearly smacked her hand away when she'd touched the scar from his old tattoo. Sleeping with her again had flayed him alive from the inside out. It was as if she could see right into where he was a fake. Where the thin veneer over his life was so flimsy it might fall away at any moment, exposing him.

He had not expected to feel that same out-of-control animalistic urge again. He'd imagined the edge would be gone from his need. But as soon as he'd had Gracie's face in his hands and her mouth under his all he'd been able to remember was the urgent need to fuse with her. The plane could have gone down into Everest and he wouldn't have noticed or cared.

And she'd met him every step of the way—even more explosively now than the first time. Rocco cursed out loud. Women did *not* get under his skin like this. His mother had taught him his first lesson by never putting him first. Whoever had been her current benefactor, or her pimp, had always been number one.

As a hormonal teenager Rocco had found that the girls he'd made a fool of himself over went with the boys with the biggest guns, the most swagger. To this day he gave thanks that he hadn't joined their ranks just to get a girl who would have soon dumped him for the next big thing. That had been his second big lesson.

His third had been when his sisters—two beautiful blonde, blue-eyed princesses—had stepped over him in the street without so much as a flicker of interest in the young man who had just confronted *their* papa, calling him *Father*. They'd not even flinched when their father had spat at him and pushed him to the ground.

When Rocco had finally left Italy and clawed his way up the ladder he'd taken great pleasure in seducing women from that world. Women who were privileged. There had been a measure of satisfaction in knowing that they would never touch an icy-cold and unbreakable part of him. The colder he was, the more he gained a reputation and a slavish following. His greatest satisfaction had come from imagining the horror and recoil on their faces if they really knew his darkest past.

But Gracie, with her serious eyes, her fierce protectiveness of her brother, and her slightly choked awe at flying over the Himalayas was fast unravelling what felt like years of block-building. He'd had no defences to pull around himself when she'd told him about the passport. Nowhere to go to hide or attack, which was what he was used to doing when he felt vulnerable.

She was connecting to a part of him long buried and denied, and he didn't like the lack of equilibrium that came with that. Rocco knew he'd be the biggest fool to believe in the track of a tear on a woman's cheek, or a cute story about a childhood dream, and yet—for possibly the first time in his life—he found a part of himself wanted to believe. Even just for a moment.

CHAPTER EIGHT

'Who are the clothes for?' Gracie asked when she stepped out of the bathroom for a second time in a towel. The sun was high now outside, and she could see brown earth far below. She felt a shiver of excitement.

Rocco must have showered in another bathroom as he was just finishing buttoning up a shirt, hair damp and looking dynamic and virile. He looked at her. 'They're for you.'

Gracie felt herself grow tense. 'But I have clothes.'

'You need suitable clothes for the weather. You have no idea how hot it's going to be. Also, I'm due to attend some functions in Bangkok and New York, so you'll need appropriate evening dress.'

Gracie bit her lip and looked at the bags warily. 'It feels weird, I don't want you dressing me.'

Rocco looked impatient now. 'It's no big deal. Luckily I realised in time.'

Fire flashed up Gracie's spine and she put her hands on her hips. 'Oh? Because you're afraid I'd embarrass you in public? Perhaps you shouldn't have been so hasty kicking your fiancée out the other night. You wouldn't have to dress *her*.'

Gracie knew she sounded petulant but she couldn't seem to stop. The contrast between her and Rocco's usual women was stark right now, and clearly she didn't measure up.

'Need I remind you that the outfit you made me wear the other evening was a size too small? But if you don't mind me parading around with my—'

'Enough!'

Gracie shut her mouth.

Rocco prowled closer and Gracie gulped. He looked dangerous. She could see a muscle throb in his jaw.

'For the umpteenth time, she was *not* my fiancée. And the company that sent the serving dress made an error on the size. I think you'll find that these will be a perfect fit, and if you don't put them on I *will* dress you myself.'

Gracie stuck up her chin. 'You don't scare me, you know.'

For a second he didn't react, and then Rocco laughed out loud, head thrown back. He looked back at her, eyes glinting and took her breath away.

'I know,' he said, with a peculiar quality to his voice. 'Believe me, you're the only one.'

When Rocco had walked out to let Gracie dress, she sucked in a deep quivery breath. The intensity of their lovemaking was still making her feel rawly vulnerable. She cursed herself for her reaction just now. The last thing she needed was that far too probing brain of his investigating why he pushed her buttons. She explored the bags of clothes and saw that they *were* the right size. Rocco had thought of everything—even make-up.

Reluctantly she packed away her own jeans and shabby shirt and, feeling like a fraud, dressed in a silk shirt, tailored lightweight linen trousers and flat shoes, and tried not to like how amazing the expensive fabrics felt against her skin.

* * *

A little later Gracie was sitting back in her seat with the belt buckled, barely able to contain her excitement as the plane descended through stormy-looking clouds into Bangkok.

The plane suddenly dipped and Gracie gripped her seat, looking at Rocco with panic. 'What was that?'

'Turbulence. It's rainy season in Bangkok, so it'll be stormy, but the rain is warm.'

'Warm?' Gracie knew she must sound ridiculous, but Rocco was reaching across the aisle for her.

'Come here,' he said throatily.

She scrambled out of her seat, more nervous than she cared to admit, and he swapped seats so that she could sit beside him at the window. She looked at him. 'But you won't be able to see.'

He gave her a funny look before replying, 'I've seen it before. It's your first time.'

Gracie finally tore her eyes away and looked down. They were just breaking through the clouds and she gasped in awe at the land below. 'It's so green. I never thought it would be so green!'

Rocco had his arms around her and his head close to hers. 'It's a mixture of jungle and paddy fields...rice paddies. It's quite a lush country—especially in the rainy season.'

Gracie was shaking her head in awe, drinking it in. She could see a huge distinctively shaped temple right in the middle of a field, with tiny stick insect people walking back and forth. 'It's so beautiful.'

Rocco's voice was amused. 'You haven't even seen it yet. Not properly.'

She turned her head. 'Will there be time...I mean, to look around?'

Rocco felt that tightness in his chest as he looked into

those brown gold-flecked eyes. He nodded. 'Sure. We can
go to the Grand Palace, and see some other things too.'

Impulsively Gracie pressed a kiss to Rocco's mouth, and
then turned away quickly before he could see the surge of
emotion she was feeling on her face.

Gracie was still reeling from the terror of her first plane
landing and the intensity of the damp heat when they'd
walked out of the plane about thirty minutes ago. The
sheer force of heat had hit her and instantly made her feel
as overdressed as someone in a ski-suit.

Rocco had looked at her when they'd got into the back of
a gloriously air-conditioned car, arched a brow and drawled
laconically, 'I told you so.'

Even in the space of those few minutes between plane
and car Gracie's shirt had begun sticking to her and her
hair had started frizzing up. Rocco looked as unfazed as
ever, and Gracie stuck her tongue out at him. 'Does nothing ever affect you?'

Rocco's face went serious and his eyes darkened as he
drawled, 'You do a pretty good job of affecting me.'

Gracie tore her gaze from Rocco's with an effort. She
was still freaked out by how quickly she lost control around
him. Luckily they were soon smack-bang in the middle of
Bangkok, and that sucked up all her attention.

The roads were wide, and tall skyscrapers pierced grey
skies. It was all at once hectic and modern and ancient.
Huge billboards written in a fascinating script showed pictures of gorgeous Thai families. Horns were screeching
and there seemed to be a million mopeds, some of them
carrying what looked like entire families. Serene-looking
women were perched on the back seat, side-saddle-style,
with babies in laps and helmets over their veils. Gracie's
eyes were huge as she took it all in.

She pointed at something. 'What are they?'

Rocco followed her gaze and said, 'They're called Tuk-Tuks. They're motorised rickshaws used as taxis.'

Gracie looked after the little vehicles wistfully, before her attention was taken by something else. Rocco stared at her face, enraptured by all her expressions, before he realised and broke his gaze away. He cursed himself. He had occasionally brought women on business trips, especially if he needed a companion for the ubiquitous social engagements. But he knew well that he'd never been so effortlessly distracted before.

He could well imagine the blasé reaction of someone like Honora Winthrop to Bangkok. Some people hated it, but it was one of Rocco's favourite cities and he couldn't help the warm feeling at seeing that Gracie looked as if she was going to love it too.

When they arrived at the hotel Gracie scrambled out of the car before the driver could open the door. She was like an irrepressible puppy. She turned around to face Rocco, a huge smile on her face. 'I *love* this heat. It's like standing in a warm shower after the water has stopped. And the smells are so exotic…'

Rocco tried not to notice how the silk of her shirt was already damp with her body heat and clung to her breasts, outlining their firm shape, the thrust of her nipples. The new clothes hugged her lithe figure, attracting attention, making him suddenly wish she was still dressed in her plain clothes.

He gritted his jaw and took her arm to lead her into the most exclusive hotel in Bangkok. It was one of the prestigious Wolfe chain of hotels, and he knew Sebastian Wolfe, the owner, personally. When they were on their way up in the lift Rocco looked at Gracie. He found that he was already anticipating her reaction to the room. And when the manager showed them in he wasn't disappointed.

Gracie walked around, speechless. She touched the backs of chairs and ran her hand along gleaming table tops. She found sliding doors and opened them, to step out onto a huge terrace which overlooked the Chao Praya river.

Rocco put down his laptop case and strolled towards the doors. The manager had left, after assuring Rocco fervently that he must call him any time of day or night if he needed anything. Rocco smiled. He didn't doubt that he had been personally informed by Sebastian to take care of him.

Rocco was reminded for a minute that Sebastian had recently married his beautiful Indian wife, and only a few weeks later she'd given birth to their baby boy. Sebastian had sent Rocco a picture of the three of them together, and it was an image of family bliss that Rocco had found almost difficult to look at. He pushed the memory aside now, frowning when he couldn't see Gracie.

Suddenly she appeared from around the corner, where a huge bamboo tree swayed gently in the breeze. 'There's a *pool*! Our very own private pool.'

He smiled and put his hands in his pockets, because he didn't think he'd be able to stop himself from touching her. 'I know.'

Her face fell, and it had an instant effect on his mood. 'Oh, of course you do. You must have been here a thousand times before.'

He gave up the effort it took to restrain himself and walked over, hating her crestfallen expression. He put an arm around her, pulling her close, and tipped her chin up. 'Not quite a thousand…a lot of times, though. You like it here?'

Gracie smiled and looked embarrassed, 'Like it? Are you crazy? This place is like Eden. I've never seen anything like it. The city is…overwhelming, breathtaking. This hotel is like…another world.'

Rocco pulled her closer and spoke without thinking. '*You're* breathtaking.'

Gracie's cheeks went a delicate pink, and she buried her head in his chest and mumbled, 'No, I'm not.' She looked up then. 'I'm just normal, and I think that's a novelty for you.'

His heart clenched. If only she knew. He lifted up a hand and kissed it, noticing that her palms had already started to soften. The realisation forced him to make his voice sound light. 'I have to meet with some clients downstairs. Why don't you have a nap and settle in? The jet lag shouldn't be too bad as we slept on the plane. We're going out tonight to a function, and then I'll be at meetings most of the day tomorrow.'

Gracie just nodded, out of her depth in more ways than one. His words sank in—one in particular. *Function.* She bit her lip.

'The function tonight…will it be very grand?'

Rocco nodded, with a serious expression on his face. 'It'll be disgustingly grand, and there's going to be a huge buffet—so you'd better bring a suitcase to fill for any needy neighbours.'

It took a second for Gracie to realise he was making fun of her. She mock-hit him, but trembled inside at his easy humour. Lord, when he turned on the charm he needed to come with a health warning.

'Seriously, though, I've only ever been to that one in London. What if people talk to me?'

'Talk back.' He quirked a dry smile. 'You didn't seem

to have a problem talking to me that night. Just don't assume everyone's security.'

And then he was letting her go and stepping away. Gracie felt ridiculously insecure, but kept her hands by her sides.

'I'll see you in a few hours.' And then he'd turned and was striding away with that mesmeric athletic grace.

That evening Gracie gave herself a last once-over. Rocco was waiting outside, in one of the suite's main lounges. They each had their own bathrooms and dressing rooms. She still couldn't take in the opulence of it all. Everything was dark wood and dimly lit. Asian antiquities were lit up in artful cubbyholes by spotlights. Gorgeous ornate silk coverings and cushions littered the sumptuous furniture and bedroom. The bathroom had two showers—one was open to the elements. The bed in their room alone would have slept a football team comfortably.

Inside the suite was almost cold with the air-conditioning, and when she stepped outside it was like stepping into a warm oven.

She took a deep breath. The dress she wore shimmered with a million varying shades of red and burnt orange. It should have clashed with her colouring, but it didn't. Made of some kind of delicate lamé material, it fell to the floor in a swirl of different colours. It was V-necked and sleeveless. Gracie looked very pale. She felt so insecure about what she should wear, but how could she ask Rocco for advice? He was a man. She should *know* these things.

She wore high-heeled strappy red sandals, and she'd made an effort with make-up. She'd dithered with her hair for ages and had finally managed to tame it into a chignon. Taking another deep breath, she turned away and picked up a small gold clutch bag. She walked out slowly in the heels, and saw Rocco standing at the now closed sliding doors. His hands were in his pockets and his back looked impossibly broad in the black suit. Hair curling a touch over his collar, exactly as she'd noticed that first night in London.

For a heart-stopping moment Gracie had an overwhelming instinct to run far away and fast. But at the same moment he must have heard her, and turned to look around. His eyes dropped and then came back up, widening imperceptibly.

Worried, she asked huskily, 'Is it okay? I wasn't sure what would be appropriate—'

'It's perfect.'

He came towards her then, hands coming out of his trouser pockets, and Gracie almost stumbled backwards at the sheer force of him in the tuxedo. She was standing by a table and he reached down and picked up a box she hadn't noticed. He opened it up, presenting it to her, and she looked down to see a plain diamond studded necklace and stunning diamond drop earrings.

She looked up at him. 'What's this?'

He frowned. 'Jewellery for you to wear.'

Gracie shook her head, backing away a little. 'It's too much, Rocco. I can't wear these. They must be worth a fortune.'

A dark shadow seemed to pass over his face, and then it cleared. Easily he said, 'They're from the shop in the hotel. They can be returned in the morning.'

She looked at him suspiciously. 'They're really only for tonight?'

He nodded, his eyes unreadable. 'If you want.'

Gracie looked at the jewels again, and after a long second nodded. 'Okay. I'll wear them.'

Rocco took out the necklace and deftly fastened it around her neck. Then he handed her the earrings. She put them in with shaky hands. The necklace felt cool and heavy around her throat, and the earrings swung when she moved her head.

Rocco held out an arm and said, 'Shall we?'

Gracie nodded and put her arm in his, and felt ridiculously as if she were walking to some kind of gallows.

Rocco kept Gracie's arm firmly in his. He could feel the tiny tremors in her body as they went down in the lift. She was *nervous*. In the reflection of the lift doors she almost looked a little ill. And despite that she looked stunning. When she'd emerged from the bedroom for a split second he hadn't recognised her. Her hair up showed off her long graceful neck. Make-up made her cheeks dewy, her eyes even bigger, lashes so long he'd seen them from across the room.

The colours of the dress shimmered around her like a hundred exotic birds, and the way the material clung to her curves showed off her petite lithe physique to perfection. With the tiniest amount of polish she had morphed into a beauty who could give any woman in his sphere a run for her money.

The diamonds were picking up the colours of her dress and flashed like fire around her neck and ears. He was so used to the routine of buying women jewellery when he took them out like this that he'd not been prepared for Gracie's reaction, and he didn't like the way it added to the clamour in his head urging him to believe in her innocence. The feeling of claustrophobia was back, but this time for entirely different reasons.

They travelled the short distance to where the function was being held in the chauffeur-driven limousine which had picked them up from the airport. When they stepped out of the car Gracie relished the warm, sultry blanket of air. Rocco was leading her into a beautifully ornate wooden building, its lines long and swooping in the distinctive Thai style. It was all so impossibly foreign. Like nothing she'd ever seen before. Gracie was drunk on the sights and smells, and the fascinatingly staccato sounds of the Thai language.

The building was open to the elements on all sides and surrounded by stunning gardens where the trees were lit up with fairy lights, giving everything a magical air. The rain had stopped and stars lit up the sky. Beautiful Thai women moved through the crowd in traditional long skirts, serving drinks and food.

Gracie refused a glass of champagne and Rocco replaced it with water, saying easily, 'You don't drink at all?'

Gracie grimaced and avoided his eye. 'My mother was an alcoholic—and my grandmother. I've never touched the stuff.'

He looked at her for a long moment. She glanced at him quickly and then away again.

She couldn't believe she'd just told him that so easily, and spoke again to distract him. 'The women are so petite. I feel like an elephant next to them.'

Rocco took her free hand and lifted it to his mouth. Gracie looked up and her breath caught when he kissed the inner palm. 'You do *not* look like an elephant. You look stunning.'

'Th-thank you,' Gracie stuttered. She couldn't really believe she was here. In this dress. With Rocco de Marco. It was as if the fantasy she'd indulged in after they'd met for the first time had been plucked out of her brain and made real. It was too much.

She knew rationally that he was only being charming because she was there to fulfil a function in his bed, because he desired her momentarily, but she couldn't help her silly heart from thumping ominously. Her mind was screaming, *Danger, danger.* Especially after what had happened on the plane, when he'd shown his deep mistrust of her. But then he'd dissolved that anger by asking her to explain about the passport. She cursed him again silently for removing her defences as though they were mere children's play-blocks.

Rocco led her further into the crowd, through the main room and out to where tables dotted the gardens, candles flickering like small beacons of light. Gracie was glad Rocco had thought to give her some mosquito repellent earlier. She could well imagine that her whiter than white skin would be a magnet on a night like tonight.

Just then a man approached Rocco and clapped him heartily on the back, and that was the start of a long evening during which people approached Rocco and talked to him about things Gracie had never heard of nor could understand. Things like market forces and trends. But she didn't mind. She'd always found it fascinating just to listen to other people talk.

'Are you bored?'

Gracie looked up at Rocco, genuinely shocked. Another man had just walked away. 'No! Why? Did you think I was?'

'No,' he said dryly. 'But you're awfully quiet and that makes me nervous.'

She shrugged. 'I don't have a clue what you're talking about most of the time.' Then she smiled. 'I would have thought that was a welcome relief.'

Rocco quirked a smile. 'Strangely enough, not as much as I would have expected.' He faced her fully then, and asked, 'That folder in your case, with the sketchings and text…what is it?'

Gracie flushed and her heart constricted. Reality intruded on the halcyon moment, reminding her why she was there. 'I should have known you'd looked at that too. Did you expect to find plans for a bank raid?'

She looked away, and then back when Rocco caught her chin with his fingers. He actually looked uncomfortable for a moment.

'I might have suspected finding something like that before…but now I don't know…'

Something inside Gracie swooped dangerously. She took a breath, and a leap into this very tenuous evidence of Rocco's trust before it disappeared. 'I did a basic art degree. I want to write children's books some day. It's just a few sketches and ideas. Nothing special.'

'I thought they looked pretty good.'

Gracie looked at him, a curious melting feeling in her chest. 'Really?'

He nodded. Gracie's heart kicked once, hard. He took his hand from her chin.

'What made you want to write children's books?'

Gracie's hands played with her bag. She'd never really told anyone this before and felt ridiculously exposed. 'I was never very good at school…not like—' She stopped herself from saying *Steven*, not wanting to jeopardise the fragile truce that seemed to exist between her and Rocco now. 'Not like most of the other kids… I always loved reading and books—the way they could they could transport you into another world.' She shrugged now, feeling silly, and avoided Rocco's piercing black gaze. 'It struck a chord and I wanted to recreate that.'

Rocco looked at Gracie's downbent head. Her hair shone like gold fire. He could imagine only too well how tantalising it must have been to lose herself in stories and magic as a child when she'd been living in such an inconstant world.

Rocco said nothing and Gracie looked up, nearly taking a step backwards at the intensity of his expression. She quickly became transfixed by his mouth, wanting to relax it from the taut line it had become.

'Don't look at me like that,' he growled.

'Or what?' Gracie asked, suddenly feeling confident in a way she never had before. It was a confidence that came from Rocco not laughing at her ambition and from being *desired*.

'Or I'll take you out of here right now and do something about it.'

Gracie looked up at him, feeling bold. 'I'm not stopping you.'

With a half-muttered curse Gracie felt her hand being taken in Rocco's and she was being led back through the throng. She felt buoyant that she could have this singular effect on Rocco. She felt buoyant with this growing ease between them.

Within minutes they were in the back of his car, the privacy window was up, and Gracie turned unquestioningly into Rocco's arms, her mouth searching desperately for his...

A short while later, when they got into the lift back at the hotel, Rocco could see Gracie's face, pink with embarrassment, reflected in the steel surface. She'd stopped him just as he'd been stepping from the car and whispered, 'They'll *know*.'

Her hair was down and dishevelled, her mouth swollen. And her hand was clasped tight in his. He'd almost taken her in the back seat of the car, a simple kiss having exploded into something much hotter within seconds.

Gracie's eyes were downcast, and he had to curb the concern he felt. He was struggling to rein in anger mixed with desire. He didn't *do* this. He didn't become so transfixed with a woman that he left functions early. And he didn't make love to women in the backs of cars. It was as if any enclosed space automatically became a provocation, an enticement to seduce her.

Only the tiniest sliver of sanity was preventing him from hitting the *Stop* button in the lift so he could hike up that dress and touch her. And also the knowledge that his friend Sebastian would not appreciate the X-rated CCTV elevator show.

When they reached the penthouse suite Gracie moved skittishly away, taking her hand out of his. Rocco's body throbbed to continue what they'd started.

He saw her hands go to the necklace. He frowned. 'What are you doing?'

'I want to take this off.'

She sounded breathless and husky and vulnerable all at once, and Rocco's chest tightened. Maybe he wasn't the only one feeling off-kilter because of this insatiable desire.

He stepped forward and gritted his teeth as her scent, musky with arousal, hit his nostrils. He told himself harshly that he could control himself. He took off the necklace and she handed him the earrings too.

She was looking around, still avoiding his eye. 'We should put them in the safe or something.'

Rocco sighed with impatience at her pragmatism, but duly found the box and put the jewellery in the suite's safe. As he went back out to the living area he yanked off his bow tie and shed his jacket. Gracie had disappeared, but the sliding doors were open. He went out. She was standing at the edge of the shimmering pool in her bare feet, shoes tumbled nearby.

Her dress glittered against the dusky night sky, her skin glowed like a pearl, and he felt as if he was falling.

* * *

Gracie heard Rocco's footfall behind her. She finally felt a little more in control. As they'd walked through the hotel lobby she'd felt as if everyone could see her shame all over her skin. *How* had she morphed into this person who felt confident enough to entice Rocco away from a party and then jump on him in the back of his car like a sex-starved groupie?

In the lift on the way up to the suite she'd been so hungry for him that she'd ached for him to stop the lift and take her right there, with her dress pushed up around her waist and her knickers ripped off.

The strength of her desire had shocked her so much that she'd felt as if she might break apart if Rocco touched her as soon as they got into the apartment. She'd focused on the jewellery to stall him, even for a moment, too embarrassed even to look at him.

Rocco was standing beside her now and she glanced at him, feeling shy all of a sudden. He was looking down at the water.

She wondered if he felt overwhelmed by this intensity too, and then had to berate herself. Rocco wouldn't feel overwhelmed by anything.

She spoke to break the tense silence. 'The air feels denser...more humid.'

Rocco glanced up at the sky. 'A storm is about to hit. The rain will start again any minute now.'

Gracie looked up and saw threatening clouds overhead. She heard the clap of thunder and flinched minutely. 'Is it really warm when it falls?'

'Yes.'

Gracie felt as if her nerve-endings were exposed. She took a breath and turned towards Rocco. 'What happened back there...at the function...and in the car. It scares me a little—the way things escalate so fast between us.'

The air went still around them, and another distant clap of thunder came.

Rocco said carefully, without looking at her, 'What do you mean?'

Gracie shrugged and turned back to curl her bare unvarnished toes over the edge of the pool. She looked down. 'I'm not sure. I just…I want you to know that I don't…I've never felt like this before.'

She felt him turn towards her and looked up. He seemed angry.

'You think this is normal for me? This…insane desire?'

Hurt lanced Gracie. 'I don't think it's insane. It's just… it feels like it's not entirely in our control…'

'You've got that right,' he said broodingly, and looked away again.

Something clicked into place and Gracie felt as if she had just stumbled on something that was fundamentally a part of Rocco's psyche. She could sense the wildness in him that he denied, and how much he hated not being in control of it; much the same thing scared her. But he really resented it. She only had to remember the icy-cool beauty of Honora Winthrop to know which he would ultimately prefer. Gracie was a mere indulgence in his dark side.

Gracie looked back at the placid surface of the water and felt Rocco's crackling tension beside her. That placid surface seemed to mock her now. A flicker of rebellion at Rocco's evident distaste of this lack of control came to life deep within her and she stepped back deliberately from the pool's edge.

Rocco said hesitantly, 'Gracie…?'

And then she ran and dived right in, barely breaking the surface, the flash of intense colour in her dress gliding away under the surface to the other end.

CHAPTER NINE

Rocco stared after Gracie, shocked. The irritation and anger he'd felt sparking when she'd tried to articulate what was between them was fading. Something else was blooming inside him, along with remorse for lashing out just now. It was a feeling of euphoria. The kind of euphoria he'd felt only once before, when he'd seen horror and disbelief dawn in his father's eyes at knowing that his worthless bastard son had surpassed even his own phenomenal wealth.

Gracie's head broke the surface of the water at the other end of the pool at that moment. Her dress, magnified under the water in a cascade of different colours, rippled out around her body. She looked impossibly wild and free, like a sea nymph, her hair slicked back in a stain of dark red.

Rocco felt the first fat drops of monsoon rain fall as he bent and pulled off his shoes and socks.

He dived in expertly, crossing the length of the pool in half the time it had taken Gracie. He saw those slim pale legs, the dress billowing around them, and reached for her underwater and pulled her down. Her eyes were wide when Rocco pressed his mouth to hers.

When they broke the surface of the water together, a few long seconds later, Gracie tore her mouth away and sucked in deep breaths. The rain was torrential now, and she tipped back her head and laughed out loud. Her arms were tight around Rocco's neck and his hands were on her waist.

She looked at him, giddy from the shock of diving into the pool and then seeing him do the same. 'The rain *is* warm!'

'Why do you believe nothing I say?' he growled, and kissed her again.

Gracie pushed away the dart of hurt at the thought it was more apt for her to say that to him, and gave up and lost herself in the kiss. She didn't want to think about what had just passed between them moments before. She didn't want to think about what it meant to lose control like this with Rocco. She just wanted to give herself up to it.

When Rocco backed her against the wall of the pool and started to peel down the stretchy material of the dress she trembled with anticipation. Even though the rain was as warm as the pool, goosebumps came up on her skin.

He pulled her dress down her arms and all the way to her waist, so that her breasts were bared, nipples tight. As he bent his head to pay homage to those peaks Gracie had to breathe in deep at the sight of Rocco, in a shirt which was now completely see-through and plastered to his strong back. His dark skin shone through in patches. Hair slicked back against his skull.

His mouth was relentless. Gracie leant back against the wall, the rain coming down into her face. The sensuality of the weather and the moment was intoxicating. The sounds of the busy city drifted up from the streets far, far below. Gracie put her arms out along the wall of the pool and arched into Rocco even more. She felt him yank the dress down over her hips and off. She could see it drift off along the floor of the pool like a puddle of bright colours.

His hand was in her panties now, his palm putting pressure on her clitoris, and one long finger delved through her secret folds, seeking where her body was already clenching in anticipation. Gracie's lower body thrust against him, silently urging him on as she lifted her hands to reach for his shirt, ripping it open in her haste. He released his hand and arms to let her yank it off, and then he pulled her panties down her legs.

Gracie was now completely naked, while Rocco still wore his trousers. His hand was between her legs again and his mouth on her breast. Warm rain drenched them, and the pool water lapped around them with increasing intensity.

'Rocco,' she said brokenly, when he slid two fingers inside her, stroking back and forth. 'I need more. I need you.'

He pulled his head back, fingers stilling. Eyes dazed, cheeks flushed. His fingers were deep inside Gracie, he could feel the wet clamp of her body, and his own ache became urgent. With a swift move he'd lifted her out of the pool to sit on the ledge. Then he pulled himself out with the minimum of effort.

He gently lifted her up into his arms and laid her down on a nearby sunbed. Pressing a swift kiss to her mouth, he muttered something about protection and disappeared for a second, only to return just as swiftly. Gracie took in the stark planes of his face. The glitter in his eyes. He put the foil-wrapped protection between his teeth for a moment as he jerkily yanked off of his soaked trousers and briefs. Ripping open the package, he smoothed the sheath onto his erection and came back to Gracie.

She felt as if she'd become one with the elements. Rocco came between her legs and said gutturally, 'I want to taste you so badly, but I need this more…'

'What do you—? *Ohhhh*…' Gracie moaned when she

felt him thrust into her. She gave up all attempts to speak or think and wrapped her legs around his waist, locking her feet behind him, urging him deeper and deeper, until they both splintered apart under the stormy clouds and driving rain.

They lay for a long time like that, with Rocco still deep within her. Little aftershocks made her tremble uncontrollably every few seconds. Eventually Rocco moved, coming up on his arms. He disengaged himself and Gracie winced slightly because she was sensitive.

He pressed a kiss to her mouth. 'I hurt you...'

She shook her head. 'No. You didn't hurt me.' Her conscience pricked at that—perhaps not physically but emotionally...she didn't want to go there.

Rocco got up and disappeared for a moment, and then came back. He held out a fluffy robe for Gracie, who took it gratefully and sat up to put it on. Rocco had tied a towel around his waist and looked down at her.

'I'm going to take a shower, join me?'

Gracie shook her head even as her traitorous mind was screaming *yes!* She needed space for a moment. 'I think I might sit out here for a bit.'

He shrugged. 'As you wish,' he said, and went inside. Gracie couldn't stop her eyes greedily devouring his lean form as he went. When he'd disappeared she sighed and pulled the robe tight around her, drawing her knees up to her chest, wrapping her arms around herself. The rain had stopped and the clouds had moved off. Stars were twinkling again. The humid air was sucking up all the excess moisture. It was as if the storm had materialised just to accompany that mad passion, and now that it was over the storm was too.

She saw the detritus of what had just happened around them. The colourful shimmer of her dress at the bottom of the pool. Her coral-coloured panties floating on the surface of the water along with Rocco's shirt. His trousers and briefs strewn on the ground. She groaned and dropped her head to her knees. One minute she'd been standing there, telling him she didn't normally do this, and within seconds she'd been ripping his shirt off like a woman possessed.

He was right. It was *insane*. She didn't doubt that with his other women—his usual women—he was a lot more civilised and restrained. None of this messy passion.

No wonder he resented it.

She'd seen the look on his face just before he'd jumped into the pool, as if he were battling with something inside himself.

Gracie felt a yearning welling up inside her. She didn't want Rocco to resent this—or *her*. She wanted a chance to make him change his mind about her properly, not just this tenuous sliver of trust that could break at any moment. She wanted to persuade him that she and her brother *weren't* just some opportunists who came from a dubious background.

She heard a noise and looked up to see him re-emerging from the suite. He had a fresh towel wrapped around his waist and was rubbing at his hair with another towel. Gracie felt exposed all over again, as if he might read that awful yearning on her face.

Brightly she asked, 'Nice shower?'

He nodded, and then smiled wickedly. 'Would have been nicer with you in it.'

He came and sat down on the lounger next to hers and his clean scent washed over her, making her belly tighten with a shaft of need. Inexplicably Gracie felt dirty all of a sudden, when she recalled their explosion of passion.

She glanced away, feeling prickly. 'I like it out here.'

His voice was wry. 'You can't stay out here all night.'

She shrugged minutely. 'To be honest, the suite…the hotel…it's all a bit intimidating. I feel like I'm tainting it with my presence.'

Rocco went still. 'That's crazy…what are you talking about?'

She glanced at him. and then away again when she saw him frowning. 'It's like I'm not meant to be here. When I was about nine one of our foster parents took Steven and I to a stately home.' Gracie smiled and said self-consciously, 'She was one of the good ones… It was a grand old house. We had to get the train from London. It had these huge rooms—so beautiful, full of antiques and paintings. After a while I got lost. The group had gone on and I couldn't find them. I wandered into a room full of tiny porcelain dolls.'

Gracie grimaced a little, remembering.

'Obviously the people who owned the house had some kind of collection. I was fascinated, and picked one up to look at. Suddenly I felt a hand on my shoulder and I got such a fright I dropped it and it smashed on the ground. This woman was standing over me, shrieking about how I was a common little thief and to get out.' She shivered at the memory. 'I was so terrified I ran and ran, and finally found the group. I kept expecting to feel that hand on my shoulder again.'

Gracie felt embarrassed. Why on earth had she even started telling this story? But Rocco just looked at her, his face obscured in the dark.

She shrugged again, properly embarrassed now. 'Earlier, when we came in, and at the function too, I felt as if a hand was going to land on my shoulder at any moment and someone would ask how I'd got in.'

A little roughly, Rocco said, 'You have as much a right to be in these places as anyone else.'

Gracie half smiled. 'Well, I don't really. But it's nice of you to say.'

Rocco stood up then, with a hand outstretched, as if to leave and take her with him. Gracie stood up too, about to take his hand, but then she stopped. His closed-off expression made something rise up within her—a desperate need for him to understand, and *see*.

'Wait. I want to tell you something else.'

He dropped his hand, his jaw clenched. 'Gracie, you don't need to tell me these stories.'

His clear reluctance galvanised her. 'They're not *stories*—and, yes, I do need to tell you.' She continued before he could protest. 'Steven...my brother...we're twins.' Her mouth twisted. 'Non-identical obviously. I'm older by twenty minutes—he nearly died when he was born. When we were small he was puny and had big thick glasses. I got used to protecting him from bullies. He was never able to deal with things like I could. He never got over our mother leaving us...'

Gracie's voice shook with passion.

'He was too smart, too quiet. He was always a natural target. It might be hard to believe because of his actions, but he never wanted that life...to be in a gang, to get involved with drugs.'

'So why did he, then?' Rocco almost sneered.

Gracie flinched minutely but stood tall. Emotion constricted her voice. 'They beat him down—literally. One day he got so badly beaten that he almost ended up in hospital. They broke him. It was easier to go along with what they wanted than to fight it. Even though I did my best to stop him. We were only fourteen. They had him hooked on alcohol within months. Drugs came soon after. He dropped out of school. Gave up.'

'And yet you defend him even now?'

Again Rocco had that slightly sneering tone. Gracie looked at him, feeling a little disembodied. How could she even begin to explain the rich tapestry that bound her and her brother together?

She nodded slowly. 'Yes, I defend him—and I would defend him for ever. Just like he defended me.'

Rocco frowned, impatience palpable in his lean form. 'What do you mean? Defended you from what?'

Gracie knew her words were going nowhere, but she couldn't stop now. 'There was one foster home—it was miraculous, really, that we got to stay together all the time.' She took a deep breath. 'There was a man in this home. He used to look at me, and touch me when no one was around. Nothing serious at first—just a pat on the bottom or a pinch on my arm. But then one night he came into my room when his wife was away.'

Gracie could feel bile rising and forced it down.

'He sat on my bed and started telling me what he wanted to do with me. Steven was in the room next to mine with another boy. I was on my own. I was so scared I couldn't move or speak. Just when the man was about to get into bed beside me Steven came in. He didn't say anything. He just waited for the man to get up and leave, and from that night until we left that house he slept in my bed, even as his own life was falling apart. He never left me alone. Not once.'

Rocco looked at Gracie's pale face. Her words were like atom bombs detonating in his head and body. He wanted to rant and rage—throw the terrace furniture out over the balcony. He wanted to hug Gracie close and never let her go ever again. He trembled with it. Emotion was thick and acrid, gripping him by the throat. To think of that man touching her. And to think of her brother and what he'd been through. That he'd been beaten viciously enough to give in to that awful wasted life. Even now Rocco could see her brother's face, clear and burning with eagerness in his office, impressing him with his zeal because it had reminded him of his own hunger to succeed.

And yet her brother had still turned around and made a fool of Rocco's gut instinct, had betrayed him.

Rocco had been through the same trials...worse. And he hadn't given in—*never*. He clung to that assertion now, like a drowning man finding a piece of floating wood in a choppy ocean. He couldn't touch Gracie right now. If he did he felt as if the emotions seething in his gut would overwhelm him completely and throw him straight back to where he'd come from, what he'd left behind all those years before.

With a huge effort Rocco thrust down the thick, cloying emotion and stepped back from Gracie and those huge eyes.

He heard the words coming out but wasn't really aware of them. 'This changes nothing. All evidence points to the fact that he *hasn't* changed one bit. Don't try my patience telling me these things.'

Rocco turned and strode back into the suite, feeling as if his insides were splintering apart into a thousand pieces.

Gracie looked at Rocco walking away and felt numb with hurt and rejection. She realised now why she'd told him more than she'd ever told anyone else. Not even Steven had ever mentioned out loud what had almost happened that night so long ago. It had been too horrific to contemplate. Yet Gracie had just told Rocco as if it had cost her nothing. But it was costing her dearly. Because she knew now what lay beneath this self-destructive desire to expose herself to him no matter what the consequences.

She was falling in love with him.

* * *

Rocco wasn't surprised when he was still tossing and turning an hour later. What he wasn't prepared for was the ache in his gut and the way the vast emptiness of the bed beside him was affecting him. He drew back the covers and sat up, his parting words to Gracie ringing in his head. He cursed her. But even as he did he cursed himself more.

All he could see in his mind's eye now was that picture of Gracie and Steven when they'd been small. Her brother's scared-looking little face with those huge glasses and Gracie looking so strong beside him. Like a little warrior. He found himself feeling *jealous*—of her brother. That she cared so much for him. That they had such a bond.

It had been easier to hurl those words at her and walk away than deal with the emotion. It opened up far too many chasms. And yet he couldn't go on like this. He felt as if he was missing a limb.

Rocco went outside to the patio. He could see her curled up shape on a sun lounger in the dim moonlight and he felt the ache in his chest intensify into a physical pain. *Damn her*. He walked over and saw that their clothes were neatly folded and piled up. Her dress was a damp stain of colour against the ground. He looked at her, steeling himself for the inevitable effect.

Her face was relaxed, her hair rippling around her, looking very red against the pale cream lounger. Legs drawn up in that foetal pose she liked. His gut clenched when he thought of how her brother had protected her, and Rocco realised that he was jealous even of that.

He fought the urge to turn and walk away again. He bent down and scooped her up into his arms. She woke up and braced herself against him, resisting him.

'Wait...' Her voice sounded sleepy and sexy.

Rocco was already responding. He gritted his jaw and

said, 'Enough. You've made your point and I've made mine.'

He set her back and looked into those huge eyes, and felt that falling sensation again.

'I didn't mean to be so sharp.' He shook his head and forced the tender feeling from his belly. 'You don't have to tell me anything, Gracie. It doesn't change the situation we're in regarding your brother.'

Her hands were on his chest. Her voice was husky with emotion. 'You mean you don't want me to tell you anything because you're not interested?'

Rocco felt that tenderness inching back, together with a need to reassure her, and crushed it, feeling more ruthless than he'd ever been in his life. He concentrated on remaining immune to Gracie's appeal.

'Why your brother has done what he has is irrelevant to me. I deal in concrete things and he stole money from me. *You*, however, are far more relevant right now, and I don't want to talk about your brother or your past any more. Deal?'

Gracie was wide awake now, and could feel Rocco's intensity reaching out and sucking her in. He desperately wanted her to say yes. She could feel it. Even now, in spite of the hurt and rejection, she could fool herself into thinking she saw something deep in his eyes. Something vulnerable and exposed. She wanted this man with a hunger that shamed her. Even as she desperately wanted to be able to reject him, to inflict pain on him the way he'd done to her. But she couldn't.

Hating herself, and the feeling of inevitability that washed through her, she said with a small voice, 'Deal.'

To her relief Rocco didn't grin with triumph, or—look mildly pleased with her capitualtion. He just looked intense and serious as he picked her up in his arms and took her back into the bedroom.

Landing in New York two days later was a different experience from landing in Bangkok. Far below them was a sea of grey buildings as far as her eye could see, vastly different from the lush green paddy fields.

Rocco was working across the aisle from her, a frown between his eyes as he studied papers.

She looked back to the view. Since the other night it had been as if a proper truce existed between them. They were careful to talk only about neutral topics. Rocco had even taken time off from his meetings to take Gracie to Bangkok's stunning Grand Palace, and she'd wandered around in complete awe at the designs of the buildings with their vast marble terraces.

The style of the palace was eclectic: soaring Palladian arches and columns mixed with traditionally ornate Thai roofs. There was an entire temple devoted to a tiny Emerald Buddha which was placed high on an altar above the crowd. There was also a large model of the Cambodian temple of Angkor Wat, one of the places that had always fascinated Gracie.

She'd spent long minutes going round and round it, and had looked up to find Rocco leaning on a nearby wall just staring at her. She still felt weak inside when she thought of that look.

He'd woken her very early the previous morning and had led her, grumbling and sleepy, outside the hotel. She'd only noticed then that he was casually dressed in shorts and T-shirt. To her delighted surprise there had been a Tuk-Tuk waiting to take them to one of the floating markets, where they'd got into a boat and seen Buddhist monks in their distinctive orange robes accepting alms from the locals.

Gracie had been deeply moved by Rocco surprising her like that with a dawn visit to the markets before the hordes of tourists arrived, and the ride back through the city with the kamikaze Tuk-Tuk driver had been exhilarating.

'What are you thinking about?'

Gracie jumped and looked at Rocco, and her heart turned over. She'd refused to let her mind go back to her revelation that she was falling for him. Far too dangerous. If she didn't think about it, she thought weakly, perhaps the feeling would go away.

She forced a smile now, and said lightly, 'I was just thinking that the last woman you took to Bangkok probably didn't enjoy the Tuk-Tuk ride half as much as I did.'

Rocco said nothing for a moment, and he sounded almost surprised when he admitted, 'I've never taken anyone to Bangkok with me before.'

Gracie's heart swelled dangerously in her chest. As if to counteract it she said lightly, 'I'm sure you've brought them to New York, though.'

Rocco looked straight at her, as if sending her a warning. She was straying into dangerous territory. Very clearly he said, 'Yes, of course I've brought women to New York. I'm here much more frequently.'

Rocco looked away from Gracie and back to his papers. He'd been pretending for nigh on an hour now to be engrossed in work, when all he'd been aware of was each minute movement she made. He almost laughed out loud at the notion that any of his previous lovers would have got into a motorised rickshaw even if he'd paid them to do it. But Gracie had loved it as it had swerved and barrelled through the chaotic Bangkok traffic. And he'd loved it too. He couldn't remember the last time he'd just taken time off to look at the sights. To enjoy a place. *Never*, came back the succinct answer.

Going into the Grand Palace, the staff had been strict about the dress code. Gracie had been wearing a vest top over shorts. The staff had a facility to make sure everyone was dressed appropriately, so she had had to put on a huge billowing plaid shirt and skirt to cover up her arms, shoulders and bare legs.

He'd braced himself for a fit of feminine pique, but she'd just been worried that she'd offended the staff and then, when assured that she hadn't, she'd giggled at how ridiculous she must look. She hadn't looked ridiculous at all. He'd ached to pull her behind the sacred *wats* and do very unsacred things with her.

Rocco welcomed the skyline of New York coming closer and closer. In this city he would feel safer around Gracie, and he would keep her at a distance if it killed him. Bangkok had been a mistake. It had been way too raw.

Just thinking of that made him picture Gracie jumping into the pool in that dress, and with a barely stifled curse Rocco forced himself to concentrate until the page he was looking at blurred.

Gracie was very aware as they drove into the city of Rocco being distant. He was more businesslike than she'd ever seen him. She refused to let his mood upset her and stared in awe at the famously iconic skyline of New York as they crossed one of the many bridges into Manhattan. As they drove onto the island and the buildings soared up around them she saw all the yellow taxis and was enraptured.

Famous designer names glittered at her on Fifth Avenue, and then the green trees of Central Park materialised. With the park to their right, the car pulled up outside an Art Deco style building with a huge awning over the pavement.

Gracie was helped out of the car by a smiling doorman in a uniform and the summer heat hit her. It was totally different from the heat in Thailand, but just as intense—even in the morning.

The doorman was greeting Rocco. 'Welcome back, Mr de Marco, it's been too long!'

They walked through a cool lobby to where the concierge was waiting with the lift doors open. They stepped in and the lift smoothly ascended and came to a halt. The doors opened straight into a private corridor and the penthouse apartment. Gracie thought she'd seen pretty much everything by now, but this was palatial and stupendous on a whole new level. Everything was cream and gold. Carpets so thick you literally sank into them. Abstract oil paintings on the walls showed Rocco's taste for mixing the old with the new again. Antiques perched on small, elaborately designed tables. Huge cream couches were piled high with cushions.

Rocco was opening French doors on the other side of the room and Gracie followed dumbly, nearly too afraid to breathe. She stepped out into the morning air to see a vast terrace stretching what looked like the length of the building, with potted trees and artfully tamed flower boxes.

Rocco was standing with his hands on his hips, watching her, and Gracie joked weakly, 'Where's the pool?'

Rocco gestured with his head. 'Downstairs in the gym on the lower level.'

'Oh.'

'It's nice,' he said redundantly. 'It has a view out onto the park.'

Gracie felt seriously overwhelmed. She walked over to the wall and looked out to see one of the most famous city parks in the world stretching away either side of her. People walked along the streets below and looked like ants.

She could see a big open green space in the middle of the park. And a lake.

Again Gracie joked. 'I'm surprised you're not in the highest skyscraper so you can see the furthest.'

She wasn't looking at him, so she didn't see how his jaw clenched. And then he replied easily, 'Ah, yes, but the Upper East Side is the best address.'

Gracie looked around at Rocco to see him glance at his watch and say, 'Look, I have to head out now. I've got back-to-back meetings all day.'

For once she was glad at the prospect of a bit of space. She nodded her head. 'Okay. I'll just…settle in…'

Rocco took something out of his wallet and handed it to her. 'Here—take this. Why don't you go shopping?'

Gracie took the black credit card automatically and looked at it. She was barely aware of Rocco peeling something else from the wallet and putting it down on the table saying, 'You'll need some cash too, for taxis. I'll have Ruben downstairs give you a map and some directions. We've got a function to go to this evening, so I'll see you back here at six…okay?'

Gracie looked at Rocco and sensed his impatience to be gone. She just nodded again, feeling a little numb. 'Fine. See you later.'

There was a moment when it looked as if he wanted to say something, but then he turned and walked out of the apartment. A few seconds later a woman appeared, wiping her hands on an apron, and introduced herself as Consuela, Mr de Marco's housekeeper.

Gracie shook her hand. The woman was clearly a huge fan of Rocco. She insisted on showing Gracie around all four *en suite* bedrooms, two dining rooms, one informal sitting room, one formal drawing room, the gym and pool, sauna room, a massive kitchen and two further bathrooms.

When her head was spinning she let Consuela get back to work and set about unpacking her things and deciding what she would do for the day. She was determined to try and not think about Rocco for at least five whole minutes. And she resolved to find an internet café and see if there was an e-mail from Steven.

At lunchtime Rocco came back to the apartment. He cursed himself for his weakness, and wasn't prepared when Consuela informed him that Gracie had gone out a couple of hours before.

He went into the bedroom but there was no note—just their bags, which had been unpacked. He cursed. Why *would* she have left a note?

He was on his way back out, feeling thoroughly disgruntled, when he noticed something on the chest of drawers. It was his credit card and the few notes he'd left for Gracie, less only about twenty dollars. As if she'd literally taken just enough to get her downtown.

Rocco laughed at himself harshly. Had he *really* expected she would head straight for the designer boutiques on Fifth Avenue? This was the woman who had personally taken the diamond necklace and earrings back to the shop in the hotel in Bangkok.

Feeling even more disgruntled now, Rocco scooped up the card and left the cash, cursing himself for even coming to check up on her and trying to ignore the tight feeling when he imagined her finding her way around or seeing the sights on her own.

It was only when he was in his car and heading back downtown that his insides went cold and he realised that he'd effectively let Gracie go. Now and in Bangkok he'd left her to her own devices, and at any moment—like *right now*—she could be disappearing into thin air.

The fact that he'd trusted her so implicitly made him extremely nervous, and to his absolute chagrin he couldn't concentrate on one thing for the rest of the afternoon until he'd got confirmation from the concierge that she'd returned to the apartment. He did not relish the relief that made him feel so weak.

CHAPTER TEN

WHEN Gracie returned late that afternoon she was exhausted but happy. Well—she made a face at her sweaty reflection in the mirror over the hall table as she put down her bag—she wasn't *happy,* exactly. She'd have been happy if she'd had Rocco with her to share the delights of climbing to the top of the Empire State Building, and she'd have been happier if she hadn't had to sit in Central Park on her own eating a sandwich.

She worried her lower lip with her teeth. And she'd have been happy if there had been an e-mail from Steven, but there had been nothing waiting for her in her mailbox when she'd found an internet café. She'd sent an e-mail to his address anyway, in the futile hope that she might hear something back.

Sighing now, she went outside to take in the majestic view of Central Park again.

She'd had to realise as she had gone around on her own that Rocco hadn't brought her on this trip to hold her hand and be her guide—no matter how nice and thoughtful he'd been in Bangkok. The sooner she remembered that the better.

Leaning on the wall overlooking Central Park, Gracie smiled to herself, feeling a little bemused. Was this how it was for Rocco normally? He'd give his credit card to his current mistress, she'd shop all day and then flaunt herself like a peacock on his arm in the evening?

'You didn't take the credit card.'

Gracie whirled around with a squeal, her heart hammering at the sight of Rocco lounging nonchalantly against the terrace door. It was as if she'd conjured him up. 'You scared me. I didn't hear you come in.'

Rocco came towards Gracie. Something in his eyes looked dangerous and she backed against the wall.

She gulped. 'No, I didn't take the card. Why would I? I don't need anything. You bought me enough clothes to last a dozen trips abroad.'

Rocco's face was hard. He enclosed Gracie by putting his hands on the wall behind her. She fought not to let his unique scent and presence weaken her.

He sounded irritated. 'You don't get it, do you? That's what you're *meant* to do. So tell me what you *did* do, then.'

Fire rose within her and Gracie matched his harsh tone. 'For your information I *borrowed* twenty dollars and went downtown, where I took some money out of a hole in the wall from my own account. Then I queued for two hours and went to the top of the Empire State Building. After that I walked all the way back to the park and bought a sandwich and ate it. Is that all right?' Gracie felt guilty for not mentioning the internet café, but Rocco seemed too volatile for her to bring Steven into the mix.

'No, damn you, it's not all right.'

Rocco's head descended and his hands closed around her arms. His kiss was harsh and demanding. Gracie tried to refuse to let him do this—take out his anger on her because she wasn't like his other women—but he was relentless, and she couldn't resist. So she fought fire with fire.

Fingers digging deep into his hair, her whole body arched towards him, hips grinding into his. At least *this* was honest between them. This transcended all thought and rationale and reduced them to base desires that had to be sated or they would die.

Their fragile truce had just been smashed.

He picked her up in his arms and Gracie couldn't help pressing kisses all over his jaw and neck. She was already opening his shirt and undoing his tie. When they got to the bedroom Rocco lowered her down onto the bed and stripped off his jacket and tie, ripping open his shirt. Gracie pulled her top over her head and yanked down the shorts she'd been wearing, kicking off her sandals.

When Rocco was gloriously naked he came down beside her and Gracie just looked at him, unable to stop her heart from swelling or from touching his stubbled jaw with one hand. She couldn't hold it back. 'I missed you today,' she whispered.

Rocco just looked at her, and something flashed in his eyes before they darkened. 'Don't say that. I don't want to hear it.'

'Well, tough,' Gracie said obstinately. 'Because I did miss you and I've just said it again.'

With a growl Rocco came over her and silenced her with his mouth, his hands roving over her body, removing her bra and panties until she was as naked as he. And then she couldn't even have articulated her name as Rocco took her with a thoroughness that had her crying out over and over again.

'And who is your companion?'

Gracie smiled tightly at the anaemic-looking woman with hair so set in a ball around her head that she feared it would go up in flames if she stood too close to a light. She could have been anywhere from forty to sixty-five, her face was so immobile and smooth.

'Gracie O'Brien,' Rocco was murmuring beside her.

The woman sent a disparaging look up and down, taking in Gracie's sparkling black floor-length dress.

'Ah, yes. Well, I might have imagined you're Irish, with the red hair and pale skin.'

Gracie smiled sweetly. 'Actually my mother was English, and I was born and grew up there, but, yes, my father was Irish.'

The woman's brows arched. 'I see.' And then, as if thoroughly bored by Gracie, and also not happy that she'd even spoken, she turned to Rocco and linked her arm with his. 'Now, Rocco darling, tell me all about Bangkok. I'm dying to hear about your deal with the Larrimar Corporation.'

The woman was expertly manoeuvreing Rocco away from Gracie, but he stalled in his tracks, forcing the woman to stop too. He smiled at her, but Gracie shivered. She'd seen that smile many a time, and was glad it wasn't directed at her for once.

He extricated his arm from the woman's claw-like clutch and took Gracie's hand, pulling her firmly to his side, saying nothing but making it very clear that she was not to be ignored. Gracie tried to ignore the jump her heart gave, and watched with amusement as the woman constantly tried to force Gracie out—only to have Rocco pull her even more firmly into his side.

Gracie tuned the conversation out. People-watching was too fascinating. They were in a function room in an exclusive hotel on the other side of Central Park from Rocco's apartment. They'd just eaten a sumptuous dinner at a huge banquet table with about two hundred guests, and had now moved into another exquisite room which led to an emormous terrace lit with hundreds of candles.

Gracie saw people milling around outside and suddenly wanted to breathe some fresh air. She tried to break free from Rocco, but his grip was like iron. She had to elbow him in the ribs before he looked down.

She smiled sweetly at the snobbish woman and said to Rocco, 'I'm just going to get some air.'

Rocco had to battle a huge reluctance to let Gracie go but finally he did. He watched her walk away through the crowd, her red hair like a glowing beacon, making people stop and turn around to look at her. She was so vibrant and alive compared to most people in the room. How had he only really noticed that now? And yet wasn't that what had caught him the very first time he'd seen her?

When they'd been driven the short distance in the car from his apartment to the hotel earlier, Gracie had said to Rocco wistfully, 'We could have walked through the park.'

Rocco had looked at her and shook his head. 'No, Gracie, we couldn't.'

She'd stuck her tongue out and said, 'Spoilsport,' and he'd remembered what she'd said earlier, about missing him, and he had all but fallen out of the car in his haste to get away. And yet just now he hadn't been able to let her go.

'She's different.'

Rocco swung back. He was afraid he'd spoken out loud. 'I'm sorry?'

Helena Thackerey was an inveterate snob, but she was also very shrewd and a tough financial negotiator.

'I said, she's *different*.'

Rocco schooled his features, defensive hackles rising. 'Yes, she is. But there's nothing more to our relationship than any other I've had.'

The older woman snorted and looked a lot more human for a moment. 'Tell that to someone who might believe you, de Marco.' She leant forward and said, *sotto voce*,

'I like her. She's got spunk. Not like those asinine up-percrust bores you usually date.'

Gracie ploughed her way through the crowd, oblivious to some of the wealthiest people in Manhattan, and made it out to the terrace. She grabbed some water from a pass-ing waiter and stood taking in the magical view of New York at night. She stretched out over the wall to try and see as far as she could.

A voice came from right behind her and sent a shiver through her. 'That's Harlem up to your left.'

Rocco stepped even closer, so her back and buttocks were flush against his front, and she could feel him hard-ening against her. She leaned her head back against his chest and said breathily, 'You're insatiable.'

He put an arm around her middle and pressed even closer. She heard a throaty, 'Let's get out of here. I've had enough of New York's finest for one evening.'

Gracie turned in his arms and looked up. She rolled her eyes and said, 'Me too, and I'm *so* over these views of Central Park.'

Rocco bit back a laugh and bent his head. Gracie hated the way she loved how she could make him laugh.

He said, close to her ear, 'That's a pity, because when we get back I want to recreate this exact position—except I want your dress gone and your legs around my waist.'

Gracie gulped and put her glass down on a table as Rocco unceremoniously hauled her from the room.

Back in Rocco's apartment, Rocco advanced towards Gracie, who was standing obediently at the wall over-looking Central Park—from the other side now. She shiv-ered with anticipation just watching him take off his jacket and bow tie, opening his shirt. He came close and the air vibrated between them, and then he took her by surprise and kissed her so sweetly on the mouth that she put her hands to his chest.

When he broke away and just looked at her Gracie suddenly wanted more than just the physical. Softly she asked, 'How can you stand socialising with people like that all the time?'

Rocco went still. 'What do you mean?'

'Well...like that woman. She was so rude.' Gracie flushed. 'And Honora Winthrop was rude.'

Rocco took Gracie's hands and pulled them down. He stepped to her side and rested his hands on the wall. Subtle tension radiated out from his body.

'Helena is not too bad, actually. A lot of her manner is bluster. She was one of the few people who helped me when I first came to New York as a green negotiator.'

Gracie frowned. She couldn't imagine Rocco ever not being completely experienced and in control.

He slid her a glance. 'She liked you. She said you've got spunk.'

Gracie smiled tentatively. 'Okay, so maybe I was wrong about her. But I wasn't wrong about Honora.'

Rocco's face got serious. 'No. She's an out-and-out bitch.'

Gracie looked up at him. 'So I don't understand how you could have ever contemplated marrying her?'

Rocco said nothing for a long moment, because he was wondering how he could explain that he'd never intended to take a wife for romantic reasons. Then he gestured with an arm towards the dark park. 'For *this*. You have to be accepted into this world to be really successful, and the only way to achieve that for someone like me is to marry into it.'

Gracie went still inside. 'What do you mean, for some-one like you? Don't you come from this world too?'

She turned around so she was facing Rocco. After a long moment he shook his head. He gestured down to the pavements far below. His voice was tight. 'That's where I'm from. Exactly like you.'

Something deep inside Gracie was slotting into place. She'd always suspected there was more to Rocco. 'What do you mean, exactly like me? You can't mean that you grew up—?'

He looked at her and his eyes were fierce. 'On the streets? Struggling to survive in a hostile environment? That's exactly what I mean.'

Rocco looked away again and cursed violently in Italian. Gracie realised in that moment that she'd rarely, if ever, heard him speak his native tongue.

After a long moment he said, 'I don't have to talk about this.'

Gracie took a metaphorical step into the dark. Feeling her way. 'Why not?' *I won't be around for much longer*, she wanted to add, but it hurt too much.

Rocco stared into the black space of the park as if it held answers she couldn't see, and then he started talk-ing in a low, emotionless voice that told her a multitude of things. He told her how he had been born and had grown up in the worst slum in Italy, in one of the poorest cities. He told her of his mother, who had been a prostitute, but a high-class prostitute—which was how it came to be that his father was one of the city's wealthiest men.

'My mother spent every penny on feeding her escalat-ing drug habit. She had targeted my father on purpose to secure a future for herself through me. She'd even been smart enough to get a swab from him, so that she could do a DNA test as soon as I was born and have proof of his paternity. But my father didn't want to know. He had two daughters and he was a megalomaniac. He didn't want a son appearing on the scene to threaten his rule. And he especially didn't want a son by a prostitute who came from the slums to sully his perfect respectable world and reputation.'

Gracie could see Rocco's hands tighten on the wall.

'You can't even begin to imagine what that world was like. The constant noise, the calls from block to block that were code for rival gangs—a murder, a drug-drop. All day and all night. They used me as a lookout for rival gangs.'

His mouth twisted.

'We didn't have a call for the police. They never came. They were as corrupt as we were. There was no social services for us. I hated the brute force of that life, the lack of intellect over chaos and destruction. My mother lurched from one passionate crisis to another. I craved a more ordered world—without that constant drama and uncertainty, the ever-present danger.'

Gracie could feel shivers of shock going through her body. 'What happened to your mother?'

Rocco went very still. 'I found her dead with a needle sticking out of her leg when I was seventeen.'

Gracie put a hand on his arm. Her voice was choked. 'Oh, Rocco....'

He shook her hand off and speared her with that black gaze. 'I'm not telling you this for sympathy. I don't need sympathy. I never have. She didn't love me. She was too in love with getting her next fix or a wealthy patron.'

Gracie swallowed the lump in her throat. 'I'm sorry.'

He looked away again, and Gracie cradled her hand against her belly.

'I confronted my father one day outside his city *palazzo*. I knew where he lived. My mother had pointed it out to me enough times. It was just after she'd died. When I confronted him he spat at me and pushed me down and stepped over me. My two half-sisters were with him and didn't even look my way, even though they'd heard me call him Father. I watched them step into a chauffeur-driven car. I watched how they could just walk away from the unsavoury truth. I envied them their ease and protection. I envied their wealth, which gave them that protection.'

He smiled then, and it made fear inch up Gracie's spine.

'My father obviously had a word with one of his *men*. As soon as the car pulled away I was dragged into a nearby lane and beaten so senseless that I ended up in hospital. It was an effective warning. I never attempted to see him again. I left Italy and I vowed that one day I would look into my father's eyes and know that I had earned my place in his world, despite his rejection.'

Gracie looked at the hard jaw and the bunched up shoulders. She saw the faint scar running from his temple to his jaw and the smaller scars. She could well imagine that meeting between father and son, and could almost feel sorry for his father. She longed to reach out and touch Rocco now, to soothe his pain. But he was like a wild animal. He was raw.

She remembered something and said, 'That scar…on your shoulder. It was a tattoo, wasn't it?'

Rocco nodded. 'It meant I belonged to a certain part of the slum.' His mouth twisted. 'A certain faction. I got it removed when I came to England.'

'That's why you never speak Italian. You hate any reminders.'

Rocco dropped his head between his shoulders and said, in a deceptively soft voice, 'Just go, Gracie…leave me alone.'

Gracie took a step back, hurt blooming out from her

heart all over her body. She was terrified she'd start crying. She ached to comfort him. She started to step away, but got to the door and looked back. She saw Rocco standing there, head down, and realised that he'd always been a lone figure. Fighting the world around him while simultaneously longing to be part of it.

Resolution fired her blood, and she kicked off her shoes and walked back over to him. She slipped under one of his arms and came up so that his body formed a cage around her.

She looked up, straight into Rocco's face and his dark eyes. 'No, I won't leave. Because I don't think you really do want to be alone.' She reached up and placed her small palm on his rigid jaw. Her eyes caressed his mouth. 'I want you, Rocco. So much.'

The tension was thick enough to touch, and then suddenly it snapped. Rocco issued a guttural, 'Damn you!' and hauled Gracie up into his body so tightly she thought her back might break, but she bit her lip. She would not say a word. She could sense the violence in him, the untamed wildness that needed release, and she wanted desperately to be there for him in the only way he would allow her to be.

Rocco demanded and Gracie gave—over and over again. His kisses were brutal and electrifying. Their clothes were shed as they moved through the apartment, ripped and torn from their bodies in desperate haste.

Afterwards, Gracie couldn't even remember how they'd got to the bedroom—only that what had happened there had shown her how restrained Rocco had become to tame the natural wildness in him. And the long-simmering anger. Her body ached all over, but pleasurably. She knew her pale skin would be bruised. Rocco had nipped her with his teeth, and she shivered now to think of how she'd wanted him to bite her harder. He'd taken her from behind, with her hands wrapped around the bedposts, and it had been the most erotic thing she'd ever felt. The heavy weight of his body on hers as he'd crushed her to the bed and thrust into her over and over again.

She lifted her head now and looked at him. The innate tension in his body told her that he wasn't asleep. 'Rocco…?'

To her surprise he put an arm over his face and wouldn't look at her. She tried to pull it down and he said roughly, 'I can't look at you. I…I took you like an animal.'

Gently but firmly Gracie pulled his arm down and then moved over Rocco's body so she was lying on his chest with her legs either side of his hips. She put her hands to his face.

'Rocco de Marco. *Look* at me.' He opened his eyes, and she could have wept at the shame she saw. She swallowed back her own emotion. 'I am fine. I liked it.'

She pressed kisses to his jaw and mouth and down his neck. He put his hands around her upper arms and forcibly moved her back, coming up so that she had to lie on her back again.

'No. I can't do this.'

His expression was unreadable in the gloom. Gracie's heart stuttered as she watched Rocco get out of the bed, his tall, naked form magnificent in the dim light.

He said, without looking her way, 'Get some sleep, Gracie. We leave tomorrow at lunchtime.'

It was the hardest thing Rocco had ever done, to walk away from Gracie in that bed. He headed straight for the pool and dived in. He'd been aching to plunge into her body all over again as she'd straddled him. *'I am fine. I liked it.'* Her fervent words had scored his insides like a serrated knife.

She'd seen too much. Got too close. He'd never told about his past. He'd been so careful not to. Yet with the smallest amount of encouragement he'd spilled it all out to Gracie. And she'd accepted it unconditionally. Embraced it.

He'd taken her brutally, and she'd welcomed him every step of the way—had encouraged him. And in the process he had assuaged his pain so that his intense anger had faded and been replaced with a kind of strange peace. Even the shame he'd felt initially was fading.

As Rocco powered up and down the pool he hoped that the physical numbness he craved would somehow numb the feelings inside him. Because these were new feelings, not dark and twisted like the old ones, and somehow they were far more frightening than anything else he'd ever known.

At lunchtime the following day Gracie still felt a little shattered. It was as if an earthquake had happened last night, and she wasn't sure where anything stood any more. She'd woken late, after tossing and turning once Rocco had walked out so suddenly, and Consuela had informed her that Rocco had gone to his office.

She heard a noise and looked up from the TV. She hadn't been able to concentrate on the rolling news channel. Rocco stood in the doorway, looking incredibly austere and stern. Her stomach fell. She didn't need to wonder how things stood after last night. It was written all over him: rejection.

Gracie told herself she shouldn't be surprised. She'd pushed Rocco too far. He'd never forgive her for making him spill his guts. He was too proud.

She stood up slowly and tried to match his cool reserve, even though she shook on the inside. 'I'm ready to go.'

Rocco held up a piece of paper in his hand. 'Do you want to explain this to me?'

Gracie frowned and glanced at the paper. 'What are you talking about?'

Rocco held it up and read aloud in flat tones. *"'Steven, where are you? Are you okay? Please contact me, I have so much to tell you. I need to know you're all right. Please, just let me know where you are. Send me a number so I can call you. We need to talk—I can help you.'"*

Gracie blanched. 'How did you get that?'

Rocco's eyes were black, and he bit out, 'It's his work e-mail address. I have someone checking Steven's inbox around the clock.'

Gracie's belly cramped. She felt guilty even though she had no reason to. 'I didn't tell you yesterday because you seemed so angry when you came back to the apartment. But I would have told you that I'd tried to contact him.'

Rocco arched a brow in a way Gracie hadn't seen him do for days. She wanted to hit him.

'You had a whole evening to tell me. This e-mail reeks of collusion. You were trying to warn him to stay away, or to arrange a meeting somewhere.'

Gracie swallowed. She could see how, in a certain frame of mind, it might read like that. If you mistrusted the person who wrote it—which Rocco patently did. She straightened her back and tried to ignore the feeling of her heart aching.

'That's how it might read to you. It's not how I meant it. I meant exactly what I said—I'm worried about him and want to know where he is. When I said I could help him I meant just that—if he gives himself up I intend to help him through whatever repercussions emerge from his actions.'

Rocco lowered the paper and smiled harshly. 'So

noble—and such lies. I think you were going to tell him you'd inveigled your way into his boss's bed and fed him stories designed to gain sympathy. Perhaps you wanted to be sure to corroborate each other's stories before he came forward like some penitent?'

Inveigled your way into his boss's bed. Stories. The words dropped into Gracie's head like poison-tipped arrows. He thought she'd set out to seduce him? The idea was laughable. She thought of the private things she'd shared with him. The fact that he saw them now as mere *stories* to gain sympathy nearly made her double over with pain.

She shook her head. It whirled dizzily. 'That's ridiculous.'

'No,' Rocco said harshly. 'What's ridiculous is that I've seriously underestimated you for so long. You're a conniving thief, just like your brother, and the lengths you'll go to to protect him are truly unbelievable.'

Gracie was shaking in earnest now. 'Need I remind you that *you* seduced *me*?'

Rocco's face was drawn from granite, the lines harsh. It was as if he couldn't hear her. 'From the moment we met at that function in London you've been playing me. You and your brother. He messed up and you're cleaning up his mess.'

Gracie looked at him. A numbness was spreading through her body. Rocco was immovable. A million miles from the raw, emotional man of last night. She wanted to accuse him of lashing out at her because she'd gone too deep and too far and exposed him. But she'd already exposed herself enough. If she displayed the emotion she was feeling it would show him that she felt something for him, and right now she would rather die than let him see that.

So she drew inwards, deep inside, to the place she'd

always retreated to for years. Whenever things got really bad. When her mother had left, and later when her nan had handed them over to Social Services. When her first lover had stood there and called her a slut for giving him her virginity. And when Steven had been taken to jail and she'd been alone.

She drew into the place where Rocco's words couldn't touch her any more and said woodenly, 'You seem to have it all figured out. What more is there to say?'

She looked at him but didn't see him. She only saw pain and anger at her own folly for thinking for a second that last night meant anything. For thinking that any of this meant anything.

His voice was clipped, harsh. 'There's nothing more to say. It's time to go.'

The journey back to London was a blur. Gracie had slept in the bedroom on the plane alone, tortured by vivid dreams of looking for Steven only to find Rocco waiting around corners with a savage expression on his face.

As Rocco's car pulled up outside his building in the cool dark night Gracie acknowledged that the effort to keep up her icy control was fading fast, and was being replaced by a flat, empty ache all through her body. She resolutely ignored Rocco when he joined her to step into the building.

For a split second she looked longingly at the empty street, and then felt her arm taken in a harsh grip. 'Don't even think about it.'

Gracie wrenched her arm away and glared up at him, her fire returning. 'Don't touch me. I'm not going to leave my brother to your mercy now.'

They were silent in the lift going up to the apartment, but to Gracie's chagrin, with the dissipation of the icy control she'd wielded all day, emotion was creeping back, and she had to consciously stop herself from remembering Rocco's tangible pain the night before, and the awful picture he'd painted of his life in Italy. He didn't deserve her sympathy. Not for one second. Especially not now.

When they got to the apartment George was there to greet them. Gracie felt like running into his huge barrel chest and blubbing all over him, but she didn't.

He handed some newspapers to Rocco and said, in a serious voice, 'There's a picture of you and Gracie in the tabloids.'

Rocco came in behind Gracie and opened out the next day's paper. She crept closer, forgetting her ire for a moment at the sight of a huge picture of her and Rocco at the party in New York and a caption underneath: *'Who is de Marco's latest flame-haired mistress?'*

Gracie felt sick. Rocco closed the paper after a long moment and said, 'Now we'll see how protective your brother really is.'

Gracie looked at him stupidly, trying to figure out what he meant, and then it hit her. Her mouth opened. She was aware of pain, even more pain, lancing her insides. 'You...' she framed shakily, 'you accused me of seducing you, but *you* set the whole thing up...taking me away with you so that my brother might see pictures of us and come out of hiding.'

Rocco's face was unreadable. His mouth thinned. 'It'll be interesting to see if your bond is as strong as you say it is.'

Gracie looked up at Rocco and couldn't see an inkling of the man she'd thought she was falling for. He'd never looked so cold and ruthless. 'You're a bastard.'

He smiled then, and it was cruel. 'You're absolutely right. I am.'

CHAPTER ELEVEN

Rocco watched as Gracie finally turned around and walked away jerkily. He heard her door close and the lock turn. He cursed and threw the paper down, and went straight to the drinks cabinet and poured himself a whisky. His hands were shaking. He'd had a red mist over his vision all day, ever since his PA had handed him the printout of the e-mail when he'd been leaving his office to go and pick Gracie up.

He'd almost ignored it, thinking it was something irrelevant, but had then read it. At first he'd seen only the surface message. It had looked innocuous enough. But then, as he'd re-read it, he'd seen more and more—until by the time he'd got back to the apartment, where Gracie had been waiting so patiently, the words of the e-mail had become a gnarled black symbol of his humiliation at her hands the previous night. Lead had surrounded his heart.

All he'd been able to think about was how excruciatingly exposed he felt. How stupid he'd been to trust her so blindly, convincing himself all along that she was innocent. When he'd thought of the burgeoning sense of peace that had settled over him after his exhaustive swim, and how in the cold light of that morning he hadn't regretted baring his soul to her, he'd wanted to punch something.

All that time she'd been trying to contact her brother

because she believed she had Rocco right in the palm of her hand. Rational thought had fled. There was no room for it in the state of paranoia that Rocco had been plunged into.

He'd said things to her that had made her pale and look sick and he'd felt nothing but numb. Even when she'd visibly retreated to somewhere he couldn't reach and kept him at that icy distance he'd welcomed it. It was only when he'd spotted her wistful look towards freedom outside his building just now that something had pierced his fierce control. It had been a primal reflex not to let her go. To keep her by his side at all costs.

And now Rocco had to face the fact that he'd reacted from a place of deep, deep pain. A pain that could only be afflicting him because an equally deep emotion was involved. And he also had to face the fact that either every one of his cynical beliefs would be proved right, or he'd just made the most spectacular mistake of his life.

The following afternoon Rocco was pacing in his office by the window. Work was far from his mind. Gracie hadn't emerged from her room, and she hadn't answered when he'd knocked on her door. Only her hoarse, *'Go away!'* had stopped him from breaking the door down. He'd just now rung up to Mrs Jones, who'd told him worriedly that she was still in her room.

He felt a curious prickling sensation on his neck and turned around to see a familiar figure walking towards his office. His heart sank like a stone. His employees had stopped to look too, because they knew what this meant. Rocco knew it meant something more, though—something infinitely more important than a million euros. His heart spasmed in his chest. As he watched Steven Murray walk into his office with a furious look on his face he knew it meant that he'd made the biggest mistake of his life.

The only thing that roused Gracie from her catatonic state was a familiar voice. She was dimly aware that it was evening outside. She heard it again.

'Gracie, come on. Open the door. It's me.'

She sat up. It couldn't be. She had to be dreaming. Feeling as if it really might be a dream, she finally moved her legs and got up and went to the door. She opened it, and saw her brother standing on the other side.

For a long moment she just looked at him stupidly, not believing her eyes, and then the emotion she'd been denying herself erupted into noisy sobs and she threw herself into his skinny arms. He grabbed her tight and stroked her back and shushed her.

Without knowing how they'd got there, Gracie found herself sitting on a couch, with Steven pushing a glass with amber liquid in it into her hand.

She sucked in a shuddery breath, her face and eyes felt swollen. 'I don't drink.'

Her brother insisted. 'You do now—go on; you need it.'

Gracie took a sip and grimaced when her insides seemed to burst into flame. She coughed a little. As the drink brought her back to life and she registered that it was really her brother sitting in front of her panic gripped her. She grabbed his hand. 'Wait. You can't be here—Rocco is just downstairs. If he finds you—'

She stopped talking when she felt her skin tingle and saw Steven look at something—or *someone*—over her head. She turned to see a pale-looking Rocco with his hands in his pockets.

'I know he's here. He came to see me first when he arrived.' Rocco smiled faintly but it looked strained.

Gracie was tense. She didn't understand Rocco's lack of anger, or her brother's lack of urgency. She tore her eyes from Rocco. 'Steven...what...?'

He smiled and looked tired. 'It's a long story. I've explained everything to Mr de Marco. I was blackmailed, Gracie, by some guys I knew in prison. They knew where I was working and they had some knowledge of fraud and inside trading. They threatened to expose me to Mr de Marco. I was terrified I'd lose the best thing that had ever happened to me... The whole thing escalated until they wanted too much money and I panicked and ran...'

Steven glanced at Rocco, and Gracie saw the respect in his face.

'Mr de Marco has promised not to prosecute if I can help him track these guys down.' He looked back to Gracie. 'Depending on how much money we can recover, I'll still owe a lot to Mr de Marco—but he's offered me a job to get me back on my feet so I can start paying him back. Gracie, I don't deserve this chance. But I'm not going to mess up again. I promise.'

Gracie couldn't believe what she was hearing. She was in shock. And then she heard Rocco say to Steven, 'Would you give us a moment, here? Mrs Jones will show you to a room.'

Steven nodded and pressed Gracie's hands. 'Are you okay?'

Gracie wanted to laugh hysterically. She'd never been less okay. But she nodded her head and watched her brother walk out of the room with his loping, slightly awkward gait.

Rocco walked into her field of vision and Gracie could only look up at him, willing down the tendrils of sensation and feelings that were too close to the surface. 'Why did you do this? Why are you giving him a chance? After everything—'

'Everything I said?' he finished for her, in a voice so harsh she flinched minutely. Rocco cursed in Italian. 'I'm sorry.' He turned away then, as if he couldn't bear for her to look at him, and said rawly, 'God, Gracie. I'm so sorry.'

He turned back after long seconds.

'I was an idiot—a stupid, blind fool. When I read your e-mail I twisted it so that I could believe the worst. Last night in New York you got too close, too deep. I'd never told anyone about myself before, and yet with you...it all came out. And you didn't turn away in horror or shock. You embraced it.'

He pulled over a chair to sit in front of her. His eyes burned.

'I didn't set up the newspaper story. You have to believe that. When I saw the picture it was the first time I thought it might flush Steven out. I hadn't even considered that possibility before. But I let you believe I had because I was so desperate to push you away.'

Rocco grimaced, and Gracie could see the wildness in his eyes—but this was a different wildness.

'I knew deep down that you were none of the things I accused you of yesterday. I seduced you because I couldn't *not*.' He shook his head, disgust with himself palpable. 'I lashed out because I've never trusted anyone in my life until you. And then when Steven turned up today and came straight to me, demanding to know what was going on between us, the sheer evidence of the lengths he'd go to to make sure you were okay humbled me. I had nothing left to hide behind.'

A tiny flicker of hope burst to flame in Gracie's heart, as if a magical thaw was starting.

Rocco said fervently, 'I should never have kept you here

in the first place, but the truth is that it always had more to do with how you made me feel rather than anything to do with your brother.'

The flame inside Gracie trembled. 'What are you saying?'

Rocco took her hand. Gracie willed down the immediate physical reaction.

'I can't stop you leaving if you want to. But I don't want you to leave. I want you to stay…for as long as you want.'

'For as long as *I* want?' Gracie asked faintly. The fragile flame inside her sputtered dangerously.

Rocco nodded. 'We have something, Gracie. Something powerful.'

Gracie pulled her hand free of Rocco's. What he meant was that they had *desire*. Physical attraction. And he wanted her to stay until it had burnt itself out.

Before she could say anything he was grimacing slightly and looking at his watch. 'Look, I've got to go to a meeting. I can't reschedule it. Think about what I've said. We'll talk when I get back…okay?'

He just looked at her, and Gracie felt numb.

He said, *'Please?'* and she realised that he wasn't going to move until she said something. Dumbly she nodded. She saw relief relax his features.

He didn't say anything else. Just stood up and walked out.

Gracie might have nodded to signify assent, but she knew what she had to do. She had to leave—to get away. Rocco wanted a brief relationship. He'd said nothing about love. And she couldn't deal with that—not knowing how she felt. Not knowing how deeply in love with him she was. He could never have hurt her so badly yesterday if she didn't love him.

She was just a temporary diversion. Rocco would

choose an ice princess to be his partner some day, and Gracie wanted to hate him for that—but how could she when she knew how badly he craved that ultimate acceptance? When she knew how hard he'd struggled to leave his past behind so he could get it? Didn't he deserve it after the tragedy and pain he'd endured? She of all people couldn't deny him that.

Moving on autopilot, Gracie packed her paltry belongings and penned two brief notes—one for Rocco and another for her brother. She couldn't even bear to see Steven right now, terrified he'd convince her to stay. When she went to the entrance of the apartment to leave a different bodyguard was on duty to let her out and she was glad. Seeing George might have shattered her brittle control completely.

Two weeks later.

Gracie was struggling through the dense crowd and had to hold the full tray of empty glasses practically over her head to get through. Even as she cursed, and sweat rolled down her back and between her breasts, she tried to stop herself from griping. With this job she would be able to afford to move out of the hostel in a few weeks and find somewhere cheap to rent. And once she had somewhere of her own she would put aside a few hours every day and work on her idea for the children's book.

Gracie heaved a sigh of relief when she saw the kitchen doors ahead. She went in and put the tray down, but was immediately handed another full tray of champagne by her boss, who said cheerily, 'They're a thirsty lot tonight.'

She stifled a weary sigh and went out again. If anything the crowd seemed even denser now, and she looked at the vast, unmoving sea of men in black and women in glittering finery and wondered how on earth she could get through.

Resolutely she started to say, *'Excuse me...'* and, *'Sorry...'* but she wasn't making much progress. Suddenly a frisson of energy went through the crowd, as if someone special had arrived, and people were whispering. People were bunching together now and craning their necks. She rolled her eyes and clung on to the tray. No doubt it was some celebrity.

Then she heard someone say, 'Oh, my God, he's getting up on a table.' And then, 'Is that really him...?'

Through the hush that had fallen in the room Gracie heard a familiar voice ringing out. 'Gracie O'Brien, I know you're in here somewhere. Where are you?'

Her heart stopped dead. It couldn't be. She was hallucinating.

The voice came again, with familiar impatience, 'Dammit, Gracie, where are you?'

Now she knew she couldn't be imagining things.

Tentatively she looked up, straining to see over taller heads, and her breath stopped in her throat when she saw Rocco way above the crowd, head swivelling back and forth, hands on hips as he stood right in the middle of one of the sumptuous buffet tables.

He turned in her direction and she ducked too late. She heard his growl of triumph and the sound of feet hitting the floor. She tried to turn and run but by now people had crowded behind her so she was truly trapped.

As if in slow motion the crowd in front of Gracie parted like the Red Sea and Rocco was revealed. Tall and dark and gorgeous. In a pale blue shirt and dark trousers. Hands on hips. Those dark eyes homing in on her like a laser. His jaw was stubbled and he looked wild. Her hands were shaking so badly now that the glasses wobbled precariously on her tray. Rocco strode forward and took the tray out of her hands, passed it to a stunned pot-bellied man who stood nearby.

Then he turned back to Gracie. She just stood there and asked, 'Why are you here, Rocco? I made it clear in my note that I'm not interested in an affair.'

His mouth tightened and his eyes flashed. 'Yes, your succinct one-line note: *"Dear Rocco, I'm sorry but I'm not interested in an affair. Goodbye. Gracie." Dio*. I wanted to wring your neck when I got that.'

The entire crowd around them was so silent you could have heard a pin drop, but Gracie could only see one man. Her body was already responding. She clenched her hands tight and kept her eyes up.

'I meant what I said. I'm not interested in an affair.'

Rocco took a step closer and Gracie moved back.

'Neither am I.'

Gracie shook her head. 'But…you only said that we had *something*.'

'We do.'

Gracie felt futile anger rise along with confusion. 'Rocco…*why* are you here? I want you to leave me alone. I'm not interested—'

He took a step closer again. 'Tell me what you *are* interested in.'

Horror filled Gracie and she lied desperately. 'I'm interested in nothing with you.'

He smiled. 'Liar.'

Immediately she exploded. 'I'm *not* a liar. I've never lied…'

Rocco's tone turned soothing. 'I know, *cara*…but I'm afraid that you are lying about this.'

To her horror and disgust Gracie could feel tears spring into her eyes, and vaguely saw a horrorstruck look cross

Rocco's face. He reached for her and pulled her into him. It was heaven and hell. She couldn't move in his tight embrace.

'Damn you, Rocco.' She spoke into his chest and then he pulled her back slightly.

His hands were around her jaw, caressing her face, catching her tears. He sounded tortured. 'Don't cry, *piccolina*...please. I don't want to make you cry. Just tell me—what *are* you interested in?'

Gracie opened her mouth. She wanted to lash out at the hurt he'd caused her, and the beautiful pain he'd brought into her life by making her fall in love with him, but she couldn't. She looked up into his dark, harsh face and could only see the man she loved.

In a quivery voice she said simply, 'I'm interested in *you*, Rocco de Marco. I'm interested in everything about you. What moves you, what you want, what makes you happy. I'm interested in making you happy. I'm in love with you, and I'm interested in spending the rest of my life with you—not just having a brief fling. I want more than that.' A kind of defiant confidence filled her now as her eyes cleared and she saw Rocco hadn't yet run screaming from the room in horror. 'Well? Is that what you wanted to hear? Is that truthful enough for you?'

Rocco smiled now—a smile like Gracie had never seen before—and she caught a glimpse of the youth he must have once been. Her heart turned over again.

He nodded. 'Oh, yes, *cara*. That's exactly what I wanted to hear. Because, you see, I love you too—only I held back from saying it that day because I was afraid of scaring you away. I knew you had to hate me for hurting you, and I wanted to woo you slowly and methodically—until you fell so deeply in love with me that you would never leave me. But when I got home you'd gone, and all I found was your note.'

He said a long stream of words in Italian then, and Gracie touched his jaw wonderingly, finally recognising the signs of strain on his face. *For her.*

'You're talking Italian.'

Rocco grimaced. 'Since you left I haven't been able to eat, sleep or speak anything else. I had hideous curtains installed in my office and banished everyone to another floor so they couldn't witness my pain.' His face was serious. 'You brought me back to life, Gracie, and the thought of a life without you in it now terrifies me more than anything else I've ever known.'

Gracie just looked at Rocco. Her whole life flashed before her eyes. She too had always felt somehow alone... until she'd met Rocco. She'd subconsciously handed control over to him from the start, because on some level she'd already trusted him.

To her utter chagrin tears pricked her eyes again, and she cursed colourfully. 'I never used to cry until I met you.'

'That's because you finally realised you didn't have to be the strong one, the protector all the time.'

Gracie nodded as tears slipped down her cheeks and he gently caught them. 'Yes, damn you, *yes.*'

In the next second she'd thrown her arms around Rocco's neck and was in his strong embrace. Her legs were wrapped around his waist and she was sobbing into his neck. And he was crooning to her in Italian, stroking her back.

She pulled away and looked down at him. 'God, I love you, Rocco.'

He looked at her and his eyes darkened. 'I love you too, Gracie.'

He was reaching up to kiss her when she pulled back

sharply and said, 'Are you sure you're not just saying this because you still fancy me and I'm normal? What if I come back and you get tired of me and realise you really do want a society ice princess?'

Rocco looked around at the open-mouthed crowd. He felt triumph surge through him to be holding the woman he loved in his arms and to know she loved him too. *This* was the pinnacle of everything he'd ever wanted, and he'd never have known it if he hadn't met her.

He looked back to Gracie and said, 'What do you think?' He saw her take in the crowd too, and realise just what he'd done. In public. For her. Among the precious peers he'd cared about for so long.

She blushed and looked at him. 'Okay, I believe you.'

'I think it's time to go home.'

Gracie's arms were tight around his neck. 'Yes, please.'

Much later, when their bodies were finally sated and Gracie didn't know where she began and Rocco ended, she took in a deep, voluptuous sigh.

Rocco raised himself up on one arm and looked at her seriously. He brushed some hair from her cheek. 'The only reason I didn't tell you I loved you the day you left was because I didn't want to scare you with the intensity I felt. I wanted to start fresh and woo you as you deserved to be wooed.'

Gracie smiled wryly. 'I think it's safe to say you've wooed me, Rocco. I'm a sure thing.'

He reached behind him to the cabinet and got something. It was hidden in his hand as he said, 'Well, seeing as how we've fast-forwarded past the wooing stage, I'm happy to jump to the next bit.'

'The next bit?' Gracie came up on her elbow too.

Rocco was opening a small velvet box, and Gracie

looked down to see a stunning emerald ring surrounded by diamonds. She looked from it to Rocco.

He said with a glint in his eye, 'You can't take this one back to the shop. It's on loan for a lifetime.'

Gracie sat up and pulled the sheet around her. She felt shaky. Rocco took her hand and placed the ring at the top of her finger and looked into her eyes. Gracie felt tears prickle and blinked them back.

'Gracie O'Brien. I love you more than life itself. Would you come to Rio de Janeiro with me next week and become my wife, with George and Steven as our witnesses?'

Gracie nodded jerkily, tears stinging in earnest now. With a choked voice she answered, 'Yes. I'd love to come to Rio de Janeiro with you and become your wife.'

Rocco pushed the ring onto her finger and pulled her into him with a growl of triumph. Their mouths met and clung.

After a long moment Rocco pulled back and said throatily, 'Good, because then we can get to the next bit.'

'What's that?' Gracie's voice was breathless.

Sounding serious all of a sudden, he said, 'Living the rest of our lives together and having a family we can love and nurture and give everything to that we were denied.'

Feeling incredibly emotional, because she knew he was waiting to see if she wanted the same thing—which, considering their histories, was not necessarily a given— Gracie touched his cheek and said huskily, 'I'd like that. A lot.'

Four years later Gracie looked over the downy head of their newborn baby—a brother to their two-and-a-half-year-old daughter, Tessa. She smiled at her husband and said jokingly, 'Any regrets, Mr de Marco?'

Tessa shifted sleepily on his shoulder as he leant

forward to kiss Gracie tenderly. Love infused the air around them.

He pulled back after a long moment and said softly, 'Not for a second.'

* * * * *

Hot reads!

These 3-in-1s will certainly get you feeling
hot under the collar with their desert
locations, billionaire tycoons and
playboy princes.

**Now available at
www.millsandboon.co.uk/offers**

14/MB472

24 new stories from the leading lights of romantic fiction!

Featuring bestsellers Adele Parks, Katie Fforde, Carole Matthews and many more, *Truly, Madly, Deeply* **takes you on an exciting romantic adventure where love really is all you need.**

Now available at:

www.millsandboon.co.uk

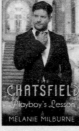

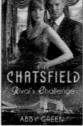

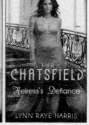

Discover more romance at

www.millsandboon.co.uk

- ♥ WIN great prizes in our exclusive competitions
- ♥ BUY new titles before they hit the shops
- ♥ BROWSE new books and REVIEW your favourites
- ♥ SAVE on new books with the Mills & Boon® Bookclub™
- ♥ DISCOVER new authors

PLUS, to chat about your favourite reads, get the latest news and find special offers:

- 🔲 Find us on facebook.com/millsandboon
- 🔺 Follow us on twitter.com/millsandboonuk
- ♥ Sign up to our newsletter at millsandboon.co.uk